Apr 2019

#5

ARIFURETA: FROM COMMONPLACE TO WORLD'S STRONGEST

ryo shirakome   takayaki

AND LIKE THAT, THE TWO WERE ONCE AGAIN LOST IN THEIR OWN WORLD, FLIRTING WITHOUT A CARE FOR THEIR SURROUNDINGS.

ARIFURETA:

ARIFURETA SHOKUGYOU DE SEKAISAIKYOU

FROM COMMONPLACE
TO WORLD'S STRONGEST

ARIFURETA: FROM COMMONPLACE TO
WORLD'S STRONGEST, VOLUME 5

© 2016 Ryo Shirakome
Illustrations by Takaya-ki

First published in Japan in 2016 by
OVERLAP Inc., Ltd., Tokyo.
English translation rights arranged with
OVERLAP Inc., Ltd., Tokyo.

Follow Seven Seas Entertainment online at
sevenseasentertainment.com.
Experience J-Novel Club books online at j-novel.club.

TRANSLATION: Ningen
J-NOVEL EDITOR: DxS
COVER DESIGN: KC Fabellon
INTERIOR LAYOUT & DESIGN: Clay Gardner
COPY EDITOR: Cae Hawksmoor
PROOFREADER: Kat Adler
LIGHT NOVEL EDITOR: Nibedita Sen
MANAGING EDITOR: Julie Davis
EDITOR-IN-CHIEF: Adam Arnold
PUBLISHER: Jason DeAngelis

ISBN: 978-1-64275-017-1
Printed in Canada
First Printing: April 2019
10 9 8 7 6 5 4 3 2 1

ARIFURETA:

ARIFURETA SHOKUGYOU DE SEKAISAIKYOU

FROM COMMONPLACE TO WORLD'S STRONGEST

#5

Presented by
RYO SHIRAKOME

Illustrated by
TAKAYAKI

Seven Seas

novel club

CONTENTS

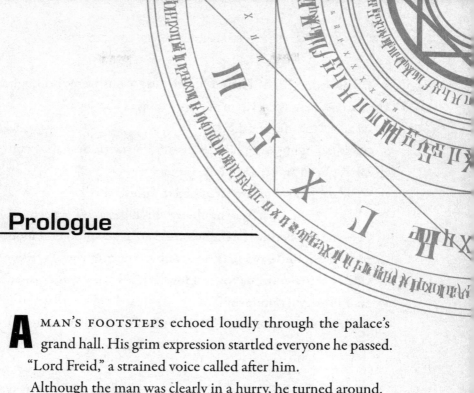

Prologue

A MAN'S FOOTSTEPS echoed loudly through the palace's grand hall. His grim expression startled everyone he passed.

"Lord Freid," a strained voice called after him.

Although the man was clearly in a hurry, he turned around. "Mikhail."

"Lord Freid. I-Is Cattleya really dead?! I heard that from the others when I returned from my mission. Tell me it's not true! Cattleya can't possibly be dead! She had your greatest monster, Ahatod, by her side, so she can't have—"

Lord Freid put a trembling hand on his subordinate's shoulder. The strength of his grip revealed everything Mikhail needed to know. It was true. Freid's beloved Cattleya had truly perished during her mission to conquer the Great Orcus Labyrinth.

"Why... How? Was the hero that strong? If they're strong enough to kill a monster of that caliber, then our hopes of winning are..."

"Calm yourself, Mikhail. Our investigations were thorough. The current hero is nowhere near as strong as Cattleya."

"Then...how did she die?!"

Mikhail clung to Freid, his eyes filling with despair. Freid shook his head and changed the topic.

"The plan to subjugate Ur ended in failure, too."

"Wha...? Did the target not betray his allies as we expected?"

"No, he did betray them. He raised an army of 60,000 monsters, and should have had no trouble burying the 'Fertility Goddess,' along with the town. However, his army was crushed by an unforeseen opponent."

"Unforeseen opponent?" Mikhail tilted his head in confusion.

Freid's eyes narrowed, and he gazed sharply at some unseen enemy.

"A small band of four people crushed the entire monster army. Reiss, who led the mission, even lost his arm. He had to use emergency teleportation to escape, and likely won't be able to return to the front lines."

"No way... Even Reiss lost? I know the monsters there weren't strengthened by your ability, Lord Freid, but could four people really take down an army of that size? Surely you jest."

Freid returned his gaze to the shaking Mikhail.

"I wish I did. At any rate, it seems those four people rushed off to the Great Orcus Labyrinth once they finished at Ur. They must have reached Cattleya around the same time she made contact with the hero party."

"So they were the ones who killed Cattleya?" A tiny red

droplet fell to the floor. Mikhail was clenching his fists so hard his nails had broken skin. Anger welled up within him.

"The enemy's strength is beyond measure," Freid warned sternly, his hand still on Mikhail's shoulder. "I'm planning to head to the volcano next. We must gain more ancient magic, no matter what the cost. It's our only hope of balancing the scales."

"Lord Freid..." Mikhail couldn't believe their strongest general would ever admit to being outmatched. He shivered, and Freid gave him a look that chilled him to the bone.

"Everything we do, we do for His Majesty, and the god we serve. Hold down the fort while I'm gone, Mikhail. The war will begin in earnest soon. Polish your skills with what little time is left."

"Ah. Yes, sir. I swear to avenge Cattleya."

Freid nodded and turned on his heel. He saw Mikhail salute out of the corner of his eye as he walked to the spot where his partner waited.

When he was finally out of sight, Freid's stern expression crumbled. He'd held his anger back from his subordinates, but there was no one to see him now.

"I don't know who you are, but you'll pay dearly for interfering with my holy mission. God is with me. The day we finally meet will be your last. Heretics have no right to live."

Freid muttered darkly to himself for a few more minutes before summoning his horde of monsters and leaving the castle.

That castle lay in the heart of Garland, the demons' capital.

Freid was the demon responsible for single-handedly destroying the delicate balance between humans and demons. And, as fate would have it, he was headed to the very same place as the monster of the abyss.

Who would the goddess of victory smile upon when they finally met?

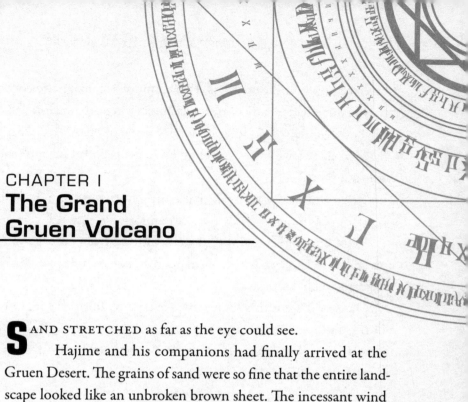

CHAPTER I
The Grand Gruen Volcano

SAND STRETCHED as far as the eye could see.

Hajime and his companions had finally arrived at the Gruen Desert. The grains of sand were so fine that the entire landscape looked like an unbroken brown sheet. The incessant wind clouded the sky with so much dust that it looked brown as well. Wherever you looked, all you saw was sand.

The only things breaking the monotony were the dunes, undulating through the desert like waves. The wind blew through them at a steady pace, making the entire desert look like one massive living creature.

The harsh sun heated the sand until it glowed red. It was easily over 40 degrees Celsius. With sand flying everywhere, the desert made for an inhospitable environment.

For normal travelers, anyway.

Brise tore through the dunes like they were nothing. And because it was completely enclosed, the sand and heat did not bother Hajime and the others. Furthermore, the magnetic compass Hajime had installed in the dashboard kept them from getting lost.

"Thank god we're not traveling on horseback. It looks miserable out there."

"Indeed. I'm not so weak that a little heat and wind would hinder me, but...it certainly is more comfortable in here."

Shea and Tio stared out of the window at the unforgiving wasteland. Tio may have been a masochist, but even she wouldn't welcome such discomfort.

"It's so different this time! Myu's eyes don't hurt, and it's not hot! Daddy's amazing!"

"That's right, Daddy *is* amazing, Myu-chan. Do you want some cold water?"

"Yeah! Thank you, Kaori-oneechan."

Myu sat happily on Kaori's lap. She was excited by how different this trip through the desert was from her first journey, when she'd been abducted.

For an aquatic species like Myu, the desert crossing must have been doubly harsh. Considering how young she was, it was a miracle the trip didn't kill her. However, she was traveling in completely different circumstances this time. Brise was air-conditioned, and kept the wind and sand out.

Moreover, Hajime had stocked up on chilled provisions for the trip. It still bothered him a little that his opinion had been completely ignored when Yue agreed to let Kaori join their party, but he was getting used to having her around.

Kaori pulled a bottle of cold water out of the mini-fridge Hajime had added to Brise.

"Hey, Shirasa... I mean, Kaori. Could you please stop calling me daddy? It just sounds really creepy."

"But Myu-chan calls you that all the time."

"It's one thing for Myu, but being called 'daddy' by someone my age is pretty weird."

Kaori had always been good at looking after others, so she had eventually taken on the role of Myu's caretaker. However, she'd also started using Myu's nickname for Hajime.

It was acceptable, if a little awkward, to have a little girl calling him daddy, but someone his own age...

Kaori had insisted that Hajime call her by her first name, until he finally gave in. She thought it was unfair that he addressed everyone else that way.

"Really? All right, I guess I'll stop... Until we actually have kids of our own, at least..." Kaori trailed off, blushing furiously.

An awkward silence descended on the car. Hajime pretended he hadn't heard, but Yue wasn't about to let it go.

"Too bad I'm going to be first. Hajime promised."

"Hajime-kun, what's the meaning of this?!"

"Is it really that surprising? It's not like I'm planning on having kids anytime soon, anyway."

"Hee hee. I'm going to introduce myself to his parents first, too," Yue continued slyly.

"Wha—?!" Kaori gasped.

"I've already planned everything out."

"Huh?!"

"Including all the dates we'll go on when we get back."

"Ah!"

Yue's words were like daggers stabbing through Kaori's chest.

Still, Kaori was a strong girl. She wouldn't break. She'd spent the better part of her time in this world believing in Hajime's survival. She even drummed up the courage to stand up to Yue. If someone hit Kaori, she hit back.

"I know all sorts of things about Hajime-kun that you don't! Like his future goals, his hobbies, and even his favorite genres! I bet you don't know his favorite anime and manga, Yue!"

"Hmph... I... that doesn't matter. None of those things exist here. I just have to learn about them when we go to Japan."

"Oh, but they do. Just look at Hajime-kun. His appearance practically screams anime."

"Gah?!"

Although Yue and Kaori were the ones arguing, it was Hajime who was suffering. That last statement was aimed right for his jugular.

"White hair, an eyepatch, even a magical fake eye... I'm pretty sure Hajime's favorite character had all of those. Even his weapons, those Cross Bits... They're definitely based off of the ones in Gundam. It doesn't matter what world we're in. Hajime-kun will always be an otaku!"

"Guh?! K-Kaori!"

"U-ugh... To think Hajime's weapons were based on entertainment..."

"Hee hee! You don't even know what kinds of things the man you love likes."

"You've got guts, Kaori. But do you know what positions Hajime likes in bed?"

"Wh-wh-what?! In bed?! Ugh... You've already gone that far...?"

"Hee hee hee. That's how big the gap is between us."

Everyone was used to ignoring Kaori and Yue when they were like this. At first, Shea had fussed over the two of them, trying to mediate and make them get along. Eventually, she'd realized that it was more trouble than it was worth... Especially since the two didn't actually seem to hate each other.

In fact, the only person really suffering from their arguments was Hajime. Almost all of the bickering centered around him, so many of his embarrassing secrets became ammunition to make a point. All the things he was self-conscious about were poked and prodded at until he couldn't take anymore.

Kaori covered her ears, trying to shut out the truth. Gripping his heart in anguish, Hajime tried to break them up. However, before he could do anything, Myu spoke up.

"No! Stop fighting, Yue-oneechan, Kaori-oneechan! I hate it when you fight!"

Myu hopped off Kaori's lap and crawled to the back, where Shea was sitting. She glared, pouting at the two girls in front. They looked at each other awkwardly. A little girl chastising them was a surprisingly effective weapon.

"Sheesh, you two. You could at least stop when Myu-chan's around. You're bad influences on her. I understand getting worked up about Hajime-san, but you could at least act like adults about it."

"Unbelievable," mumbled Kaori. "To think I'm being scolded by Shea..."

"I-I'm sorry, Myu-chan... Shea." Never in her wildest dreams had Yue thought she would sink so low.

Despite the fact that Shea was Yue's best friend, Yue treated her like a younger sister. Although both girls were vying for Hajime's affections, Shea loved Yue just as much. It was a slightly different relationship than the one Yue had with Kaori.

On the other hand, Tio was just a pervert.

In a sense, Kaori was the first true love rival Yue ever encountered. However, Yue was confident that her bond with Hajime was stronger than anything. She had unwavering faith that she was the only one special to him. So, at first, she'd seen Kaori as a mere challenger, and believed that it would be easy to beat Kaori down.

And, although her confidence remained unshaken, Yue occasionally noticed Hajime and Kaori reminiscing about their lives in Japan.

That was Kaori's one advantage over Yue. She'd known Hajime longer. It was the one thing that let her fight Yue on equal footing.

Kaori, meanwhile, was jealous of the fact that Yue was Hajime's current lover. However, she was too honest and good-natured to try anything underhanded.

Because neither Yui nor Kaori wanted to "cheat" their way to victory, their squabbles never escalated. However, they bickered so frequently that it grated on the others. Today, Myu and Shea had finally had enough.

Normally, Hajime put an end to most arguments by professing his love for Yue, but he'd taken too much damage in a short span of time. He simply stared off into the distance, ignoring everyone.

"Hm? What could that be...? Master, there appears to be some commotion to your right."

Hajime, who was repeatedly muttering "I'm not an otaku" to himself, suddenly returned to his senses and turned to his right. Kaori and Yue stopped trying to show Myu how well they really got along, and turned to see what was happening. Shea, too, craned her neck for a better look. They could all see something in the distance.

A large number of sandworms—earthworm-like desert monsters—were congregating on a dune. Their heads poked above the hilltop.

Sandworms were around 20 meters long. Some of the really large ones grew up to 100 meters. They could only be found in the Gruen Desert. Normally, they lived underground, and only surfaced to swallow prey with their triple-layered jaws. Travelers who crossed the desert lived in fear of their nigh-imperceptible sneak attacks.

Fortunately, the sandworms were not very perceptive. Travelers wouldn't be spotted unless they were unlucky enough to walk over a lair. *If they're all surfacing now, they must have found some sap to prey on, Hajime mused. But from the looks of it...*

"Why are they circling around like that?"

If the sandworms had just come up to feed, Tio wouldn't have considered it worth pointing out. Hajime's skills let him sense incoming attacks, and Brise could easily outpace a sandworm. What was strange about this particular colony of worms was that they'd surfaced, but were hesitating to attack their supposed target. They simply circled around the hill.

"They seem uncertain, as though they aren't sure whether their prey is safe to eat," Tio replied.

"Looks like it. Does that happen often?"

"Not to my knowledge. They can eat most anything, so they normally don't hesitate."

Tio might have been a masochist and a huge pervert, but she had lived even longer than Yue. And since, unlike Yue, she hadn't been sealed away for most of her life, her vast knowledge of the world encompassed obscure monsters' habits. If this had even Tio confused, it was definitely worth noting.

But there was no reason for Hajime to get involved. He decided to leave before the party got wrapped up in something troublesome.

"Wha—?! Hang on tight, guys!"

Hajime gunned Brise's accelerator. A second later, a giant brown creature erupted from the earth, grazing them. A sandworm had just tried to swallow them whole. It looked like Hajime and the others were on the menu, too.

Hajime swerved sharply, zigzagging through the dunes. Sandworms erupted one after another from the ground, each emerging from whatever spot Brise had occupied seconds before.

"Ahhhhhhhh!"

"Eeek!"

"Whoa!"

Kaori, Myu, and Shea screamed. Worried about Myu, Kaori turned to check on her. At the same time, Hajime made another sharp turn. Kaori lost her balance and tumbled forward... Right into Yue and Hajime. She collapsed with her butt in Yue's lap and her head in Hajime's.

After a few surprised blinks, Kaori blushed and clung to Hajime's waist, much to his chagrin. His expression stiffened, and he tried not to think dirty thoughts. The lower half of Kaori's body still sprawled across Yue's lap.

"Hey, Shira... Kaori! What are you doing?!"

"It's dangerous! I'm hanging onto you for safety!"

"Kaori, you vixen! To think you would cozy up to Hajime while curtailing my movements... You're craftier than I gave you credit for."

Even though they were fleeing for dear life, Yue and Kaori were still only interested in winning. Yue spanked Kaori's defenseless behind, but Kaori refused to loosen her grip. Instead, she buried her face in Hajime's crotch.

Having failed their initial ambush, the three sandworms began an overland pursuit of Brise. They moved far more swiftly than their size suggested.

Had Hajime and the others been riding a normal carriage, they would have been toast. However, Brise was an artifact imbued with all of an otaku's ingenuity. Even if the sandworms managed to swallow it, it wouldn't suffer a single scratch.

"Come to think of it, this is a good chance to test that thing out." Drifting hard enough to start driving in reverse, Hajime poured mana into another of the attachments he'd installed on Brise.

A series of metallic clunks reverberated through the car. Brise's hood slid back to reveal a quadruple rocket launcher.

The launcher swiveled back and forth, seeking out its prey. After a few seconds, it locked onto the nearest sandworm. With a flurry of red sparks, the launcher unleashed its salvo.

A glowing trail of orange followed in the rocket's wake. The missile sailed into the sandworm's open mouth and exploded. Chunks of flesh rained from the sky, spattering Brise's windshield.

"Bleh... Shea, cover Myu's eyes, please."

"Already on it. Ah...! Myu-chan, I know it hurts, but don't pinch me there!"

Shea buried Myu's head inside her ample bosom to shield her from the horrors Hajime inflicted on the monsters. However, Myu found it too suffocating, and pinched Shea in a rather sensitive spot. Hajime did his best to ignore the moaning coming from the back of the vehicle. Dealing with his own comrades was more draining than fighting monsters.

It didn't help that Kaori was still clinging to his waist. After a herculean effort, Yue finally pulled Kaori off and strapped her in with her seatbelt, locking Kaori in place. Kaori was blushing bright red, surprised at her own boldness.

"U-umm, Hajime-kun. Sorry about that. I acted on instinct... I wasn't purposely trying to do something dirty. I just wanted to know what it felt like to hug you once..."

"And, if you saw your chance, you'd push him down then and there?" Yue interjected.

"Exact... No! Yue, please don't say such strange things. I'm not as lewd as you."

"You're calling *me* lewd? Well, I suppose I can't really deny it, considering the things Hajime and I do at night."

Hajime blasted the rest of the nearby sandworms to bits. Hearing the explosions, the sandworms atop the dune turned to look at Brise. Hajime steeled himself for another fight, but Kaori and Yue's arguing distracted him. Their constant bickering was sapping his mental fortitude. He'd finally hit his limit, and snapped at Yue.

"Could you two shut up for a second? And, Yue, quit talking about our sex life."

Still, everything Yue had said was true. Hajime doubted that anyone could beat her when it came to simple sexiness. Kaori could tell what he was thinking about, and tears welled up in her eyes.

Yue smiled victoriously and licked her lips. Kaori groaned, lamenting her defeat. Hajime's annoyed outburst had only fanned the flames of their feud.

Shea leaned forward and patted Kaori's shoulder sympathetically. "I know how you feel, Kaori-san."

Hajime ignored them, gunning Brise toward the dune. He could tell there were more sandworms moving underground. The sand bulged slightly with their movements, so it was clear that the beasts weren't trying to be stealthy anymore. Right now, speed would avail them more than stealth.

Retracting his rocket launcher, Hajime activated a new weapon. This time, a long rectangular box came out of Brise's hood. Metal grated against metal, and the box transformed itself into a long-range rifle. It looked strikingly similar to Schlagen.

Red sparks ran down the length of the gun barrel. The robotic arm supporting the weapon adjusted its aim and fired. A dazzling streak of red cut through the muddy brown air.

The sandworm slammed into the ground, and a plume of sand rose into the sky. Chunks of flesh and droplets of blood rose with it. Hajime's bullet had found its mark.

Hajime reloaded and fired again and again. Each bullet caused another eruption of sand and blood. The sandworms were obliterated before they even surfaced.

"Hajime-kun, look over there!" Kaori shouted.

"Is that...a person?" Yue asked uncertainly.

Hajime retracted his rifle. Yue's guess was correct. Some distance away lay a humanoid figure, clad in white. In all likelihood, that was the person the sandworms had been trying to eat. However, from this distance, Hajime's party could see nothing out of the ordinary. Nothing to indicate why the sandworms hesitated.

"Please, Hajime-kun. I'm a Priestess..." Kaori said, looking up pleadingly. "I have to at least try and help him."

Since Hajime was interested in learning why the sandworms hadn't attacked the man, he saw no reason to refuse. "Might as well, I guess. I'm kinda curious, honestly."

It was possible the man had some unique item that warded

off monsters, or knew some unknown magic. After all, if things like verdren crystals existed in the sea of trees, who knew what other strange wonders this world contained? The man might even possess something with more potent effects than those crystals.

Hajime made a beeline for the collapsed figure.

The stranger wore something resembling a jellabiya—a traditional Egyptian garment back on Earth—with a big hooded overcoat on top. The hood covered his head, and, since he lay face-down, it was difficult to discern his features.

Kaori hopped off Brise, dashed over to the man, and rolled him onto his back.

"What on..."

Lowering the figure's hood, Kaori discovered that he was young, probably in his early twenties. However, what surprised her was the state he was in.

His face was locked in a painful grimace, sweat beaded on his forehead, and his breath came in short, shallow gasps. He was so feverish that steam rose from his body. His blood vessels strained against his skin, as if they pushed out from inside. Blood dripped from his eyes and nose. Something was obviously wrong, and it wasn't just heatstroke.

Hajime was worried Kaori might get infected, but as she was the healer, he left the situation to her.

Kaori cast Magical Diagnostics on the man. The spell used her mana to investigate her target's condition, and displayed its findings on her Status Plate.

The results were unexpected.

"What'd you find, Kaori?" Hajime asked.

"L-Look," whispered Kaori. "This is what it says..."

Kaori showed her Status Plate to the rest of the party.

◊ STATUS

The target's mana has overloaded and he is incapable of releasing the excess.

SYMPTOMS: Fever, fainting, body pains, and capillary vessel ruptures.

CAUSE: Foreign liquid in the target's body.

"Mana overload?" Hajime said. "His mana's going berserk because of poison in his body?"

"My guess is that he drank something poisonous, and it's making his mana go berserk," Kaori replied. "Because he can't get rid of it, it's destroying his body from inside. At this rate, all his blood vessels will rupture, and he'll die. Even if that doesn't kill him instantly, blood loss will. Heaven's providence, grant succor to the doomed—Renewal!"

Kaori cast the healing spell Renewal. It was an intermediate-rank healing spell that dispelled status debuffs.

However...

"Oh no, it barely had any effect," Kaori lamented. "How come? This spell can cure almost all status effects... Does that mean the poison is too deeply ingrained?"

Although it prevented the spread of the poison, Kaori's

Renewal spell couldn't cure him. The man groaned feebly. His bleeding hadn't stopped, either. Kaori ground her teeth in frustration. She couldn't think of a way to heal him, so for now, she began to administer emergency treatments to keep his condition from worsening.

"May the grace of light bless you in this holy sanctuary. No evil shall pass so long as I hold the gates—Sanctorum!"

The high-level light spell, Sanctorum, allowed everyone in a set area to exchange mana. Normally, Kaori used the spell to transfer mana to her allies, and support them if they didn't have enough of their own left.

However, there was no restriction on who could transfer mana to whom. Furthermore, the caster could forcibly transfer mana from one target to another, if they wished. In other words, Sanctorum could function as a mana-draining spell. But it took more time to drain mana *from* a target than to transfer mana *to* them. Because of that, it normally wasn't suitable in combat.

Thanks to Kaori's extensive training, however, she'd shortened the incantation to the point where it was fast enough to be practical in either case. Hajime could guess how hard she'd worked to reach that level of proficiency.

With Sanctorum in place, Kaori began siphoning mana from the young man. Although the Status Plate had said it was impossible to release his excess mana, Kaori hoped a powerful light spell could forcibly drain it out.

Purplish-white light enveloped the young man, making him look ethereal.

It was a wondrous sight. Kaori closed her eyes and placed her hands on his chest. After a few seconds of furious concentration, the same lavender light enveloped her.

Yue and Tio murmured at Kaori's impressive skill. As fellow mages, they were even more appreciative of her abilities than Hajime.

"So pretty," Myu muttered in Shea's arms.

Kaori didn't even notice their praise. She focused fully on her task, diverting the drained mana into the mana-absorbing brace-let Hajime had given her. He gave her a bracelet, rather than a ring, because he didn't want to be misunderstood again. Either way, it appeared Kaori's magic could overcome whatever symptoms were preventing this unknown man from venting mana.

The man's breathing became less labored. His blood vessels stopped swelling, and his eyes and nose ceased bleeding. Once she'd siphoned off most of his mana, Kaori dispelled her Sanctorum spell, and cast Heaven's Blessing to heal his internal injuries.

"He should be good for a little while, but I've only alleviated the symptoms," she explained. "I still don't know how to cure him. If I took too much of his mana, he would've died from exhaustion, so I could only drain a little bit. His mana might surge up and go berserk again... Or he might start leaking mana until he dies. I've never seen these symptoms before, so I'm not sure, but... Yue, Tio, do you two have any idea what this could be?"

Kaori turned to them for help. A temporary fix like this was pointless if they couldn't cure the underlying cause.

The two girls searched their vast memories, but nothing came to mind. In the end, they still weren't sure what was wrong.

"Kaori, could you check us too, just in case? It's possible that whatever he's sick with is infectious. If it's just something that makes mana go berserk, then Myu's safe, at least."

"Yes, that should be the case."

Kaori nodded and began diagnosing the rest of the party. Fortunately, none of them seemed to be infected. Whatever the disease was, it certainly wasn't airborne. Everyone breathed a sigh of relief.

The young man groaned and opened his eyes. It seemed he'd recovered sufficiently to regain consciousness. He looked around slowly, his gaze stopping on Kaori.

"A goddess? I see, you've come to take me..." he mumbled.

He reached out a shaky hand. However, the heat and sand made Hajime even more irritable than usual, and he kicked the unfamiliar man in the stomach.

"Urgh!"

"H-Hajime-kun?!"

Hajime ignored Kaori's outburst, and asked the man what had happened.

From what Hajime remembered, the man's clothes were traditional Ankajian garb. Ankaji sat at the largest oasis in the desert. All that knowledge Hajime had amassed when he was still "useless" was starting to come in handy. If Ankaji was been struck by some unknown disease, that would make Hajime's crossing much more perilous, so he was a lot more interested in the man's circumstances now.

Hajime's kick brought the man back to his senses, and he took a closer look at his surroundings. Seeing Brise almost sent him into shock again, and he didn't calm down until Kaori explained what was going on.

"I thought that me and the dukedom were both doomed, but it seems God hasn't abandoned me yet," the man muttered.

I wonder what he'd think if he learned that god of his was actually a heartless monster? Hajime looked up at the sky. If anything, his disease was probably a "present" from his god.

"Hajime-kun. Let's move him to the car for now."

The poor man had difficulty even standing. The desert heat had left him dehydrated. Hajime still had questions to ask, so he couldn't let the man die just yet.

Sighing, Hajime nodded. He tossed the young man over his shoulder and carried him to Brise, laying him down in the air-conditioned backseat.

"Is this the land of the gods?!" the man exclaimed in surprise.

Looks like he's still got some life left in him, thought Hajime.

After chugging a few bottles of water, he finally recovered enough to speak coherently.

"First, let me thank you for saving my life," said the man. His expression grew grim. "Had I died back there... Ankaji would have been finished. My name is Bize Feuward Zengen. I'm the son of Ankaji's duke, Lanzwi Feuward Zengen."

Well, that's a surprise. Didn't think he'd be royalty.

The Dukedom of Ankaji was responsible for transporting all of the marine goods that came out of Erisen, which accounted for

80 percent of the northern continent's marine products. In other words, Ankaji had a near-monopoly on humanity's seafood supply. Their nobility was highly respected, even within the Heiligh Kingdom.

Bize was just as surprised to hear his saviors' credentials. Kaori was one of Ehit's warriors, while Hajime, Yue, Shea, and Tio were all gold-ranked adventurers.

"I see now, God! You sent your messenger down to save me!" the man exclaimed upon learning who Kaori was.

Kaori stared at him blankly. She didn't realize he was addressing her.

Activating Intimidation, Hajime once again pressed Bize to explain what was going on. Sweating profusely, Bize cleared his throat.

Four days ago, many Ankaji residents had succumbed to a fever of unknown cause. It came out of nowhere, and it struck 20,000 of the city's 270,000 citizens on the first day. Of those, 3,000 had symptoms so severe they lost consciousness. Doctors worked around the clock to discover the cause, but it eluded them. All they could do was delay the symptoms, like Kaori had.

As days passed, more and more people got sick. Worse, many of the doctors fell prey to the fever as well. Soon, not enough doctors remained to look after everyone. Finally, casualties started appearing. The remaining doctors couldn't siphon all the patients' mana, and those who went untreated for too long died. The city despaired. No one had heard of a disease that killed within two days.

On a hunch, one of the city's pharmacists cast Appraise Liquid on the city's water supply. Upon doing so, he discovered that the municipal wells had been tainted with a poison that made mana go berserk. Fearing the worst, the city quickly assembled an investigation team to examine the oasis. As they expected, it too had been poisoned.

Oases were the lifeline of desert cities like Ankaji. Ankaji's was guarded day and night, and maintaining it was the city's highest priority. It would have been impossible for an intruder to sneak past the guards and poison it.

The investigation team couldn't fathom who would do such a thing, or why. However, they had bigger problems. The city's only drinkable water was whatever they'd gathered before the poisoning. And they still had no idea how to save the poisoning victims.

Actually, that wasn't strictly true. They knew of one thing that might save them.

Stillstone. A special mineral that could silence mana. It grew in small quantities inside the Grand Gruen Volcano to the north, and was extremely valuable. Magical researchers often used it as a safeguard against accidents. By crushing it into a powder, they could feed it to the patients, calming their rampaging mana.

However, the distance between the city and the volcano was great. A round trip would take at least a month. And all of the adventurers skilled enough to delve into the Grand Gruen Volcano were already incapacitated by fever. Most of them didn't even possess enough strength to make it past the eternal sandstorm that raged around the volcano.

Even if they *had* capable adventurers left, not enough water remained to last through the journey. The only remaining option was to ask the kingdom for help.

Of course, the possibility of the kingdom providing Ankaji with enough water to slake the city's thirst for a month was unlikely. Hoping that they would dispatch adventurers capable of harvesting stillstone in the meantime was even more of a longshot. Ankaji might have been a vital outpost, but it would still be normal for the kingdom to send an investigation team first. By then, it would be too late.

Hence, it was necessary for a member of the influential Zengen family to personally ask for aid.

"Father, Mother, and even my sister were infected on the first day. We used what little stillstone we had left to cure them, but they still haven't fully recovered. They're definitely in no state to travel. So, I left Ankaji with my guard yesterday and headed to the capital. Since I hadn't shown any symptoms, I thought I hadn't been infected... But I guess my symptoms were just delayed. Onset must vary from person to person. I was so preoccupied with the city's crisis that the possibility never even occurred to me. I should have taken some stillstone, too, just in case. Every second wasted is another precious Ankaji life gone... I can't believe I was so foolish!" He slammed a fist against his knee, lamenting his helplessness.

To make matters worse, his guards died protecting him from the sandworms. Nice to see that the next duke of Ankaji cares about his people, Hajime mused.

In a way, Bize was lucky to be infected. That was the only thing that kept the sandworms from eating him. The poison had made him collapse, but it also kept him alive, and led Hajime towards him. Fate truly was a fickle mistress.

"I would—that is to say, the dukedom of Ankaji would—like to formally submit a request to you. Please, lend me your strength." Bize bowed his head low. Silence fell inside the car.

The sound of sand hitting the windows seemed unnaturally loud. As a duke's son, Bize knew that bowing his head to others wasn't done lightly. But this might be his only chance to save his countrymen. He couldn't let pride get in the way.

Everyone turned to look at Hajime. Although they left the decision to him, Kaori and Shea obviously wanted to help... Kaori, especially. As a Priestess, she felt duty-bound to assist those in need. Tio and Yue didn't seem to care one way or another. Myu, however, was even more direct than the others.

"Daddy, we're going to help him, right?" Myu asked, with all the innocence of a small girl. She honestly believed that Hajime could do anything, no matter how absurd. He was her hero.

Seeing that both Myu and Kaori were clearly in favor, Hajime shrugged helplessly. "Guess that settles it."

Shea and Tio giggled happily. Hajime turned to Yue, and found her staring at him with the same deadpan expression as always.

No matter what Hajime chose, Yue would always support his decision. Even if she didn't say it, he knew that was what she was thinking. He gently brushed Yue's cheek, and turned to Bize to accept his request.

Hajime had planned on visiting the Grand Gruen Volcano anyway, and he wanted to leave Myu in Ankaji while he did so. Strong as he was, he didn't want to bring a four-year-old girl somewhere so dangerous. He could easily pick up the stillstone Bize needed during his quest to reach the volcano's center, and, since Myu was from a beastman tribe, she would be safe from the epidemic ravaging Ankaji. She had no mana, after all. However you looked at it, Hajime could solve all of Bize's problems without going out of his way.

"Hajime-dono, since you are a gold-ranked adventurer, I have no doubt you could easily procure the stillstone I need. However, we also need to solve my city's water problem. Can anyone operate this Artifact, or only you, Hajime-dono?"

"Well, everyone here except Kaori and Myu can drive it, but... there's no need to go to the capital. I can do something about your water, so let's head back to Ankaji for now."

"What exactly do you mean by that?"

Bize did not doubt Hajime's prowess, but he was skeptical that even a gold-ranked adventurer could procure enough water to sustain hundreds of thousands of people out of nowhere. His uncertainty was understandable. However, there was one way to procure water that Bize hadn't thought of: using strong water magic to collect moisture in the atmosphere.

Of course, most mages couldn't draw nearly enough water for that many people. However, Hajime had a genius magician in his party... Yue. And, because she knew multiple ways of restoring her mana quickly, she wouldn't get tired. At the very least, she'd be able to provide the town with water long enough for Bize or his father to appeal to the kingdom for aid.

When Hajime told Bize as much, he was skeptical. However, it was also true that he was in no condition to reach the capital. With a little persuasion from Kaori, one of Ehit's trusted warriors, he finally gave in and agreed.

Bize was shocked to see how much ground Hajime could cover in Brise. However, by that point, it was just one surprise in an endless parade. He didn't know why a warrior of Ehit was traveling with these adventurers, why they had a Dagon girl with them, why she called Hajime daddy, or why there were a rabbitman and a black-haired woman who seemed happy to be insulted. What he did know was that there was still hope left. That hope allowed him to hold his head high as they continued their journey.

After a short drive, the walls of Ankaji shimmered into view. They were truly a sight to behold, towering higher than even Fuhren's impressive ramparts. The walls and buildings were all built from the same milky-white material, in stark contrast to the brown that surrounded them.

Pillars of light jutted from the walls at regular intervals. They curved into each other and converged high in the sky, creating a dome that covered the city. Whenever anything hit the dome, ripples spread from the point of impact, as if someone had thrown a stone into a pond. It was a wondrous sight.

As far as Hajime could tell, the dome seemed to protect the city from the elements. The desert experienced fierce sandstorms every few months, so the dome was a necessity. It could turn a raging storm into no more than a cloudy day.

Hajime and the others approached the city gates, shrouded in a veil of light. It stood to reason that even the gates would need to be ensorcelled if they wanted to keep the sand out. The gate guards were mildly surprised to see Brise, but their reactions were far more subdued than most.

Ankaji's plight likely occupied most of the guards' attention. They were barely focusing on their job. When they saw their lord sitting in Brise's backseat, however, they instantly snapped to attention.

Ankaji's gate stood at a higher elevation than the rest of the city. Apparently, it had been built that way on purpose, so that the first thing visitors saw was the entire city in all its splendor.

The great oasis lay to the east, sparkling in the early afternoon sun. Great palm trees grew all around it. It was the first bit of green Hajime had seen since entering the desert. Small canals branched out from the oasis, crisscrossing the rest of the city. Although Ankaji lay in the middle of the desert, most people seemed to travel by boat. More trees dotted the streets, and entire squares had been converted into gardens.

To the north was the city's agricultural district. Hajime had read that many fruit species thrived in Ankaji's warm climate, and it seemed that was no exaggeration. The fruit groves stretched past the horizon, farther even than Hajime could see with his Farsight. To the west was the royal palace. Unlike the milky stone that seemed to be favored in the rest of the city, the palace was made of pure white marble. That set it apart, as the architect likely intended. However, the effect was diminished by the crude rectangular structures surrounding the palace on all sides. Hajime assumed they were administrative buildings.

Ankaji lay in the middle of a desert, but there was more water here than Hajime had seen in any other city.

"It looks...amazing," Hajime muttered, stunned.

"Yeah... It's a beautiful city," Yue whispered back, equally astonished. The others exclaimed in awe as well.

"But...it feels empty," Myu said quietly. She was right. Despite its magnificent appearance, an air of gloom hung over the city.

Normally, the squares would be bustling with traders haggling over fruit and fish prices, and tourists exploring the city's marvels. Now, however, the streets were practically empty. Everyone was hiding in their houses, as if waiting out a storm. An eerie silence filled the streets.

"I wish I could have shown you what the city looked like before the plague," said Bize. "At any rate, my apologies, but we have no time to waste. I promise I'll show you around the city once this crisis has been averted. For now, though, I need to report to my father."

Hajime nodded, and they headed toward the palace.

.⁕. .⁕. .⁕. .⁕. .⁕. .⁕. .⁕. .⁕. .⁕. .⁕. .⁕. .⁕. .⁕.

"Father!"

"Bize! What happened...? Wait... What in Ehit's name is that?!"

Thanks to Bize, the party could head straight to the audience hall without being asked any questions. Although he was still weak from the poison, Lanzwi had continued working, relying on a combination of healing magic and guts.

His son had gone out to request aid just yesterday. That wasn't nearly enough time to make it to the capital and back. However, what surprised Lanzwi more was his son's condition. After all, Bize was levitating.

To be precise, he was lying on a levitating Cross Bit.

Although he'd recovered a little during the ride to Ankaji, Bize was still in no state to walk. Kaori had offered her shoulder, but Bize had refused, giving excuses like, "I couldn't possibly ask one of Ehit's chosen warriors to carry me." Hajime hadn't liked the bashful look their guest gave Kaori, so he interrupted them by forcibly putting Bize on a Cross Bit.

Hajime wasn't jealous. That was what Kaori thought, but in truth, he just didn't want to deal with people envying her affection for him. He'd had enough of that with Kouki and Hiyama.

Bize clung to the Cross Bit, afraid of falling, as he explained what had happened. Once he outlined the situation, a butler came and gave him a small vial of powdered stillstone. The stillstone, combined with Kaori's healing magic, was enough to get Bize back on his feet. He wasn't fully recovered, but his condition was still a far cry from his state minutes ago.

The biggest issue was that Bize still wasn't cured. The stillstone could suppress his symptoms, but their root cause, the poison, still ran through his veins. Although it was possible his body would eventually expel the toxin, all they could do for now was wait and see.

"All right, let's get moving. Kaori, Shea, you two check up on the patients. Take the empty magic stones with you. The rest of us are going to get the city some water. Lord Lanzwi, is there a wide open space anywhere nearby? At least two hundred square meters, if possible."

"Huh? Oh, yes, there's one in the agricultural district."

"That's where we're headed, then. Shea, once the magic stones are saturated, bring them to Yue." Hajime swiftly delivered his orders.

His plan was simple. Kaori would use her Sanctorum spell to drain the infected people's mana, just as she had with Bize. Then, she'd siphon that mana into empty magic stones. Once they were full, Shea would pass them to Yue, who'd use the mana to create water.

Hajime would then use Transmutation to create a makeshift storage reservoir, after which he would investigate the oasis. If he could analyze the poison successfully, he'd solve the city's problem at that point. If he couldn't, he'd head to the volcano, as originally planned. Simple, but efficient.

Everyone set about their respective tasks.

Kaori and Shea headed off to the makeshift hospitals set up near the palace while Lanzwi, along with his guards and attendants, led Hajime, Yue, Tio, and Myu to Ankaji's largest open area.

The field was over three times the size Hajime had specified as a minimum. It was normally used to grow crops, but had been left fallow this year, to let the soil replenish.

Lanzwi still wasn't convinced Hajime could do what he claimed. If it turned out Hajime's plan was all some sort of elaborate trick, he would order Hajime executed. Lanzwi's town was in desperate need of water, and he had no time to waste on charlatans. He'd only agreed to this crazy idea because he had no other option. Fortunately for everyone involved, Lanzwi's suspicions proved unfounded.

Although there was no wind, Yue's hair started to flutter. The air became so saturated with mana that it glowed gold. Yue was using one of the spells she created with the ancient magic she acquired.

"Asura," she murmured. A swirling black sphere appeared above the empty farmland.

The sphere stretched and flattened until it morphed into a rectangle 200 square meters in size. After a brief pause, the rectangle silently sank into the ground, crushing the earth beneath it. A massive depression formed where the rectangle had been.

Asura had gouged the earth with such force that it caused a localized earthquake. The shaking stopped relatively quickly, the earth's cries of protest fading away.

In an instant, Yue created a massive reservoir to store all the water she was about to summon.

Hajime snuck a glance at Lanzwi, and saw that the older man's jaw had nearly hit the floor. He and his attendants were flabbergasted. They were at a loss for words, which was the only reason they weren't screaming in shock.

Yue breathed a tired sigh. She'd only unleashed Asura at half strength, so it hadn't drained all her mana. However, the spell still took a lot of effort.

She could replenish her mana using the jewelry set Hajime had given her, but she wanted to save that for the volcano. There wouldn't be time to restock in between, so the more she used now, the less she'd have later. And, since she wasn't in the middle of a fight, she had time to replenish her mana by other means.

Yue let her body fall backward. She didn't bother taking a falling stance. She knew she wouldn't hit the ground. As she expected, Hajime caught her.

He lifted Yue up and turned her around. Yue smiled faintly and wrapped her arms around his neck. She brought her face close to his. "Thanks," she whispered, then bit into his neck.

Blood flowed forth. Yue ran her tongue down Hajime's neck, making sure to lap up every last drop. Yue always seemed more mature than her appearance suggested, but she looked downright seductive while drinking Hajime's blood.

The bloodsucking went on for a good few minutes. The way Yue moaned softly between gulps made it seem almost erotic. Although having their blood drained should have seemed fearsome, most of the men present watched Hajime with longing expressions.

Only Lanzwi had the presence of mind to maintain an austere expression. Recovering from his surprise, he organized his thoughts. His breathing was labored, and his eyes slightly bloodshot, but he surely wasn't thinking anything lewd.

Off to the side, Tio watched with an ecstatic expression. But at least she still thought to cover Myu's eyes. Some things were too stimulating for a four-year-old girl to see.

Myu squirmed and complained, but couldn't break free from Tio's boob prison.

Once her mana was fully replenished, Yue removed her fangs from Hajime's neck. She looked up at him and kissed him, her lips still stained with his blood.

The two gazed deeply into each other's eyes for a few seconds until a loud cough brought them back to reality. Lanzwi couldn't bear much more. His self-control would crumble. Hajime and Yue smiled awkwardly at each other, then turned away from the group and kissed again.

Lanzwi was so nonplussed that he dropped his regal facade. "Wait, wait, wait, wait," he ordered. "Whether we can see you or not isn't the problem. There's a mountain of things I'd like to ask about the bloodsucking and all, but first, could you get us that water you promised?!"

Shrugging, Hajime and Yue reluctantly got back to work.

Hopping down into the reservoir, Hajime brought Brise out of his Treasure Trove. He drove the vehicle around the reservoir, using his Ore Desynthesis skill to separate out the soil's water-absorbing components. Once that was done, he coated the surface of the reservoir with a thin layer of metal.

After Hajime finished, Yue stuck her arms out and cast a high-level water spell. "Tidal Wave!" As its name suggested, Tidal Wave blasted opponents with a wave of water.

Normally, the wave wouldn't be *that* huge, but Yue's spells were on a completely different level. She summoned a wave 150 meters wide and 100 meters tall. It flowed into the reservoir, filling it up a few centimeters. The basin could hold 200,000 tons of water. Yue repeated this process multiple times, stopping every so often to suck Hajime's blood. But he didn't have an infinite supply, and by the time the reservoir was half-full, he was starting to feel anemic.

If he lost any more blood, he'd probably faint. Fortunately, just then, Shea came running. Her arms were laden with magic stones Kaori had filled. Although she'd only drained a little mana from each patient, she'd already treated thousands. That had produced quite a lot. Even more impressively, it was only two hours since Kaori had begun. Considering Hajime and the others' ridiculous abilities, it was easy to forget that Kaori was pretty overpowered herself.

Shea handed Yue all of her magic stones, then ran back to help Kaori. A few hours later, the reservoir brimmed with pure, drinkable water.

"This is unbelievable," Lanzwi muttered to himself. He was staring at a reservoir of water nearly as large as the oasis. And it had been made from nothing, in the span of a few hours. He didn't even know what to say.

"This should last you guys a while. All that's left now is to investigate the oasis... If we can't purify it, you should contact the capital for help. The water here should be enough to sustain you until then."

"O-okay. I still have a mountain of questions for you, but...

Thank you. Truly. You've saved my people. Let me guide you to the oasis."

Lanzwi still hadn't completely recovered from his shock, but he knew now that Hajime and his friends were trustworthy. He no longer suspected them of having ulterior motives.

The party headed east, toward the great oasis. They arrived at a vast, sparkling expanse of pure blue water. It was so clear, it was hard to believe it was poisoned. However...

"Hm? Hajime?"

Hajime narrowed his eyes, focusing his gaze on a specific location. Yue tilted her head, noticing the slight shift in his demeanor.

"It's just... My Demon Eye sensed something. Duke, what areas did your team investigate?"

"According to their report, they examined the oasis itself, the rivers that flow from it, and the nearby wells. They also examined the underground reservoir. I'm sure my son already told you what we found. The underground reservoirs were the only places that hadn't been poisoned. Basically, we examined everything within a few meters of the oasis... Although we haven't explored its bottom yet."

"Is there an artifact or anything at the bottom of the oasis?"

"Huh? No. We use a few artifacts to secure the oasis, but nothing inside the oasis itself. Normally, the barrier artifacts would make it impossible to pollute. This is the first incident of its kind."

The barrier artifact Lanzwi referred to was known as the Judgment of Truth. It produced the dome of light that protected Ankaji.

It allowed through things essential for life, like air and water, while keeping sand and other nuisances out. The wielder of the Judgment of Truth decided what could and couldn't pass through. Not only that, it could be used as a sensor. Like its barrier component, it was set according to its wielder. As it incorporated dark magic, the Judgment of Truth could even be set to react to certain thoughts.

In other words, if Lanzwi set the artifact to detect anyone who meant the oasis harm, it should have reacted when the person who poisoned the oasis entered the city. That was *if* Lanzwi had set it that way. Only he knew how he'd formatted the Judgment of Truth. At present, security around the oasis was thin. It had already been polluted, and so many people were going to and fro, Lanzwi saw little point in keeping a tight guard.

"Huh. So, what's that, then?"

Hajime turned away from Lanzwi, who was clenching his fists in frustration, and pointed to the center of the oasis. His Demon Eye sensed something emitting mana from the bottom.

Lanzwi looked up in surprise. He couldn't believe there was something there that he wasn't aware of.

Hajime walked up to the water and pulled something shaped like a bottle from his Treasure Trove. He started pouring mana into it. Once he was done, he casually threw it into the oasis, backing up toward Yue. Lanzwi shot him a questioning stare, but Hajime said nothing. Just as Lanzwi was about to run out of patience, there was a huge explosion, and a massive pillar of water erupted from the center of the oasis. Lanzwi's jaw dropped.

"Tch, it's faster than I thought... Or, wait, maybe its defense is just really high?"

Hajime pulled out a dozen more bottle-shaped explosives and tossed them into the oasis. A few seconds later, another massive spout of water erupted from the center.

What he'd thrown were actually custom torpedoes of his own design. He'd made them to prepare for their expedition into Melusine. According to Miledi, the sunken ruins were, shockingly, underwater, so Hajime had designed a few prototype torpedoes. This mystery object was a perfect test dummy. So far, it appeared that his torpedoes lacked speed and tracking capabilities, although their firepower was sufficient. *Guess I need to refine my design.*

Hajime had added ore enchanted with Sense Presence and Tracking to his torpedoes. Once they locked onto a target, they would chase it until they got within the blast radius. Then they would explode. Right now, he'd had them lock onto the mysterious thing in the water.

"Hey! What are you doing, Hajime-dono?!" Lanzwi exclaimed. "Ahh! You just destroyed the pier! There are chunks of fish floating up from everywhere! The whole oasis is turning red!"

"Tch. Still not good enough? Fine, maybe fifty will do the trick..."

Hajime ignored Lanzwi's anguished screams and stepped forward, preparing an even grander attack. Lanzwi's guards clung to Hajime, begging him to stop.

They couldn't see the thing Hajime was trying to destroy. To them, it looked like he'd randomly started throwing explosives.

He'd already destroyed the pier and killed countless fish, and they needed to stop him before the damage got any worse.

Since the Judgment of Truth didn't react, Lanzwi could tell Hajime wasn't trying to harm the oasis. However, that only made his destructive actions more confusing. Besides, Lanzwi and his guards had to protect the oasis.

Annoyed, Hajime brushed Lanzwi's guards off. But before he could throw his next batch of torpedoes—

"Wha...?!"

Countless tentacles of water suddenly shot from the oasis and headed straight for Hajime.

Hajime pulled out Donner and Schlag and started shooting the tentacles down. Yue froze as many as she could, while Tio evaporated the rest with fire magic.

Lanzwi stared, slack-jawed. Infuriated by Hajime's constant bombardment, the water rose up. Seemingly defying gravity, it created a mound ten meters high.

"What...in Ehit's name..." Lanzwi's hushed voice carried surprisingly far.

The water morphed from a mound into a horrific creature. Wriggling tentacles covered its body, and a red mana crystal glowed at its center. It resembled the slimes Hajime had seen in video games.

However, its size was on a completely different level. It was ten times larger than any such monster Hajime had ever seen. Also, the slimes Hajime remembered hadn't possessed the ability to manipulate water. Nor had they shot water tentacles at people.

"What...what kind of monster is this? Some kind of... Bachulum, maybe?" Lanzwi tried to make sense of what he was seeing. Bachulum was the scientific name for Tortus' slime monster species.

"Well, it doesn't really matter what it is. That's the thing polluting your oasis. Its unique magic probably has something to do with releasing toxins."

"That would certainly make sense, but how will you defeat it?"

The Bachulum continued its attack, even as Hajime and Lanzwi spoke. However, Yue and Tio kept its tentacles at bay.

Hajime too fired Donner and Schlag continually. He was trying to find an opening to shoot the Bachulum's core, but the monster kept moving around inside the slime, making it difficult for Hajime to get a clear shot. It was as though it had a will of its own.

Lanzwi was so used to being surprised that Hajime's guns didn't even faze him. Instead, he calmly asked whether Hajime had a plan to deal with the Bachulum.

"Hmmm." Hajime barely registered Lanzwi's question, and only gave a perfunctory reply. "Ah, don't worry. I've got it." His entire focus was on the whizzing mana crystal inside the slime. After a few seconds, he holstered Schlag, and held Donner with both hands.

Hajime wrapped his left arm around his right, bent his left elbow, and spread his feet, right foot slightly forward. He was copying the Weaver Stance he'd seen back on Earth. To hit the mana crystal, he'd need ungodly precision.

Hajime's eyes were as sharp as a hawk's, and he'd finally grasped the crystal's movements.

He held the stance for a few seconds, waiting for the perfect opportunity.

Bang! A single streak of light trailed through the sky. The mana crystal moved directly into the bullet's path, as though magnetically pulled.

It was a clean hit, and the crystal shattered into a thousand pieces. With the slime dead, there was nothing left to control the water, which splashed back into the oasis. Waves rippled from the point of impact, as if signaling an end to the town's pollution.

"Is it over?" Lanzwi asked hesitantly.

"Should be. I don't sense any mana in the oasis anymore. Although I don't know whether getting rid of the monster also purified the water."

Lanzwi couldn't believe Hajime had solved their crisis so easily. Ankaji had verged on ruin, and this stranger just waltzed in and fixed everything. An attendant hurried over to the water and appraised the oasis' quality.

"How is it?"

"The water's still polluted."

The attendant shook his head, dashing Lanzwi's hopes. People who drank directly from the oasis had gotten sick as well, so everyone had known it was poisoned from the start. Still, it was disappointing that killing the slime hadn't purified it.

"Now, now, there's no need to be so depressed. Now that the source is gone, poisoned water will stop spreading. The underground reservoir should still be clean, so if you dispose of all the infected water, you can replace it with that. Then, you'll have your old oasis back."

Tio tried to comfort Lanzwi and the others. Their gloomy expressions perked up a little, and they started thinking about how to revive their city. Their determination and unity showed Hajime just how much the citizens and their lord cared. Even in these dire straits, no one was thinking of abandoning Ankaji.

"But what kind of monster was that Bachulum-like thing…? Some new species that found its way to the oasis through an underground tunnel?" Lanzwi tilted his head and stared at the oasis.

Hajime provided his answer. "It was…probably the demons' work, right?"

"Demons?! Hajime-dono, you must have some basis for that accusation." Quickly recovering from his surprise, Lanzwi pressed Hajime for more information. After seeing how swiftly Hajime dealt with both the water and the monster, Lanzwi respected him greatly. Never again would he doubt Hajime's abilities.

Since the Bachulum they'd encountered was a type no one had seen before, Hajime guessed it must have been some new species, which the demons created with their ancient magic. The slime's many peculiarities matched those of the monsters that attacked Ur, and the ones that attacked Kaori in Orcus. Chances were, the demons were building up their monster army. They apparently wanted the humans as weak as possible before the war started, so they were striking preemptively at the most important human assets. Aiko had the potential to revolutionize the kingdom's agriculture, and the heroes the Holy Church had summoned were humanity's strongest trump card. The demons would want to eliminate them as soon as possible.

Ankaji, too, was an important lifeline for the kingdom. It was a major crossroads, and almost all of the northern continent's seafood passed through its borders. Best of all, since it was in a desert, it was comparatively isolated. It was a perfect target. That was why demons were Hajime's first thought.

When he explained as much to Lanzwi, the man groaned.

"I've heard about the other monster attacks," he admitted. "We conducted our own investigation into the affair, but...we never thought they could launch an attack like this. We were too naive."

"Don't beat yourself up. Even people in the capital couldn't have guessed that the demons were making new species of monsters. The hero party was only attacked a few days ago. The whole kingdom's probably in an uproar. There hasn't been time to share information."

"I guess the demons are finally making their move. Hajime-dono, you said you were an adventurer. But given your inhuman strength and those artifacts you carry, I can only assume that, like Kaori-dono, you are one of Ehit's warriors."

Hajime shrugged. Lanzwi guessed that Hajime had his own reasons for not elaborating, so he didn't pry. Regardless of what secrets Hajime was hiding, he was still Ankaji's savior. Besides, there were more important matters to deal with.

"Hajime-dono, Yue-dono, Tio-dono. I, Duke Lanzwi Feuward Zengen, humbly thank you for saving the city of Ankaji and its people. We will forever be in your debt." Lanzwi and his attendants bowed to Hajime and the others.

It was rare for the duke of a city to bow their head to anyone, but Hajime had earned that honor. It didn't matter whether he was one of Ehit's warriors, since his actions had saved thousands of lives. Hajime hadn't known Lanzwi long, but he could tell the duke cared deeply for his people and country. The duke's attendants knew that as well. When Lanzwi bowed to Hajime, they didn't stop him, but elected to join him instead. Hajime could tell who Bize took after. Even their mannerisms were similar.

Hajime grinned to himself. "That's right, you guys owe me now," he said. "Don't forget it."

He could make use of their gratitude. When it came to turning things to his advantage, Hajime had no shame.

Lanzwi expected Hajime to be humble, while covertly trying to curry favor, so he was taken by surprise when Hajime just laid out the facts. Still, he planned to repay his debt regardless, so it wasn't a big deal.

Honestly, Hajime didn't feel as though he'd done anything altruistic. Saving Ankaji was Kaori's request, and he had a personal stake in ensuring the city's safety. After all, he needed to leave Myu there while he explored the Grand Gruen Volcano.

However, if Lanzwi felt obligated to him, he would be a fool not to capitalize on that. The more allies he had when the time came to deal with the Holy Church, the better. Lanzwi had planned to return Hajime's good faith regardless, but as a politician, he understood that it was important to officially promise such things.

"Y-yes, of course. I'll never forget your service to us... Unfortunately, my city is still suffering. Could I request your help in healing the patients?"

Lanzwi had grown accustomed to dealing with odd people during his time as a politician, so he recovered from his surprise relatively quickly. Smiling ruefully, he agreed to Hajime's demands for repayment. However, Lanzwi wanted his citizens restored to good health before doing anything.

"I was planning on heading to the Grand Gruen Volcano anyway, so I don't mind," Hajime replied. "How much stillstone do you need?"

"Thank you so much," Lanzwi sighed in relief. "Hey, someone get me the medical reports!"

Lanzwi ordered one of his attendants to get him the reports on how much stillstone they'd need to cure everyone. It turned out they needed quite a bit.

"We'll require a lot. Would you like me to send porters with you?"

"Nah, no need. I've got a transportation artifact that merchants would kill for."

Lanzwi threw his arms up in amazement. "At this point, you could tell me you command the heavens themselves, and I'd believe you. It must be the blessings of Ehit that guided you here." He smiled wryly as he looked at Hajime. *Is there anything this boy can't do?*

Around the same time, Kaori and Shea were working frantically to treat the patients.

Starting with the ones in the worst condition, Kaori absorbed mana in batches, her Sanctorum reaching everyone within a radius of ten meters. Her healing spells had about the same effect range, so she could cast healing magic at the same time.

Meanwhile, Shea carried the patients Kaori had already treated away, and carried in new ones. She filled an entire cart with people and transported them en masse. Instead of running through the buildings, she hopped over the rooftops to save time. It was faster to bring critically ill patients to Kaori than to have Kaori run around to every makeshift hospital.

It was quite a sight, watching a diminutive girl carry entire carts of people across rooftops. Many of the patients thought the disease had made them hallucinate, and a fair few panicked. Some hospitals descended into chaos.

The doctors were amazed at how effortlessly Kaori juggled multiple high-level healing spells. Before long, she took charge of the entire treatment operation, and all the healers received orders from her.

She was still in the middle of healing patients when Hajime and the others showed up. Seeing Lanzwi following behind, the patients and healers tried to bow to the duke. However, he raised a hand to stop them.

"Listen to me, everyone! Just now, we eliminated the source of the poison! It will take some time, but we can reclaim our oasis! Not only that, we have secured a new source of water! It's large enough to sustain us until relief arrives. Best of all, this gold-rank adventurer has agreed to harvest stillstone for us! Hang on for just a few more days, everyone! Together, we'll weather this storm!" Lanzwi's deep voice echoed through the room. Hajime could see why the kingdom had entrusted such an important city to his rule. He possessed both wisdom and charisma.

At first, the patients were confused, but Lanzwi's smiling face convinced them that this was not a joke, or a white lie to raise their spirits.

Cheers rang throughout the hospital. The citizens had despaired, but now, hope colored their faces. This ordeal could end without more lives being lost. Families hugged each other, weeping openly. Healers patted each other on the back, relieved that their efforts would not be in vain. People thanked Hajime and Kaori for saving them.

Lanzwi glanced over at Hajime. Noticing his gaze, Hajime turned, grimacing. "Duke, you..."

"Don't look so concerned. If you don't come back, we'll simply despair."

The implicit message hung in the air. *If you don't save us, we're all dead, so you better not let us down. You promised you'd fulfill my request, so you better hold your end of the bargain.* Although he was grateful to Hajime, Lanzwi had no one else to rely on. He wanted to know that Hajime would keep his word. Hundreds of thousands of lives were on the line, after all. Thus, Lanzwi appealed to Hajime's conscience. He hoped it would make Hajime feel too guilty to run away.

"You're a crafty one, huh?"

"You have to be, to survive as a noble."

Hajime smiled ruefully and Lanzwi shrugged his shoulders. In truth, Hajime wasn't really mad. He'd expected something like this. If the duke hadn't tried to secure some kind of insurance, Hajime would have doubted his competence. Still, Hajime wouldn't feel terribly guilty, even if he did flee. The destruction of Ankaji, and the death of its citizens, wouldn't weigh on his conscience.

Hajime turned away and walked to Kaori.

"Kaori, we're gonna head to the Grand Gruen Volcano now. How long do you think you can keep this up?"

"Hajime-kun..." Kaori smiled, but her expression grew serious as she ran the numbers in her head.

"Two days," she replied, once she'd done the math. That was the longest she could keep the patients alive.

"Hajime-kun, I'll do everything I can here to heal the patients, so please, bring the stillstone back as soon as possible. I'm sorry... I know you don't care about this world's people, but I still..."

"It was on our way, so it's not a big deal. Besides, I agreed to help. I can hardly leave Myu behind in a city filled with corpses."

"Hee hee! That's right. She's relying on you. Don't worry, I'll look after Myu-chan while you're gone."

Hajime had explained everything he went through to Kaori while they drove through the desert. She knew about the mad gods and the fact that Hajime prioritized going home over everything. If she couldn't accept that, she was free to return to Kouki's party. But of course, she'd elected to stay.

Even if Hajime abandoned Ankaji, Kaori still wouldn't leave his side. She would try to persuade him, but if he insisted, she would accept his decision.

That said, she still wanted to help the people of Ankaji. Fortunately, her puppy-dog look convinced Hajime. She wasn't conceited enough to think that she could manipulate Hajime with her charms, but she was glad to know that her opinion had some influence.

At the same time, she felt bad for forcing him to go along with her desires.

That was why she'd apologized. However, Hajime apparently wasn't that bothered by the decision. He saw through Kaori's worries, and told her that it was his decision. Kaori could tell he was just trying to be considerate. She smiled at him, her gaze full of trust and love.

"I'll do my best here, so come back safely, all right? I'll be waiting."

"G-gotcha."

Kaori sounded like a housewife sending her husband off to war. It was surprisingly touching, and Hajime was at a loss for words.

Even back in Japan, Kaori had always been straightforward. She'd talked to Hajime every day in class, ignoring Kouki's warnings and the jealous stares. Eventually, Hajime got used to it, but she'd grown even more bold since confessing to him.

Hajime blushed and looked away, only to find himself face-to-face with Yue.

She gave him a frigid glare. Hajime shivered. Turning back, he saw Kaori smiling at him again. Hajime despaired, trapped between two predators. Then Myu complicated things.

"Kaori-oneechan, are you going to kiss Daddy like Yue-oneechan did earlier?"

"Oh, you saw that, Myu?"

"Huh? I could see through the gaps in your fingers, Tio-oneechan. Yue-oneechan looked really cute. Myu wants to try kissing Daddy too."

"Hmm... Even I have not kissed Master yet. Myu, you'll have to wait until you're older before you can do such things."

"Aww..."

Hajime glared at Tio, although there was no way she could have stopped Myu from peeking. As always, Tio derived immense pleasure from being glared at, but Hajime didn't have any time to spare for her.

That strange sword-wielding demon had appeared behind Kaori again, and it looked angrier than ever. That logic-defying creature's arrival was always bad news.

"Whatever could Myu be talking about, I wonder? Didn't you set out to fix the oasis, Hajime-kun? So, how come you were kissing Yue? What happened to doing your job? Or was kissing her part of your job? Don't tell me you two were off having fun while I was working myself to the bone treating patients. You couldn't possibly have done something so cruel, right? You didn't just leave me to get some alone time, did you?"

The darkness in Kaori's eyes terrified Hajime. Cold sweat

dripped down his forehead. He tried to explain, but before he could say anything, Yue stepped forward.

Hajime mistakenly believed that she would solve the misunderstanding, but expecting anything from Yue when she was like this was a mistake. She put her hands on her hips and puffed out her chest, grinning triumphantly.

"It was great," she said simply.

"Aha ha ha ha ha ha!"

"Hee hee hee hee!"

Kaori and Yue's laughter echoed through the hospital. Before that point, the doctors and patients all considered Kaori some kind of saint. Now that they saw her true colors, they backed away, pale.

It was impossible to believe someone possessing such a demonic spirit could be a saint. Worse, a giant thunder dragon had started forming behind Yue. Everyone was terrified to see what happened next.

Sighing, Hajime walked between the two women and flicked both of them on the forehead. It was just a flick, but he put considerable force behind it. Kaori and Yue crouched in pain, clutching their foreheads. They looked up at him reproachfully.

"Kaori. I didn't suggest we split up so I could spend time with Yue," he tried to explain, exasperated. "You should know that. Besides, Yue's my lover. You don't have any right to complain about what we do. You agreed to those conditions when you decided to come along."

"Um... I know, but...I can't control my feelings..." Kaori hung her head, but still tried to argue back.

Hajime sighed again and turned to Yue.

"And you, stop picking fights with her every chance you get."

Yue turned away, sulking. "This is a fight between women. You have no right to interfere, Hajime."

"Is it just me, or am I being ignored more often now?" Shea lamented.

Tio, still lost in the throes of ecstasy, missed the confrontation entirely. Myu, however, wasn't happy to see Kaori and Yue fighting again.

It took some time for Hajime to calm everyone down, but finally, they were ready to depart for the Grand Gruen Volcano. Since Kaori would be busy tending to the patients, Hajime asked Lanzwi to help her look after Myu. Lanzwi was still stunned by the group's convoluted relationships. Nevertheless, he happily agreed.

Hajime had told Myu that he needed to leave her behind while he explored the volcano, but she still wasn't happy. He bent down and patted her on the head.

"I'm going now, Myu. Will you be a good girl while I'm gone?"

"I...I will. So, please, come back soon, Daddy."

"Don't worry. I'll be back as soon as I can."

Myu clung to Hajime's shirt, trying her best not to cry. He comforted her just like a real father. People began to relax. Hajime gave Myu's back a little push, and sent her off to Kaori. Then he turned to Yue, Shea, and Tio.

However, before he could leave, Kaori stopped him.

"Ah, Hajime-kun... Stay safe."

"Will do. Take care of Myu for me."

"I will. Also, umm... Could you give me a kiss? A...goodbye kiss?"

"Definitely not. Where'd that idea come from?"

"Not even on the cheek? Please?" Kaori blushed, but her voice remained firm. She knew that she needed confidence to stand any chance against Yue. She'd been bold even back in Japan, but all of her restraint had disappeared after her confession.

"Oh, give me one too!" Shea tried to grab Hajime's attention, but he ignored her. He opened his mouth, planning to refuse, but Myu butted in.

"Myu wants one too. Myu wants Daddy to kiss her!" She had decided she wanted to join the fun. Hajime tried to explain why he couldn't, but his words didn't get through. "Do you hate me, Daddy?"

Hajime could feel his heart melting.

In the end, he kissed Kaori, Myu, and for some reason even Shea on the cheek. The doctors and patients watched fondly. Feeling too awkward to remain even a second longer, Hajime hurriedly left for the Grand Gruen Volcano.

Tio also asked for a kiss, but Hajime ended up just slapping her. Her panting creeped him out too much.

•/• •/• •/• •/• •/• •/• •/• •/• •/• •/• •/• •/• •/•

The Grand Gruen Volcano was approximately 100 kilometers north of Ankaji. It was around five kilometers in diameter at its base, and it rose to the modest height of 3000 meters. It was dome-shaped, rather than conical like most volcanoes. However, its summit was flat. It seemed more like a hill than a mountain. A really, really big hill.

Although the Grand Gruen Volcano was one of the few well-known labyrinths aside from the Great Orcus, it wasn't nearly as popular. It was more dangerous than the Orcus Labyrinth, and the monsters roaming its depths contained less valuable mana crystals. However, the main reason for its unpopularity was that it was difficult to reach.

And not just because it was in the middle of a desert.

"It looks like Laputa."

"Laputa?"

Yue and the others had no idea that Hajime was referencing a famous movie. Hajime just shrugged and stared at the whirling sandstorm surrounding the volcano.

Just as Laputa had been surrounded by a veil of thick clouds, the Grand Gruen Volcano was wreathed by a massive sandstorm. The wind and sand were so thick that they looked more like a spinning wall than a tornado.

However, that wasn't all. Sandworms and other deadly monsters lurked within the storm. Fighting them off would prove difficult in low visibility. Hajime could see why most adventurers weren't qualified to even make it past the sandstorm.

As they stared out the windows at the howling storm, Shea and Tio murmured their appreciation for Brise.

"I'm so glad we didn't decide to do this trip on foot."

"Even someone as sturdy as me wouldn't enjoy marching through that."

They couldn't take their time conquering this labyrinth. The stillstone deposits on the volcano's surface weren't large enough to cure all of Ankaji, so Hajime would need to harvest the stone deep below. If this was anything like the other labyrinths, there'd be a shortcut leading back outside from the center. It'd be faster to conquer the whole thing than to fight halfway down, then double back. Once they were out, making it back to Ankaji would be easy.

Hajime wasn't invested in saving Ankaji's citizens, but if it was possible to save them without risking himself, that sounded good. If nothing else, that would spare him from Kaori and Myu's tears.

Hajime gunned Brise's accelerator and charged into the storm.

Inside, their vision was blocked by the wall of brown that surrounded them on all sides. Like the mist they'd encountered in the Haltina Woods, the sandstorm reduced their visibility to practically nothing. Since the sand could physically harm them, it was even more dangerous. Even with magic barriers and good equipment, breaking through while surviving attacks would be no easy feat.

The sun's rays didn't penetrate the storm. The only source of light was Brise's green glowstone headlights. Hajime slowed down to about 30 kilometers per hour. At that speed, he estimated they'd be out of the storm in five minutes.

Shea's bunny ears perked up, and a second later, Hajime's eyes narrowed.

"Hang on tight!" he yelled, gunning the accelerator.

Three sandworms burst from the ground behind them.

Hajime swerved from side to side, dodging their attacks. Once he was clear, he sped up again.

Considering Brise's speed, it made more sense to push straight through than try to fight the monsters.

Two more sandworms erupted from the ground on either side of Brise, bearing down in a pincer attack. Their aim was perfect, and they headed straight for Brise's side doors. The impact itself wouldn't break the armor, but Hajime didn't want the car to flip over. He was just about to turn into a drift when Yue and Tio stopped him.

"Hmm... Leave this to us."

"Indeed. We can handle this, Master."

Hajime nodded and straightened the steering wheel. The sandworms were so close the party could see the beasts with their naked eyes.

Just before the worms slammed into the truck, they stopped.

"Wind Blades."

Yue summoned a barrage of blades that cut through the storm, heading straight for the sandworm on the left. The blades sliced right through, cutting it in half. Blood spurted everywhere as the sandworm split down the middle.

The one on the right suffered a similar fate as Tio's spell tore it to shreds.

"A wonderful display, Yue. You executed your magic magnificently."

"You're pretty good too, Tio. I didn't think you could use the sandstorm's winds like that."

Wind Blades was a beginner-level wind spell, but the mana Yue and Tio poured in gave their magic the force of intermediate spells. Furthermore, they utilized the sandstorm's winds to further increase the spells' force. Skilled magicians didn't just have vast amounts of mana. They also knew how to use their environment and pick the best spell for a situation. It sounded simple, but was easier said than done. Yue and Tio had both spent years practicing.

The three sandworms from earlier caught up to Brise. Their underground speed was truly impressive. Annoyed by their persistence, Hajime activated one of Brise's weapons. There was a loud clang from the back of the truck, and a couple of black, round objects rolled out from underneath.

The moment the round objects got close to the sandworms, they exploded. The force shook the ground, and chunks of sandworm flesh flew through the air. Hajime threw out another handful of grenades, finishing off any survivors. One sandworm was blown in half. Its head whirled through the sky before the sand swallowed it.

Shea was watching from the rear window. "Wow, that was amazing. Hajime-san, how many different things did you add to Brise?"

Hajime grinned wickedly. "It can also transform into a giant, human-shaped golem to fight."

"......"

That sounded unbelievable, but knowing Hajime, he might really have done it. Shea, Yue, and Tio all started looking around the car for hints as to how it would transform.

"I'm kidding. Even I wouldn't go that far... Although I did want to," Hajime added with a smirk. The girls were certain he'd do it eventually.

As they drove farther into the storm, they came under attack from giant ants and spiders. However, the combination of Yue and Tio's magic, and Brise's built-in weapons, made short work of all of them. The monsters didn't even have a chance.

Shea sulked in the back, lamenting her own uselessness. Hajime and the others ignored her, breezing through the sandstorm that repelled so many adventurers.

A few minutes later, they burst through the other side. Up close, the volcano looked like Ayers Rock, scaled up. The center was surprisingly silent. Without the wind whipping the sand everywhere, they had a clear view of the dazzling blue sky. *So, this is what the eye of a storm is like?*

The volcano's entrance was at its peak, so Hajime drove Brise up the gentle slope. The dark red rock sizzled and sputtered, steam rising here and there. Although this was an active volcano, it had never erupted. That probably had something to do with the fact it was a labyrinth.

Finally, the mountainside grew too steep for Brise, and Hajime reluctantly put it away. They'd have to finish on foot.

"Whoa. I-It's hot."

"Mhm," grunted Hajime.

"Yeah. The stone's hotter than the sand was. Even if we didn't have a time limit, this is one place where I wouldn't wanna spend much time."

"Hmm... Personally, I find this temperature quite agreeable," mused Tio. "It certainly is a shame that I cannot suffer the heat as you can."

"Want me to drop you in some magma? Then you can suffer too."

Everyone but Tio found the volcano's temperature suffocating. The effects were made worse by the stark contrast from the air-conditioned car. *I probably shouldn't have spent all my life in Japan holed up in my air-conditioned room. You reap what you sow, I guess.*

Aware the clock was ticking, the group hurried up the mountainside, complaining all the while. They reached the summit in less than an hour.

At the top, they found boulders strewn all about, creating a complex rock maze. The juxtaposition of jagged, glossy boulders with polished, smooth ones resembled a science museum's geology exhibit. The sandstorm looked close enough to touch.

One boulder stood out among the mass of stones. It had been shaped into an arch at least 10 meters high.

As he approached, Hajime spotted a staircase descending into the volcano below. He stopped at the top of stairs, looked back at Yue, Shea, and Tio, then gave each of them a confident nod.

"Let's do this!"

"Okay!"

"You got it!"

"Very well!"

◦│◦ ◦│◦ ◦│◦ ◦│◦ ◦│◦ ◦│◦ ◦│◦ ◦│◦ ◦│◦ ◦│◦ ◦│◦ ◦│◦ ◦│◦

Hajime thought the interiors of the Great Orcus Labyrinth

and Reisen Gorge were ridiculous, but they paled in comparison to the Grand Gruen Volcano's absurdity. The monsters weren't tougher, but the volcano's construction was absolutely awe-inspiring. It was like nothing he'd ever seen.

What he was most surprised by was the magma floating in the air, filling the space before him. It wasn't like the treetop aqueducts Hajime had seen in Verbergen. There was quite literally a stream of magma floating in the air. It snaked and swerved like an actual river, until it looked like a giant red dragon flying through the volcano.

Magma flowed through the passageways and rooms as well, so challengers had to be wary of lava both above and below them.

Furthermore...

"Ahhhh!" Shea yelped.

"Whoa," Hajime said. "You okay?"

"Yikes! Thank you, Hajime-san. I didn't think lava would spew out like that... It took me by surprise."

As Shea said, magma erupted at irregular intervals from spouts in the wall.

There was no warning, so it was hard to prepare. Nature had provided perfect traps for this labyrinth. *Thank god I have the Sense Heat skill,* Hajime thought. Without it, the volcano would have been slow going.

However, what really made the labyrinth grueling was the heat. Not just how hot the surfaces were, but the atmosphere itself. The abundant magma created the atmosphere of a superheated sauna. *This must be what an egg feels like when it's getting cooked.*

Sweat poured off them in buckets as they headed deeper.

They had to be careful to avoid magma droplets from above and the spouts from the side, but they made steady progress. After some time, they arrived in a room that was clearly man-made. It had been hollowed out with a rough tool, likely a pickaxe, and there was a glowing pink jewel slotted into one of the walls.

"Hm? That's...stillstone, right? That glowing thing?"

"Indeed it is, Master," Tio replied, drawing upon her vast knowledge. This appeared to be the excavation site most adventurers used to harvest stillstone.

"So small."

"All the others are only as big as pebbles, too..."

All of the stillstone they could find came in chunks no bigger than their pinky fingers. *I guess this section's been almost completely harvested.* There was no way they could acquire enough by only searching the upper floors. Their best bet was to make it to the bottom and find a large stash.

Hajime used Ore Appraisal on the stillstone, just in case. His magic confirmed what Tio had said, and they grabbed all the stillstone within easy reach before hurrying on.

They descended another seven floors, their irritation at the heat growing stronger with each new passage downward. According to the records Hajime had read, the seventh floor was the farthest any adventurer had gone. Or, at least, the farthest any adventurer had gone and returned. Steeling themselves, the party descended the next staircase.

As they stepped onto the eighth floor, they were buffeted by a searing gust of wind. A second later, a massive spout of fire bore

ARIFURETA: FROM COMMONPLACE TO WORLD'S STRONGEST

down on them. It shot toward them in a spiral, illuminating the orange walls.

"Spatial Severance." Yue reacted instantly with a defensive spell. A swirling black sphere materialized in front of them. This was another of Yue's gravity spells, but it wasn't used as an attack.

The conflagration, hot enough to melt bones, was sucked into Yue's sphere, and vanished without a trace. Actually, "vanished" wasn't the proper term. Yue's gravity sphere exerted a gravitational field strong enough to suck in its surroundings. Yue had calibrated it so it wouldn't affect those she was trying to protect, making it an ideal shield.

Since the flames no longer blocked their line of sight, Hajime and the others could see what attacked them.

Magma covered the ox monster's entire body, and it stood in a pool of the stuff. Its two curved horns were wickedly sharp, and each breath it exhaled was accompanied by a small fireball. *I don't care how strong you are. Nothing should survive getting slathered in magma.*

The Magma Ox kicked the ground angrily, sending drops of fire flying. It prepared to charge, angry that they had managed to repel its flames.

Yue snapped her fingers. Her gravity sphere sped toward the beast, and shot the absorbed flames back at the monster who'd cast them. Compressed by Yue's gravity sphere, they came out like a barrage of lasers.

Yue's bombardment spoiled the Magma Ox's charge. Ironically, it was stymied by its own flames.

With a loud boom, the magma blew away under Yue's bombardment. The ox went with it, flipping through the air a few times before crashing into the wall. It screamed in pain, but quickly got back up and charged. It wouldn't let these intruders live.

"Mrgh... I guess fire won't work on a fire monster." Yue sounded unhappy.

"I mean, it's already covered in magma, so...yeah?" Smiling wryly, Hajime made to pull out Donner, but Shea stopped him.

"Leave this to me, Hajime-san!" Shea had already unsheathed Drucken. She was breathing quickly.

She's being unusually assertive today. Hajime's Demon Eye detected the part of Drucken Shea was sending her mana to. Apparently, she wanted to try out the new feature he'd added. After a moment's hesitation, Hajime nodded.

"All right, say your prayers, you cow!"

Shea leaped fearlessly at the charging ox. She spun around in the air, adding centrifugal force to her swing before bringing it down. Her aim was perfect, and Drucken slammed into the Magma Ox's skull. Ripples of blue mana spread from the point of impact, each one a powerful shockwave. The ox's head went flying as though it had been blown off.

Shea used the force of her swing to flip the headless beast over, and landed safely on the ground.

"W-wow. Hajime-san, that was amazing. I did that myself, and *I* can't believe it happened. This upgrade is crazy!"

"Yeah, looks like it. I wasn't sure how well the shock converter would work, but that was..."

Even Yue and Tio were impressed. Shea's increased strength was all thanks to the shock converter.

Shock Conversion was a skill derived from Mana Conversion, and it allowed the user to convert their mana into pure force.

Hajime had acquired it from one of the new monsters he'd eaten. It came from the horse-headed beast he saved Kaori and the others from, back in the Orcus Labyrinth. When he recovered his pile bunker from its corpse, he took some meat with him as well.

Normal monsters had long since stopped giving Hajime new skills, or even improving his stats. However, since Kouki hadn't managed to defeat the horse-head, even with his Overdrive, Hajime guessed it must have been strong. As he expected, it possessed a new skill. His stats hadn't jumped too much, but the new skill had been worth it. He'd added Shock Conversion to Drucken using creation magic.

Hajime wanted to examine the ox's head, but Yue hurried him on.

As they continued downwards, the monsters grew more varied. They encountered bats that shot burning hot magma from their wings; eel-like creatures that swam through the walls, melting the stone as they passed; porcupines that fired flaming spines; chameleons that attacked with whip-like tongues from the magma; snakes that ignored gravity by swimming in the magma rivers... The list went on.

Not only did the magma coating provide an excellent defense against most low-level spells, the beasts used it as camouflage to launch surprise attacks. Even touching one would kill most humans. And, because the creatures could utilize the magma in their surroundings, everything was a potential weapon. On the off-chance the battle went poorly, they could also retreat into the magma.

Even adventurers who could clear the sandstorm wouldn't stand a chance against them. Now Hajime understood why no one had made it past the seventh floor. Not only was it dangerous, the reward didn't match the risk. The monsters themselves were no stronger than the ones on the Great Orcus Labyrinth's 40th floor, they just had magma to enhance them. That meant their mana crystals weren't too large, and the amount of stillstone to be found wasn't much more than on the higher floors.

Worst of all, the heat kept growing.

"Haaah...haaah... It's so hot."

"Saying that out loud will only make you feel hotter, Shea. Just imagine that we're swimming through water... Nice, cool water. Heh heh heh."

"M-Master! Yue's finally snapped! Her eyes have glazed over!"

Everyone but Tio took most of their damage from the heat. Hajime pulled out all the cooling artifacts he possessed, but it was like trying to push back a storm. Drenched in sweat and barely conscious, Yue, Shea, and Hajime were nearing their limits. *We're going to need a break,* Hajime thought, wiping sweat off his chin.

In the next room, Hajime transmuted a hole onto the wall furthest from the magma. Once everyone was inside, he closed it, leaving just a small airhole. Then he used Ore Desynthesis and

Compression Synthesis to coat the walls with superdense metal, so that stray eels or magma jets had no chance of getting in.

"Phew... Yue, can you make some ice? We'll take a short break here. If we press ahead like this, we'll slip up sooner or later."

"Mmm... Okay."

Although her eyes were still glazed over, Yue summoned a massive ice block into the center of the room. Tio cast basic wind magic to circulate the cold air. The temperature began to drop.

"Haaawaaah... It feels so good! I feel alive again!"

"Ahhh...!"

Yue and Shea sank to the floor, enjoying the cold breeze. They looked like half-melted snowmen.

They're cute like that, Hajime thought as he pulled towels out of his Treasure Trove and passed them around.

"Yue, Shea, relax all you want, but wipe yourselves off first. If you don't, you'll get too cold."

"Okay."

"Roger."

Tio walked up to Hajime.

"You don't seem to be having a hard time, Master."

"I wouldn't say that. You're probably the only one who's not affected. This heat's killing me. I should have made better cooling artifacts."

"Hmm... If it's bad enough that even *you're* suffering, then... It seems heat is this labyrinth's theme."

Even Tio, who hadn't been affected at first, was starting to sweat. She wiped herself off with the towel.

"Theme?"

"Indeed. From what you told me, Master, the labyrinths are all trials, correct? Trials to determine who is worthy to challenge the gods. Based on that description, it seems that each has its own theme. For example, the Great Orcus Labyrinth is filled with various monsters. It's designed to help challengers obtain different types of battle experience. The Reisen Gorge is designed to force challengers to clear obstacles without magic. And it appears this Grand Gruen Volcano is designed to see whether challengers can focus and respond to constant surprise attacks under extreme stress. In this case, the stress is heat."

"I see." Hajime nodded in agreement. "I figured I'd have to clear them all eventually, so I didn't give it much thought. But... now that you mention it, the trials certainly seem to be lessons the Liberators left behind for us."

Underneath her perverted exterior, Tio was quite the scholar. She was also exceptionally beautiful, with golden eyes and long black hair. *It's a shame her personality puts all that to waste.*

Hajime watched as a bead of sweat trailed down Tio's neck and vanished into her voluptuous bust. Embarrassed, he turned away. Unfortunately, Yue and Shea sat on his other side, their clothes so drenched with sweat that he could see their skin. This time, he was captivated by Yue's alluring figure.

She'd unbuttoned the top of her white shirt to wipe off the sweat underneath. Her skin was slightly flushed with the heat. Glistening with sweat and panting slightly, Yue looked seductive without even trying.

Hajime found himself unable to look away. Yue looked up, and their eyes met. Berating himself for letting his lust distract him, Hajime tried to look away, but Yue's captivating smile held him in place. He couldn't turn away even if he wanted to. Shirt still unbuttoned, Yue crawled toward him. Her back arched like a cat. Hajime's eyes darted between her inviting gaze, her flushed cheeks, and her nearly-exposed breasts. When she reached him, Yue looked up.

"Will you clean me up, Hajime?" she pleaded.

Those were dangerous words. Hajime silently accepted the towel. He still couldn't look away.

Crap, I'm screwed now. There's no way I can get myself out of this. Hajime smiled bitterly to himself and moved his hand toward Yue's neck. Before he could do anything, however, Shea interrupted them.

"*You two!* This isn't the time or the place for fooling around! We're in a hurry, and this is a labyrinth! Sheesh... I can't believe you guys!"

"Uhh, well, I mean, it's not my fault. Yue's just too seductive. How am I supposed to refuse her?"

"Hajime's cute when he's staring at me like that."

"Reflect on your actions! Also, how come you don't look at me like that, Hajime-san? I was sitting right next to Yue, drenched in sweat too... *hic*... I'm starting to lose confidence. Come on, Tio-san, you say something too."

"Hmm, those two seem quite deeply in love to me. I'm not sure there's anything to say. After all, I too wish to be berated, no matter the time or place. Besides...Master seems at least a little interested in my breasts. For me, that is more than enough. Hee hee."

As always, Tio's masochistic nature shone through. However, she had shrewdly noticed Hajime's interest.

"But he didn't even glance at mine!" Shea wailed, and began stripping.

It seemed she'd already forgotten why she'd yelled at Yue. Wanting to join in the fun, Tio started taking off her clothes as well. Hajime stopped them both with a rubber bullet from Donner.

Thank god Kaori isn't here to see this. Shea writhed on the ground, her breasts in plain view. Meanwhile, Tio squirmed in pleasure as Yue continued wiping herself down.

⁂

Hajime guessed that the Grand Gruen Volcano was likely fifty floors deep.

Coincidentally, that was about how many floors they'd descended already. He only thought it was "likely," despite having gone that far, because their current situation was a little unique. It was hard to tell exactly what floor they were on.

Hajime and the others were riding a dark brown boat down one of the volcano's magma rivers.

"This must be what Indiana Jones felt like on his adventures," Hajime muttered as he marveled at the absurdity of his situation.

It was Hajime's fault they ended up like this. They'd been progressing through the floors, harvesting stillstone wherever they found it. At one point, Hajime noticed that the magma moved in strange ways.

Although there were no boulders, the rivers parted around the air as if there were. In some places, the flow slowed, although there was nothing to impede it. And it only dripped down from above in certain spots.

Normally, it dripped away from the path, where it wouldn't be an obstacle to their progress, so Hajime hadn't paid it too much attention. However, he'd used his Ore Perception skill near a dripping section of river, and discovered that stillstone was causing the unnatural behavior. Mana was propelling the magma through the air. The stillstone neutralized that mana whenever the river got too close, causing it to act erratically.

Of course, it stood to reason that large quantities of stillstone were deposited in places where the river dripped. Upon investigating, Hajime found out he was right. Thanks to this new discovery, the party quickly managed to collect enough stillstone. To make sure they had enough to spare, Hajime and the others headed to where they assumed they'd find another deposit.

The river gave this section of wall a wide berth, so Hajime figured it contained stillstone. He transmuted a makeshift staircase and, using Ore Perception, found that there was a large quantity of stillstone in the wall.

Hajime quickly used Ore Desynthesis to remove the stillstone. However, the constant heat and the ease of the previous extractions caused him to drop his guard. He wasn't paying attention to what was inside the wall.

Only after he put the harvested stillstone into his Treasure Trove did he realize his mistake. Without the stillstone to stop it, a huge fountain of magma erupted.

Hajime jumped out of the way, but there was a lot of magma dammed up on the other side. More and more burst through, flooding the area.

Surrounded on all sides, they acted fast. Yue erected a barrier to protect them temporarily, while Hajime fashioned a boat so they could ride out the flood. The extreme heat burned through the boat quickly, but Hajime used Diamond Skin's derivative skill, Diamond Protection, to strengthen it. That allowed the boat to ride the magma without melting.

When the boat first threatened to sink, Shea used her gravity spell, Fluctuator, to make it float. Fluctuator let Shea regulate the gravity of anything she touched, much as she did her own weight.

The flood joined up with the magma river, and soon the party took the express route down to the volcano's center. After braving a few rapids, Hajime and the others arrived at the section of the river they now traversed.

"Ah, Hajime-san. Look, it's another tunnel."

"By my calculations, we should be nearing the volcano's base. It's likely we'll find something on the other side."

Hajime looked where Shea was pointing and saw a massive hole in the wall, with the magma river running through it. The magma doubled as illumination, so everyone could see the tunnel angled downward. Every time they'd gone through a tunnel, they found themselves one floor farther down. At least the river was a much faster route than descending normally.

The party nodded grimly to each other as the current carried them through. On the other side, they found that the floating magma river snaked its way down through a massive cavern. The flow grew slower as they descended, stopping at a curved section, where it suddenly turned into a waterfall of magma.

"Not this again... Everyone, hang on tight!"

The girls nodded and hung onto the edges of the boat, or Hajime himself. Hajime's stomach churned. It was just like riding a water coaster, except the water here was fatal. Finally, they plunged over the falls.

The wind roared in their ears. Shea's gravity magic and Tio's wind magic kept stray splashes from pelting them. Despite magma's supposedly viscous nature, they accelerated at a breakneck pace.

Hajime transmuted the bottom of his shoes into spikes to hold himself in place while he examined his surroundings. He didn't want to be caught off guard. Knowing the Liberators, this was where they'd set an ambush.

"Tch... I knew it."

Hajime clicked his tongue, pulled out Donner, quickly took aim, and fired. There were three loud bangs, and three streaks of red light. A flock of magma bats had swooped down to attack.

On their own, the bats weren't much of a threat. They could fly pretty fast and shoot fireballs, but that was about it. To Hajime and the others, they were small fry.

In a group, though, they became more of a threat. Where there was one, there was sure to be more. They swarmed out of the walls like cockroaches, dozens appearing from every crack and crevice.

Hajime shot down three, but he could hear many more flapping toward them... Enough that the sound of bat wings drowned out the wind.

"Hajime, leave the left and the back to me."

"You got it. Shea, Tio, make sure our boat doesn't fall apart."

"Roger!"

"Leave it to me. May I ask for a spanking as a reward?"

Hajime couldn't figure out if Tio was serious, so he ignored her. Yue and Hajime stood back to back, angled diagonally. As always, they were in perfect sync.

The magma bat colony bore down on the party in a coordinated rush. They were so close to each other that they looked like one giant flaming dragon. Their burning red wings melded together.

As they approached, the bats split into two groups. One attacked from the front, while the other circled behind. Weak as they were individually, they made for formidable foes en masse. Most people wouldn't have enough ammunition to take them all.

Unfortunately for the bats, they were facing one of the most overpowered parties in existence... One that had fought a far larger group of monsters back in Ur.

"Fight numbers with numbers. Eat lead, you flaming freaks!"

Hajime pulled his gatling gun, Metzelei, from his Treasure Trove. He braced it against his hip, took aim, and pulled the trigger.

The distinctive *ratatatata* of machine gun fire echoed through the cavern as Hajime mowed down the bats. The deadly hail of gunfire pierced even the most distant waves of monsters. Metzelei fired with such force that the far wall was riddled with holes.

However, there were more magma bats than even Metzelei could handle, so Hajime pulled Orkan out with his free hand and started firing rockets into the bunched-up group of monsters. The rockets left a trail of sparks as they struck, blowing dozens of the beasts to smithereens.

The bats never stood a chance. A torrent of chunks fell to the ground. Hajime had quite literally made it rain blood.

The magma bats behind him suffered a similar fate at Yue's hands.

"Storm Serpent."

A giant green globe of wind appeared before Yue's outstretched hand. The globe elongated and sprouted wings, transforming into a dragon. The dragon eyed its prey for a moment before opening its maw and charging.

The bats split into smaller groups, trying to avoid it. They pelted it with fireballs as they flapped out of the way. However, Yue's dragon was made of gravity magic. It couldn't be hurt by fire. Wind blades swirled around inside the dragon. Once it had set its sights on something, its target couldn't escape.

Like Yue's Draconic Thunder and Sapphire Serpent, Storm

Serpent exerted a gravitational field that drew enemies nearer. The magma bats were sucked in, and the wind blades ripped them to shreds. Yue chose a wind dragon because the bats were resistant to heat. Ripping their wings off with wind seemed the most efficient way to deal with them.

After the dragon swallowed up most of the bats, it flew to the center of the room and burst. The trapped wind blades flew out in all directions, cutting down the few bats lucky enough to avoid being sucked in.

"However many times I see it, Yue and Master's ability to annihilate hordes of enemies never ceases to amaze me."

"Yeah, they're incredible."

Tio and Shea exchanged a glance as they continued to steer and fortify the boat. Hajime put Metzelei and Orkan back into his Treasure Trove. Yue puffed her chest out proudly. Hajime patted her on the head, then turned to see what lay ahead. Yue went back to keeping watch.

Tio and Shea were pouting, angry that Hajime had taken yet another chance to flirt with Yue and ignore them. Feeling a little guilty, Hajime sheepishly scratched Shea's bunny ears and pinched Tio's cheek.

It seemed rather odd that such simple acts were enough to pacify her.

Hajime and the others had little difficulty dispatching monsters as they made their way through the rapids. However, after a few minutes, something changed. The river began angling upward instead of down.

Climbing a few dozen meters, the party could make out a light in the distance. The cavern's exit. Unfortunately, the river came to a dead halt right in front of it.

"Hang on, guys!"

Everyone clung to the edges of the boat again. They fell down the steepest drop yet as their boat rushed toward the exit.

Hajime felt momentarily weightless. However, he quickly reoriented himself, and examined his surroundings. The room they found themselves in was even more vast than the floating arena where they fought Miledi.

But this room wasn't spherical. It seemed to follow the rock's natural contours, making it difficult to grasp its exact size. The floor was covered in magma, with a few boulders jutting out here and there for footholds.

The walls also had protrusions large enough to stand on, and in some spots, sunken walls formed alcoves. Numerous rivers of fire crisscrossed each other in the sky, each spilling into the sea of magma beneath them.

Fountains occasionally spewed up from below. If there was a cauldron in hell, it might have looked like this. Hajime and the others exclaimed in wonder.

What was even more amazing was the island sitting in the center. It was made of the same rock as everything else, and rose a good ten meters above the boiling magma. What was special about it was its giant dome of magma. From afar, it looked like the island housed a mini-sun. It certainly wasn't an everyday sight.

"Updraft!"

The fall tossed the boat nearly upside-down, and Tio righted it with her magic. Once in place, Hajime and the others leaped through the air back onto the boat. Yue adjusted their speed with her own Updraft.

As they floated across the magma, Hajime and the others looked around warily.

"Is that where this labyrinth's Liberator lived?" Yue pointed to the island with the magma dome.

"Considering how far we've descended, it seems likely. But, then, that also means..."

"This is where we will have to face the guardian?"

Tio finished Hajime's sentence, scanning the room like a hawk. Sometimes Hajime almost forgot that she was a hopeless pervert. Shea didn't let her guard down, either, but tried to take a more optimistic view.

"Maybe we skipped past it by taking a shortcut?"

Hajime turned to follow Shea's gaze and saw a staircase leading to a raised platform. Chances were, that's where they would have emerged if they had taken the normal route down.

It might have been unthinkable to the labyrinth's designer that anyone would try and ride the magma. Still, Hajime doubted that they were careless enough to let anyone skip the final guardian. Even Shea didn't really believe they somehow slipped past it.

Unfortunately, they were right to be skeptical. Without warning, bullets of magma shot out of the sea, heading straight for the boat.

"Hmph! Let me handle this!"

Tio summoned her own balls of magma from the sea, and fired them at the oncoming bullets, neutralizing them.

However, that first attack was just an opening volley. As the shattered bullets dropped to the ground, another salvo came at them. This time, it also came from the rivers above.

"Tch... Everyone scatter!"

If they stayed on the boat, they'd be burned to ashes in no time. They leaped away onto the nearby boulders. A second later, their boat was bombarded, and sank into the fiery ocean.

The party landed on their footholds, and beat back the barrage of magma balls. The bullet waves weren't too numerous, but they soon grew irritated at the endless hail of magma. Part of that was the heat. The sky had grown so thick that it began to blur.

Hajime needed to do something fast. He finished reloading his revolvers and, without turning around, aimed Schlag behind him. He fired buckshot from his artificial elbow to clear the bullets closest to him, also shooting down the ones closing in on Yue.

Yue realized what Hajime wanted her to do. She used the reprieve to cast one of her gravity spells.

"Spatial Severance."

A black sphere materialized at a spot directly between the four of them. It sucked all the magma balls into itself. Inside the sphere, the magma was crushed under the immense pressure.

Now that he no longer had to worry about fending off magma bullets, Hajime was free to move. He leaped through the air with Aerodynamic, heading for the island.

The most dangerous thing about the endless barrage was that they could see no obvious way to halt it. This was obviously the Grand Gruen Volcano's final trial, but unlike the other labyrinths, the volcano contained no actual guardian to defeat. Hajime had no idea what they needed to do to clear it. The only clue was the strange island in the center.

"I'm going to investigate the central island," he told the others via Telepathy. "Cover me."

"Mmm... Okay."

As Hajime left the effective range of Yue's Spatial Severance, magma bullets headed towards him. Yue shot them all down with her own magma, maintaining Spatial Severance all the while.

Tio backed her up, supplementing Yue's magma balls with a few of her own. Shea pitched in too, shooting down bullets with Drucken's shotgun mode.

With everyone's help, Hajime was able to move quickly. However, just before he could make the final leap onto the central island, he was interrupted.

"Graaaaaaaaaaaaaaaaah!"

"Huh?!"

A bestial roar shook him to the very core. A second later, a giant magma serpent flew out of the sea, its jaws open wide.

Their surroundings were so hot that Hajime's Heat Perception hadn't sensed it. And since the entire sea was filled with mana, his Mana Perception skill didn't detect it either. For the first time since leaving Orcus' labyrinth, he was truly caught by surprise.

Hajime reacted with superhuman reflexes. He twisted to the

side and barely managed to dodge the serpent's jaws. It flew past him, its mouth closing over the spot where he'd just been.

Hajime used Aerodynamic to flip himself around and fired at the serpent as it passed. His bullets sped toward its head, each finding its mark.

"What the?!" Hajime yelled in surprise.

The serpent was still alive.

Hajime's bullets passed straight through its head, dislodging a bit of magma. The beast was hollow. All the other monsters Hajime had faced in the volcano possessed physical bodies underneath their lava. This was his first time facing a creature created purely from magma.

He quickly recovered, and tried shooting at other sections of the serpent, just in case. Unfortunately, the rest of its body was hollow as well.

"Man, what a pain. I don't have time to deal with you."

Hajime fired enough bullets that the dragon could no longer maintain its shape. Once it was rendered ineffectual, he slipped past it and sped off toward the island.

Still, the serpent wasn't done with him. Although the magma comprising its head and much of its body had been shot away, it could still move. It lurched toward Hajime, trying to tackle him.

Hajime used his elbow shotgun's recoil to push himself out of the way. Chills ran down his spine. Trusting his instincts, Hajime fired two more shotgun blasts, pushing himself even farther back. He augmented his movement with an Aerodynamic-powered leap, trying to gain as much distance as possible.

Barely a second later, multiple magma serpents shot out of the sea below, each chomping down where he'd been.

Hajime beat a hasty retreat and landed on a nearby platform. Yue alighted next to him. The storm of magma bullets had stopped once the serpents showed up.

"Are you all right, Hajime?"

"Yeah, I'm fine. Looks like this is gonna be the real test."

Yue placed a hand on Hajime's arm. He kept his gaze fixed straight ahead, but put his hand on top of hers. More and more magma serpents appeared.

"I guess that basically confirms that the central island's our goal. If we want to make it there, we'll have to destroy all the serpents."

"But the one you destroyed is regenerating already. How are we going to get rid of them?"

There were more than twenty serpents now, and they had the party surrounded. Just as Shea said, the one Hajime shot holes through had already begun to regenerate. When they found the regenerating golems in the Reisen Gorge, Shea had panicked, but now she had enough experience to think the problem through. Her rabbit ears twitched as she considered their options. Hajime smiled, proud at how far she'd come. Then he offered a suggestion of his own.

"I think they're like that giant slime we fought. There should be a core somewhere, controlling the magma. But because there's mana in everything, I can't use my Demon Eye to search for it... We'll probably just have to smash everything."

Everyone nodded, and the twenty-plus snakes attacked.

The magma serpents spat fireballs that shone as brightly as solar flares. The fireballs closed in from all sides, followed closely by the serpents themselves. Any normal party would have been swallowed by the flames and burnt to a crisp.

"It's been some time since I went all out! Behold my power!"

Jet-black mana swirled around Tio's outstretched hands. She compressed it into a single point and fired off a pitch-black laser... Her prized dragonbreath.

It was the same ability that had forced Hajime onto the defensive. The black stream cut through the fireballs and vaporized the serpents in front of her. She turned slowly, her breath cutting through everything like a massive black blade. Within seconds, eight serpents lay dead.

Hajime and the others used the opening to escape their confines.

They thought that if they vaporized the serpents, they'd definitely destroy the mana crystal powering them, too. Sadly, things were never that easy in a labyrinth.

The remaining serpents crashed into the platform where the party had been standing, pulverizing it, and sank into the sea. When they emerged once more, their numbers were replenished.

"You've gotta be kidding me! I saw their mana crystals shatter. Does this mean defeating them isn't the goal?"

Hajime tilted his head in thought. He'd used Riftwalk to watch Tio's breath rip through the serpents in slow motion. He'd seen a mana crystal inside each one, and he'd seen her breath vaporize them.

"Hajime-san, look at that!" Shea shouted, pointing to the central island and jolting Hajime out of his musings. "The boulder's glowing!"

"What?"

Hajime turned to look. Part of the boulder was indeed aglow. He hadn't noticed before, but some strange rocks were buried on the island. A few now shone bright orange.

Hajime used Farsight to examine the island more closely. More of those rocks seemed to be buried at regular intervals within it. They were almost the same color as the island, so it was hard to make them out. The island was cylindrical, and Hajime guessed, based on its circumference and the distance between each glowing rock, that there were around one hundred in total. Of those hundred, eight were glowing. *And Tio killed eight of serpents.*

"I see... We have to kill a hundred of these things to clear this trial."

"So, it's meant to be a battle of endurance in the heat. It seems I guessed this labyrinth's theme correctly."

Anyone who made it this far would be exhausted by the constant surprise attacks and ever-present heat. And yet, this final trial required more concentration and focus than any up to that point. It was just like the Liberators to ramp up the difficulty at the very end.

Even Hajime and the others were beginning to grow weary. Still, they were all smiling. They were sure that they could beat the trial, as long as they knew how.

Knowing their goal revitalized everyone. They readied themselves for the next charge. The magma bullet barrage began once more, and the serpents started acting unpredictably, keeping the party on their toes.

The group split up again, deciding it would be easier if they counterattacked individually.

Tio sprouted dragon wings from her back and took to the skies. She unleashed a tornado that shot a deadly volley of wind blades. She'd cast the intermediate-rank wind spell, Infinity Gust.

"That's the ninth one! It looks like I'm in the lead, Master! If I destroy the most, will you please punish me? Of course, it will have to be just the two of us, all night long!"

Tio shredded her ninth serpent with a smile. Hajime tried to tell her that he wasn't going to do that, but Shea cut him off.

"Wha...?! It's no fair if only you get a reward, Tio-san! Let me join the contest! Hajime-san, if I win, you have to spend a whole night with me instead!"

Shea leaped into the air and smashed Drucken down onto a serpent's head. Blue ripples spread from the point of impact, creating shockwaves. The blow's force was so great that even some of the magma below blew away. Glimmering fragments of the serpent's crystal floated in midair for a few seconds before falling into the sea.

A magma bullet hurtled toward Shea, who still hung in mid-air. She fired Drucken's buckshot, using the recoil to dodge. However, one of the serpents had predicted her leap backward, and waited with open jaws.

Shea didn't seem worried. She focused her mana into her boots. The metal plates in her soles began to glow, and shockwaves of pale blue light spread from her feet. Shea leaped off the mana platform she'd created and soared through the air.

Since Shea was the only one who couldn't fly naturally, Hajime had enchanted a pair of boots with Aerodynamic for her. And because she could render herself weightless with gravity magic, she could utilize it even more effectively than Hajime.

The magma serpent passed by. As it did, Shea took aim with Drucken and pulled the trigger. It wasn't her usual buckshot that came out, but a high-caliber shotgun slug.

Not just any shotgun slug, either. Hajime had crafted it out of a special material and enchanted it with Shock Conversion. It unleashed powerful shockwaves on impact. In terms of pure power, it was more destructive than his grenade launcher.

The slug slammed into the serpent, blowing its head and body apart in a massive explosion. Fragments of another shattered crystal flew through the air.

"Hey, you two," Hajime yelled. "Don't just go deciding that on your—"

"Then, if I win, you have to go on a date with me," Yue interrupted before he could finish. Considering how many comrades they had now, Yue rarely had the chance to spend time alone with Hajime. She had him all to herself at night, but she wanted to spend a day with him as well.

Smiling faintly, Yue once again proved that she was a fearsome mage. She pulled out her favorite spell, Draconic Thunder.

Instead of just one dragon, however, she summoned seven. Her practice was finally beginning to pay off. Each dragon picked a target and flew away. Their howls shook the walls. The hunter became the hunted as the magma serpents heading for Yue found themselves swallowed up. Their mana crystals burnt to a crisp.

"I knew Yue-san was the one I should watch out for!"

"Now, that's hardly fair! Yue is too strong!"

Grumbling, Shea and Tio launched even more ferocious attacks. They were *not* going to let themselves fall behind.

"I guess it's fine. Everyone looks like they're having fun, at least," Hajime shrugged. He shot down the magma serpent closing in from behind without even turning around.

The bullets all landed at once, shockwaves blowing away the serpent's magma body. Its crystal flew through the air, exposed. Hajime dodged its head nimbly and shot the falling mana crystal with Donner.

He had loaded Schlag with shockwave shells similar to the ones he'd given Shea, although they lacked Drucken's power, as he'd made them small enough to fit Schlag's chambers. If he wanted power, he could always pull out Schlagen, but he wanted to see how well these new bullets worked with his handguns first.

His revolvers didn't have enough force to destroy the serpents and their mana crystals at the same time, so he adopted a two-shot strategy. He used Schlag to get rid of the magma, then sniped the mana crystal with Donner. Schlagen could have pierced both the magma coating and the mana crystal in one shot, but it possessed too much piercing power, which made pinpoint shots too hard.

Hajime flipped through the air, dodging two more serpents. Upside-down, he took aim with Schlag, and fired.

There was only a single bang, but Hajime had fired four times. The serpents didn't have time to notice Hajime wasn't there before his bullets scattered their bodies.

Hajime fired Donner twice, destroying the exposed crystals.

He glanced down at the central island and was surprised to see that they only had eight more serpents to kill. Barely ten minutes had passed since they'd begun.

If, as Tio suspected, this labyrinth's theme was to see how well challengers could handle a prolonged battle requiring intense concentration under strenuous conditions, then Hajime and the others must have completely surpassed the creator's expectations.

Tio's breath mowed down another pair of serpents.

Six more to go.

Shea's shotgun slug took out two serpents at once.

Four more to go.

Another team of serpents tried to pincer Yue. One rose from below, while the other bore down from above. They found themselves stopped short by another of Yue's thunder dragons, which coiled around her. Then they were surrounded by four more, and summarily destroyed.

Two more to go.

A magma serpent rushed Hajime and unleashed a slew of fireballs. He danced through the air like a leaf riding the wind, firing on it with Schlag as it opened its maw to swallow him. The serpent was blown back, and Hajime shot its mana crystal without even aiming.

The last serpent tried to launch a sneak attack from beneath the magma sea. Hajime leaped up with Aerodynamic and fired Schlag into its open mouth.

Red shockwaves spread out from the point of impact, pushing the serpent back. Its mana crystal glinted in the red light.

Hajime took careful aim with Donner. Yue and the others watched with satisfaction as Hajime finished off the trial.

"And now it's over." Hajime glanced at the others before pulling the trigger that signaled the end.

An aurora of light poured down from above.

What the...?! Crap, I can't dodge in time—

Hajime's eyes were glued to the light. It looked just like the rainbow that nearly killed him back in the Great Orcus Labyrinth.

Judging by its brightness, it might be even more dangerous...

It felt as if the air was being torn apart. The labyrinth's creator had timed this trap to activate when everyone was at their most defenseless... Right when they thought they'd won.

The light of destruction swallowed Hajime whole, and he vanished without a trace.

"H-Hajimeeee!" Yue let out a bloodcurdling scream.

Shea and Tio stood in place, stunned. Yue's scream brought them back to their senses. They'd never heard her so much as raise her voice.

The giant wall of light swallowed up the remnants of the magma serpent Hajime had killed, then crashed into the sea. The impact sent magma flying, and for a second, the volcano's base was visible.

The light grew fainter as it bored through the rock. Eventually, it faded entirely, vanishing without a trace.

Yue flew, rushing to find Hajime. As the light faded, she saw him, still floating in the air. His clothes were a tattered mess. He'd used his arms to protect his face and torso, keeping his vitals intact. However, he no longer had the strength to remain airborne, and plummeted toward the magma.

"Updraft!"

Yue used magic to keep his limp body afloat. It looked like he'd lost consciousness. Once she got close, she grabbed him and carried him to a nearby platform.

"Hajime! Hajime!"

Shea and Tio seldom saw her so panicked. Yue fumbled through her pockets, pulled out a vial of Ambrosia, and fed it to him.

He was in pretty bad shape. His right arm was so burned that bone showed, and his artificial left arm had melted. His eyepatch was ripped off, and the right side of his face bled profusely. Worst of all, his stomach was burnt black. The fact that his organs were intact showed how much stronger he'd grown since fighting the Hydra.

Just before the aurora struck, Hajime had twisted his body away while activating Diamond Skin's derivative skills, Focused Hardening and Diamond Protection. Thanks to that, he was able to protect his head with his hardened left arm, while saving his lungs and heart with his right. His stomach was protected by monster leather, enchanted with Diamond Protection. Most importantly, his ridiculously high Magic Defense kept the aurora from melting right through him. His wounds were certainly terrible, but not fatal.

"Mmm... It's taking too long." Yue's impatience showed on her face. The Ambrosia was barely healing Hajime.

Back when they fought the Hydra, this same light had demolished Hajime while protecting Yue. She swore on that day never to let something so terrible happen to him again. Yet, it had happened. Her mouth twisted in grief, frustration at her inability to save Hajime written all over her face. Unfortunately, their enemy didn't give her time to grieve.

"Fool! Above you!" Tio shouted in warning.

"Ah! Oh no—"

Countless beams of light rained down on Yue. They were miniature versions of the blast that hit Hajime. Most of them hardly had a tenth of its strength, but even that was enough to kill most people.

Yue had been too caught up in feeding Hajime Ambrosia to notice. She only looked up when Tio cried out. There wasn't time to cast a spell; the light would have hit far too quickly. *If only I had three... No, one more second...* Yue desperately tried to cast a defensive spell anyway.

"I won't let you! Cloudburst!"

Fortunately, Tio managed to buy the time Yue needed. Cloudburst was an intermediate-rank wind spell. It created a wall of compressed air, which Tio used to hold back the deadly light. The wind wall bent inward as the light hit it. Normally, the wall would repel whatever struck it, but faced with an attack this powerful, all Tio could do was keep it from shattering. Even then, she could only hold it for a few seconds.

Still, that was more than enough.

"Hallowed Ground!"

Yue cast the strongest barrier spell she knew. If she had time, she would have used Spatial Severance instead, but gravity magic still took her longer than the other elements. Practice had shortened that preparation time, but Hallowed Ground was faster. It was the best option.

A bright barrier of light appeared in front of her outstretched hands. It spread into a dome, protecting Yue and Hajime. A split second later, Tio's Cloudburst shattered, unable to hold back the barrage. Their fury undiluted, the beams of light slammed into Yue's barrier.

Thud! Thud! Thud! Thud! A hailstorm of light pounded against Yue's Hallowed Ground, cracking it.

"Gwaaaaaah!" Realizing that the barrier wouldn't last, Yue transformed it from a dome into a shield guarding the space above them. The less area it covered, the stronger it would be.

No longer protected by Yue's shield, the ground was pelted by rainbow-colored light. The auroras destroyed the boulder, except for Hajime and Yue's location.

The light seemed to focus on Hajime. A few beams fell toward Shea and Tio, but only enough to keep them busy; the bulk attacked Hajime and Yue. That said, it took a lot to occupy Shea and Tio. Keeping Tio, Shea, and Yue on the defensive simultaneously was no small feat.

"Hajime-san! Hajime-saaan!"

"Calm yourself, Shea! If you leave my barrier, you'll end up killing yourself!"

"But Hajime-san is in trouble!"

Tio tried to restrain Shea while maintaining Cloudburst so that they wouldn't drown in deadly rainbow light.

Tio was just as worried about Hajime as Shea was. She understood wanting to run over and help him, but also knew that jumping into a barrage of light powerful enough to nearly kill Hajime wouldn't do any good. Tio grabbed Shea by the collar and pulled her back to the safety.

Time slowed to a crawl. Tio couldn't tell if ten seconds had passed, or a minute.

After what seemed like an eternity, the barrage finally abated. Most of the boulders had been pulverized, and white smoke rose from the few that hadn't.

Yue and Tio panted heavily, their mana nearly spent. They used the respite to drain their magic accessories.

As they recovered, a man's voice spoke to them from above. He sounded almost impressed.

"Your strength is certainly formidable. Ambushing you here was the right choice. You four are too dangerous to let live. Especially that man over there."

The three girls looked up at the ceiling. Their eyes opened wide in surprise. Countless dragons filled the air. One was far larger than the others, pure white from snout to tail. A red-haired, dark-skinned, pointy-eared demon rode atop it.

"To think he could survive even a direct hit from my Uranos' breath... Plus, those strange weapons the report mentioned are even stronger than I imagined, just like you girls. It's amazing that you withstood a concentrated barrage from fifty Ash Dragons. Who are you people? How many ancient spells have you acquired?"

The demon's eyes glowed golden, like Tio's. He glared pointedly at them. He seemed to be mistakenly assuming that their strength resulted from the number of labyrinths they'd cleared.

"How about you tell us your name before asking questions? Or do demons have no manners?"

It was Hajime. The demon furrowed his brow.

"Hajime!" Yue shouted.

"Hajime-san!"

"You're alive, Master!"

Hajime managed to prop himself up, but looked as though he was ready to collapse at any second. Yue rushed to help him. Tio and Shea leaped over to what remained of the crumbling platform for a closer look.

Hajime smiled to reassure everyone and rose to his feet. He was in no condition to fight. The effort of standing made him sweat. Even so, he looked the demon in the eye and smiled fearlessly.

"I have no reason to give my name to those who are about to die."

"I know what you mean. I just figured I'd play out the cliché. To be honest, I don't care who you are. By the way, how's your friend doing? I did him a favor, if you ask me. It was a pretty ugly arm."

Hajime was purposely goading the demon to buy time until

he healed. From this demon's mention of a report, and the fact that it was waiting to ambush them, Hajime guessed that the demon who barely escaped from Ur had told this one about them. Presumably, he'd been sent to deal with them.

The demon's eyebrow twitched. He growled in a low tone.

"I've changed my mind. Carve this name into your memories, scum. I am Freid Bagwa. A faithful apostle of god, sworn to bring divine judgment to the heretics."

"An apostle of god, huh? Someone sure thinks highly of himself. What, you think knowing some magic from the age of the gods makes you their apostle? That magic doesn't let you control monsters, does it? There aren't enough of them in the world capable of shooting out those auroras. Your magic must let you create them somehow. If you could create an unbeatable army, maybe you'd be qualified to call yourself their apostle."

"You're a sharp one. That's right, the gods spoke to me when I obtained the ancient magic. They told me I was their apostle. I decided then to devote myself to them, and work to see their wishes granted. I denounce you, who dare to stand in my lord's way."

He reminds me of that pope, Ishtar. Only a fanatic would denounce us for a reason like that.

Hajime's smile didn't waver. The Ambrosia was working slowly, but Hajime augmented it with one of Mana Conversion's derivative skills, Healing Conversion. That let him stop the bleeding, at least. His left arm was useless for now. His right arm was burned to the bone, but it wasn't broken. He could use it if he really had to. *I can still fight!*

"Stole the words right from my mouth. Anyone who stands in my way is an enemy. And...I kill all my enemies!"

Gritting his teeth against the pain, Hajime raised Donner and fired at Freid.

His arm screamed in pain at the recoil, but Hajime ignored the agony, focusing his energy solely on killing the enemy before him. He activated Riftwalk and sent out his Cross Bits. Yue, Tio, and Shea attacked at the same time. Yue used Draconic Thunder, Tio fired her breath, and Shea shot another shotgun slug.

A number of the creatures Freid called Ash Dragons flew in front of him. They created multiple layers of triangular, dark red barriers to defend against the attack.

The barriers shattered, one after another, in the face of the powerful barrage. However, more Ash Dragons flew in and supplemented the defense. With so many shields to break through, even the party's best attacks began to peter out. Hajime noticed turtle-shaped monsters riding the Ash Dragons. Their shells glowed dark red. Hajime assumed they were casting the barriers.

"Did you think I only brought dragons with me? You won't be able to break through my defenses that easily. Now, let me show you the other power I've obtained. This is the true might of magic from the age of the gods!"

Freid began chanting a spell, falling almost into a trance. *If it's magic he just recently gained, it's probably what you receive for clearing the Grand Gruen Volcano.* Hajime and the others knew the danger of magic from the age of the gods firsthand. They focused their attacks, determined to stop Freid before he could finish.

Every time they destroyed a barrier, however, a new turtle appeared to craft one in its place. Normally, Hajime would have charged forward to attack Freid directly, but he still wasn't fully recovered, so he limited himself to ranged attacks. He ground his teeth, frustrated.

Holstering Donner, Hajime pulled out Orkan instead. He unleashed all four of its rockets, but only managed to kill a few dragons. None of the explosions reached Freid. His Cross Bits were too weak to even penetrate the barriers.

Before Hajime could set up any other attacks, Freid finished his spell. Their time was up.

"Cosmic Rift!"

Freid and the white dragon disappeared. Specifically, they vanished inside a veil of blinding light.

"Behind you, Hajime-san!"

Hajime whirled around, reacting to Shea's warning.

Directly in front of him was the white dragon, its gaping jaws inches from his face. Freid glared coldly down at him from its back. Massive amounts of heat and mana radiated from the dragon's mouth.

Hajime held Orkan in front of him, shielding himself from the point-blank aurora blast.

"Gwaaaaaaaaah!"

The force of the light sent Hajime flying backward. Injured as he was, his body couldn't take much more. He screamed in pain as the aurora's shockwaves buffeted him.

"Hajime!"

Yue and the others tried to attack the white dragon, hoping to distract it from Hajime. But before they could, the Ash Dragons above them fired a barrage of light, forcing them to defend themselves.

Although it wasn't a direct hit, the force of the blast reopened Hajime's wounds. Blood soaked the ground at his feet.

Fuck, that hurts. At this rate, we're done for.

Hajime came to a decision. There was no point holding anything back. It was time to use Limit Break.

Dark red mana swirled around his body. He felt his strength multiply.

"Raaaaaaaaah!"

Hajime wrenched Orkan upward, deflecting the aurora toward the ceiling. He was unable to deflect it all, however. A few traces slammed against him, gouging into his wounds.

The white dragon followed up with a wave of mini-aurora balls. Its attack patterns were almost identical to those of the Hydra. But the dragon's aurora was more powerful, which meant its mini-auroras would be as well. Hajime couldn't afford to take any more hits.

"Cross Bits!"

Hajime's concentration was so intense that the world around him passed by in slow motion. He wove through the aurora balls with expert precision, sometimes dodging by only a hairsbreadth. Some scraped past his clothes, but he didn't let himself get distracted. He needed to stay focused if he wanted to mount a counterattack.

Hajime tossed Orkan, mostly destroyed by the aurora, back into his Treasure Trove. He pulled out Donner, firing a short burst while summoning his Cross Bits. They also fired at Freid, supplementing the barrage.

"Such persistence! To think you could keep dodging for so long!"

Freid retreated behind the safety of his barriers. He hadn't expected the wounded Hajime to put up such a fight. He flew backwards, and started chanting another spell.

"Not this time!"

Freid was so focused on keeping his distance from Hajime that he forgot about the others. He turned in surprise as a deep voice roared next to him. Before he could see what was happening, something crashed into his side.

Freid clung to his dragon, barely keeping himself upright. The shock was enough to break his chant. When he realized what hit him, his jaw dropped.

"Impossible. A black dragon, here?!"

"Don't be so proud of those mock dragons of yours! I will not allow you to hurt Master any longer!"

Tio had transformed into her dragon form. She knew it was dangerous to expose her existence to a demon, but she'd taken the risk anyway. She was smaller than Freid's white dragon, but she exuded a far greater pressure.

Tio joined Hajime's party because she liked him, but she'd also wanted a better idea of what these people from another world were like. To do that, she had to hide the fact that she was a dragonman.

If the world found out dragonmen still lived, her village would be in danger. Although each dragonman was strong individually, they were helpless against humanity's sheer numbers. Tio learned that lesson the hard way five hundred years ago.

But Hajime, the one person she'd believed utterly invincible, had almost died. Seeing him crippled shook her.

She was a fool. Strong as Hajime was, he wasn't invincible. A moment's carelessness could get him killed.

How could she forget? Only now did she realize what her oath really meant. She'd sworn to serve Hajime. Not just because she found him interesting, and not just because he was her Master.

It was because Tio didn't want to lose him. He was an irreplaceable friend, and the man she loved.

So, she threw caution to the wind, and revealed her dragon form. If she prioritized her mission over her friends' safety, then she had no right to travel with them. Nor did she have any right to call herself a Guardian. Even if this decision led to her clan's persecution, she had to do it. Whatever happened, Tio Klarus would never put her safety above the lives of her friends.

"Behold, boy. This is what a true dragon's breath looks like!" Deadly black light gathered in Tio's mouth. She unleashed it with a roar. The light closed in on Freid with unbelievable speed.

The white dragon turned to face Tio and countered with its own breath. White and black clashed, sending out massive shockwaves. Waves of magma spread beneath the point of impact.

At first, the two beams of light seemed evenly matched, but eventually Tio's started pushing the white dragon's back.

"Gah... To think I would run into the remnants of the dragon-man clan here... It seems I have no choice. It's dangerous, but I'll have to blow this entire—"

"You won't be doing anything."

"Huh?!"

Freid was genuinely surprised that Tio was a dragon. That fact hadn't been mentioned in his reports. He began chanting a new spell, hoping to create an opportunity to retreat, but was stopped once more.

He felt something hit his back, and stumbled forward.

He turned to see Hajime, bleeding from multiple wounds, level Donner. In a few short seconds, Hajime had gotten behind him. Now, the human fired another six rounds. They all landed at once, each with pinpoint accuracy.

The turtles surrounding Freid put up a barrier, but it was no match for the bullets. It shattered, leaving him defenseless. Hajime leaped forward, closing the distance between them.

He wreathed Donner with a Gale Claw and swiped at Freid.

"Gwaaaaaah?!"

Freid stumbled backward, narrowly avoiding being cut in half. Hajime's claw gouged deep into his chest, leaving him severely injured. Hajime didn't let up, following up with a Shock Conversion-enhanced roundhouse kick.

"Gaaah!"

Freid blocked with his left arm, but couldn't kill the force of the attack. Hajime's kick shattered Freid's arm, damaged his internal organs, and sent him flying from his dragon.

Distracted by what was happening to its master, the white dragon stopped its aurora attack, and Tio's breath punched through.

It slammed into the dragon a second after Hajime jumped off the beast's back, sending it flying.

"Graaaaaaaaaaaaah!"

Although heavily injured, the dragon managed to straighten itself and fly toward the ceiling. Freid awaited it there, riding an Ash Dragon. Once the two were level with each other, Freid hopped off the Ash Dragon, and onto the white one.

Hajime tried to chase after him with Aerodynamic, but—

"Ngh?! Gah!"

The red mana swirling around him vanished, and he coughed up blood. His Limit Break was over. His injuries meant that it didn't last as long as usual, and there was more recoil as well. Unable to keep up Aerodynamic, Hajime plummeted toward the magma sea.

"Master, get ahold of yourself!"

"Guh... T-Tio..."

Tio soared down and caught Hajime on her back. He was barely conscious, but managed to struggle to his knees. Eyes still burning with determination, he glared up at Freid.

The Ash Dragons that had attacked Yue and Shea clumped around him.

"Hajime!"

"Hajime-san!"

Free from the barrage, the women rushed toward Hajime.

Tio landed on a nearby platform to let him down. Considering his state, she couldn't fight with him on her back. He'd fall. Shea and Yue arrived to help him stand.

"Your combat prowess is truly impressive. And the women with you are quite strong themselves. The dragonmen should have died out, yet one travels with you. Furthermore, you have a mage who can cast spells without incantations, and a rabbitman with strange precognitive powers. I didn't think anything could press me this hard, now that I have ancient magic. Had my surprise attack failed, I likely wouldn't have stood a chance." Freid spoke quietly, but there was fire in his eyes. His breathing was ragged, and he covered his wounded chest with his good hand.

"You say that like you've already won. I'm nowhere near done yet." Hajime glared at Freid. Although he could barely stand, his bloodlust remained undiminished.

"So it seems. No matter how badly I injure you, your determination doesn't waver. What's truly frightening about you isn't your physical strength, but the inexorable persistence you show... No, perhaps it would be more apt to call it your will to survive."

Freid looked down for a moment, steeled himself, then turned back to Hajime.

"I didn't want to have to use this. But if that's what it takes to get rid of someone as dangerous as you, it's a price I'm willing to pay."

"What are you going on about?"

Freid didn't respond. Instead, he whispered something to the bird-shaped monster sitting on his shoulder.

A series of loud noises followed. *Dundundundundun! Thud! Crash!* The entire volcano shook, and the magma sea began to seethe.

"Whoa!"

"Hm?!"

"Kyaaa!"

"Nuoooh?!"

The impact knocked the party off-balance, and they struggled to regain their footing. The rumbling grew into an earthquake. Pillars of magma rose from the sea.

"Hajime-san, the magma's rising!"

Hajime looked down. The amount of rock left for them to stand on was rapidly shrinking.

"What did you do?" Hajime yelled at Freid, who was obviously behind this. Freid flew to the center of the room, directly above the island.

"I just destroyed the keystone."

"The...keystone?"

"Didn't you ever find it strange, looking at all this magma? The Grand Gruen Volcano is clearly active, and yet, it's never erupted. That can only mean something in the volcano controls the magma."

"And that was the keystone... Wait, don't tell me—?!"

"You guessed it. Now that I've destroyed the keystone, the labyrinth will be submerged in magma. It's a shame I cannot share this ancient magic with my comrades... But this is the only way to destroy you. Sink into the depths, along with this labyrinth!"

Freid held up the pendant hanging from his neck and glared

down at Hajime. Cracks started appearing in the ceiling. One opened near the center, revealing a circular passage heading straight to the summit.

He probably obtained that pendant by clearing the labyrinth. And that's the shortcut back out, Hajime realized.

Freid looked at Hajime one last time before turning his dragon around and flying through the opening.

The magma sea had turned into a raging whirlpool, and pillars erupted from the center, one after another. Magma poured down on the boulder where they stood. It was as if they were watching the world end.

Hajime closed his eyes and considered his options. He came to a decision and struggled to his feet.

Although Freid had retreated, he'd left behind his Ash Dragons. They started bombarding Hajime and the others with aurora balls once more. He wasn't taking any chances.

Yue cast Spatial Severance to keep them at bay, while Tio prepared to fire another breath attack. Hajime grabbed his Treasure Trove and tapped Tio's cheek to get her attention.

"Tio, listen to me. Take this and escape through that passage in the ceiling."

Her expression went from confused to hurt as she realized what Hajime was saying. She growled, full of rage. She would not abandon her comrades and escape by herself.

"Master, are you saying I alone am unworthy to fight with you until the end? Are you truly asking me to abandon you all? I will not—"

"That's not it, Tio. We don't have much time, so I'm only gonna explain this once. I haven't given up. We're gonna get the ancient magic from this labyrinth, and we'll get back at that bastard soon enough. We have to keep our promise to bring still-stone back to everyone, too. But I can't do it all alone. I need your help. Only you can get back to Ankaji in time. Please, Tio. I need you to do this."

Hajime stared into Tio's eyes. This was the first time she'd seen him look so serious. Hajime, who was always self-confident, was asking someone else for assistance. In order to fulfill his promises, in order to come out ahead, he needed her help. Without Tio, they'd fail.

Hajime had no intention of giving up, and this wasn't part of some noble self-sacrifice.

When Tio realized that, her face lit up with joy. The man she'd fallen for had entrusted her with an important mission. If she couldn't live up to his expectations, then she didn't deserve to travel with him.

Filled with determination, Tio nodded. "Leave it to me!"

Hajime stuck the Treasure Trove into a gap between Tio's scales. He positioned it so that, when she transformed back into a human, it would already be in her hand.

Tio made sure it was secure, and nuzzled Hajime's head. In this form, that was all she could do to show affection. Hajime patted her gently, and she took to the skies. Tio glanced down at Yue and Shea. They nodded back at her resolutely. They hadn't given up either.

"Tio, tell Kaori and Myu that we'll see them soon. I'm counting on you."

"Hee hee! I shall."

Tio smiled at the casual tone of Hajime's message. A second later, she wrapped herself in a gust of wind, and shot toward the ceiling. The Ash Dragons focused their fire on her, but she avoided the aurora balls with a barrel roll and slipped past. Realizing how dangerous it would be to let her escape, the Ash Dragons turned to give chase.

Tio deflected the next barrage with her breath, but the continuous bombardment made it difficult to keep all the missiles at bay. Before their attacks could overwhelm her, however, many were wiped out by a beam of their own light.

Yue had sent a powered-up version of their attacks back at them, using the light she'd absorbed into Spatial Severance. Shea followed up with a wave of shotgun slugs. Their shockwaves blew quite a few dragons apart.

The passage which Freid and the white dragon had used to flee began to close. Realizing she didn't have much time, Tio shot forward, focusing only on speed. Now that she was no longer engaging the Ash Dragons, some of their aurora balls struck her.

"Hmph, this is nothing! In fact, it feels good! Bring it oooooon!"

Tio increased her speed, the aurora balls giving her a boost. She was using one of Draconfication's derivative skills, Pain Conversion, which transformed the damage into a stat boost. She'd learned it back when she met Hajime. It was the first derivative skill she'd acquired in centuries. It really had opened the door to a world of new possibilities when Hajime beat her senseless.

Even the Ash Dragons were astonished by her speed. Tio broke through the aurora storm, shooting through the opening just before it closed. Above her, she could see a faint light. The surface. She'd have to pass through a number of doors first, and they were all closing.

Tio poured all her remaining mana into the wind that pushed her forward, keeping only enough to maintain Draconification.

She flew faster than the raging wind, faster than she ever had before.

Tio blew past a door, then another, then another. There was just one door left between her and the summit. She blasted forward, surrounded by a storm of jet-black wind. Rainbow-colored light rained down on her from overhead.

Freid noticed Tio's escape attempt, and launched one last attack to slow her down. The door was almost closed. She had to decide now if she would dodge, or take the hit and push through.

The white dragon had burned through most of its mana, so the aurora wasn't as strong as before. Tio guessed it was only half as powerful. Even so, it would be far more devastating than the Ash Dragons.

If she tried to intercept or dodge, however, she'd lose speed. She wouldn't make it through the door in time.

"Let's see what you've got!" Tio prepared herself to take the hit and convert the pain to speed.

But just before it reached her, a few small shadows flitted past, interposing themselves between her and the light.

Tio recognized the shapes: Hajime's Cross Bits. He'd sent them after her.

Three of the Cross Bits glowed dark red and angled themselves to deflect the blast. The light quickly melted through them, but they held on long enough for Tio to push through. The remaining four stuck close to Tio, protecting her as she flew.

"What a surprise! Master, I truly love you!" Even surrounded by a rising magma sea, Hajime had managed to control his Cross Bits to protect her.

She'd never met anyone strong enough to protect her before. Even in her village, she was the strongest. She'd always been the one who protected others. She never knew just how wonderful it was to be defended by someone else.

"Graaaaaah!" The white dragon let out a mighty roar as Tio slipped through the final door. A swirling black gale shot up into the sunlight. Although the sandstorm raged all around Tio, the eye of the storm was calm.

"You managed to escape under those circumstances?! You truly are a pack of monsters. But even a black dragon of your caliber must be weak after sustaining so many injuries. I'll have no problem—"

Freid tried to prepare a follow-up attack, but stopped short. The remaining four Cross Bits had surrounded him.

He ordered the turtle he'd brought to create a barrier. He'd learned earlier that the Cross Bits couldn't break through. Had Hajime loaded his Cross Bits with the same exploding shells he'd put into Drucken, Donner, and Schlag, that might have been a different story, but he hadn't had time. His primary weapons, and Shea's, had taken priority.

What Freid didn't know, however, was that the Cross Bits had another powerful attack. Certain that the Cross Bits couldn't harm him, Freid let his guard down. In that instant, Hajime chose to activate their trump card.

Freid only had a second to wonder why the Cross Bits were glowing more brightly.

There was a huge bang.

Shockwaves assailed Freid from all sides, followed by a hailstorm of bullets. The explosions released the Cross Bits' remaining ammo in a deadly barrage.

"Gaaaaaah!"

"Graaaaaaaaaaaaaaaah!"

Demon and dragon screamed as they were blasted into the distance. With the last of her mana, Tio added her own powerful tornado to the mix, to make doubly sure they got him. She wanted to use her breath to guarantee the kill, but she no longer had enough mana.

Tio watched the direction Freid had fallen, in case he miraculously got up. Once she was certain he wasn't coming back, she looked back down at the oddly silent volcano.

"I believe in you, Master, Yue, Shea." Tio turned toward the sandstorm, her whisper carried away by the wind. She needed to deliver what had been entrusted to her. She vanished into the sandstorm, destined for Ankaji.

A few minutes later, the Grand Gruen Volcano shuddered.

A massive eruption followed, temporarily blowing away the surrounding sandstorm. Black smoke rose from the volcano's peak as it spat magma and chunks of white-hot rock. Forks of lightning flashed within the smoke.

This was the Grand Gruen Volcano's first known eruption. The historic event faded from view as the sandstorm veil covered the volcano again.

Although the volcano itself was obscured, the plume of smoke rising from its peak could be seen as far away as Ankaji.

The two girls awaiting Hajime's return watched anxiously.

• *•* *•* *•* *•* *•* *•* *•* *•* *•* *•* *•* *•* *•*

"There's just something cool about going out in a blaze of glory," Hajime grinned.

"Hajime?"

"Hajime-san?"

Yue and Shea stared at him in confusion. The Ash Dragons were still pelting them with aurora balls. Hajime just shook his head and, with Shea and Yue's help, managed to leap onto the central island.

In the few minutes since Tio's departure, the magma had gotten more violent. Only the central island was still above the writhing sea of death. In another five minutes, even the island would be submerged.

Yue's Spatial Severance did a perfect job of dealing with the aurora balls, and the Ash Dragons were getting desperate. They dove down, trying to attack the party directly, but Shea swatted them away. Another ten dragons fell.

The magma dome that covered the center of the island had vanished, revealing a jet-black building. Next to that, a disk floated a few centimeters from the ground. It probably transported people through the shortcut, back to the surface.

There were so many magma pillars now that the Ash Dragons cut their attacks short to keep out of the way. Hajime watched them from the corner of his eye as he walked to the building.

There didn't seem to be a door, but one wall bore the familiar Liberators' crest.

When the party stopped in front of it, the wall fell away to reveal an opening.

They stepped inside just as magma started flowing over the island. The door closed behind them seconds before the magma would have reached them.

The party watched the door warily for a few seconds, but it didn't melt. Everyone breathed a sigh of relief. Hajime had guessed that anyone who built their house in a place like this would make it impervious to magma, in case something happened. It was just a guess, though, and Hajime was relieved to discover the building really was magma-resistant.

"Looks like we can rest for a bit now. I can't believe this room even dampens the shaking," Hajime marveled.

"Mmm... Hajime, there," said Yue. "A magic circle." It was more complex than most, and would likely grant them this labyrinth's ancient magic. The three nodded to each other and walked into it.

Just like the circle in Oscar's room, this one read their memories, tracing their path through the labyrinth. Once the circle confirmed that they defeated all the magma serpents, it imprinted the knowledge of this magic onto them.

"So, this labyrinth held spatial magic." Hajime wasn't even surprised at the magic's ridiculous power. *Looks like it's some pretty crazy stuff too.*

"We can teleport with this," Yue realized, thinking back to their earlier fight.

Shea nodded, remembering. "Yeah, that's how he got behind us, isn't it?"

Freid probably used that magic to launch the first surprise attack, too. Hajime would need to test it before he could be certain whether it actually enabled teleportation, or just the warping of space. Either way, it was unbelievably powerful. If not for Shea's Future Sight, that first attack would likely have killed Hajime. *He really got me good.*

As the magic circle's glow faded, a section of the wall fell away with a dull clunk, revealing a small alcove. Glowing letters appeared inside.

I pray the day comes when people can be free—Naiz Gruen

"Short and sweet, I see," Hajime said.

Looking around, they noticed Gruen's hideout was rather Spartan. Unlike Orcus' place, there wasn't even any furniture, nor any appliances. There was just the magic circle.

"I guess he put his affairs in order before coming here."

"Yeah, it looks like the only thing Naiz-san left for us here was the circle."

"Come to think of it, Oscar's diary said Naiz was a pretty quiet guy."

Leaving Shea to support Hajime, Yue walked to the alcove. She groped inside it and pulled out a pendant. It was slightly different from the other items they'd received as proof of clearing a labyrinth. The circular pendant was inlaid with an ornate pattern. Yue walked back and put it around Hajime's neck.

"All right, we've got the magic, and we've got our crest. Now we just have to get out of here," said Yue.

"Any ideas?" asked Hajime.

"You have a plan, right? The whole place must be filled with magma by now," said Shea.

Both Yue and Shea were confident Hajime could get them out of this mess.

Happy that they trusted him so much, Hajime began to outline his plan. "We're going to swim through the magma."

Has the blood loss finally gotten to him? the two girls thought. His suggestion definitely didn't seem sane.

"Hm?"

"Come again?"

"Hold on, I'm not crazy, I swear. I'll explain, so don't give me that look. The truth is, I left a submarine outside. I figured it made sense to create one, since Melusine comes next. I wasn't sure whether it'd survive the magma, but since our strengthened boat did, I think the submarine's probably all right. I'm glad I tried that out."

"When exactly did you have time to..."

Shea stared at Hajime in shock. Even Yue's eyed widened a little.

When Freid announced that he'd destroyed the keystone, Hajime had pulled his submarine out and dropped it into the magma. If it had melted, Hajime would have told everyone to ride Tio out, and forced his way through. However, he tracked the submarine's movements with the spirit stone he'd placed in it, and saw that it was perfectly fine.

However, given how chaotic things were getting, it was possible they wouldn't make it back in time to save Ankaji. They'd have to take risks to move quickly enough, and Hajime wanted to avoid that. So, he sent Tio on ahead just in case. He knew she could make it back with time to spare.

"As for the route, we have the shortcut Freid took. Yue, I'll need you to make a barrier against the magma until we're in the sub. Can you handle that?"

"Yeah... No problem."

Yue nodded and deployed a tri-layered Hallowed Ground. The shimmering dome surrounded them. They nodded to each other. Hajime clutched the handle and slid the door open.

Burning hot magma rushed into the room. Yue's barrier protected them, but they couldn't even see two inches in front of their faces. Although he'd planned for the situation, Hajime was still amazed. They were seeing a volcano from inside. Chances were, they were the only people in the whole world to have experienced something so strange.

"It's not far. Let's go!"

"Okay."

"R-roger!"

At Hajime's command, they walked forward. Although they couldn't see anything, the submarine really was only a few feet from the room. Yue extended Hallowed Ground to create a path.

The three of them ran to the entrance hatch and hopped inside. There, they relaxed.

Just then, a massive quake ripped through the volcano. At the same time, the magma rushed violently forward. Its flow carried the submarine, and Hajime and the others rolled around inside like bowling balls.

"Gwaaah!"

"Hwaaa?!"

"Huuuuh?! Owww!"

They cried out in pain as they slammed into the bulkheads, floor, and ceiling. Yue deployed a miniature version of Spatial Severance to keep everyone from flying around. The gravity field stabilized them enough to regain their balance.

"Th-thanks, Yue."

"Thank you very much, Yue-san."

"Mmm... Anyway..."

Yue used Spatial Severance to drop Hajime into the cockpit. He poured mana into the submarine's control system, but made little headway trying to steer it. The magma's thickness, and the speed of its flow, made stabilizing the sub very difficult.

"Tch... If only this meant that the volcano was erupting. We would have our express ticket out."

"It's not?" Yue tilted her head quizzically.

"No, it's not. I added lodestones to the Cross Bits when I sent them out. That way, I'd always know which direction we were going in. I dropped them on the summit before I blew them up, so I know where the shortcut comes out. But we're getting farther from there, not closer."

"Wait. Does that mean the magma's taking us deeper underground?"

"Yeah. It's traveling on a diagonal, but we're still descending. I wonder where we're heading. Yue, Shea... It looks like we won't be making it back anytime soon. All we can do is see where this takes us."

Yue and Shea smiled gently and sidled up to Hajime.

"All I want is to be with you. If I can have that, I don't care what else happens," Yue murmured.

"Hee hee...! So, this is what 'through hell and high water' really means... As long as I can be with you two, I don't care where we go!"

"I see. Fair enough," Hajime smiled.

The three huddled together in the submarine as the ocean of magma pushed them along.

◦┼◦ ◦┼◦ ◦┼◦ ◦┼◦ ◦┼◦ ◦┼◦ ◦┼◦ ◦┼◦ ◦┼◦ ◦┼◦ ◦┼◦ ◦┼◦ ◦┼◦

Meanwhile, Tio flew through the sandstorm. Her silhouette was the only feature in the brown sky.

"Mmm. This does not bode well. Unbelievable, to think that charlatan's breath would... I suppose I have no choice. Master, please forgive me."

Even with Hajime's protection, some of the white dragon's aurora had hit Tio as she pushed through. Now, its insidious poison ate away at her wounds. At the rate things were going, she would collapse long before she reached Ankaji. Tio reached into the Treasure Trove and pulled out one of Hajime's few remaining Ambrosia vials. Then, she popped the whole thing, vial and all, into her mouth, muttering an apology for taking it without permission.

The vast amount of mana Tio had spent regenerated at an alarming rate. Her poisoned wounds didn't start healing right away, but the aurora's effects were diminished.

After flying for a few hours, she finally spotted Ankaji in the distance. If she got any closer, Ankaji's lookouts would see her.

Tio considered changing back to human form. "Well, now that the white dragon tamer has seen me, I guess there's no point in hiding."

Besides, if I'm going to continue traveling with Master, a time will come when we need my dragon form again. In the end, Tio decided to carry on.

Her hidden village wouldn't be easily found. Even if it was, her clan was notoriously hard to kill. Most importantly, she had Hajime. If, by some chance, the whole world turned against them, she could count on him. He tried to act tough, but Tio knew he'd do anything for those he cared about.

Only a few kilometers remained between her and Ankaji. When she looked down, she spotted the lookout panicking and pointing in her direction. Tio didn't want to have to deal with them accidentally attacking her, so she angled herself toward the main gate. She landed there, kicking up a massive dust cloud.

A contingent of Ankaji's soldiers waited for her. She glanced up and saw another squad of soldiers aiming their bows and staves at her from the walls.

The wind swept away the dust cloud, revealing Tio's silhouette. The soldiers gulped nervously. However, when the sand finally cleared, all they could see was an exhausted woman.

Kaori pushed past the bewildered soldiers and ran to Tio.

Bize and the soldiers tried to stop her, but she ignored them. She only stopped when she was next to Tio, who had doubled over, panting.

Kaori knew Tio was a dragon, so the moment the lookout reported one, she ran to the main gate.

"Tio, are you all right?!"

"Oh, Kaori. Despite how I look, I shall be fine. I'm just a little tired."

Kaori paled as she saw that every inch of Tio's flesh was covered in wounds. She knelt beside her friend and examined her injuries. When she realized the damage was caused by an unknown poison, she cast a cleansing spell, followed by a healing spell.

"How come... Why can't I purify you?"

The aurora's poison was so potent that even Ambrosia took some time to flush it out. Kaori's skills weren't nearly enough to get rid of the toxin.

However, she was far better than any other healer. The combination of her magic and the Ambrosia healed most of Tio's more serious injuries. Tio smiled and patted Kaori's head.

"Don't worry, child, the rest will heal soon enough," she said.

Kaori smiled in relief as Tio's wounds begin to close. It seemed there really wasn't any need to worry. Still, her expression grew anxious again as she noticed Tio was alone.

"Tio... Umm, where's Hajime-kun? Did you come back alone? And what was that eruption?"

"Relax, Kaori. I will explain everything. But first, can you please calm those soldiers, and find somewhere we can talk privately?"

"Oh, uh, of course."

Kaori turned back, as if she'd only just noticed the soldiers behind her. Still a little worried, she reassured them nonetheless. The only reason she wasn't panicking was because Tio didn't seem sad.

Kaori explained the situation to Bize and Lanzwi, then took Tio somewhere they could talk in peace.

•¦• •¦• •¦• •¦• •¦• •¦• •¦• •¦• •¦• •¦• •¦• •¦• •¦•

"In that case, Hajime-kun and the others are..."

"Indeed. They should join us soon. Master didn't seem worried. I didn't have time to ask for details, but I am certain he has a plan."

Kaori clenched her fists, pale as a ghost. The worry she'd felt when she first saw the eruption returned with a vengeance.

Tio placed her hands over Kaori's and gazed sternly into her eyes.

"Kaori, I have a message from Master."

"From Hajime-kun?"

"Yes. Well, technically, he said it was for both you and Myu. Regardless, the message is 'We'll see you soon.'"

Kaori had expected him to say something reassuring, like "Don't worry" or "I promise I'll come back." Not something casual, like "We'll see you soon." Hajime made it sound like he was just going to get groceries.

An image of him smiling fearlessly flashed in her mind. She could just imagine him saying "Come on, this isn't even worth getting worried over." He was the kind of person who'd overcome any hardship with a grin. Kaori smiled wryly. *He must have said that because he knew it'd reassure me more than a serious promise.*

"I see. Well, I guess he's fine, then."

"Precisely. Master is the kind of man who can overcome any hopeless situation and make it look easy. You can't help but trust him."

"Yeah... As long as Hajime-kun's there, they'll be fine. I should focus on my job here while I wait."

"That you should. Allow me to assist you."

Although Kaori felt the same despair she had when Hajime fell into the Orcus Labyrinth's depths, she told herself he would be fine, and focused on what she could do. She wiped her eyes and stood up. Lanzwi and his attendants had likely finished crushing the stillstone, and would be distributing it to the patients. In the meantime, she needed to heal the people in critical condition, so that they could recover.

On her way to the hospitals, Kaori stopped by the palace and explained everything to Myu. Lanzwi's daughter, fourteen-year-old Ailee, was taking care of her.

Myu started crying when she learned Hajime hadn't returned, but Tio shushed her, saying Hajime's daughter had to be strong, and strong girls didn't cry. After that, Myu held in her tears.

Although Myu was a Dagon, everyone treated her kindly. That wasn't only because she was one of Kaori's companions. Once they got to know her, no one could resist being moved by Myu's adorable nature. Ailee especially had taken to her.

Lanzwi and the others were surprised to learn Tio was a dragonman, but they didn't seem to hate her for it. In the end, she'd risked her life to save theirs, and they owed her for that.

Two days later, Hajime still hadn't returned.

Kaori was busy healing patients, but she knew she couldn't distract herself with work for much longer.

Tio flew back and forth between the city and the volcano multiple times, but didn't find any trace.

On the evening of the third day, Kaori made a suggestion.

"I finished healing the critically-injured patients. The others will heal naturally, given time, or Ankaji's doctors can look after them. So, I think it's time we start looking for Hajime-kun."

"We're going to find Daddy?"

"Hmm... I suppose we should. I was thinking of going to look for him myself."

Myu leaned forward eagerly, while Tio lapsed into thought.

"But we can't really take Myu with us to the Grand Gruen Volcano, can we?" Kaori wondered.

"Indeed. Master left her here because it was too dangerous to bring her along. Besides, searching the area will be difficult, since the volcano just erupted."

"Yeah. I agree. I think we should take Myu to her mom in Erisen first, then turn back to look for Hajime-kun."

"Hmm, that does sound sensible. Very well. It will be faster if you ride on my back. By air, Erisen is only a day's journey from here. We should arrive tomorrow evening if we leave early enough."

Myu watched the two of them with a puzzled expression. The conversation moved too quickly. Kaori knelt and explained what they were talking about. The girl frowned when Kaori said they couldn't look for Hajime right away. However, she really wanted to see her mother again. Reluctantly, she agreed to go home and wait for Hajime.

Tio and Kaori smiled ruefully at how calculating Myu was in her decision. She'd picked between Hajime and her mother, just as Hajime would have done in her position.

They set off the next day. Lanzwi seemed reluctant to let them go, and Bize saw them off with tears in his eyes. Kaori and Myu climbed onto Tio's back, and the three headed off to the west. The townspeople cheered them as they went, voices resounding through the desert.

Kaori was determined to find Hajime. She'd done it before, and she could do it again.

Little did she know they'd be reunited very soon.

•ı• •ı• •ı• •ı• •ı• •ı• •ı• •ı• •ı• •ı• •ı• •ı• •ı• •ı•

Around the same time, back in Heiligh, Kouki had thrown himself wholeheartedly into training.

It wasn't because he wanted to improve his skills. He still didn't know if he could really kill someone when the time came, and tried to find the answer as he trained.

However, there was no way training could hold such answers. Although his skills improved, Kouki was no closer to knowing.

In a way, he realized he was just trying to distract himself from facing the problem. His irritation at himself grew with each passing day. Although he had to make a decision soon, he couldn't bring himself to do it.

Thanks to Kouki's indecision, the other students—even the ones who hadn't participated in combat since the Orcus Labyrinth— began to feel more stressed. Gloom hung over the castle.

Training ended for the day, but someone was still present at a less-popular training area.

"Hmph... Faster."

A series of sword strokes cut through the air. The jet-black sword moved so quickly that it was back in its sheath before the afterimages disappeared. A second later, it shot back with such speed, you couldn't even see it being drawn.

Each stroke of the sword could have cut steel. Every time Shizuku Yaegashi swung her blade, her ponytail swayed from side to side.

She was training alone in the deserted practice grounds, swinging the sword Hajime had given her. Finishing her flurry of strokes, Shizuku took a deep breath and closed her eyes.

A woman's face appeared in the back of her mind. Red hair and dark skin. The demon who nearly killed them. She'd controlled a horde of monsters and used powerful earth magic.

She was a member of the army that drove the humans into a corner. Shizuku could still remember every detail of that fight. When she looked down, she noticed her right hand trembling.

I'll cut them down. Next time one shows up, I'll do it. If I don't kill them, it'll be my friends who end up dead. Shizuku tried to steel her resolve. Back then, a miracle had saved them. Hajime had swooped in, like a fairytale hero. However, miracles didn't happen often. Shizuku couldn't count on another. She knew she'd lose someone precious to her if she didn't take this seriously. That was why she was training.

"Haaah!"

She let out a yell and slashed at the air with all her might. Her sword cut through the imaginary demon. Still, that wasn't good enough. Her own weakness had made her hesitate. In a real fight, her attack would have been too slow. She couldn't afford to be weak, so she struck again.

"Go forth, Gale Claw!"

A faint breeze blew along the blade's length. This skill was imbued in the sword Hajime had given her. Originally, it would have been impossible to invoke without manipulating mana directly. However, the kingdom's best alchemists had worked tirelessly to modify the weapon.

The masterfully crafted black sword transformed Shizuku's image into a spell, and this time, she cut through the imaginary demon without hesitation. A second later...

"Ugh...!" Groaning, Shizuku dashed to the corner of the practice grounds and threw up.

"Bleh...haaah...haaah... Sheesh. I can't believe this happens every time I train. What a waste of good food. Although I guess eating only healthy foods that look and taste like crap isn't really a good thing, either."

Shizuku sighed and smiled bitterly at herself.

She tottered over to the sandwich and water bottle she'd left underneath the shade of a tree. She'd expected to throw up. And even if she wasn't hungry, she needed to replenish her energy, or risk collapse. She'd force the food down her own throat if she had to.

Shizuku sat on a protruding root and took a big gulp of water. The refreshingly coolness washed away the bitter taste in her mouth.

"Haaah..." Breathing another sigh, she looked up at the sun setting in the west. Just then, she heard something unexpected.

"Meow..."

"Huh?"

Looking down, she spotted a chestnut-colored cat purring

next to her. Cats in Tortus apparently looked just like cats back home. They were equally prevalent too.

"Where'd you come from, little fella?"

The practice grounds were inside the palace complex. In other words, they were surrounded by tall walls on three sides, and the mountain behind. There was no way a cat should have been able to get in. Shizuku tentatively reached a hand out, and the cat didn't shy away. It seemed content to let Shizuku pet it. Its fur was clean and well-kept.

"Must be some noble's pet. Did you run away from your master?"

"Meow!"

Shizuku scratched its neck. The cat purred happily and nuzzled against her. It seemed to enjoy Shizuku's petting.

"S-so cute..." Shizuku murmured, smiling. Both her irritation at herself and her burning bloodlust vanished. She was totally absorbed by the cat.

The constant training had exhausted her, so it was understandable that Shizuku, who prided herself on her reputation as an aloof and mysterious beauty, allowed herself to cut loose.

"You're so cuuute! But you can't run away from your owner. Bad kitties like you need to be scolded."

If any of the noble ladies who'd taken to calling Shizuku "Neesan" had spotted her conversing with a cat, they would likely have doubted their sanity. Or possibly developed a nosebleed.

Shizuku continued petting the cat as she talked, exhausted.

After a few more minutes, the cat padded over to the basket holding Shizuku's sandwich, and poked its nose inside.

"Oh? Do you want meow sandwich?" Shizuku cooed.

The cat gazed longingly at her.

Its cuteness melted Shizuku's heart. Naturally, she wouldn't refuse. However, her sandwich was too big, and she needed to cut it into smaller chunks.

"Wait just a little bit. I'll cut it up meowcely for you."

No one was around to ask why she was cutting the sandwich with her sword, and not just ripping it with her hands, or even why she took a battle stance to do so. Adopting the same stance she used when cutting imaginary demons, she threw the sandwich into the air and prepared to draw.

All this drove home an already-clear point: Shizukat was extremely tired.

"Go forth... Gale Claw!" Hajime could never have guessed that she would use his sword to cut a sandwich. But cut one it did, and splendidly.

The sandwich still looked whole when it fell back into Shizuku's hand. The moment she sheathed her blade, however, it fell apart into even squares.

Shizuku struck a pose, as if her swordsmanship would somehow impress the cat.

"Meow that's what I call a cut."

Turning around, Shizuku locked eyes with Princess Liliana, who stared at her with a dumbfounded expression.

"......"

"......"

Shizuku's smile froze. The princess said nothing. Silence

stretched on for a few minutes. The cat finished its meal and ran off.

After an ominous gust of wind, the princess finally broke the silence.

"Meow that's what I call a cut?" She asked.

"M-meoooooow!" Shizuku replied loudly.

She was still talking like a cat.

"Don't look at me. Please, don't look at me! In fact, just kill me right now."

"C-calm down... It's not that big a deal. In fact, I thought you looked rather cute, Shizuku."

Shizuku buried her face in her hands. Liliana squatted next to her.

It took some time before Shizuku would look her in the eye. Once Shizuku finally calmed down, she glared at Liliana. "So, what were you doing here, Liliana? Did you have some business with me? I can't think of any other reason you'd come to this practice ground."

Liliana grimaced. "It's true that I had business with you, but... I didn't see you with Kouki-san and the others."

She'd been worried that Shizuku wasn't with her comrades. Shizuku smiled.

"Thanks for being concerned about me, Lily. But I'm fine, don't worry."

"Then why were you here alone...?"

Because I wanted to be alone. Shizuku swallowed those words. Unfortunately for her, Liliana grew up in the ruthless world of court politics, which made her very good at reading people.

"Shizuku, you always push yourself too hard. Perhaps that's presumptuous of me, when I'm one of the people making you fight for our cause, but..."

"I don't think it is. We all know just how hard you work for our sakes, Lily. And I'm not pushing myself. It's just that Kouki and the others can be a bit difficult. Sometimes I just need to get away for a while."

Liliana knew that couldn't be everything, but pressing any further would just make things harder for Shizuku, so she decided to let Shizuku change the topic.

"They can definitely be a handful sometimes."

"Yeah. It's not easy to get over the defeat we suffered in the labyrinth. It's worse for Kouki, because of what happened with Kaori."

Shizuku stared westward, thinking of her best friend.

"Are you lonely?"

It didn't show on Shizuku's face, but Liliana guessed how she felt.

"I'm not exactly lonely. Even if she's not here, I'll always be connected to Kaori. Yeah... I'm sure of that. Besides, I have a princess worrying about me right here, don't I?"

Shizuku smiled playfully, and Liliana blushed. She felt like one of those noble girls who thought of themselves as Shizuku's little sisters.

"You really are like everyone's big sister."

Shizuku pinched Liliana's cheek. She wasn't happy about everyone else calling her Oneesama. That said, most of the other girls considered a pinch from Shizuku a reward. Liliana could imagine how jealous they would be.

"So, what do you need me for?" Shizuku asked, tired of talking about herself.

Liliana blushed again. "I was wondering about the change in the demons, and about Nagumo-san."

"I should have known. Have the king and Holy Church come to a decision?"

Ever since the heroes' return from the labyrinth, the country had been in an uproar. It was only natural. Their report stated that the demons could control an army of extremely powerful monsters, strong enough to defeat the hero party. If that was true, humanity was doomed.

Hajime had also caused widespread panic. Supposedly, he annihilated monsters that cornered the hero party.

Also, reports from Ur described him destroying an entire monster army, even before the battle in the labyrinth. Most people didn't really believe the claims. The events at Orcus lent more credence to those tales, however.

Everyone was interested in the boy who was once labeled "worthless." His unbelievable strength, along with his unknown artifacts, likely held the key to saving humanity.

Yet he hadn't returned to his old comrades. Instead, he struck out on his own.

Neither the king nor the pope was happy about that. They'd spent the past few days discussing how to deal with Hajime. However, they had yet to come to a conclusion.

Shizuku hoped Liliana might have news about a verdict, but Liliana just sighed uncharacteristically.

"They still haven't made a decision. All they've been talking about is how they need Kouki-san and the others to get stronger as fast as possible. I think they want to reexamine everyone's jobs, too. They're hoping that, if one student could control monsters, there might be more. They don't understand that the problem is mental and not physical. They think, because you were chosen by Ehit for this mission, that you should be happy to fulfill it. To them, killing demons isn't a big deal."

Like all humans, Liliana was a devout follower of Ehit, so it surprised Shizuku that she spoke so irreverently of her god.

Sensing the unspoken question, Liliana smiled bitterly.

"I think it's important to be able to separate your emotions and your beliefs when examining a problem objectively."

That was one thing the princess was good at; a core part of her personality. Shizuku was amazed a girl of fourteen could be so mature.

"Also, I feel as though the priests weren't this radical before. Perhaps it's a sign that they feel cornered. Regardless, you should be careful. The Holy Church may try something drastic. Kouki-san and the others are still uneasy, so the pope will probably take the opportunity to push them in a dangerous direction. I thought I should warn you."

"That certainly makes sense. Okay, we'll be careful. Thank you, Lily."

Just being prepared for something made a world of difference.

Knowing it was coming would let you ride it out, and keep your thoughts from getting muddled.

"What about Nagumo-kun?"

Liliana hesitated. Shizuku suddenly had a bad feeling. It turned out to be true.

"They're considering declaring him a heretic."

"You're serious, aren't you?"

That would mean any human was allowed to kill him. Hajime would be branded an enemy of Ehit, and would no longer possess any rights. Worse, other humans would be forbidden to aid him. The world would effectively turn against him.

"It isn't set in stone yet. They're still just considering it. They can't brand him one for refusing to obey the Holy Church. It takes more than that. Still, rumors are going to spread. Even if it was something one of the bishops said in the heat of the moment, word will get out, and people will talk. The mere fact that he's considered a potential heretic will ruin his reputation."

"So, you want us to stop those rumors, before they go too far?"

"Yes. Humanity's fate was at stake, and a bishop got too heated and made a careless remark. That was the only reason Nagumo-san's name was brought up. Please try and keep the story to just that. I suspect the official decision will come after Aiko-san returns and gives her report."

Shizuku understood why Liliana was trying so hard to save Hajime's reputation. She wanted to make sure Hajime had somewhere to return to. Not just for his sake, but for Kaori's. She

ARIFURETA: FROM COMMONPLACE TO WORLD'S STRONGEST

didn't want Kaori to suffer the pain of seeing her beloved become a hunted man.

"Thank you so much, Lily." Shizuku said sincerely.

"Although it may have been Ehit's decree, it's still our fault you're wrapped up in this. If I don't do everything I can to help you, then how will I ever face Ehit in the afterlife? Besides...you and Kaori are my friends."

Liliana blushed and turned away. Shizuku hugged her.

"Not just any friend... One of my best friends!"

Liliana's face grew even redder.

After getting the heavy topics out of the way, Shizuku and Liliana spoke about more trivial matters. Liliana had to support a nation, while Shizuku had to support her troublemaking classmates. They both had endless worries. Still, it was precisely because of their duties that they could talk so candidly.

Those healing conversations came at a price, however. Namely, the dignity of the people they talked about.

Liliana complained about how Lundel came crying every night because the love of his life, Kaori, ran off with Hajime. Meanwhile, Shizuku regaled Liliana with tales of how Lundel accused Kouki of being a coward for letting Hajime steal Kaori. The conversation left Kouki writhing on the ground.

Liliana described how she left Lundel afterward by saying the exact same thing. At some point, the conversation shifted to Hajime's appearance.

Had Kouki, Lundel, or Hajime been present, they likely would have cried themselves to sleep. Conversations between girls were something the men of the world were destined never to know about.

"Well, Shizuku, I should head back now. Please don't overdo it."

"Mm-hmm. I know. I think I'll go back to my room, too. Thanks for everything, Lily."

The sun had long since set, and the stars twinkled in the night sky as the two girls finally finished talking. They were smiling, glad of the opportunity to let off some stress.

They walked back to the castle together, then parted where the corridor forked. Shizuku watched her closest friend in this world vanish down the hallway. Content, she turned towards her room.

"Huh?!" For the briefest moment, she felt a terrible chill.

Placing a hand on her sword, and falling into her battle stance, she observed her surroundings for a few seconds. She saw nothing in the dimly-lit corridor.

"Was it just my imagination?" She tried to magically sense other beings, but discerned nothing.

I'm probably just nervous because of what Lily told me. Shizuku sighed and took her hand off her sword.

She walked toward her room, her pace faster than before, as if something pushed her on.

ARIFURETA:
ARIFURETA SHOKUGYOU DE SEKAISAIKYOU

**FROM COMMONPLACE
TO WORLD'S STRONGEST**

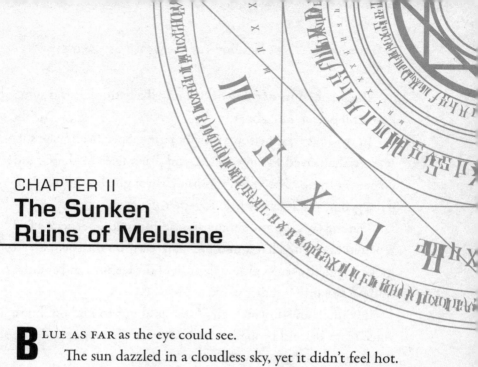

CHAPTER II
The Sunken
Ruins of Melusine

BLUE AS FAR as the eye could see.

The sun dazzled in a cloudless sky, yet it didn't feel hot. In fact, the weather was positively pleasant. A gentle breeze blew past, moderating the temperature.

There was nothing in sight, making the scene somewhat lonely. But then, this was the middle of the ocean.

A single boat drifted gently through the waves. Although perhaps "boat" wasn't the best way to describe it. At the very least, this world's people wouldn't have considered it one.

The not-boat was jet-black, narrow, and had no visible place to board. Two wings jutted from its side in a V, its rear had a propeller of some sort, and its rudder looked like a tail. However, it wasn't in the best shape. The entire thing looked like it'd been ravaged by a fierce storm. From a certain angle, it almost resembled a flattened whale.

The inhabitants of this world would likely think it was some kind of monster, not a boat.

In truth, it was the top of a submarine. Specifically, the submarine that saved Hajime, Shea, and Yue's lives in the Grand Gruen Volcano. The vessel's journey through the magma had damaged it, and it barely held together.

Hajime lay atop the submarine, admiring the scenery. He'd repaired his melted left arm using material from the sub. Now it looked as good as new, although most of the features and abilities he'd packed into it didn't work.

"Hajime, how do you feel?" He was about to nod off, but a voice from behind brought him back. Yue's head popped into view. She looked at him worriedly.

Hajime had taken quite a bit of damage from the aurora, and the poison had slowed his healing.

"Pretty good. My wounds have all closed up. They'll probably be fully healed in another day or so. How about you, Yue? You were pretty exhausted after that fight, right?"

"Mmm... I'm fine. Shea let me drink some of her blood." Yue climbed out of the hatch and crawled over to where Hajime was lying. Then, as if it were the most natural thing in the world, she straddled him. Her plump butt fell directly over a very sensitive part of Hajime's body.

"Yue, why are you climbing on top of me?"

"Because you're there?" Yue said, copying a certain mountain climber's quote, and stared seriously down at Hajime. However, her aura wasn't seductive.

"Don't move..." she said as she bent over his neck. She ran her tongue along his skin before sinking her fangs inside, lapping up the blood that welled out.

"Mmm, I think the poison's mostly gone. You should be fine."

It seemed Yue could tell the state of Hajime's body by tasting his blood.

"I told you I was fine."

"Mmm... But I was still worried. I'm glad you're finally able to rest, even if it's in the middle of the ocean."

"Yeah. To be honest, I never expected things to move so quickly. I can't decide if it was good luck or bad." Hajime smiled wryly and Yue arched an eyebrow.

Neither could decide whether they should be grateful that they made it out alive, or consider it bad luck that they went through so many horrible events before riding the magma torrent into the ocean.

They spent almost an entire day floating atop the underground magma channel after the eruption.

Hajime underwent a sleepless night, worrying that the current might take them into the planet's mantle. Around that time, their journey changed.

Their submarine was hit by an impact far stronger than any before. So strong, in fact, that it broke through the Diamond Skin defense and damaged the hull directly. The force sent the sub flying.

Hajime hurried to make sure there weren't any leaks. When he checked the exterior, he discovered an unbelievable sight. They were no longer surrounded by magma on all sides. Instead, they found themselves at the bottom of an actual sea, encircled by spiraling ribbons of magma.

The channel had carried them into an underwater volcano. The impact they felt was a phreatic eruption that spat them into the sea.

The eruption damaged the submarine badly, but fortunately, the hull wasn't breached. Hajime's expert engineering probably had more to do with that than luck.

Hajime and the others breathed sighs of relief at finally reaching the surface, but their troubles had only just begun. The propeller and rudder were both broken, forcing them to move the submarine with mana as deep-sea monsters attacked them.

First, they had to grapple with a giant squid. It was thirty meters long and had over thirty tentacles. Hajime dubbed it the Kraken.

The Kraken continually assaulted the submarine as they tried to rise to the surface. It nearly caught and ate them, but Hajime's torpedoes and Yue's magic somehow managed to fend it off.

Next, a school of sharks hounded them, wrapping water around them like a tornado. After that, they faced a giant marlin with a revolving horn. Then, a giant turtle that spat mines out of its ass... The list was endless.

Eventually, Hajime's weapon reserves ran dry, and they were entirely reliant on magic. Yue drained all of her magic accessories, and since Hajime was still weak from blood loss, she drank Shea's blood to replenish her mana.

The strain from their earlier fight at the Grand Gruen Volcano had taken its toll, and they were barely able to fight the creatures off. Shea, who hated being powerless, gave so much blood to Yue that she fainted.

Once they made it into relatively safe waters, Hajime sent Yue and Shea to rest as he guided the submarine back to the continent. It had been half a day since then. The weather was perfect and the sea was calm. Since there was no immediate danger, Hajime decided to stop the sub and treat himself to a little sunbath. It was his first proper rest in quite a while.

It really had been one thing after another since they cleared the Grand Gruen Volcano. No other party would have survived. Hajime could understand why a certain anime character, who punched people into living their lives correctly, was always complaining about his misfortune.

"How's Shea?" Hajime brought himself back to the present and looked up at Yue.

"Still sleeping. I drank a lot of her blood, so she probably won't wake up for a while."

According to Yue, the amount of mana she got from Hajime's blood and the amount she got from Shea's blood were different. She'd made a blood oath with Hajime, so his blood gave her exponentially more mana.

Yue's blood oath was a double-edged sword. She gained far more mana from the person she made the oath with, but the amount of mana she obtained from others fell.

"I see. Well, we can take it easy for a bit. We have no idea how far we are from the continent, so there's no telling how long it'll take to get back. It's better to rest now, while we have the chance. Who knows what else we might have to deal with later."

"Yeah."

The ocean lay to the west of the continent, so Hajime was sure they'd reach their destination by heading east. Yue could make water for them with her magic, and they could catch fish. There wasn't a fish in the sea that could escape Hajime's submarine and Yue's magic, so although they were stranded in the middle of the ocean with nothing, they could get by. Plus, it was safer to wait until night, so they could use the stars to confirm their direction.

Hajime laid back and relaxed. Yue watched him closely.

"Yue, may I ask what you're doing?"

"I'm giving you energy." Yue smiled seductively and leaned in close. She was definitely giving him energy, but only to a certain body part. As Hajime stared into her eyes, all thoughts of resisting melted away.

"Mmm... Hee hee! Looks like you're ready."

"Never thought I'd do this in the middle of the ocean half a year ago."

Hajime and Yue enjoyed themselves thoroughly, savoring the feeling of still being alive. For a while, the submarine rocked from more than just waves.

•¦• •¦• •¦• •¦• •¦• •¦• •¦• •¦• •¦• •¦• •¦• •¦• •¦•

"It sounded like you two were having fun."

Shea, glaring, met them as they entered the submarine.

"Hm? I didn't know you'd woken up. How're you feeling?"

"Thanks for glossing over that like it never happened. All of your rocking and moaning woke me up. All my loneliness and sadness gave me strength, so I'm feeling a lot better now. Well enough to smack you, in fact."

"That's good."

Shea groaned at how casually Hajime took her words. Realizing he was being too cold, he smiled and invited Shea to sit next to him.

She felt really left out when she woke up to the sounds of Hajime and Yue having sex, and made up for it by clinging even more tightly to Hajime than usual.

Yue also took a seat beside Shea, instead of her customary place by Hajime. She stroked Shea's ears in an attempt to improve her mood.

With that, Hajime poured mana into his sub and propelled it eastward. Monsters still came out to attack them, but Yue fended them off with ease. Hajime drove them through the night, and finally spotted land around dawn.

He'd triangulated their position from the stars during the night. By his estimate, they were somewhere north of Erisen. That meant, if he followed the coastline south, he'd eventually reach Erisen, and the port that connected the sea to the Gruen Desert.

Relieved, the party followed the coast south for two days. Around noon on the second day, Hajime stopped the submarine, and the group went up to the deck to eat.

Lunch consisted of fish, as it had for the past two days. It reminded Hajime of his days in the abyss as he used Lightning Field to grill it. Since he'd given Tio his Treasure Trove, they didn't have any seasonings or dishes.

Still, the three enjoyed their meal as they gazed out at the sea. In a way, the spectacular scenery provided flavor, the same way food tasted different on a beach, or at a festival.

Just as Shea finished off some unknown species, her ears twitched. She began to move.

A split second later, Hajime noticed it too. His mouth full of giant fish, he turned toward the water.

A number of human-shaped silhouettes surrounded the submarine. They leaped from the water and pointed their tridents at the three.

They were dagons, and there were at least twenty of them. Hajime noticed they all had emerald-green hair and fins for ears. They watched Hajime and the others warily.

The one standing directly in front of Hajime thrust out his spear.

"Who are you people? Why are you here? And what is that thing you're riding?"

Hajime's mouth was still full of fish, so he couldn't answer. That was rather unfortunate, as he had no intention of fighting these dagons, but the fish was surprisingly tough and hard to chew. It would take some time to swallow it all.

Hajime wanted to take this conversation seriously, but he knew it must look like he was making fun of them. Instead of talking, he was just casually eating his lunch.

A vein pulsed in the dagon's forehead. His anger seemed a bit overblown. Realizing the situation could blow up at any minute, Shea tried to placate him.

"U-umm, please, calm down. We're just—"

"Silence! A mere rabbitman like you has no right to speak!"

Even outside the sea of trees, rabbitmen were apparently looked down on by the other beastmen. The dagons wanted Hajime himself to answer. They thought he was insulting them. The head dagon turned his trident on Shea and thrust at her.

His attack would likely not even have scratched her, due to her body strengthening, but she still dodged out of the way. He'd aimed for her cheek, hoping that injuring Hajime's comrade would make the human take the encounter more seriously.

The dagon seemed almost desperate. From what Hajime remembered, dagons weren't an aggressive race.

But regardless of what drove them to such aggression, they shouldn't have turned on Shea. Even if the attack was just a warning, Hajime didn't like anyone attacking his friends. He unleashed a wave of Intimidation so strong that it sent ripples through the ocean.

The lead dagon turned to Hajime, his eyes nearly bulging out of their sockets. A second later, there was a loud thud. The dagon flew through the air in a tailspin. He bounced off the ocean's surface a few times before sinking into the sea.

The other dagons looked back at Hajime. He was holding a grilled fish as though he'd just smacked a golf ball with it.

The sea glimmered in the sunlight. Hajime's dead fish glimmered, too.

"Wh-what?"

The dagons still couldn't grasp what had happened.

Hajime slung the half-eaten fish over his shoulder and glared at the next dagon, who was already scared senseless by Hajime's Intimidation. The added pressure of the human's glare made him snap. He charged forward with a wild yell.

"Zaaaaaah!"

It was perhaps the dagon's most noble moment. In the face of certain death, he unleashed the strongest attack he could. However, Hajime blocked it with his dead fish. The dagon's trident stuck fast inside the fish's mouth.

"Huh? Wh-what the..."

Hajime spun the fish, pulling the trident clean out of his hands. Its shaft struck the other dagons as it spun, leaving them reeling.

As they clutched their bloody noses, Hajime swung the fish again.

The dagon who lost his spear stared, dumbfounded, at this human boy, glowing dark red and slapping them around with a fish.

"Bwah?!"

Hajime sent the next one flying the same way. A faint stream of water trailed behind the dagon as he flew off into the ocean.

"*Gulp.* Okay, now I really don't want to fight you guys. Let's calm down and talk this through. I won't hold back if you try to hurt my comrades, but I went easy on those guys, so they should still be alive."

Hajime lifted his Intimidation, and the red glow surrounding him faded. He didn't want to fight Myu's people. He couldn't face her if he accidentally ended up killing her neighbor or something.

However, the dagons didn't seem interested in talking. Even if he hadn't killed their comrades, he'd still knocked them around. More importantly, it hurt their pride that Hajime didn't even consider them worth fighting, especially since he was the one at a disadvantage at sea.

They were still wary of humans and didn't trust Hajime's words. They weren't going to let their guards down. The dagons backed up and prepared to throw their tridents.

"Is this how you tricked her? Are you here to kidnap more of our children?!"

"We won't let you use magic again! The sea is our domain! Don't think you'll make it home in one piece!"

"We'll get her location out of you, even if we have to rip your limbs off!"

"Don't worry, we won't kill you. We need you as a hostage to trade with the kingdom, after all."

There's definitely something strange going on here. They weren't just wary of Hajime, they hated him. Judging by what they'd said, Hajime guessed it had something to do with Myu. *Did they mistake us for the criminals that kidnapped her?* They'd come in on some strange machine, with what appeared to be a rabbitman slave in tow. It was only natural the dagons would suspect them.

Beastmen societies were known to be extremely close-knit. They were protective even of other species, but especially of their own.

The Haulia tribe abandoned the sea of trees for Shea, and the bearmen ignored the council's decision to take revenge for their leader. The dagons were no exception. Each was protective of Myu, even if she wasn't their daughter.

She had all these guys to choose for her dad. Why'd she pick me? Hajime smiled bitterly to himself. He decided to bring up Myu to solve the misunderstanding.

"Uh, about that kidnapped girl—"

"Get him!" Before he could continue, the dagons threw their tridents.

They all swam in the ocean, and yet still managed to throw with considerable force. Since they aimed at his shoulders and legs, Hajime guessed they didn't really plan to kill him. They shook the submarine as they attacked it from below.

Any normal opponent would have lost their balance and been unable to dodge. They might even have fallen into the sea to be torn apart. Of course, Hajime was no normal opponent.

"Liquid Rampart!" The ocean rose around them, knocking down the tridents. While the dagons marveled at Yue's ability to cast magic without an incantation, she created twenty balls of electricity.

As the walls of water crashed back into the sea, the dagons saw electricity flying at them.

"Wha...?! T-take coveeer!" a dagon cried. Their faces paled, and they quickly tried to swim away, but it was already too late.

The balls homed in on each dagon and hit with a powerful shock. They spasmed and screamed for a few minutes before floating limply to the surface.

"Nice job, Yue."

"Yeah. Hajime, the thing they were talking about..."

"They probably meant Myu."

"You just have to cause a commotion wherever you go, huh? I guess I should expect this by now. We haven't visited a single town without making a stir..."

"Oh, come on, Shea. To be honest, I feel a little bad about this. Damn... This wouldn't have happened if we had Myu with us."

Hajime sighed and started collecting the unconscious dagons.

Hajime dumped the dagon men into the impromptu trunk he crafted into the submarine, then headed toward the city.

Yue had held back, so the dagons woke up relatively quickly. Once they were awake, Hajime explained the situation.

A few of them still thought he might be the culprit, because he could describe Myu so well. They tried to jump at him, but he slapped them silly with a fish until they calmed down. Eventually, they were convinced.

Patience is an important virtue when it comes to persuasion.

Swollen-cheeked, the dagon men were finally willing to listen. When Hajime told them Myu was waiting in Ankaji, they requested that he first stop by Erisen, and choose a few members to accompany him.

Although they still weren't sure they could trust him, they chose to believe his words. However, they planned to accompany him to make sure.

Hajime agreed, and steered the submarine to Erisen.

Along the way, he learned that all of the dagons who attacked him knew Myu personally.

Myu's kidnappers had also hurt her mother badly, so the men held a deep-seated resentment against them. Hajime didn't want Myu to see her friends with unkempt hair and bruises, so he reluctantly healed them all.

After a few hours, they spotted Erisen.

"Ah, Hajime-san! There it is! I can see a city, and people!" Shea pointed excitedly.

"Hm? Wow. It actually is in the middle of the ocean."

The city literally floated on top of the sea.

Hajime headed to one of Erisen's many docks. Dagons, visiting human tourists, and traders watched in awe as his mysterious vessel rode past. Hajime ignored them and stopped at an empty dock.

The dagons, in particular, murmured worriedly when they saw their unconscious brethren in the trunk.

"Hey, explain the situation to them. The more time we waste dealing with stuff here, the longer it'll take to get Myu."

"O-okay!"

A young dagon nodded, trembling. He didn't want to face Hajime's fish slaps again.

Spotting a contingent of human and dagon soldiers making their way over, the youth quickly intercepted them. Hajime was anxious to rendezvous with Tio, Kaori, and Myu, so he didn't want to waste any time here. He watched impatiently as the young dagon talked to the soldiers.

Sadly, things were never simple. The soldiers shoved the youth aside and marched up to the sub. They surrounded Hajime, trapping him on the tiny dock.

"Until we know your intentions, we have to detain you. Don't resist."

"Hey, did you even listen to that guy?"

"Yes." The man spoke curtly. "We will send some of our men to confirm your story. You, however, will stay here."

Hajime didn't like his attitude one bit, but he restrained himself. *Remember, this is Myu's home.*

"Okay, look. I've got comrades waiting for me. I was planning to head straight back there, but I took a detour to deliver these guys to you. They're the ones who attacked me, you know."

"We have yet to verify whether they were justified. If the kidnapped child isn't in Ankaji, you're just a suspicious boy who arrived on an unknown vessel. What proof do we have that you won't run?"

"That'd be kind of pointless, don't you think? If I wanted to run, I could have just left these guys in the ocean and gone somewhere else."

"About that. You are within our territory without permission. Furthermore, you attacked one of our patrols. We cannot let you move freely within the city."

"They're the ones who attacked, without even listening to us. What, did you want me to just sit there while they chopped my limbs off? Gimme a break."

He narrowed his eyes dangerously. The man frowned,

seemingly unperturbed by the enormous pressure radiating from Hajime.

Hajime recognized the crest on the man's uniform. It was the Heiligh Kingdom's coat of arms. That meant this stranger was the captain of the peacekeeping force assigned to Erisen, which explained why he wasn't affected by Hajime's glare. Hajime hadn't used Intimidation yet, after all. Although the dagon captain's face paled, he held his ground.

Hajime really didn't want to cause a stir here. Not only was this Myu's hometown, he would likely spend time here searching for the entrance to the Sunken Ruins of Melusine. That was another of the Seven Great Labyrinths, so he needed to conquer it.

He knew Myu was in Ankaji, so he wasn't worried that they wouldn't find her. But after everything this world had thrown at him, fighting back was almost instinctive. He'd sworn he wouldn't back down to anyone when he crawled out of the abyss. He didn't feel like breaking that oath here.

However, he also didn't want to cause an uproar, which made the situation rather dicey.

Just when Hajime had convinced himself that he should accept their conditions, for Myu's sake, he heard something.

"Hm? What's..."

Shea's bunny ears perked up and she scanned the sky.

Hajime turned away from the captain and followed her gaze. "What'd you see?" he asked.

Before she could reply, Hajime heard a familiar voice.

"...dy!"

"Huh? What was that?"

"...dy!"

"Wait... No way...!"

"Daddy!"

Hajime looked up and saw a vaguely human-shaped figure falling from the sky. She was smiling happily, arms spread wide.

"Myu?!"

It was indeed Myu, seemingly skydiving without a parachute.

He noticed Tio, in her dragon form, following closely behind, Kaori riding on her back.

Hajime's body moved automatically. He activated Air Dance and Supersonic Step, then shot into the sky.

The force of his jump destroyed the wooden dock. The soldiers screamed as they fell into the sea, but Hajime didn't notice.

He used Aerodynamic to propel himself farther upward, then activated Riftwalk. He caught Myu in slow motion and expertly controlled the speed of their descent to negate the impact.

With Myu safely in his arms, he zipped back to the ground. Cold sweat covered his whole body.

"Daddy!"

Unaware of Hajime's panic, Myu happily nuzzled his chest. Tio had probably told Myu she'd spotted him.

Then, either by accident, or perhaps on purpose, Myu had fallen. Judging by her smiling face, she'd had no doubt that Hajime would catch her.

Still, it took a ridiculous amount of courage to jump off a

flying dragon's back. *What kind of four-year-old does that?!* Hajime frowned, scolding Myu for her recklessness.

⁕ ⁕ ⁕ ⁕ ⁕ ⁕ ⁕ ⁕ ⁕ ⁕ ⁕ ⁕ ⁕ ⁕

"*Hic...hic...*"

Myu stood next to the destroyed dock, crying. The area was filled with onlookers and soldiers, but none said a word.

The kidnapped girl had fallen from the sky, and a young boy caught her in midair with superhuman abilities. Not only that, there was a dragon flying overhead. But what surprised everyone most was that the boy was scolding Myu, and that Myu called him her father.

"*Hic...* I'm sorry, Daddy!"

"Do you promise not to do anything that dangerous again?"

"I promise..."

"Then it's fine. Now, give me a hug."

"Daddy!"

Hajime knelt down, and Myu launched herself into his chest. The whole exchange looked exactly like a father scolding his daughter. In many ways, Hajime really was Myu's father.

Everyone watched with dumbfounded amazement. They would never have expected a kidnapped dagon girl to call a human boy her father.

What the hell is going on?

Hajime lifted Myu in his arms and patted her back. As if it was some signal, the onlookers all started talking at once.

Hajime ignored the commotion and started walking when he

felt someone hug him from behind. He turned around, and Kaori rested her head on his shoulder. She was trembling.

"Thank goodness... I'm so glad you're okay."

Now it was Kaori's turn to cry. Although she acted strong, she'd been worried sick. She believed Hajime was still alive, of course, but that didn't stop her from worrying... Especially since he disappeared shortly after they were finally reunited. She'd been through a lot.

"Sorry I made you worry. But as you can see, we're all fine. So... please don't cry. If a certain someone found out I made you cry... Well, she'd probably kill me."

"Waaah... *Hic...* Th-then, let me stay here like this for a while longer...!"

Hajime looked away awkwardly, and gently patted Kaori on the head with his free hand. Her tears didn't stop, and she buried her face in Hajime's shoulder, hugging him with all her might.

"Hey, you. What on earth is going on? I demand an explan— bwah?!"

"Hm? Oh, my apologies."

The captain dragged himself out of the water and stalked up to Hajime, dripping wet. Before he could start yelling, he was knocked back into the water by Tio. She'd turned back into a human upon landing and, in her haste, accidentally bumped into the captain.

Tio didn't seem sorry. She grabbed Hajime's head and pulled him into her bosom.

"Whoa?! Hey, Tio!"

"I believed in you. I believed...you would return. Still, you made me wait quite some time, Master."

Hajime extricated himself from Tio's massive chest and looked up at her face. Tears dripped from her eyes. She hugged Hajime tight, as if he would vanish. He'd put Tio through a lot, so he let her do as she wished.

Myu joined in as well, hugging Hajime around the neck. Yue and Shea didn't feel like being left out, so they crowded around Hajime and joined in the fun.

Hajime was buried underneath a pile of girls of all ages and sizes.

The confusion gradually faded from the onlookers' faces, replaced by a gentle warmth. Even the dagons who attacked Hajime lowered their weapons, although a few others picked up weapons of their own. As always, some people were jealous of Hajime's harem.

"You bastard... Not once, but twice now! Interfering with a royal soldier's duty is a criminal offense!"

The captain dragged himself from the water again and stalked toward Hajime. He readied his weapon.

Considering Myu's attitude, it was unlikely that Hajime was the kidnapper, but there was still a lot about this situation that didn't make sense. Thus, the captain wanted to interrogate Hajime.

Since escorting Myu back to Erisen was an official request from Fuhren's branch chief Ilwa, Hajime hadn't worried about being arrested. A proper explanation would have cleared things up. The only problem was, he hadn't had any proof of the request. Fortunately, he now possessed such proof.

Tio gave Hajime his Treasure Trove. He pulled out his Status Plate and the letter Ilwa had given him.

"What? Just showing me your identity now won't... Wait, you're a gold-rank adventurer?! And you have a personal introduction from Fuhren's branch chief?!"

Hajime pulled out the letter detailing his request and handed it to the captain. The letter was originally addressed to the mayor and the captain of the guard, so Hajime would have given it to him eventually.

The captain scrutinized the document. Once he was done reading, he sighed. After a moment's hesitation, he shrugged his shoulders and saluted.

"I verify that you have indeed completed the assigned task, Hajime Nagumo-dono."

"Glad to be cleared of suspicion. I'm sure there's a lot you want to know, but we're kinda busy here. Could you hold off on your questions for a bit? I want to bring Myu to her mother first. Is that all right?"

"I suppose so. However, I cannot overlook that dragon, those unbelievable abilities of yours, and this strange boat."

The captain was no longer talking down to Hajime. In fact, he was almost respectful. But still, he had a job to do, and it required him to investigate those things.

"It's fine if we talk about all that later, right? We're planning on staying in Erisen for a while, so it's not like we're going anywhere. Besides, there's no point sending a report to the capital. They already know all this."

"Hmm, I see. In that case, as long as we can talk, I'll be satisfied. You said you want to take the little girl to her mother, but... do you know what kind of state her mother is in?"

"No, but that shouldn't be a problem. We've got some of the best medicine in the world and a top-class healer here."

"I see. Very well, then. In that case, I shall return once things have settled down."

The captain gave Hajime his name, Salze, and got to work dispersing the onlookers. He seemed very dedicated to his job.

Everyone acquainted with Myu came up to talk to her, but Hajime silenced them with a look. He appreciated their enthusiasm, but if they started wishing her well now, the party would never reach Myu's mother.

"Daddy! Daddy! I wanna go home. Mommy's waiting! I wanna see Mommy!"

"Yeah. Let's go see her."

Myu took Hajime's hand and dragged him excitedly toward her house. She'd last seen her mother nearly two months ago. She'd laughed and smiled around Hajime and the others, but at night, she cried for her mom.

As they made their way to Myu's house, Kaori walked up to Hajime, looking worried.

"Hajime-kun. About what that soldier said earlier..."

"Well, it seems her life isn't in danger, at least. Her wounds are pretty bad, though, and it must have been a shock to lose her daughter. Seeing Myu again will help with the latter. I count on you for the former."

"Don't worry. Just leave it to me."

Their conversation was interrupted by a commotion farther down the street. A woman, and several men.

"Remia, calm down! You can't go anywhere on that leg!"

"He's right, Remia-chan. We'll bring Myu-chan to you!"

"No! She's my daughter! I have to be there to greet her! I have to!"

The men tried to hold her back. It seemed someone had told Myu's mother about her return.

When she heard her mother's voice, Myu's face lit up. She called out to the twenty-something woman collapsed in her house's entryway and dashed off toward her.

"Mommy!"

"Huh?! Myu?! Myu!"

Myu tottered up to her mother and leaped into her arms.

Mother and daughter embraced tightly, and the onlookers watched with smiles on their faces. A few even teared up.

Remia apologized to Myu over and over. Hajime couldn't tell whether she was apologizing for taking her eyes off Myu, or not coming to get her. It might have been both.

Tears streamed down Remia's cheeks. She was both relieved to have her daughter back, and angry at her inability to protect her. Myu patted her mom's head reassuringly.

"It's okay, Mommy. I'm here. It's okay."

"Myu..." Remia stared. She hadn't expected to be consoled by her daughter.

Myu peered back at her mother, worry etched over her face.

Before she'd been kidnapped, Myu had been a spoiled child, quick to throw a tantrum. Despite that, and although she must have suffered far more, she was the one worrying about others.

Myu smiled, and Remia hugged her tight. She'd spent many sleepless nights agonizing over the horrors her daughter might be facing, but while Remia fretted, Myu grew stronger.

Remia smiled, admiring the little girl's growth. Her tears dried up, and the tension drained from her shoulders.

The pair hugged again, but Myu suddenly shrieked.

"Mommy, what happened to your legs?! Do they hurt?!" Myu had finally noticed Remia's bandage-wrapped legs. Her wounds looked pretty serious.

Hajime remembered what Salze and the dagons who'd attacked him said. Not only had the slavers kidnapped Myu, they hurt Remia so badly that she couldn't walk.

No one saw Myu go missing, so at first, they weren't sure she had actually been kidnapped.

However, their suspicions were confirmed after Remia ran into the kidnappers.

She'd gone searching for her missing daughter, and found a group of shifty-looking men trying to cover their tracks at the beach. She didn't want to approach them, but she needed all the information she could get. She went to ask if they'd seen her daughter, and they attacked.

Realizing they must have taken Myu, Remia evaded the men's attacks. She tried to get her daughter back, but she had no combat skills to speak of. She could only dodge for so long, and eventually, one of the mages' fireballs hit her legs. The attack sent her flying backwards into the ocean, unconscious.

Worried when she didn't return, the other dagons sent out a search party. They found Remia floating in the sea and brought her back.

They managed to save her life, but her injuries were grave, and she would likely never be able to walk or swim properly again. Naturally, Remia tried to keep looking for her daughter, but with her legs the way they were, she was left with no choice but to leave the search to the others.

Even now, Remia could barely stand. But she didn't want to worry her daughter, so she smiled reassuringly and just murmured that she was fine.

Still, Myu had Hajime on her side now, and he could do anything. She turned to him for help.

"Daddy! You have to help Mommy! Her legs are hurt!"

"Wha...?! M-Myu...? Did you just say..."

"Daddy, hurry!"

"Huh? Daddy? Myu, who's Daddy?" Remia stared at her daughter, confused.

The other dagons started whispering.

"Did Remia...remarry? No way."

"Remia-chan's finally found a new husband! How wonderful!"

"No way. Someone tell me this isn't real... My Remia-san..."

"Daddy?! She didn't mean *me*, did she?!"

"It's probably just a nickname or something. I'm sure everyone calls him that."

"Guys, we need to hold an emergency meeting! Gather the members of the Remia and Myu Protection Committee!"

It seemed the mother and daughter were quite popular in Erisen. Remia was still young, and although she'd grown gaunt in the months since her daughter's disappearance, you could tell she was originally quite pretty. Once she regained her health, she'd likely turn heads in the street again.

Hajime grimaced. I really don't want to deal with those guys.

He was sure if he explained that Myu had started calling him that because she didn't have a real father, and that he wasn't interested in marrying Remia, the other men would understand. However, rumors often spread quickly.

Still, this was a stroke of good fortune. Hajime could leave Myu with her mother and continue his journey without worry. Once they cleared the Sunken Ruins of Melusine, he'd have to say his farewells. Myu clung so tightly to Hajime and the others because there was no one else she could trust, but now that she was back with her mother, she'd soon forget about them. She'd cry at first, but she'd get used to it in time. Especially since the other townspeople seemed to care a great deal for her.

"Daddy, hurry! You have to save Mommy!"

Myu looked over at Hajime, and everyone else stared, too. Many had only just noticed his presence. Hajime resigned himself to dealing with this misunderstanding and walked over.

"Daddy, Mommy's..."

"It's all right, Myu. We'll heal her, so don't cry."

"Okay..."

Hajime patted Myu's head and turned to Remia. She stared blankly back at him.

The whispers grew even more heated. For now, Hajime figured he should focus on healing Remia. That'd be easier to do inside her house.

"Sorry about this."

"Huh? Wha...?!"

Hajime effortlessly hoisted Remia in his arms and followed Myu inside. He could hear some of the guys screaming behind him, but he ignored them. Remia was too flustered to say anything at all.

As they entered the living room, Hajime spotted a sofa, so he put Remia down on it. He sat next to her and called Kaori over.

"Kaori, how's it look?"

"Let me examine her. Remia-san, I'm going to need to touch your legs. If it hurts, please say something."

"O-okay? Umm... What's going on?"

Not only was Myu calling some guy daddy, he was surrounded by a bunch of beautiful girls. Remia's confusion was understandable.

Kaori finished her examination and told Hajime that, while the injuries were serious, she was capable of healing them.

"But it'll take some time. A lot of fragile nerve endings were damaged, so I'll need a few days to heal her completely," Kaori added. "It might be a little inconvenient, Remia-san, but please bear with it. I promise I can cure you."

"Oh, my... I didn't think I would ever walk again. I don't know how to thank you."

"Heh heh. It's fine," said Hajime. "We can't leave Myu-chan's mom like this."

"About that... What kind of relationship do you have with my daughter? Also...umm...why is Myu calling you daddy?"

As Kaori began healing Remia, Hajime explained everything that had happened since Fuhren, including the events at the slave auction that led to Myu's nickname for him.

When he finished, Remia bowed her head. She thanked Hajime over and over again, tears in her eyes.

"I don't know how to thank you... It's because of you that I can see my daughter again. I swear, I will repay the favor, even if it takes my whole life. If there's anything I can do for you, anything at all..."

They told her not to worry about it, but Remia insisted. She couldn't accept doing nothing for the people who saved her daughter's life.

Eventually, Kaori's treatment reached a point where she could stop safely for the day. Hajime and the others began discussing where they would stay for the night, and Remia urged them to use her house.

"Please, at least let me do this for you. Fortunately, my house has plenty of space. There's enough room for all of you. As long as you're in Erisen, think of my home as yours. I'm sure Myu would be happier that way, too. Isn't that right, Myu? You want them to stay with us, don't you?"

"Huh? Are you going somewhere, Daddy?" Myu, who'd been dozing in Remia's lap, got up groggily and looked at Hajime in confusion. She was apparently certain that Hajime would stay. In fact, she couldn't even understand why her mother bothered to ask.

"I was thinking it might be better to spend some time away, now that she's back with you."

"Oh, my... Don't you know a father should never leave his daughter?"

"Well, I mean, I told you before, we're..."

"I know you'll leave on your journey eventually, but that's precisely why I'd like you to act as her father as long as you're here. Don't you think saying farewell after spending time apart would be even more sad?"

"Well, I guess you've got a point."

"Hee hee! You're welcome to stay here as her father forever, too, if you wish. I did say I would do anything to repay you."

Remia blushed and put a hand to her cheek. Normally, Hajime would have been reassured by her smile, but he could feel the room temperature dropping.

"Please don't joke around like that. A certain someone might kill me if you do."

"Oh, my! I see you're quite popular already. Still, it's been nearly five years since my husband passed away... And Myu seems to be pining for a father."

"Huh? But Daddy's already my daddy."

"Hee hee! There you have it, Daddy."

If the room got any colder, Hajime would freeze to death. It felt like he'd just stepped into the tundra.

Remia didn't seem to notice, or rather, didn't seem to care.

She continued joking with Hajime despite the cold glares Yue, Shea, Tio, and Kaori gave her. She weathered their ire with a smile; she was surprisingly strong-willed.

In the end, Hajime and the others decided to stay at Remia's house. She caused another stir later by saying, "Husband and wife are supposed to sleep in the same room, right?" Myu only made things worse by following up with, "Daddy and Mommy are going to sleep together!"

It was late by the time Remia and the girls finally stopped feuding.

They'd start their hunt for Melusine tomorrow, so Hajime wanted to spend the night repairing his damaged gear, creating new weapons, and testing the ancient magic they'd acquired. However, he also wanted to make the most of his remaining time with Myu, so he made sure to play with her. By the time he crawled into bed, he was dead tired.

Five days passed after Myu was reunited with her mother.

The dagon men were extremely jealous of Remia and Hajime's apparent closeness. Hajime had to fight a number of them off, and deal with the neighborhood gossip. Thanks to that, his usual companions came on to Hajime even more aggressively, and Yue spent every night pinning him to the bed. In the end, they didn't get any real exploring done, but were finally ready to embark.

Even though this parting would only be for a short while, Myu was still sad to see Hajime go. She clung to him for dear life, but Hajime eventually managed to pull her off, and head to his newly repaired submarine.

Myu waved and shouted goodbye as Hajime ducked through the entrance hatch.

"Goodbye, dear!" Remia shouted. Hajime still couldn't tell if she was being serious. It certainly looked as though his wife and daughter had come to see him off to work.

He could feel the other girls' sharp glares behind him. In front, the dagons glared jealously as well. *Maybe I should just leave right after we clear the ruins.*

⁂

They traveled roughly 300 kilometers northwest.

That was where the Sunken Ruins of Melusine were hidden, according to Miledi Reisen.

However, they hadn't gotten its precise location before she flushed them out. On top of that, she mentioned something about the moon, and needing Gruen's crest.

Hajime had decided to find the ruins, and go from there. They arrived at the location around noon, and began searching the bottom of the ocean. Unfortunately, they found nothing of note. Since it was a sunken *ruin,* Hajime expected to see some trace of it on the ocean floor, but there was nothing.

The only difference was the depth. The surrounding area was around 100 kilometers deep, but the ruins' supposed location was slightly shallower.

They reluctantly cut their search short, and decided to do as Miledi said, waiting patiently for the moon to come out.

The sun had almost completely sunk beneath the horizon,

and illuminated the sky with the its last rays. Both the sea and sky were dyed a dazzling shade of vermillion. A single streak of light ran through the water, connecting the horizon and the sun.

No matter the world, nature's beauty was unchanged. Hajime anchored the sub and headed up to the deck. *Maybe if I follow that ray of light all the way to the sun, it'll lead me back to Japan,* Hajime thought idly. *Heh, how ridiculous.* He smiled at his foolishness.

"What're you thinking about?" Kaori walked over to him.

She'd just gotten out of the shower he installed, and her hair was damp. Yue, Shea, and Tio followed behind.

It seemed they'd all taken a shower. Each woman was slightly flushed, with damp hair. It was quite an alluring sight. The shower poured hot water directly from the ceiling, so it was possible for them all to rinse off together. *Guess they're getting along now.*

Hajime had come up to the deck so that he didn't get roped into joining them.

Tio had actually invited Hajime to take a shower with her earlier, which of course meant Yue, Shea, and Kaori insisted on joining in.

Hajime made it clear that the only person he wanted to see naked was Yue. However, Kaori and the others completely ignored him. Tio and Kaori pinned Hajime down, while Shea attempted to knock him out with Drucken.

In the end, he'd fled to the deck, fearing for his life. He was beginning to wonder if he was a loser for refusing their advances. Hajime shook his head, banishing such dangerous thoughts, and turned to Kaori.

"I was just thinking about Japan. We have the same kind of sunset back home."

"I see. Yeah, you're right. It's exactly like the sunsets we used to see... How nostalgic. I can't believe it's only been half a year since we came here."

"It feels like the days stretch on forever."

Kaori sat down next to Hajime and nodded, gazing off into the distance, thinking back.

Lonely at being left out, Yue tottered over to Hajime and sat down on his lap. She leaned back and looked up at him.

Her eyes begged him to let her into the conversation. She was curious about Hajime's homeland. Although Yue was hard to resist, Hajime could feel Kaori's temper rising again. He leaned over and pinched her cheeks.

That seemed to be enough to improve her mood, although that wasn't what he was going for. He couldn't understand why they were all so obsessed with him, especially since he'd made his intentions clear. But he didn't say anything. It would be a betrayal of their feelings to ask something so crass.

Shea came up to Hajime too, her eyes sparkling. She obviously wanted his attention as well. He patted her bunny ears with his spare hand. She grinned and leaned closer.

Tio sat down, leaning against his back. She didn't ask for anything, but he could tell from her posture that she was completely relaxed. He expected her to ask for something perverted, so he was surprised when she didn't give him a reason to chuck her into the sea.

Before long, however, Tio's breathing grew heavy. It seemed that just sitting next to him was arousing. The five of them sat quietly, enjoying the sunset. There was still some time until the moon came out. Hajime decided to tell everyone stories of his homeland.

Yue and the others listened with rapt attention, while Kaori chimed in with stories of her own.

Time passed in the blink of an eye, and the sun set before they knew it. The moon appeared in the sky, shining brightly.

Hajime pulled Gruen's pendant out of his pocket and held it up. The pendant was engraved with a woman holding up a lantern, framed in a circle. The lantern had been cut out, leaving a hole.

In Erisen, Hajime had tried pouring mana into the pendant or holding it up against the moon, but nothing happened.

He still couldn't figure out what he was supposed to do, but he tried holding it up to the moon again, just in case. He angled it so the moon shone through the lantern-hole.

He kept the pendant like that for a while, but nothing changed. Sighing, he lowered it, and thought of other ways he could use it.

Just then, it began to glow.

"Look, the lantern's shining. It's so pretty," cooed Shea.

"You're right," Kaori agreed. "How strange. There's a hole there, but it's glowing."

Kaori and Shea examined the pendant with great interest. The glowing lantern had seemingly absorbed the moonlight. Now, pale, silvery light filled the hole, spreading like wispy liquid. Yue and Tio leaned in, and Hajime held the pendant aloft for them.

"It didn't do that last night," mused Yue.

"Hmm," Tio murmured. "I suspect it only activates in this location, Master."

Tio's probably right.

Once the entire lantern was saturated, it shot a stream of light directly downward, to the bottom of the ocean.

"That's an impressive trick. Better than Miledi's, at least."

"Totally. This is like something straight out of an RPG. It's pretty cool."

Hajime and Yue watched in awe as the moonlight literally showed them the way. Shea, who'd been with them for the Reisen Gorge, seemed impressed as well.

There was no telling how long the light would last, so they decided to hurry. They scrambled back into the submarine and followed the trail.

The sea was even darker at night. Practically no light made it past the first few kilometers. It grew pitch black, and Hajime turned on the sub's headlights. Those, and the light emanating from the pendant, were the only sources of light.

The pendant's light easily shone through the transparent crystal Hajime had used for the front windshield.

As they approached the sea floor, Hajime realized the light was pointing to a rocky section of the bottom. Countless massive boulders rested next to each other, creating an underwater mountain range of sorts. When they explored that section in the

CHAPTER II: THE SUNKEN RUINS OF MELUSINE

afternoon, there was nothing there. The light hit part of a boulder, and the entire formation began to shake with an ominous rumbling.

Part of the rock crumbled away, revealing an almost doorlike passage leading farther inside. The passage was pitch black, resembling the gateway to some hellish underworld.

"I get it now. No wonder we couldn't find anything, no matter how hard we looked. It was all a waste of time."

"We had time. Anyway, it was fun."

"Yeah. Sightseeing at the bottom of the ocean in another world was a great experience."

Hajime slumped his shoulders dejectedly, but Yue and Kaori seemed to have enjoyed the adventure.

Hajime steered the submarine into the newly-revealed passage. The pendant still contained about half of its light, but once they entered the passage, it suddenly stopped shining. All that remained were Hajime's headlights.

"Hmmm... I've been thinking about this since I heard the ruins were underground. Normal people would be unable to even reach the entrance."

"Yeah. You'd need a really strong barrier."

"On top of that, you'd need to create air, and light, and hold back the waves at the same time."

"You can't even enter unless you've cleared the Grand Gruen Volcano, though. If you can beat a labyrinth, you're already someone special."

"I guess you'd have to use air magic to make it down here."

As they continued down the passage, they discussed how they would have reached their location if Hajime hadn't built a submarine. Considering you'd need a party of extremely skilled mages just to make it to the entrance, I'm betting this labyrinth is harder than the others.

Hajime and the others steeled themselves, staring warily out the windshield. Then—

"Whoa!"

"Hm?!"

"Waaah!"

"Kyaaa!"

"My word!"

Something hit them from the side, sending them spiraling in the other direction. Once again, the submarine flipped around in the current, but this time, Hajime had countermeasures in place. The weightstone on the bottom of the ship's hull grew heavier, stabilizing the sub.

"Ugh! I was hoping we wouldn't have to deal with this again." Shea paled and shook her head. She hadn't enjoyed the ride out of the Grand Gruen Volcano one bit.

"Don't worry, I stabilized us already. The real question is where this current is taking us." Hajime grimaced and looked out the windshield.

The green glowstone headlights chased away the darkness. From the looks of things, they were being pushed down a long tunnel.

Hajime stabilized the sub, but otherwise, let the current steer them. After a while, his alertstone picked up a number of dark red, glowing creatures.

"Something's coming toward us. It's probably monsters. Nothing else glows like that."

"Should I kill them?" Mana gathered in Yue's hands as she casually offered to wipe them out. Her cute face contrasted starkly with her harsh words.

"Nah. Let's try out my new weapons. I wanna see how effective they are."

Hajime activated one of the mechanisms he'd added to the rear of the sub. A barrage of small torpedoes shot from the stern. He'd painted images of smiling sharks on them.

The torpedoes had to fight the current, so they didn't travel very fast. Thus, they ended up sitting in place, creating a minefield behind Hajime.

The monsters closed in, and the party got a good look at them for the first time. They were shaped like flying fish, but were much larger. They swam headfirst into Hajime's torpedoes.

The resulting explosion was so massive that it made the entire tunnel shake. A cloud of frothy water enveloped the flying fish. The explosion tore them apart, and chunks of flesh whipped past the submarine, pulled along by the current. There had been so many fish that the water was red with their blood.

"Yeah, this is definitely better than before. Looks like my upgrades worked."

"Whoa, Hajime-san. I think I just saw a dead fish's eyes staring at me."

"You probably did. I killed a lot of them."

"I've been thinking about this for a while... The artifacts you make are really something, Hajime-kun."

The group ran into more schools of monster fish, but had no problem dispatching them.

Since they were underwater, Hajime had no way of tracking the time. Eventually, though, he felt a subtle change. The current had carried them to a place where the walls were severely damaged. Dead eyes stared at Hajime from the cracks in the rock, and he realized the fish he'd blown up were stuck there.

"Have we been here before?"

"Seems like it. Guess we're going in circles?"

They'd just been looping around. Hajime thought he'd been advancing through the labyrinth, but it turned out they'd just been shunted into an underwater cavern. He stopped letting the current carry them, and carefully searched the cavern as they advanced.

Upon inspection, they realized there was more to the place than met the eye.

"Ah, Hajime-kun. There's something there, too!"

"That's the fifth one."

They'd been finding fifty-centimeter stretches of wall engraved with Melusine's crest: a five-pointed star, with a line running from the top vertex to the crescent moon in the center. There were five crests total.

Hajime moved the submarine back to the first one they'd found, and examined it more closely. The current was strong, so it took effort to keep the sub anchored in place.

"So, we've got five five-pointed stars and this half-lit pendant."

Hajime held the pendant up to the crest. As he expected, the lantern glowed. The moonbeam hit the crest, which absorbed it, and began to glow too.

"This would be pretty hard for people who came here using magic. You'd have to catch on quick, or your mana would run out."

Kaori was right. Completing these steps while struggling to keep yourself from drowning would not be easy. It seemed this labyrinth was designed to test one's limits in a completely different way.

They went around lighting the remaining crests, and it wasn't long before they reached the last one. The lantern had lost a bit of light at each crest, and had just enough left.

As Hajime lit the last crest, part of the rock slid away with a rumble, revealing yet another passage.

They advanced to find a passage heading straight down. Hajime angled the sub downwards and descended. As they entered the passage, something pushed them forcefully. The sub fell so quickly, everyone felt weightless.

"Whoa!"

"Mmm."

"Hwaaah?!"

"Nwoooh!"

"Waaah!"

All five yelped as they fell. Hajime felt the same tingling in his crotch as he did on a roller coaster.

The submarine landed on something solid with a resounding

thud. Everyone groaned, especially Kaori, who was the weakest physically.

"Ugh! Kaori, are you all right?"

"Urgh... I-I'm okay. Where are we?" Kaori grimaced and looked out the windshield. They weren't surrounded by water anymore. There didn't seem to be any monsters nearby, either, so Hajime and the others tentatively stepped out of the sub.

They found themselves in a large, dome-shaped cavern. Directly above them was the hole they'd fallen through. Due to some magic trick, water didn't cascade through it. Not a single drop fell through. Instead, the water undulated within the top half of the hole.

"I guess this is where things get serious. Looks like we're not underwater anymore, either."

"It's better that it's not all underwater."

Hajime put the submarine back into his Treasure Trove.

"Yue!"

"Okay." Yue immediately deployed a barrier around them.

A second later, jets of water slammed down from above. It was the same Rupture spell Yue had used back in the Reisen Gorge. The water jets possessed enough force to cut people to ribbons, but Yue's barriers, even the makeshift ones, were made of tougher stuff. This barrier easily deflected the water jets' barrage. Hajime had detected the surprise attack, and Yue picked up on his thoughts. Their superhuman teamwork made surprise attacks largely ineffective. Shea and Tio had sensed the attack coming too, so they weren't surprised in the slightest.

However, Kaori wasn't on that level.

"Kyaaa!" She screamed in surprise and staggered backward. Hajime caught her as she stumbled.

"I-I'm sorry!" She glanced at Hajime, pale-faced.

"Eh, don't worry about it."

Normally, Kaori would blush at the opportunity to rest in his arms, but right now, she was just depressed to be the only party member shaken by the attack.

She was also still shocked by Yue's magic.

Back when she'd been in Kouki's party, Kaori had often supplemented Suzu's barriers with her own, so she knew a fair amount about defensive magic. She trained herself ruthlessly to reduce her barrier spell casting time to Suzu's level.

Compared to Yue, though, Kaori's skills were nothing.

She felt like this when Hajime saved her back in the Great Orcus Labyrinth too. She'd pushed down that sense of inferiority to convince herself she was fit to travel with Hajime.

Am I just slowing everyone down? The thought whirled around her mind.

"What's wrong?"

"Huh? Oh, it's nothing." Kaori forced herself to smile.

"If you say so." Hajime narrowed his eyes, but didn't say anything.

Kaori was both a little disappointed, and a little relieved, that he didn't push. She noticed Yue, still fending off the torrent of deadly water, staring at her. It felt as though Yue saw right through her. Angry, Kaori glared back.

She wouldn't let Yue make fun of her feelings any longer. If Yue walked all over her, she wouldn't be fit to call herself Yue's rival.

She absolutely couldn't let that happen.

Yue just smiled faintly and turned her attention back to the ceiling. Tio unleashed a stream of flame at the same time, caking the ceiling with fire. Monsters dropped to the ground, burnt to a crisp.

At a glance, they looked almost like barnacles. They had likely unleashed those water jets. They were hiding in the ceiling cracks, so Kaori hadn't noticed them. Now that they'd burned to death, they looked rather disgusting.

It seemed the sea creatures were especially weak to fire. Tio's Spiral Blaze had taken them all out in one shot.

With the barnacles dead, the party was free to advance farther. The passage was narrower than the cavern they'd landed in, and filled knee-deep with water.

"Grr..."

Yue growled to herself. She was so short that the water came up to her waist, which made walking difficult. Hajime nodded, then lifted her onto his shoulders.

"H-Hajime... This is a little embarrassing."

"But it looks like the water gets deeper farther in. Besides, don't you like it more up here?"

"I guess..."

The party continued wading. Yue blushed, feeling like a child. She wrapped her thighs around Hajime, hugging him tight. Shea and the others didn't seem jealous. In fact, they were snickering. They gave Yue looks full of pity.

Yue felt even more embarrassed, and cringed. Hajime had never seen her like this.

"Heh heh heh... You look really cute right now, Yue-san."

"Ugh..."

"I see you've taken over Myu's favorite spot."

"Ngh..."

"Hee hee hee! Should we call you Yue-chan from now on?"

Yue blushed with embarrassment, but when Kaori joined in on the ribbing, her glare turned stone-cold. "Do you want to die, Kaori?"

"How come I'm the only one you're yelling at?!"

Hajime watched the exchange with a laugh.

Their lighthearted banter abruptly ended when another wave of monsters assaulted them.

These monsters resembled shuriken. They came spinning at Hajime and the others. Hajime calmly unholstered Donner and shot them down. As they fell lifeless to the ground, Hajime realized they were actually starfish.

Yue noticed a horde of sea snakes slithering toward them, and skewered the lot of them with ice spears.

"Aren't these a little too weak?"

Everyone except Kaori nodded.

Normally, labyrinths contained monsters that were dangerously powerful, possessed abilities that made them annoying in groups, or both. However, the monsters here were around the same level as the ones who attacked the sub when the underwater volcano spat them out. In fact, they might have been a little weaker. Certainly, nowhere near labyrinth level.

Only Kaori, who didn't have any experience with labyrinths, wasn't confused by their weakness. But the party didn't have to ponder for long. The answer was revealed in the next room.

"What the..."

The corridor opened into a massive chamber. As they walked inside, a translucent, jelly-like substance blocked the passage forward.

"I'll get it! Rryaaah!"

Shea leaped forward and smacked the wall with Drucken. The jelly on the wall's surface scattered, but the blockade itself remained in place. Some of the jelly splashed onto Shea's chest.

"Hwah! What is this stuff?!" she screamed in surprise. Hajime and the others turned to her. The jelly was melting through her clothes. Her voluptuous cleavage came into view as the cloth covering it dissolved.

"Shea, don't move!"

Tio burned away the jelly with masterfully controlled fire. A few stray flames singed Shea's skin, turning it red. Otherwise, it only hit the jelly, which appeared to have caustic properties.

"Watch out!" The party leaped away from the wall, but this time, countless tentacles came down from the ceiling. The tentacles were pointed, like spears, but they were made of the same jelly as the wall, which meant they were just as dangerous. Yue jumped off Hajime's shoulders and deployed a barrier above them. Tio cast her flame breath at the same time, burning the tentacles away.

"Man, the combination of Yue's barriers and Tio's fire is awesome."

An ironclad wall, combined with one of the most powerful attacks... Frankly, Hajime was impressed.

Confident that Yue and Tio could handle things, Shea sidled up to Hajime and puffed out her mostly-visible chest. She blushed and looked up at him.

"Umm, Hajime-san. I got burned a little here, so could you put some medicine on it?"

She never missed an opportunity to come on to him. Truly a clever bunny girl. Sadly, Hajime just gave her an exasperated look.

"Is this really the time?"

"Well... I mean, Yue and Tio are unbeatable, so it should be fine. If I don't show off at times like these, I'll start losing to even Kaori-san."

Shea showed off her breasts' numerous small burns. Just then—

"Grant respite to these divine warriors—Divine Blessing!" Kaori healed Shea's wounds with a smile.

"Nooo! My chance to let Hajime grope me!" Shea wailed, but everyone just stared at her coldly.

"Hm...? Hajime, this jelly can melt magic, too."

Hajime looked. The tentacles were indeed seemingly melting the barrier wherever they touched it.

"Ah, that explains it. I was wondering why my flames had so little effect. It seems the tentacles can disintegrate the mana my fire is composed of."

If what Tio said was true, this jelly was far more dangerous than Hajime initially thought. Plenty powerful, and plenty annoying. That was what he'd come to expect from labyrinths.

Just then, the monster controlling the jelly showed itself.

It squeezed out of a crack in the ceiling, and expanded in midair. It was translucent, and roughly humanoid. Although its limbs were shaped like fins, its entire body was covered in miniscule, glimmering red flecks. There were two feelers of sorts growing out of its head.

The way its limbs floated in the air reminded Hajime of a sea angel. A sea angel that was ten meters long and oozed caustic jelly was a pretty monstrous sight, though.

Without warning, the sea angel's body launched a barrage of tentacles. At the same time, it spat a shower of jelly from its head.

"Yue, you focus on attacking! I'll protect us! Hallowed Ground!" Kaori's derivative skill, Delayed Activation, allowed her to cast a spell she'd chanted ahead of time. Yue nodded curtly and combined her strength with Tio's. The two shot a barrage of flames at the sea angel.

The flames found their mark, and disintegrated the monster. Yue turned back to Hajime proudly, but instead of praising her, he yelled out a warning.

"It's not over! I'm still sensing something. Kaori, keep that barrier up. What the hell is this? I can sense it everywhere in the room..."

Hajime's Sense Presence picked up a reaction from every corner. When he checked with his Demon Eye, he saw the entire room covered in dark red. It was almost as if the room itself was a monster. Hajime looked around warily. He'd never seen anything like this.

His fears were well-founded. The giant sea angel reformed itself in the center of the room. Upon closer inspection, Hajime noticed many of the starfish and sea snake monsters they'd defeated earlier melting inside the sea angel's stomach.

"I see... So, the monsters we found too weak were just this creature's sustenance. Master, if it keeps regenerating indefinitely, it'll wear us down. Where is its mana crystal?"

"Come to think of it, how come we can't see it? The thing's transparent."

Shea nodded and looked at Hajime. Hajime focused his Demon Eye on the sea angel, but what he saw only confused him.

"Hajime?"

He scratched his head. "There isn't one. I can't find one anywhere inside it."

Everyone stared at him in shock.

"H-Hajime-kun? If it doesn't have a mana crystal...does that mean it's not a monster?"

"Beats me. I guess, if I had to say, its whole body seems like a mana crystal. The entire thing shows up dark red on my Demon Eye, and so does the rest of the room. Be careful, guys. It's possible we're already inside the thing's stomach!"

The sea angel attacked again as Hajime finished explaining. This time, it fired chunks of its body like torpedoes, in addition to the tentacles and jelly rain.

Hajime pulled a giant black rifle out of his Treasure Trove. There was a compressed gas canister where the magazine would normally go. It was too large in radius to be a bullet of any caliber.

Which made sense, since it wasn't actually a rifle. It was a flamethrower.

He'd created it from liquid flamrock. *Whooooooooosh!* The flamrock ignited as it left the barrel, spreading unquenchable, white-hot flames everywhere. Hajime didn't target the giant sea angel, nor the jelly. Instead, he aimed for the walls of the room. He knew Yue and the others could handle the sea angel.

It turned out the sea angel could use camouflage as well. When Hajime's flames hit the wall, parts of it peeled away, transforming into jelly as it burned. Hajime breathed a sigh of relief. *Thank god the whole room isn't the monster.*

But no matter how much jelly Hajime burned, more kept oozing out of cracks in the walls and floor. Hajime's shoes sizzled.

Yue and the others redoubled their attacks on the sea angel. It seemed to finally be taking them seriously, and an unbelievable amount of jelly trickled out of every crack and hole in the room. The water level began to rise as well. At first it only came to their knees, but now it was up to Hajime's waist, and Yue's chest.

No matter how many times Yue and Tio destroyed the sea angel, it just absorbed nearby jelly and regenerated. There didn't seem to be an end in sight.

Unless they found a way to eliminate it for good, they'd be wasting their strength. On top of that, the rising water levels meant they'd soon be fighting underwater. They couldn't even hole up and hold out. Neither Yue's barriers nor Hajime's submarine would last long against that caustic jelly.

It might be best to retreat for now. The problem was, all the exits were covered by jelly. Hajime desperately examined his surroundings. He noticed a small whirlpool above a fissure in the floor.

"Let's retreat and regroup! There's a room below us, although I don't know where it leads. Be prepared for anything!"

"Okay."

"Roger."

"Understood."

"All right!"

Hajime swung his flamethrower, burning all the jelly around him. Once the area was clear, he transmuted the floor around the fissure. It grew wider, forming a hole large enough for them to jump through.

Hajime ducked underwater and pulled a small, fifteen centimeter cylinder out of his pocket. It had a snorkel and a mouthpiece attached. The canister was actually an oxygen tank. He'd used creation magic to enchant it with air magic. The air-filled space inside was much larger than it seemed.

He'd originally wanted to make the space as large as his Treasure Trove, but didn't have time. In Erisen, he prioritized repairing his damaged equipment, but he found enchanting things with air magic extremely difficult. As it was, a single canister only contained 30 minutes of air.

Keeping the time limit in the back of his mind, Hajime

continued transmuting the hole, digging deeper until he finally hit open space. Then, he pulled out his pile bunker. He anchored it underwater and began charging.

It let out a loud hydraulic hiss as the mechanism engaged. A second later, it bored through the floor Hajime had weakened.

The water muffled the sound, but everyone felt the vibrations.

Water rushed through the massive pit he'd created. The current was so strong that it knocked everyone off their feet and carried them into the hole.

Hajime pulled a massive boulder and a few incendiary grenades out of his Treasure Trove. He held fast against the current long enough to toss them before letting himself be swept away.

The boulder blocked the hole he'd made, while the grenades exploded around the sea angel. Though Hajime had no way of telling if that actually bought them time, it felt like the smart thing to do.

"Ugh... Ack..."

"Haaah... Haaah... You all right, Kaori?"

"Y-yes. Somehow... How's everyone else...?" Kaori looked around, coughing up water. She noticed Hajime holding her up, and realized that they were on some sort of massive sandy beach. A dense jungle stretched out in the distance, and water floated near the ceiling above. Kaori didn't see anyone else nearby. Some sort of barrier seemed to keep this area clear.

"Looks like we got separated. Well, I've given everyone mini Treasure Troves, so they should be fine."

"Yeah..."

Hajime put Kaori down and scratched his head. He could tell that he hadn't really reassured her.

Kaori watched as Hajime got changed right in front of her, then thought back to how they'd gotten here.

They'd had to retreat from the giant sea angel. The huge room they'd fallen into had dozens of holes in the floor. Seawater gushed from some, but flowed into others. The water's currents were unpredictable and wild, like a storm. The group tried to stay together, but the water mercilessly tore them apart. Yue tried to control the current with magic, but it was so random that she didn't make much headway. Shea managed to use gravity manipulation and Drucken's natural weight to fix herself in place and somehow link up with Tio.

Hajime wanted to pull out his submarine and herd everyone inside, but the current made it impossible. And so, he gritted his teeth and pulled some extremely dense rocks from his Treasure Trove. He'd hoped to use their weight to anchor himself as Shea had.

Luckily, Yue was carried toward him. If he could just stay in place, they'd collide with each other. Tio and Shea had already fallen down a hole and vanished from sight.

Hajime was about to reach Yue when he spotted Kaori being swept away. His eyes met hers. He turned back to Yue, whose hand stretched out to him.

He had two options.

If he caught Yue, Kaori would likely be swept down a hole, alone. And if he caught Kaori, Yue would be alone.

Hajime could only grab one of them. Time slowed to a crawl as he deliberated. He exchanged one last glance with Yue, and made his decision.

Hajime pulled more stones out of his Treasure Trove and sank like a rock. On his way down, he grabbed hold of Kaori. He decided to prioritize her.

Kaori's eyes opened wide in surprise, but she shut them a second later, as the current beat against her. Hajime held Kaori tight as the undertow sucked them down a hole.

He activated Diamond Skin as they fell, then covered Kaori, protecting her from the stray boulders that hit them on the way down. Finally, the current weakened, and Hajime saw a light above. He floated up to it.

When he surfaced, he found himself at the coastline of the beach they now stood on.

"Hey, Hajime-kun. Why...did you save me?"

"Huh?" Hajime had his back turned to Kaori, still in the middle of changing. *Where'd that come from?*

"Why did you save me and not Yue?"

"I mean, if you fell by yourself, you'd probably die. I figured Yue'd be fine on her own. Yue wanted me to save you too. I could tell from her eyes."

"You really trust her, don't you?"

"Of course I do. We're partners."

"......"

Kaori's expression grew even more glum. She noticed a shadow above her, and looked up. Hajime looked down at her, his face inches from her own. They were practically touching. If he moved just a little closer, they'd kiss. She stared into Hajime's eyes. The moment was ruined as he grabbed her cheeks and pulled.

"Owww! What was that for?!" Tears sprang to Kaori's eyes.

Hajime ignored her protests and continued toying with her cheeks. By the time he was done, they were red and swollen. She looked at him reproachfully, and Hajime snorted.

"There's no time to sit around moping. We're in the middle of a labyrinth here. How long were you planning to stay in those soaked clothes? Or were you hoping to earn my sympathy by walking around like that?"

Kaori blushed at Hajime's rebuke. It was as if he'd just told her she didn't belong here.

"Th-that's not it! I just spaced out for a bit. I-I'll change right away. Sorry."

"……"

Kaori hurried to her feet and pulled a spare change of clothes from the mini Treasure Trove Hajime had given her. He'd made one for everyone at Erisen, although they were far smaller in scope than Oscar's. Hajime nonchalantly turned around. Normally, Kaori would have tried to flirt with him, saying something like "It's fine if you want to watch." But right now, she wasn't in the mood.

"I-I'm done. So, what are we going to do now?"

"Let's see. Even if we went back, we'd have no idea where the others are, so I guess our best bet is to keep searching for the end of the labyrinth. Yue and the others are probably doing the same."

Hajime stared at the jungle for a few seconds before turning to Kaori. She smiled and nodded, trying to hide her melancholy. Hajime narrowed his eyes suspiciously, but in the end he said nothing.

Sand crunched underneath their boots as the pair made their way to the jungle. Thick grass and dense bushes barred their way forward, and Hajime pulled out a machete to hack through. Kaori followed silently behind.

After a few minutes, Hajime suddenly came to a halt and turned around. He wrapped a hand around the back of Kaori's head protectively.

"Huh? U-umm, Hajime-kun...? Th-this is a bit sudden..." She blushed, but when she saw the thing Hajime pulled off her neck, the blood drained from her face.

The spider was as big as Hajime's hand, with twenty legs. Purple liquid dripped from its fangs. Feet grew not only from its abdomen, but also from its back. Kaori had never seen anything so disgusting.

"Don't let your guard down. These labyrinths are way deadlier than the upper floors of the Orcus. If you assume the monsters you face here will only be as strong as the ones you fought there, you'll end up dead."

"O-okay. I'm sorry. I'll be more careful."

"......"

The spider didn't have a mana crystal. That meant it was just a very ugly spider, and not a monster. Kaori felt even more depressed. She had almost been killed by something that wasn't even a monster. On top of that, Hajime had to save her again.

In Kouki's party, she'd been one of the best mages. But here, she was just dead weight. That fact continued to nag her. She kept a more vigilant eye on her surroundings as they advanced, not even breaking her concentration to talk to Hajime. The two continued silently through the jungle.

Eventually, they found something.

"Is this a...ship graveyard?"

"Amazing. I never realized ships were so huge."

Once they made it out of the jungle, they found themselves on a rocky plain. A number of massive sailing ships nestled among the boulders, masts rotting and sails tattered. Every one of them must have been at least a hundred meters long. Some of the larger ones were more than three times that.

The pair stopped in their tracks to admire the surreal sight, but couldn't gawk forever. Eventually, they shook off their awe and started walking.

They marched around the boulders, climbing the ones they couldn't circumvent. At times they walked across the ships' decks as well. Although the ships were rotting, they hadn't decayed enough to fall apart completely.

"You know... These look like warships."

"Yeah. That really big one in the back looks like a passenger ship, though. It's all decorated and stuff."

The warships here didn't have gunports like the ones Hajime was used to seeing back on Earth. He guessed they were warships because of their battle scars. From the looks of it, they'd been bombarded with magic. Some of the masts had been cut clean through, while others had burn scars all over their wooden decks. Some even had petrified sails and ropes.

Since there were no gunports, Hajime imagined long distance battles between warships had been fought with magic in the past.

It turned out he was right. About halfway through the graveyard, they were attacked.

"Uwoooooooooooooh!"

"Raaaaaaaaaaaaaaaah!"

"Wh-what the...?!"

Hajime and Kaori stopped in their tracks. Hajime heard the screams of countless men, and his surroundings began to warp. Everything blurred, and a second later, they stood on the deck of a ship.

"Hajime-kun, look around us!"

They were no longer on the plain. Instead, they were in the middle of the sea. Hundreds of ships faced off against each other, and men yelled as they brandished their weapons.

"Wh-what on..."

"H-H-Hajime-kun? Am I dreaming? Are you seeing this too? You are, right?"

The two of them were so shocked, all they could do was blankly examine their surroundings.

A flare rose in the sky, and a mass of ships advanced. Another flare rose from the other side, and those ships advanced as well.

Once the two sides were close enough, they began exchanging volleys of spells. Neither side slowed, and it looked like they planned to ram each other.

"Whoa!"

"Kyaaa!"

Fireballs raked the deck, burning holes through the wood. A raging tornado attempted to splinter the mast. The ocean froze over in chunks, stymieing both sides. Gray spheres flew through the air, petrifying any sails unlucky enough to be in the way.

The deck Hajime and Kaori stood on had caught fire. Sailors hurried to cast water magic and put it out.

This was a war. That was the scale of the battle. A chilly breeze rolled past the combatants. Then, a fireball hurtle toward Hajime. If he didn't do anything, it would hit him head-on, but he was still dumbfounded.

How on earth did we wind up in the middle of a naval battle? The question whirled around inside his head as Hajime pulled out Donner and fired.

A streak of red light struck the fireball, but contrary to Hajime's expectations, it didn't disappear. In fact, his bullet passed right through and vanished into the sky.

"What?!" he let out another yell of surprise, reaching to grab Kaori and dive out of the way.

"Wait, I'll stop it! Light Wall!" She deployed a beginner-level light barrier.

Hajime figured it'd be best to dodge, since even shooting through the spell's core hadn't dispersed it, but he didn't want Kaori to feel useless. So he stood there, activating Diamond Skin, just in case.

However, Hajime needn't have worried. Kaori's barrier stopped the fireball.

Did I miss? Hajime thought dubiously. He tried again, aiming for yet another fireball. He watched with his Demon Eye, making sure he shot precisely through the spell's core. But once again, his bullet passed cleanly through, vanishing in the distance.

"So, that's how it is."

Hajime knew why his attacks hadn't worked, and attempted a different tactic. He stopped Kaori, who was about to put up another barrier, and wreathed his revolver in a Gale Claw. Then, he leaped out of the way and sliced through the fireball. This time, the attack connected and dispersed the flames.

"Umm, Hajime-kun?"

"It looks like this isn't just a hallucination. Though it's not exactly real, either. Physical objects can't interact with the vision, but mana can. I still have no clue what the hell is going on."

Hajime sighed and shook his head. Just then, he heard a man scream behind him. He turned to see a youth double over, holding a cutlass in one hand and his own stomach in the other. There was a pool of blood at his feet and a bloody icicle on the ground next to him. He had been hit in the earlier barrage.

"Are you all right?!" Kaori rushed over and began casting healing magic on him. Lavender light enveloped the youth. A priest of Kaori's skill should have been able to heal a wound like that instantly, yet that didn't happen. The moment Kaori's healing magic touched him, he faded away.

"Huh? What? Wh-why did he..."

Hajime lapsed into thought. After a moment, he explained his hypothesis.

"I think, when mana touches any part of this illusion, it'll fade. It doesn't matter what kind of spell you use."

"Then that means I-I...killed him..."

"Kaori, none of this is real. It's an illusion that we can interact with, that's all. I mean, you can hardly call something human if it literally disappears from being healed."

"Hajime-kun... you're right. I'm sorry. That surprised me a little, but I'm fine now."

Hajime wasn't blaming Kaori, but she still slumped her shoulders and apologized. However, she quickly recovered as well, and smiled at him. Hajime thought back to how she'd been earlier too, and muttered something.

"Always an apology, huh?"

"Huh? Did you say something?"

"It's nothing."

Hajime turned away. Not because the conversation was over, but because he sensed something coming.

He looked around and noticed quite a few sailors staring darkly at them.

Kaori noticed the change in Hajime's attitude and looked around as well. With a resounding battle cry, the sailors attacked.

"My life for Ehit!"

"Glory to Ehit!"

"You damned heretics! Die in the name of our lord!"

The men had gone completely mad. Their eyes were bloodshot

and spittle sprayed from their mouths. They obviously weren't thinking clearly.

Hajime had already guessed this was some dispute between two neighboring countries, but now he understood the reason. It was a holy war. He could hear similar cries coming from the other side. The only difference was the name of their god.

Kaori was stunned into silence.

Hajime pulled her close and started firing Donner over his shoulder. Instead of physical bullets, he shot rounds of pure mana.

Mana Manipulation's derivative skills, Mana Emission and Mana Compression, let him do that. Since the mana wasn't structured behind a spell of any kind, normal enemies wouldn't take any physical damage. They would just have their mana shaved off.

Both humans and monsters were unable to move once their mana dried up, so it was a great way to immobilize targets without harming them. Until now, Hajime's enemies had all been too dangerous to immobilize, so he hadn't used it much.

In this situation, though, it was perfect. Streaks of red light shot through the battle-crazed sailors' heads. Each mana bullet pierced multiple sailors, dissipating them.

"Kaori, I'm gonna jump! Make sure you don't bite your tongue!"

"What? Kyaaaaaaaaa!"

Hajime didn't want to deal with being surrounded on the narrow deck, so he grabbed hold of Kaori and leaped into the sky. She hadn't expected him to shoot upwards with such force, and screamed in surprise.

Hajime shot down the sailors on the crow's nest and appropriated it for himself. The sailors below glared at him with bloodshot eyes.

They'd been busy fighting each other, but now, for some reason, they focused on Hajime and Kaori. Although they'd been enemies seconds before, they were united in their hatred of the pair. The madness spread like a disease. At first, only a small knot of sailors targeted them. Before long, however, the entire ship was after them.

Sailors locked in combat with each other froze and turned to face Hajime and Kaori instead. Then, with the same fanatical battle cries, they pointed their cutlasses. The insane spectacle left Kaori pale.

"Now then, how are we supposed to get out of this crazy vision?"

"Is there an exit somewhere, maybe?"

"We're in the middle of the ocean, remember?"

"Maybe one of the ships has a portal out? You know, like the Anywhere Door?"

Hajime raised an eyebrow as Kaori brought up a certain blue cat robot's convenient tool.

"There's around 600 ships here. I don't think we can check all of them. The battle would end before we finished."

"Hmmm... It looks like some ships are already sinking, too. Maybe we're supposed to end this war?"

"End it...? I see. I get it now. You're saying we've gotta kill everyone, right? You're pretty sadistic, you know that?"

"Huh? No, wait. That's not what I—"

"Yeah, that's gotta be it. I can't really think of anything else, and this suits my style anyway."

Hajime casually shot down a few sailors who tried to swing to the crow's nest using mast ropes. *I should have made some mana bullets for a situation like this.* He used the derivative skill Remote Manipulation to neutralize a barrage of incoming fireballs.

"Kaori, I know you're not really skilled at offensive magic, but even healing magic'll kill these guys. I'm still not totally sure killing them's how we get out, but since they're coming at us, we've got no choice but to take them down."

"O-okay!" Kaori berated herself for hesitating and began to chant. The insanity in the ghost soldiers' eyes shook her, but she didn't want to break down in front of Hajime, so she held her ground and fought.

Hajime surveyed his surroundings, protecting Kaori from any attackers.

Looking down, he noticed pockets of sailors still fighting. Unlike the ones he killed, the illusions bled when they cut each other.

Gutted entrails and hacked-off body parts littered the ship's deck. It made for quite a grotesque sight. The men happily killed each other in the name of their gods.

The wind picked up, and a bloody mist rolled across the deck. Despite their losses, the sailors targeting Hajime and Kaori didn't let up.

Whenever anyone got too close, Hajime mercilessly shot

them down. He'd set up a pseudo-barrier of bullets to circle around him, destroying any illusion he missed, and to block any magical attacks sent his way.

That didn't deter the sailors, who kept rushing to their deaths.

A few dozen soldiers used air magic to fly over the crow's nest and attack from above. More came from either side, using the mast's netting to close in. With his Demon Eye, Hajime could see a number of casters on other ships targeting his own. They were all casting high-level spells.

Just as Hajime considered shooting them down, Kaori finished casting her strongest spell.

"Divine Mother, smiling down from heaven, encompass all in thy heavenly embrace—Aetherflow!" Ripples of light spread across the battlefield. They extended a full kilometer from Kaori. Whoever they touched was wrapped in a faint halo of light.

This was one of the highest-rank healing spells, Aetherflow. It healed everyone in a massive radius.

The actual range of the spell depended on the caster's skill, and how much mana they used, but its minimum reach was 500 meters. Furthermore, if the caster marked certain targets beforehand, they could direct the spell to affect those targets specifically. Normally, this spell required a few dozen people's combined mana, a ridiculously long chant, and a huge mana circle. It was a testament to Kaori's strength that she'd cast it in two minutes all by herself.

Aetherflow's light covered the battlefield, destroying every illusion it touched.

Kaori stumbled once her spell ended, her mana spent. Hajime caught her before she fell.

"Wow, it's like we're floating in a sea of ghost ships now. Nice one, Kaori. I knew you had it in you."

Kaori blushed at Hajime's sincere praise. Still, she was certain Yue would have done a faster and better job.

"Ah, um, i-it was nothing, really. You guys are way more powerful than me, anyway." She smiled bitterly to herself and looked away.

Changing the topic, she muttered something about needing to recharge, and Hajime handed her a magic stone pendant. Kaori couldn't control mana directly, so Hajime had engraved the pendant with a magic circle she could use to drain it.

Hajime opened his mouth to say something, but shut it again when he saw another wave of enemies approach. They could talk about it later.

Normally, fighting an army of illusions who could only be hurt by mana would have been extremely difficult, doubly so on the deck of a swaying ship. However, Hajime and Kaori were anything but normal.

They decimated the two countries' combined armies in just one hour.

•/• •/• •/• •/• •/• •/• •/• •/• •/• •/• •/• •/• •/•

"Ugh... Sorry."

"It's fine. Don't worry about it."

Once they destroyed the last of the illusions, Hajime and Kaori found themselves back in their original location.

Hajime breathed a sigh of relief, glad that killing all the sailors had been the solution. A second later, Kaori doubled over and started retching. It was some time since she last ate, so she didn't throw anything up, but it still didn't look pleasant.

Tears in her eyes, Kaori held up a hand, begging Hajime not to get any closer. He walked over anyway and gently rubbed her back. She hadn't wanted him to see this side of her, but she was reassured by his warm hand. Before she knew it, she fell into his arms. It didn't take long for her to calm down and stop gagging.

Hajime pulled out a pack of apple juice from his Treasure Trove and passed it to her. She gulped it down greedily, and the color began returning to her face. The juice's sweetness washed away the taste of bile in her mouth.

"I'm really sorry..."

Hajime narrowed his eyes.

"It's totally understandable. I found them pretty disgusting myself. I can't believe people would let blind faith turn them into something like that. Let's take a short break. I used up a lot of my mana, too, so I need to rest."

"Okay... Hey, Hajime-kun. What was that? Did it have something to do with all of these rotting ships?" Kaori sat on a nearby boulder. Hajime thought for a few seconds.

"I'm guessing that war actually happened in the past, and whoever made this labyrinth recreated it with magic. I imagine the part where the sailors attacked any intruders was their own addition. That might have been part of this labyrinth's theme."

"Its...theme?"

"Yeah. Tio mentioned that in the Grand Gruen Volcano. She thought each of the liberators designed their labyrinth around a certain theme. If she's right, then..."

"This one's theme is the tragedy the gods brought upon Tortus?"

"Yeah, looks like it."

Chills ran down Kaori's spine as she thought back to what they saw. She shivered, her face pale. The madness had disturbed her enough to make her throw up. She'd never seen such religious fanaticism. Their fervor, their actions, and the fact that their faith led them to slaughter each other disgusted her.

Worst of all, they'd been *laughing* as they fought. Some dying sailors had even ripped out their own hearts to offer to their heartless gods. Others stabbed right through their comrades for a better chance at hitting Hajime and Kaori.

It was an unbelievably gruesome sight, especially because it was all done in the name of god. Hajime sat next to Kaori and took her hand. He couldn't just watch her grapple with atrocities like that.

Kaori looked up at him in surprise, but after a moment, she smiled and tightened her grip.

"Thank you, Hajime-kun."

"Don't worry about it. I know how painful it feels...to think you're going crazy. I nearly lost myself when I fell into the abyss."

"How did you manage to stay sane? Actually, I don't even need to ask. It was Yue, wasn't it?"

"Yeah. If I hadn't met her back then...who knows what I would have become." Hajime looked into the distance, reminiscing.

ARIFURETA: FROM COMMONPLACE TO WORLD'S STRONGEST

Kaori felt as if a vice was squeezing her heart.

"It's so frustrating. I wanted to be the one to protect you, Hajime-kun... The one to save you. Although I don't know if I could have done it, if it was me down there. I couldn't even keep my first promise to you. Ha ha... I guess it's going to be tough to beat Yue."

Hajime narrowed his eyes. Normally Kaori's smile was warm, but right now it was bitter, full of self-loathing.

"You've been apologizing a lot since we got here. You've been smiling like that a lot, too."

"Huh? Umm..." Kaori tilted her head in confusion.

Hajime's next words crumbled her forced smile.

"Hey, Kaori. Why'd you come with us?"

"So, I really am in your way?"

Hajime sighed, and changed the topic. This was going nowhere.

"I still remember what you told me that night, when you came to my room and we drank my shitty tea. That's why I don't understand why you still like me so much, after how I've changed."

"Hajime-kun, I..." Kaori opened her mouth, but Hajime cut her off.

"Still, I have no intention of denying your feelings, or saying they're a lie. I'm sure you have your own reasons for loving me. No one else has the right to deny you that, or your determination. I already gave you my answer, and if you say you love me despite that, then that's fine. It's not like Shea's any different. In fact, she's so persistent that I'm worried she'll just attack me one night."

Shea's physical abilities had only continued to grow in the

time they'd traveled together. Hajime was worried he wouldn't be able to fend her off if she tried to overpower him. Kaori smiled wryly and nodded.

"Yeah... Even I'm amazed at how outgoing and positive Shea is."

"I have to admit, I was pretty mean to her in the beginning. Yue was the only person I cared about, so I just wanted Shea to give up."

"......"

"But no matter how roughly I treated her, no matter how much I told her she had no chance, she still seemed to be enjoying herself. Sure, she cried, and got mad, and yelled at me, but she never looked unhappy. Even though she had no aptitude for magic, and wasn't nearly as strong as Yue, she never stopped looking forward. She never let herself wallow in her own inferiority."

"I-I'm not wallowing..." Kaori trailed off weakly. She wanted to protest, but even she knew he was right.

"Have you noticed that all you've done since we got here is apologize? Even the way you smile has changed."

"What?"

"Hey, Kaori. Quit looking down. Look me in the eye."

It was only when he said it that Kaori realized she'd been avoiding eye contact, although she'd always met his gaze before. She looked up with a start.

"I'll say this one more time. I love Yue. Even if other people become important to me, they'll never be special, like she is. If it really hurts that much, if comparing yourself to Yue brings you nothing but pain, then you should leave."

"Ah..." Kaori looked down again. Hajime wasn't done yet, though.

"Back then, I agreed to let you come because I thought you were like Shea. I figured that was what you really wanted. That you thought this was best for you. I told you I loved Yue, but you insisted on coming anyway. So I thought, sure, you'd be happier this way too. But that's not how it seems now."

Hajime let go of her hand.

"I want you to think about this seriously. Decide for yourself what has you so down, and whether you really want to keep traveling with me. You're not like Shea. Shea loves Yue just as much as she loves me. If you think it's better to leave, I'll make sure to bring you back to Yaegashi safely, don't worry."

"I-I..."

Kaori looked down at her hand. She wanted to say something, but the words wouldn't come out. Things had grown awkward between them, but they still needed to move forward. This was a labyrinth, after all. They continued until they reached a massive passenger ship. It was more than 300 meters long, and at least ten stories tall. Taller, probably, since part of it was buried underground. It was ornately decorated, and although partly rotted, it still looked magnificent.

They stopped for a moment to admire it. Even on earth, few ships were this big, and those that were didn't look quite so elegant.

Kaori stared in awe, while Hajime admired its craftsmanship.

"I'm amazed they managed to make something this big from wood."

He was still a Synergist at heart. *Whoever managed to make that deserves respect.*

Hajime grabbed Kaori and used Aerodynamic to jump all the way up to top deck terrace. As he expected, the air began to warp.

"Looks like we've got another vision to go through. Prepare yourself, Kaori. We're probably not going to like this one, either."

"It's okay... I'll be fine."

Kaori took a second to reply. Hajime mentally berated himself. He should have saved that conversation for after they left the labyrinth.

All he'd succeeded in doing was spoiling her mood. He needed to confront her eventually, but he could have picked a better time.

Still, he couldn't bear seeing Kaori smile sadly any longer. *But I could have waited until we cleared the Sunken Ruins of Melusine.* Hajime scratched his cheek awkwardly.

Their next vision put them in the middle of a luxurious passenger ship.

It was night, and the moon was full. Lights glimmered all along the deck. Decorations hung from every railing and mast, and tables of refreshments were laid out buffet-style. A large crowd of people milled about, sampling the rich food and chitchatting.

"Is this...a party?"

"Looks like it. A fancy one too... Did I get Melusine's theme wrong?"

Hajime was caught off guard by the distinctly welcoming

sight in front of him. He and Kaori stood atop a raised terrace overlooking the deck.

As Hajime gazed over the partygoers, the door behind him opened, and a few sailors stepped out. They lounged around, talking with each other. *I guess they're here for their break.*

Hajime listened in on their conversation. He gathered that the party was celebrating the end of a war. It seemed the war had gone on between these two countries for years, and ended not with one country annihilating and invading the other, but with a treaty. The sailors seemed happy. Upon closer inspection, Hajime noticed that humans, demons, and beastmen were all in attendance. They mingled together, with no regards to race.

"I guess a time like this existed too."

"They must have worked really hard to make this peace happen. I don't know how long it's been since the war ended, but I can't imagine that no one's holding a grudge. And yet, they're all smiling and laughing together..."

"I'm sure the people here fought for peace. There's no way they'd be able to laugh like that with people they'd been fighting."

"Yeah..."

Hajime and Kaori smiled as they watched. After some time, a middle-aged man climbed up onto the podium at the end of the deck and waved to everyone. The talking quieted down and people turned their attention to him respectfully.

Behind him was someone Hajime guessed was his aide, and a hooded figure. Hajime thought it was rather rude to go onstage in a hood, but none of the partygoers seemed to mind.

Once the ship was completely quiet, the man began his speech.

"Ladies and gentlemen, all of you who gathered here today are heroes. Brave heroes who fought, not to make war, but to make peace. I am honored and humbled that you all agreed to come here. I cannot tell you how happy I am that this war has ended. Peace between our two nations has been always been my dream."

Everyone listened raptly. The man continued, talking about the missteps along the way, the trials they faced to overcome suspicion, and the lasting cornerstones of peace that they'd finally built. He spoke of the friends they lost, and tears sprang to many guests' eyes. Some looked off into the distance, while others recalled nostalgic memories.

This man seemed to be the humans' king. He'd spent his entire life working toward this peace. Hajime could see why everyone respected him.

Finally, his speech wound to a close. He roused everyone with a spirited finale. The audience burst out in cheers. However, a sudden premonition struck Hajime. He recognized the king's face from somewhere.

"Now, after a year of peace, I've realized something... How worthless it truly is."

Everyone glanced about in confusion. They looked to each other, wondering if they'd misheard. Everyone had thought the speech was finished, but it continued.

"Indeed, utterly worthless. Raising toasts with beasts and consorting with heretics... What is it, if not folly? Do you understand, ladies and gentlemen? You are a pack of fools."

"Wh-what are you saying, Aleister?!" A demon stepped forward to protest. "What's gotten into—gah?!"

The demon coughed up blood. A sword stuck out of his chest.

The demon's eyes widened in surprise. He turned around to see a human behind him holding the weapon. From the demon's expression, Hajime could tell the two must have been close friends. The demon fell to the ground, disbelief frozen on his face.

Everyone started talking at once. Cries of "Your Majesty, please!" rang out. Few of the guests could comprehend what was happening.

"Now then, ladies and gentlemen. Like I said, I am honored you all agreed to come. You have made my job that much easier. It grated me, day after day, to watch you ungodly heretics attempt to create your own nation. As if the monsters who turned their backs on Ehit, the world's sole creator, could ever be our equals. But that all ends today. You barbarians do not deserve to exist on Ehit's holy Tortus. We will only have true peace when vermin like you are eradicated! If only you knew the joy it brings me that this world's leaders willingly gathered here today. Believers of Ehit, bring down the iron hammer of retribution on these nonbelievers! Lord Ehit, are you watching?!"

King Aleister sunk to his knees and gazed up at the heavens in prayer. The sailors took off their uniforms, revealing gleaming soldier's armor. They surrounded the guests.

In the center of the deck was a massive mast. The terrace was built atop that mast, providing the soldiers positioned there an unobstructed view of the entire deck. Unless the guests could somehow escape into the sea, the soldiers had an overwhelming advantage.

The lords and ladies of every country realized that, and despair colored their faces.

A second later, the soldiers loosed magic at the undefended guests. Their targets tried to fight back, but outnumbered and outmaneuvered as they were, the desperate struggle amounted to little.

A few managed to escape, but in seconds, most lay in puddles of their own blood.

Just a short while ago, they were happily eating and drinking. Some tried leaping into the ocean, but Aleister had prepared for that. Small boats packed to the brim with soldiers lay in wait, and killed anyone who jumped. The water around the ship turned crimson.

"Ugh...!"

"Kaori..."

Kaori leaned against the railing, one hand over her mouth. She tried very hard not to throw up. This vision was even more horrific than the last. Hajime gently patted her back.

Once the slaughter was over, King Aleister went below deck with his soldiers. He was probably going to hunt down the few guests who escaped into the bowels of the ship.

His aide and the hooded figure trailed behind him.

However, before heading downstairs, the hooded figure turned to look at the terrace. Hajime caught a glimpse of silver hair in the moonlight, or at least, he thought he did.

Their surroundings warped again. It seemed there was no test in this vision. Melusine just wanted to show it to them.

"Kaori, rest for a bit."

"It's okay, I'm fine. That was a bit graphic, but... Is it over? It ended without us doing anything."

"This is the end of the ship graveyard. We could craft a barrier and explore the ocean, but judging from what we saw, I assume we're supposed to go inside now. At least, the vision seems to be leading us there. Melusine wanted to burn these atrocities into our memory before letting us continue, I guess. Can't say it's a very pleasant experience. It'd probably be even worse if we were from this world."

Almost all the humans in Tortus worshipped Ehit. It'd be quite a shock to see what monsters their faith could turn them into.

To conquer this labyrinth, powerful magic was a necessity. The ability to use magic depended greatly on the user's mental state. In many ways, this was the complete opposite of the Reisen Gorge. Fortunately, Hajime and Kaori weren't from this world, so it wasn't like their entire worldview was shaken.

Still, the massacre was horrific. They looked down at the deck, which had soaked up so many people's blood, and thought back to what they saw. Hajime was annoyed that Melusine was putting them through all this crap.

Once they prepared themselves, he took them down to the deck and they entered the same door Aleister had used.

The interior was pitch black. It was bright outside, so Hajime expected light to pour in through the windows, but for whatever reason it didn't. He pulled a green glowstone lamp out of his Treasure Trove.

"About that vision from before... The king betrayed them after they'd already made peace, right?"

"I guess. But don't you think that was a little weird? It looked like everyone really respected the guy... Would they really look up to him if he secretly hated all beastmen and demons?"

"You're right. Based on what he said, the war had ended a year ago. Something must have happened to change him. The question is, what?"

"There's no doubt the gods were involved. You heard him. He sounded pretty crazy."

"Yeah. He reminded me of Ishtar-san... It was like he was in a trance. It was almost pitiful."

Hajime almost felt a little bad for Ishtar. A high school girl thought the pope of the Holy Church was cringeworthy.

They walked until Hajime's lamp illuminated something white and fluttering.

The pair stopped in their tracks. Hajime pointed the light upward. It revealed a little girl wearing a pure white dress. She swayed back and forth, her head tilted downward.

Hajime and Kaori both had a bad feeling. Kaori's face was frozen stiff.

Hajime had no idea what a child was doing here, but he pulled Donner out anyway. He wasn't taking any chances in a labyrinth.

Just then, the girl crumpled to the floor. Her joints bent at inhuman angles, and she started scuttling toward them like some grotesque spider.

"Kakakakakakakakaka!"

Ominous laughter rang through the hallway. Her eyes, partially hidden by her bangs, glowed with an eerie light. She looked like something straight out of a horror movie.

"Aaaaaaaaaaaaaaaaaaaaaaaaaaaaaaaaaaaaaaah!"

"Whoa! Calm down, Kaori! Let go of my arm!"

This was as clichéd as it got, but that didn't make it any less scary. Kaori clung to Hajime's arm for dear life. Hajime tried to shoot down the monster, but Kaori ruined his aim.

"Kgyaaa!"

With a strange scream, the monster girl leaped at Hajime's face.

Hajime gave up trying to shoot her and kicked her in the stomach. He enhanced the kick with Steel Legs in case it wasn't enough.

The girl doubled over as she flew backward into the darkness. She bounced off the walls like a pinball, landing in a crumpled heap at the end of the hall. Her limbs bent at even odder angles, and she didn't get back up. Instead, she melted into the ground and vanished.

Hajime sighed and patted Kaori's trembling head. She jumped at his touch and looked timidly up at him. There were tears in her eyes, and her lips quivered. *Damn, I guess that really scared her.*

"Are you bad with horror stuff, Kaori?"

"Is there anyone who isn't?"

"Just pretend they're all monsters."

"*Hic...* I'll try."

Kaori finally let go of Hajime's arm, but kept hold of his shirt hem.

Hajime's words had given her a lot to think about, and she'd been less clingy after their discussion. However, now that ghosts and the like had shown up, she threw her reservations out the window. She wouldn't let go until they were out of here. She was absolutely terrified. Even more so than when she first confessed to Hajime.

They encountered a number of unsettling events after that. Bloody handprints on doors, noises from behind walls, water dripping down from the ceiling, ominous scratching, a strange monster with a severed head and an axe, the list went on. Hajime easily shot and kicked his way through most of them, but it was slow going.

The events left Kaori clinging to Hajime in a childlike state. "I hate this. I want go home. Shizuku-chan, I want to see you again!"

She wanted Shizuku to come save her because, when Kouki had taken them all to a haunted house long ago, Shizuku protected her. Kaori trusted her the most.

The creator of the Sunken Ruins of Melusine, Meiru Melusine, had been determined to unnerve challengers to her labyrinth. Hajime had already spent months in the darkness of the abyss, surrounded by monsters who attacked without warning, so he wasn't too affected. He couldn't imagine Yue or Tio being scared, either. However, he had to admit a normal person would be pretty unsettled.

What happened to all those serious visions about the folly of man? Despite her fear, Kaori was holding up pretty well. She mowed down hordes of supernatural apparitions with her Binding Blades of Light as they moved forward. Hajime had to keep her from fainting a few times, but her grit still impressed him.

After some time, the two arrived at the ship's hold. Hajime pushed open the heavy door and stepped inside. There was still cargo scattered here and there. The pair picked their way around crates and barrels as they headed farther in. Once they were about halfway, the door slammed behind them.

"Wahhhh?!" Kaori shrieked, turning back.

"......" Hajime wondered if she even remembered what they talked about. He really didn't want to have that conversation again.

He sighed and patted Kaori's shoulder. Then he noticed something odd. A thick fog sprang up around them.

"H-H-H-H-H-Hajime-kun?!"

"Your voice is starting to sound pretty weird. Don't worry. It doesn't matter what we're up against, all we've gotta do is blow it away with magic, like everything else."

There was a sharp whistling noise, and something flew out of the fog, heading straight for Hajime. He raised his left hand to block, and found a very fine thread wrapped around it. More whistling noises followed. This time, they came from all directions.

"A physical trap after all those magical ones? God, what a pain! Why'd the Liberators have to make such annoying dungeons?!"

"Guardian of light, lend us thy aid—Holy Shield!"

Although the attack's physical nature took Hajime aback, he quickly recovered. He broke the threads easily, while Kaori protected herself with magic. A second later, fog swirled around, and a powerful gale struck.

Hajime transmuted spikes from the bottom of his shoes to lock himself in place. He tried to grab Kaori too, but her shields worked against her. He missed by a split second, and the wind carried her away.

"Gahhhhh!"

The gust dragged her into the center of the fog. Hajime clicked his tongue and tried to pinpoint Kaori's position with Sense Presence.

However, the fog possessed the same properties as the mist surrounding the Haltina Woods. It interfered with your sense of direction, and nullified sensory magic.

"Tch... Kaori, don't move!"

Before Hajime could do anything, a knight stepped forward, sweeping away the fog with his longsword. Hajime didn't know what style the knight was using, but he was clearly proficient.

Hajime blocked the oncoming strokes with Donner. Then, once he saw an opening, he stepped in and fired a magic bullet at point-blank range with Schlag. It punched a giant hole through the knight's stomach. He vanished without a sound.

After that, Hajime found himself up against a gauntlet of powerful knights, each a master of their chosen weapon.

"God, what a pain." Hajime grumbled and set a number of magic bullets to circle around him.

He activated Supersonic Step, and went about defeating the knights. He was worried, since Kaori hadn't responded.

Around the same time, Kaori was trembling in fear. She couldn't see Hajime.

Horror was the one thing she couldn't deal with. She froze up whenever she encountered anything remotely scary, and she hadn't been able to overcome her phobia. Kaori wanted to prove to Hajime that she wasn't wallowing in her own inferiority, but she'd just ended up clinging to him again. She hated her weakness.

Kaori berated herself for being so pathetic and forced herself to stand.

Just then, something laid its hand on her shoulder. Kaori hoped it was Hajime. He had a habit of tapping her shoulder, so that wouldn't be surprising.

"Hajime-k..."

She was about to turn around, but realized the hand on her shoulder lacked warmth. In fact, it was ice-cold.

A shiver ran down her spine. *That's not Hajime behind me, is it?* She was sure of it.

So, then, who was behind her? She turned her head slowly, her neck creaking like a badly-oiled door. A girl's face stared back at her. It was no ordinary face, though. Her eyes, mouth, and nose were dark, bottomless pits.

"Eyaah!"

Kaori was so overwhelmed that her brain did the only thing it could to protect her. It shut down.

In only two minutes, Hajime succeeded in destroying almost fifty knights. Each knight only lasted a few seconds.

As the fiftieth knight met his end, Hajime stopped. *Was that all of them?* However, the trial wasn't over. Another figure appeared from the fog. This knight was massive, and carried a greatsword taller than Hajime himself.

Hajime sidestepped the knight's giant swing. The knight had seemingly predicted that Hajime would dodge. He utilized the rebound as his sword slammed into the ground, and followed up with a lightning-quick attack.

Hajime leaped into the air and used his Diamond Skin-enhanced prosthetic arm to grab the sword. He swung himself onto the flat of the blade and fired a mana bullet at the knight's head.

As the giant knight disappeared, the nearby fog began to fade as well. *All right, now it's definitely over.*

"Kaori! Where are you?!"

Hajime cast Sense Presence, although that proved unnecessary. He spotted her almost immediately.

"I'm over here, Hajime-kun."

"Oh, good, you're safe."

Hajime breathed a sigh of relief as Kaori walked towards him. She smiled cheerfully and sidled up close.

"I was so scared..."

"That bad, huh...?"

"Yep. Won't you comfort me?" She wrapped her arms around Hajime's neck and hugged him. Her face was so close that their noses practically touched. She looked up at him with pleading eyes and leaned in closer. Hajime casually pressed Donner against her forehead.

"Wh-what are you doing?"

She looked at him in confusion. There was murder in Hajime's eyes.

"Isn't it obvious? Killing my enemies, just like you tried to do to me."

He pulled the trigger without hesitation. A crimson mana bullet shot straight through Kaori's forehead, sending her sprawling backward.

A rusty knife fell to the ground with a clang. It had been hidden up Kaori's sleeve.

Hajime walked over to Kaori's prone figure. She raised herself into a sitting position and looked up at Hajime with fear in her eyes.

"Hajime-kun, why are you doing—"

He fired another bullet into her mercilessly.

"How dare you use Kaori's voice? How dare you take over her body? I can see right through you. Trash like you has no right to even touch her. Don't speak. Don't even move."

Hajime's Demon Eye could see the female specter possessing Kaori. The ghost grinned wickedly. Now that Hajime had discovered her identity, there was no reason to continue pretending.

"Hee hee. So what if you know? This woman is already mi—"

Hajime knocked Kaori to the ground and straddled her.

"Wait! What do you think you're doing?! This woman is your lover, isn't she?! Can you really bring yourself to hurt her?!"

"You're not a very good listener, are you? I said, don't speak, and don't move. Don't worry, I won't hurt Kaori. These mana bullets pass right through physical things. The only one suffering right now is you."

"If you destroy me, you'll destroy this girl's soul! Are you willing to take that risk?!"

Hajime hesitated. It was possible she was bluffing, but he had no way of knowing. If he thought about it logically, he would surely hesitate to strike again. The specter was counting on it. She grinned and ordered Hajime to get off.

However, contrary to her expectations, he shot her with another mana bullet.

The specter's pain showed in Kaori's twisted expression.

"Are you insane?! Don't you care what happens to her?!" she yelled, panicking.

"Shut up, ghost. If I stop attacking, you'll keep Kaori's body forever. Besides, if killing you will destroy Kaori's soul, then I can do anything to you as long as you remain alive, right? I'll just have to torture you until you beg to leave."

The specter was at a loss for words. She'd never faced anyone so hell-bent on killing her.

"You hurt someone important to me. Don't think you'll get off lightly. Trust me, I have ways to make sure you won't die, no matter how much you suffer. I'll make sure you're perfectly lucid for every minute. Hell will seem like paradise once I'm through with you. You're my enemy... But, hey, at least you won't die."

Ribbons of dark red mana swirled around Hajime, and his white hair stood on end. His gaze was as cold as ice.

Hajime was more furious than he had ever been. Just killing this specter wouldn't be enough. He would make her suffer every way he knew.

The specter stared at Hajime, frozen in terror. She couldn't even muster the courage to say anything.

She had realized too late that she should never have picked a fight with this monster. Now, she had no choice but to pay the price.

Hajime pressed Donner against Kaori's forehead. The specter began to pray. *Please, let this end quickly.* The mere thought of what Hajime would do left her wishing she was dead, except she already was.

She was nothing more than a remnant of a particularly powerful human grudge. Now, though, she was willing to forgo that grudge to leave this plane of existence.

I don't want to exist anymore! I don't want to exist anymore! I don't want to exist anymore! I don't want to exist anymore! I don't want to exist anymore! I don't want to exist anymore!

Just before Hajime pulled the trigger, Kaori's body glowed. She was enveloped in the light of the healing spell Consecration. It was one of the delayed-cast spells she held in reserve for emergencies.

The specter looked down in surprise.

Don't worry, I'm exorcising you. This way, you'll be able to pass on.

The light surrounding Kaori grew brighter. It wrapped itself around the specter, and she floated to the ceiling. Her consciousness faded, and her spirit along with it.

A second later, Kaori opened her eyes. It seemed the specter had been banished.

Hajime looked down at Kaori. He'd confirmed the specter's disappearance with his Demon Eye, so there was no reason to be on guard. He checked her over, making sure the possession hadn't left any lingering effects.

Kaori could feel the intensity of Hajime's gaze. She could tell how worried he'd been. His serious look almost surprised her.

She met his eyes and lifted herself up. Then, she brought her face close to his, and kissed him on the lips. It was brief, but it was Kaori's first kiss.

Hajime was too distracted with protecting Kaori's soul to dodge. After a moment of surprise, he pulled away.

"What're you doing?"

"Giving you my answer."

"Your answer to what?"

"Remember, you asked me why I came along…? Well, I found the reason I decided to travel with you, and why I'll keep traveling with you."

She smiled, and it was the usual bright smile Hajime had missed. This was the first time since entering the labyrinth that he'd seen her smile like that.

The whole time Kaori was possessed, she'd been conscious. It was as if she was locked inside her own mind, forced to watch her body act against her will. However, since she was aware of everything, she saw how mad Hajime got for her sake. She heard him describe her importance to him.

Seeing him like that really moved her. She remembered how she felt when she'd confessed.

No matter what anyone said, no matter how much trouble it caused, this was the one thing she wasn't going to give up on. She would earn his love. Her determination hadn't changed.

She didn't want to be the only one left out of Hajime's group, or the only one not by his side. Even if she wasn't as strong as Yue or the others, she wanted to prove that her feelings were every bit as deep.

"I love you, Hajime-kun. I love you so much. That's why I want to stay by your side."

"Won't that just hurt more? Like I told Shea, I have no intention of being with anyone besides Yue."

"Maybe. I do want all your attention. I want to be the only one who's special to you. I'm jealous of Yue, and I feel like she's better than me. It'll definitely be painful if I stay."

"Then you should..."

"But I know, if I back down, I'll regret it for the rest of my life. I'm sure of that. You're right. Coming here, I saw the difference between me and everyone else. I started to lose faith. I began to doubt whether coming with you was for the best. But I'm not worried anymore."

She cupped Hajime's cheeks and smiled.

He wasn't sure how to react. In the end, it was Kaori's decision.

If she truly wanted this, he wasn't going to refuse. Happiness had a different meaning for everyone. It wasn't for Hajime to decide what would make Kaori happy, nor to dictate such things.

"I see. If that's what you've decided, I won't argue."

"Good. I know I'll cause you a lot of trouble, but please don't resent me for it."

"Bit late to be asking that. You caused me heaps of trouble back in Japan, even. You're more of a troublemaker than you seem."

"Hey, that's mean!"

"Well, it's true. You'd always come talk to me in school, completely oblivious of what everyone else thought. You didn't even notice that the other guys wanted to kill me every time you said something remotely suggestive. Plus, you came to my room at night wearing nothing but a negligee!"

"Ugh... I-I didn't think anything of it back then. I just wanted to talk... And that time I went to your room, I got super embarrassed afterward."

Kaori buried her face in her hands. Smiling wryly, Hajime helped her up. He patted her on the shoulder, and the pair made their way to the end of the hold. There was a glowing magic circle there.

Kaori grabbed Hajime's sleeve, holding him back. She was still shaking. Clearly, being possessed had been quite an ordeal. However, it seemed not to have left any lasting effects, so it wouldn't take Kaori long to recover.

"Let's take a short break."

Kaori decided to make the most of it, and jumped onto Hajime's back.

"What are you doing?"

"It's better to hurry, right? There's no telling how long that magic circle will stay active. If we stay here too long, the fog might come back, so isn't this more efficient?"

She's got a point. Hajime reluctantly allowed her to ride on his back. Kaori wrapped her arms around his neck and hugged him tight.

Hajime had a hard time concentrating with her pressing so tightly against him. Her whispering into his ear only made it worse. Her hot breath tickled.

"Hajime-kun... Can you say that again?"

"Say what again?"

"What you said when you got angry at the ghost. Remember?"

"Hmm... Can't say I do."

"Come on. You could at least say it one more time."

The two continued flirting amicably as Hajime stepped into the circle.

⁕ ⁕ ⁕ ⁕ ⁕ ⁕ ⁕ ⁕ ⁕ ⁕ ⁕ ⁕ ⁕ ⁕

In a completely different place, pale light illuminated the ocean's surface as waves lapped against the ceiling.

In the room's center was a shrine supported by four massive pillars. It had no walls; the ceiling was held by the pillars alone. An altar lay in the center, with a detailed magic circle engraved on its face. Seawater surrounded it, and four floating paths jutted out along the cardinal directions. Each ended at a circular platform with magic circles carved into its floor.

One of the four magic circles started glowing faintly. A second later, it exploded into light, and two figures stepped out: Hajime and Kaori.

"Where are we? Hm...? Wait... Is that the final magic circle? Don't tell me we beat this labyrinth already."

"Umm, is that bad?"

"Nah. I just didn't think we'd finish so fast. It feels like this was too easy compared to the others... I thought that sea angel thing might come back, but I don't sense it anywhere."

Hajime was a little disappointed that they'd reached the end so easily. Kaori poked her head out from behind Hajime's shoulder and grimaced.

"You know, Hajime-kun, I'd say what we went through already was hard enough. First, we had to find our way into an underwater cavern. Most people don't have submarines in this world, right? They'd have to use a lot of mana just to get here. If you messed up, you'd drown before even stepping inside. Then, we had to fight that crazy sea angel monster, and after that, we fought a bunch of illusions. They couldn't even be hurt by physical attacks, so we had to use mana again. After that, at the end, you had to battle an army while exhausted. I wouldn't call that easy."

"Hm... You've got a point, but still..."

"The people of this world are pretty devout. Seeing something like that would probably have broken them."

"Yeah, it's possible just watching them go crazy would have been too much for someone else to handle."

Kaori meant that Hajime was just too strong. When he thought about it, he realized the Grand Gruen Volcano had been a piece of cake, too. If not for Freid's surprise attack, they would have cleared the volcano without a single injury.

I guess it's possible the labyrinth was so easy that we cleared it even before meeting up with Yue and the others again. Hajime thought. Just then, the magic circle on the platform to his right began to glow.

Once the blinding light faded, Yue, Shea, and Tio stepped out. *Perfect timing.*

"You guys got here just in time," said Hajime. "Is everyone okay?"

"Yeah. Did you...run into difficulties?"

"Uh, are you all right, Kaori-san?"

"Hm? You aren't injured, are you? Shouldn't you be able to heal yourself?"

Yue and the others responded cheerfully. When they saw Kaori on Hajime's back, though, their expressions became concerned.

Kaori hurriedly reassured them. "Thanks for worrying about me. But I'm fine. I'm just being a little lazy."

Kaori smiled. Yue glared at her, and Shea muttered jealously.

"Wow, lucky you. Let me have a turn too."

Tio, on the other hand, grinned knowingly. "I see."

"Wait, Kaori. You can stand now?"

"Hee hee! To be honest, I could have walked from the start. Sorry."

"Haaah, just get off."

Kaori smiled guiltily, and Hajime shrugged her off his back. The group joined up where the paths connected, and headed to the temple.

"So, what's transpired between you two? Come on, Master, you have to tell us. Something happened with you and Kaori, did it not? Don't try to hide it now, I can—bweh?!"

Tio's persistence got on Hajime's nerves, so he slapped her. Tio sank to the ground, a look of pure ecstasy on her face. She panted heavily.

"I-It has been a while since I felt such pain. Haaah... Haaah... Mmm... Master, will you please punish me more? You can even kick me if you like."

Hajime ignored her expectant gaze and continued walking.

"One more! Just one more slap, please! I beg of you!"

Tio pleaded with Hajime, but everyone ignored her.

"So? What happened?" Yue asked.

However, her question was directed at Kaori, not Hajime. Kaori met Yue's gaze and beamed. Her smile had the same warmth Hajime used to see in the classroom.

"We just kissed."

"I see." Yue's voice had an angry edge.

Shea, however, seemed excited for Kaori. "What?! Really?! Who started it?! Did you kiss him or... Wait... Did he kiss you?!"

"I kissed him. After seeing Hajime-kun get so angry for my sake, I couldn't help myself."

"Wow, it's just like what happened with me! I did the exact same thing before. We're comrades now, Kaori-san!"

"Hee hee, I guess so, Shea. Shall we steal him together, then?"

"If we do, we have to make him ours for good!"

It almost sounded as if they planned to kidnap him. Cold sweat poured down Hajime's face. True, they were just joking, but their eyes glimmered dangerously. It scared him to see a pure girl like Kaori and a cheerful bunny girl like Shea stare as if they were wolves. He never knew Kaori, especially, could be so aggressive.

"I thought you'd run away with your tail between your legs." Yue looked probingly at Kaori.

She had noticed Kaori letting her inferiority complex eat away at her. Honestly, she expected the labyrinth to break the human woman's spirit. If that had happened, Yue certainly wouldn't have tried to console her. After all, if Kaori's feelings for Hajime were that shallow, she had no right to be here.

However, Kaori had evidently managed to survive. More than that, her resolve was even firmer. Yue was curious as to how she'd managed it.

"I thought so too. Hajime-kun even said I should leave. Still, it's a bit too late to care about trivial things like...how much stronger you are."

"So, you're determined, then?"

"I guess you could say that. But you know, I was determined from the start. I just lost sight of that when I saw how much stronger you all were. I won't be so pathetic anymore."

"It would have been better if you'd given up."

"Hee hee... Scared? Worried I'll steal Hajime-kun?"

"Don't get ahead of yourself, you troublemaker."

"Hajime-kun called me a troublemaker too. But I don't think I really am one."

Kaori frowned. It was a little disheartening that both the man she loved and her rival thought she was trouble. Still, she got over her distress quickly enough. To be fair, Yue and the rest of Hajime's group were pretty big troublemakers. Sadly, Yue herself wasn't aware of that.

"Well, maybe you're right, Yue... But at least now I know I'm important to Hajime-kun. All that's left is to steal your status as 'special.' I won't give up, no matter what anyone says."

"I see. Then, as before, I accept your challenge."

"Yep! Oh, by the way, I don't hate you or anything. In fact, I feel like we're just friends that fight a lot."

"Friends? I'm your friend?"

"Yep, you're my friend. In Japan, there's a lot of people like that. They show their friendship by fighting. Just like us. We're rivals in love, but we're still friends, right?"

"Japan... That's Hajime's home. The more I hear about it, the stranger it sounds. But...I like it."

"Glad to hear it. Hee hee! Let's try and get along, okay?"

"All right."

It should have been a good thing that the girls were finally getting along, but for some reason, it made Hajime feel lonely. He was the only one being left out.

Their conversation reminded Hajime of the dialogue between certain Monogatari characters, but he didn't mention that.

Hajime was patient, so he knew when it was time to wait his

turn. Once they reached the altar, the party stepped into the giant magic circle together. As usual, it examined their memories to ascertain whether they'd actually cleared the labyrinth. However, this time, each group saw the other's memories. That allowed Hajime and Kaori to see what Yue, Shea, and Tio went through.

It seemed they had traversed the ruins of a giant underground city. Like Hajime, they witnessed magical illusions. In their vision, two armies fought in the streets of the city. At first, the invading demon army attacked the human defenders. But once Yue used magic, both sides turned their blades onto the party, just as they had in Hajime's vision.

Yue and the others made their way to the city's castle, defeating enemies along the way. Inside, they overheard a discussion among the country's leaders.

It sounded as though the demons had overrun a human village and slaughtered everyone. Because of that, the humans declared war. However, the attack was orchestrated by the human leaders. They wanted an excuse to eradicate demons from the planet. Before the schemers knew it, the flames of war spread beyond their control. Soon enough, the humans were losing, and being pushed back to their capital.

A high-ranking priest from the Church of Light apparently pushed hardest for war. The Church of Light, which was behind the attack on the human village, was apparently the predecessor of the Holy Church Hajime and the others had encountered.

Driven into a corner, the humans turned to desperate tactics. They attempted to use sacrifice to appease their gods and gain favor. A hundred little girls were invited to the church's grand cathedral and summarily slaughtered.

Yue and the others were appalled at what they saw. Their faces paled as they were forced to re-watch those memories. Shea looked ready to vomit.

The memory scan finished, and the circle concluded that they had indeed conquered the labyrinth. It inscribed another branch of magic from the age of the gods into their minds: restoration magic.

"So, this is where we were supposed to obtain the power of restoration," Hajime muttered, cursing the long-dead Melusine. "Stupid Liberators! Of course they'd put this magic here. This is the other tip of the continent, goddammit!"

Hajime recalled going to the Grand Tree in the Haltina Woods. The stone tablet said they would need the power of restoration. In other words, to conquer the labyrinth on the eastern tip of the continent, one needed magic obtained by clearing the labyrinth on the western tip. For Hajime, who'd gone east first, that was unbelievably annoying. At least he had a car to drive. Normal challengers would have been forced to make another year-long trek.

The Liberators just keep getting more and more irritating. As the magic circle's light faded, a rectangular block rose from the ground. It was like a miniature version of the altar. It glowed with faint light, and a second later, a vaguely humanoid shape formed above it. Like Orcus, Meiru Melusine had seemingly left a message.

ARIFURETA: FROM COMMONPLACE TO WORLD'S STRONGEST

The light coalesced until Meiru's features could be made out. She sat on the block, wearing a white one-piece dress. She had long, emerald-green hair, and her ears were shaped like fins. Surprised, Hajime realized Meiru Melusine must have been a Dagon.

Like Oscar, she introduced herself and began explaining the Liberators' true goal. She seemed gentle. There was a look of profound sorrow on her face as she spoke of the atrocities the gods had committed. Otherwise, her speech was not too different from Oscar's. As she wound down, she gave Hajime and the others a final warning.

"Please, don't cling to the gods. Don't rely on them. Don't grow accustomed to what's given to you. Struggle on, and grasp your desires with your own hands. Decide your own path in life, and walk down it with your own feet. Remember, no matter how bleak things look, you'll be able to find the answers inside of yourself. Only you have those answers. Don't be deceived by the gods' honeyed words. Only when you live by your own free will can you find true happiness. I pray the path you walk will be forever showered in fortune."

With that, Meiru Melusine's apparition faded. As the light from the magic circle dissipated, Hajime spotted a coin engraved with her crest resting atop the altar.

"This is our fourth marker of strength, Hajime-san. Now we should be able to challenge the labyrinth in the sea of trees. We'll finally go back, won't we? I wonder how my dad's doing."

Shea gazed nostalgically towards her home. When she

remembered how her father and the rest of her family had transformed into gangsters, however, she shook herself back to the present.

Hajime put the coin in his Treasure Trove and likewise tried very hard not to think about the gangster Haulia tribe.

The moment the coin disappeared into his Treasure Trove, the temple began to rumble. A second later, the water level rose.

"Wha...?! Tch... Looks like we're getting another rough exit. Everyone, grab onto me!"

"Okay."

"Waaah, not so rough!"

"I don't want to go through another Reisen Gorge!"

"Water torture...sounds rather fascinating."

They were completely submerged in seconds. Hajime didn't even have time to pull out his submarine. He handed everyone oxygen masks in case this trip lasted a while, then had them huddle together.

The ceiling opened, just as it had in the Grand Gruen Volcano, and water flowed inside. The party was carried upwards by the powerful current, and found themselves heading for the hole.

Hajime assumed this was the shortcut out. Still, he would never have guessed that kind, gentle woman could come up with such a violent way to remove them. Especially since it was essentially involuntary. *Maybe she was way more ruthless than she looked.*

After a while, Hajime realized that, at the rate they were rising, the current would smash them into the roof.

Hajime activated Diamond Skin and moved to shield Yue

and the others from the shock. However, just before they hit the ceiling, it too slid away to reveal a hole. The current bore them out and spat them into the sea. Now, Hajime was sure Meiru Melusine was nowhere near as gentle as she appeared.

Once they were in relatively calm waters, Hajime pulled out his submarine. He motioned for everyone to get inside.

Before they could move, they were interrupted by the worst possible enemy.

"Huh?! Everyone, get out of the way!" Hajime called out with Telepathy.

A giant translucent tentacle slammed into the submarine, sending it spinning.

Hajime turned back to see the same enemy they'd failed to defeat, the giant sea angel. It looked like a fairy, but its jelly melted anything it touched, and it could regenerate indefinitely. It seemed utterly unaffected by water resistance, and shot its countless tentacles at the party at unbelievable speed.

I can't believe we have to deal with this thing even after beating the labyrinth. Hajime ground his teeth and called out telepathically to Yue.

"Crystal Coffin!" She immediately created an ice barrier around them, freezing the surrounding water in place.

The tentacles slammed into the ice globe protecting Hajime and the others. The impact was so strong, the party rattled like dice in a shaker.

"How will we handle this, Master?!"

Fortunately, Hajime had a plan.

"Yue, we've gotta make it to the surface. Underwater, it'll beat us down slowly. I'll buy you the time you need!"

"All right."

Hajime used the spirit stone-imbued ring on his finger to remotely control the submarine. It stopped drifting aimlessly and charged headfirst at the sea angel. Performing an underwater barrel roll to avoid the tentacle barrage, the submarine launched a salvo of twenty torpedoes. Honestly, it was almost overkill. However, Hajime wanted to be absolutely certain he'd buy them enough time, so he launched the sub's remaining salvos. He set the submarine circling the sea angel with its hull pointed toward its target. The unnatural movements almost made the sub look like it was drifting.

All in all, Hajime launched a grand total of 48 torpedoes at the monster. They came from all directions, and each and every one found their mark.

Boom! Boom! Boom! Boom! Explosions blossomed, displacing massive amounts of water. Jets broke the surface of the ocean one after another. That's how powerful the torpedoes were.

While the sea angel was distracted, Yue manipulated the current to carry them to the surface. No matter how fearsome the sea angel's powers of regeneration, Hajime was sure that would keep it out of commission for a few minutes.

Unfortunately, he underestimated its strength.

"Yue, above us!"

"No... I can't stop in time!"

Hajime looked up and saw a jelly membrane covering the area

above them. In a matter of seconds, the jelly had reformed, and now the sea angel was above their heads.

It opened its mouth wide and swallowed the ice sphere whole. They were inside the sea angel's stomach.

"Shit! It regenerates too fast!"

"This isn't good, Hajime-san. We're surrounded by jelly now!"

The sea angel had been spreading jelly since it appeared. It had planned this exact situation.

"Hajime, my barrier won't last long! There's no water inside this thing's stomach, so I can't freeze more to reinforce it, either!"

"Tch... Everyone, brace for impact!"

Yue did her best to slow the her ice sphere's corrosion. Hajime helped as well by coating the ice in Diamond Skin. At the same time, he pulled numerous torpedoes and explosives from his Treasure Trove. He placed them outside the barrier, but inside the sea angel's stomach.

Once again, the sea angel's body was blown to bits, its pieces scattered to the four winds. The barrier had nearly corroded away at this point, and the explosion blew it to pieces, sending Hajime and the others flying.

They were once again in the middle of the ocean. Hajime called his submarine back, hoping to at least get Shea and Kaori to the surface. Those two were even more helpless underwater than the others.

However, his submarine had been caught. The sea angel latched some jelly onto the bottom, producing a huge hole. Filled with water, Hajime's submarine was too slow to maneuver.

Crippled as it was, the sea angel easily surrounded it with more jelly, rendering it completely immobile.

Worse, the sea angel realized they were trying to make a break for the surface, and created a translucent jelly barrier directly above them. Considering how quickly it regenerated, Hajime knew it wouldn't be easy to break through.

He inwardly cursed as the sea angel devoured his prized submarine.

"Yue, you're going to have to use your trump card."

"I'll need forty seconds."

"I won't let it touch you. This is our only way out."

"Okay... Leave it to me."

Yue closed her eyes and concentrated. Kaori and Shea supported her, making sure the current didn't sweep her away.

Tio's rapid barrage of mini breath attacks just barely held back the encroaching tentacles. However, she couldn't keep it up for long. Breath attacks consumed a lot of mana, and down here, they were hampered by water resistance. Moreover, because they were linear attacks, they pierced the tentacles instead of destroying them. In a few seconds, Tio would be overrun.

Hajime pulled massive quantities of ore out of his Treasure Trove and transmuted another globe-shaped barrier around them.

"Master, I cannot hold them back any longer!"

"You held out long enough, Tio! Everyone, get inside!"

Hajime made the sphere large enough to fit all five of them. They scrambled inside, Tio coming last. Once they were in, he sealed the entrance. Dark red mana surrounded the metal sphere.

Hajime had strengthened it with Diamond Skin. Furthermore, he'd incorporated weightstone into the barrier's design, so it wouldn't sink.

Numerous tentacles slammed against the sphere. The mana-corroding jelly ate away the Diamond Skin. Before long, the metal itself was being dissolved. Red sparks ran down the most worn-out sections, and they filled with new metal.

By continually transmuting more ore into the barrier, Hajime kept it mostly intact. Thankfully, he'd stockpiled mountains of extra ore. He continued replenishing the barrier's walls for the full forty seconds Yue needed.

"Cosmic Rift!"

Yue finished casting her teleportation spell. An elliptical ring of light appeared next to the party.

The teleportation spell, Cosmic Rift, was one many spatial magic skills they'd learned at the Grand Gruen Volcano. It connected two points in space, creating a warp gate. As Yue had only acquired it recently, it still took her nearly a minute to cast.

"Everyone, get in!"

At Hajime's command, everyone jumped into the warp gate. Hajime went last, transmuting the barrier until everyone had entered. The gate vanished after he leaped through, and seconds later, the sea angel's tentacles dissolved the barrier.

As they passed through the gate, they were assailed by a sense of weightlessness. That was mostly because Yue had teleported them into the sky. To get them as far away from the ocean as possible, Yue placed the exit point of her Cosmic Rift a hundred meters in the air.

Tio instantly transformed into her dragon form and caught the others on her back. Yue slumped over, and Shea and Kaori hurried to lift her up. Casting that spell took all of her mana. She began replenishing her reserves using the magic accessories Hajime had given her.

"Thanks, Yue. I knew I could count on you... Although spatial magic looks pretty difficult."

"Haaah...haaah... Yeah. I did it, but I'm not good enough yet to use it in combat."

Yue found spatial magic far harder than even gravity magic. Under normal circumstances, she couldn't use it in combat. She was forced to use Image Composition to create an imaginary magic circle instead of simply controlling her mana directly. On top of that, spatial magic consumed twice as much mana as her highest-rank spells, just to teleport them a hundred meters into the air. Its mana consumption was still highly inefficient.

Still, they were able to escape. Yue blushed as everyone, even Kaori, praised her skills. They all smiled in relief, but a second later, those smiles froze.

Splaaaaaaaaaaaaaash! A massive tidal wave bore down on them from behind.

No, massive didn't do the wave justice. It rose so high that it blotted out the sky, towering over them, although they were a good hundred meters above the water. At a guess, Hajime put it at 500 meters tall, and at least a full kilometer wide.

"Tch... Tio!"

"Understood!"

Tio flapped her wings and shot forward. They couldn't dodge left or right, and spatial magic wouldn't work in time. The only option was to flee. Tio flew with a speed rivaling her escape from the Grand Gruen Volcano.

"Divine Shackles! Hallowed Ground!"

"Hallowed Ground."

Kaori cast the spells she had stocked up while they waited for Yue. She joined everyone together with her chains while she and Yue simultaneously cast the same barrier. Shea closed her eyes and concentrated. A second later, her eyes opened wide, and she shouted out a warning.

"Tio-san, watch out! That thing is hiding inside the tsunami! It's going to send tentacles at you!"

She relayed what she'd seen with Future Sight. Tio instantly twisted out of the way. Countless tentacles lashed at the spot she'd occupied.

They'd evaded the first attack. However, the distance between them and the tsunami had shrunk. Hajime fended off further attacks with his flamethrower, but Tio couldn't recover enough speed to get away.

"Shit! Everyone, brace for impact!" Hajime hugged Yue, Shea, and Kaori protectively. A second later, the gargantuan tsunami crashed into them.

Thanks to Yue and Kaori's barriers, they withstood the impact. Still, the tsunami tossed them around, and before they knew it, they plummeted back into the ocean.

Moreover, the tsunami's force completely shattered one

Hallowed Ground, and filled the other with cracks. Had Yue and Kaori only deployed one barrier, they would have been sleeping with the fishes.

Hajime shook his head, clearing the dizziness. When he looked up, his expression grew grim.

"You're not gonna let your prey go, huh?"

The sea angel had caught up to them. It had gotten bigger, too. Now, it was over twenty meters long, but apparently, it didn't think that was big enough. It continued gathering translucent jelly from its surroundings, growing even larger.

"Y-you've gotta be kidding me. It doesn't die, it can melt anything, and it can even control the sea," Kaori said, despairing. "How are we supposed to beat it?"

"Hajime-san, can you kiss me? I'm not joking. I want to at least enjoy being kissed by you once before I die."

"In that case, Master, I too wish for a kiss before death."

Shea and Tio smiled faintly, looks of resignation on their faces.

When they looked up at Hajime, shivers ran down their spines. Even now, his eyes glimmered with determination. Bloodlust, so thick it was palpable, rolled off him in waves. He glared at the sea angel, completely undaunted.

He hadn't given up. The thought hadn't even crossed his mind. All he was thinking about was how to kill his enemy and emerge alive.

The sea angel was unbelievably powerful. But if Hajime was the type who gave up because the enemy was too strong, he wouldn't have made it so far. He would have died in the abyss.

Yue had walked through the abyss with him, so she understood. She, too, only thought of how to defeat their foe. Surrender wasn't part of her vocabulary.

Kaori, Shea, and Tio held their breath as they watched Hajime. They stayed like that until the sea angel, now thirty meters long, attacked and brought them back to their senses.

Kaori hurriedly put up another Hallowed Ground. Shea tried to use Branching Paths to find a way out of this mess. Tio fired her breath at the sea angel. If Hajime hadn't given up, they wouldn't, either. If they didn't show their grit here, then they had no right to travel at his side.

Yue couldn't come up with a solution, so she added her strength to theirs, hoping to buy time.

Hajime stood stock-still, thinking furiously. He'd activated Riftwalk to accelerate his thought processes even further. He knew he needed to find a solution soon, or they were all dead. He reviewed all the information they'd gathered on the enemy. He examined every detail, in case it offered a potential solution. There was one point he came back to: their initial escape from the sea angel. *Why didn't it pursue us back then? It could have chased us down easily. What changed between then and now? We're not...*

"We're not using enough fire."

Last time, both Tio and Yue blasted the sea angel with fire spells. The fire withered its tentacles, and the burned jelly hadn't regenerated.

Finally, Hajime saw a ray of hope. He wasn't one hundred

percent certain, but he had a hunch the sea angel couldn't re-generate indefinitely. It just appeared that way because it had so much jelly.

Furthermore, the sea angel could likely produce more jelly, given enough time. Creating fresh jelly probably took a lot more time than regenerating what was already there, though. That was why the sea angel took so long to recover after they burned it. They were able to escape because it prioritized replenishing its jelly reserves over chasing them.

To defeat the sea angel, they simply had to do the same thing again. Burn it faster than it could regenerate. However, they were surrounded by ocean. Fire magic wouldn't be very effective around all this water. Tio's breath was powerful, but she couldn't keep it up long enough to burn away all the jelly. They had no weapons that could manage that.

In that case...

"I just have to make one."

Hajime pulled lots of ore and torpedoes from his Treasure Trove and started transmuting.

"Hajime? Did you think of something?"

"Yeah. This is the only way we'll be able to use fire around water. If this works, we can kill it."

"Do you really mean that, Hajime-kun?!"

"I knew I could trust you, Hajime-san! I never doubted you for a second!"

"Shea, weren't you asking Master for a kiss before you died just moments ago? At any rate, good job, Master!" Tio joked.

"It's gonna take some time, though," Hajime warned. "I'm counting on you guys to hold it off."

Tio and Shea relaxed a little. The man they trusted said they'd make it. There was no reason to worry. All that was left to do was live up to the trust *he'd* shown in *them*.

Hajime smiled fearlessly, and the others smiled back. He activated both Riftwalk and Limit Break while he worked. Bolstered by those skills, he transmuted faster than ever.

Hajime finished one weapon and quickly started on the next. This new weapon required unprecedented precision and skill to craft, so he couldn't mass-produce it like a bullet. However, he needed a lot of them to burn away the sea angel's jelly. Firing them off one after another would just delay the party's inevitable demise. Either he'd get it all at once, or not at all. Limit Break caused dark red mana to swirl about him. It looked as though he was caught in a small crimson tornado.

Unfortunately, their situation still looked rather bleak. Overpowered, Yue and the others couldn't hold back the sea angel for long. The advantage the ocean gave it was too great.

The women tried their best to hold on, but it didn't look like they would last long enough.

"Three more minutes, that's all I need!" Hajime telepathically shouted to the others.

The sea angel was almost right on top of them. It opened its mouth wide to swallow the party whole.

Hajime reluctantly decided to fire off what he'd made so far.

It wasn't enough, but there was no point saving it if they were about to die.

Just then, a grizzled old voice spoke to them via Telepathy.

"Yo, Young Haj. You seem to be in a spot of trouble. This old man'll help you out."

"W-wait. I recognize that voice! Is that you, Fish-san?!"

"That's right. It's me, your friend Fish-san."

To Hajime's disbelief, the fishman he freed back in the aquarium at Fuhren had arrived. Hajime looked around in surprise, and saw a giant silver silhouette tackle the sea angel. The sea angel, taken completely by surprise, flew off to the side.

The familiar human-headed fish monster appeared beside Yue's barrier, stunning Yue and the others. Yue, Kaori, and Tio had never seen the fishman before, and even Shea hadn't expected him here.

"You're the guy from back then!" Shea exclaimed, while Kaori shrieked in fear.

"Have you been well, Shea?"

"Wha...?! Umm, y-yes! I'm doing fine!"

"Excellent, excellent. Quit spacing out, Young Haj. You said you needed three minutes to beat that oversized Devourer, right? Get to work, then. I can't hold it off for long."

"A-All right, all right. I'm still not sure what's going on, but thanks for saving us, Fish-san."

Hajime got back to work.

The giant silver silhouette continued fighting the sea angel, dodging its attacks and keeping it away from Tio. Upon closer inspection, Hajime realized that what he took for one silver creature was actually a huge school of fish. Not monster fish; just regular, everyday fish. However, there were hundreds of thousands of them. With those numbers, even the tiny fish could hold their own against the sea angel. Still, they wouldn't be able to endure for long; thousands of fish died in every attack.

Why on earth is a fishman here? Shea stepped up to ask what everyone else was wondering. It was rare to see Yue huddling behind Shea and not the other way around.

"U-umm, Fish-san? Is it all right if I call you that? Uhh... What exactly are you doing here?"

"Hmph! I wasn't doing anything. I was just minding my business, swimming along, when I sensed a huge mana explosion. I heard your Telepathy, so I rushed over, only to find a giant Devourer about to eat Young Haj. I didn't really know what was going on, but my friend was in trouble. I wouldn't be a man if I didn't help him out."

"Umm, what about those fish...? Also, what's a Devourer?"

"That thing you're fighting is known as a Devourer. They lived in the sea long ago... Actually, they're more natural disasters than creatures. People say they're the ancient ancestors of monsters. Oh! And I'm controlling those fish with Telepathy. My species' Telepathy lets me communicate with all sea creatures to some extent, even the ones without mana."

Shea's jaw dropped. Fish-san was a fishmancer. As he finished his explanation, the last of his fish army melted away. The

Devourer turned again on Tio, determined to swallow them whole.

Fortunately, Fish-san had bought them the three minutes Hajime needed.

Hajime set his super-sized torpedoes around the edges of Yue's barrier. In three minutes, he'd crafted roughly 120 of the weapons. A number of small circles, equal to the number of torpedoes, floated next to him.

Hajime poured his mana into the spirit stone and launched all the torpedoes simultaneously. They left a trail of bubbles in their wake as they sped toward the Devourer. These were no normal torpedoes. Simple explosives wouldn't do any lasting harm to the Devourer, after all. It would just regenerate all the jelly they blew apart.

Irked at the interruption, the Devourer sent a barrage of tentacles to swat down the torpedoes. However, Hajime guided the torpedoes, which wove through the tentacles. With his Limit Break, he could just barely control all 120 at once.

"You're not gonna dodge, are you? Hope you like my present, then," Hajime muttered viciously.

He figured that, since the Devourer dissolved anything that got close to it, it never bothered dodging. He was right. After making it through the forest of tentacles, Hajime's torpedoes smashed into the Devourer. It hadn't even tried to move.

However, there was no explosion. The torpedoes slowly melted into the Devourer. The black dots sticking from its body made it look like it had been poisoned.

Hajime needed to hurry and complete his preparations before the torpedoes melted completely. He pulled a large amount of sticky black liquid out of his Treasure Trove: liquified flamrock. He poured the flamrock into the circles floating around him.

A second later, the Devourer was dyed pitch-black. The blackness spread through its body like ink over paper. Black liquid filled every inch of the translucent jelly.

The circles were transporting the flamrock into the Devourer's body. They were actually all miniature warp gates connected to their respective torpedoes. Whatever fell into the circles appeared in the corresponding torpedo's location. His torpedoes hadn't actually been the weapon; they'd just delivered it. Their shells only existed to protect the warp gates inside them from corroding away instantly.

Naturally, the liquid flamrock itself began to dissolve inside the Devourer, but the creature couldn't get rid of all of it in time. It tried to split itself into pieces to prevent the flamrock from filling its entire body, but Yue and the others weren't about to let that happen. They used barriers, ice spells, and breath attacks to keep the Devourer busy. Hajime hadn't asked Yue to make the gate, since he knew she wasn't magically skilled enough to accurately open one inside a moving target. For now, the best she could do was connect two points in space.

The Devourer had gathered all its jelly in one place to give itself an advantage over Hajime, but that had backfired. It would die precisely because it had gone all-out. Hajime kept pouring flamrock until he was sure the Devourer was thoroughly saturated.

He grinned wickedly, a sharp glint in his eyes. There was a small, burning object in his hand.

"Let me show you what hell feels like." Hajime flicked the object into a warp gate with his thumb. It stuck to the flamrock, pouring through and reappearing inside the Devourer. White-hot flames spread to cover every inch of the monster's body, enveloping it.

The creature turned from black to red in the span of a few heartbeats. Once the flames were inside it, the Devourer had no way to fight back. It could only watch in horror as fire ate its body away.

Soon, it couldn't contain the flames, and fire shot out of its body, causing it to catch fire both outside and in. The flames were so hot that they evaporated the ocean's surface, and a large cloud of steam covered the Devourer.

Jets of water shot up as hyper-pressurized steam rose to the surface. The sea roiled and bubbled as the Devourer burned away. Yue's barrier kept the choppy waves off them while the party searched the area, making sure no traces remained.

They combed their surroundings for a while, but they didn't see any more jelly. Hajime used his Demon Eye and Farsight to check even more thoroughly, but still didn't spot anything.

Now he was certain. The ancient monster of the depths, the Devourer, was no more.

"Gah... That was hard."

Hajime's warp gates lost their glimmer and fell to the ground as he stopped powering them. The swirling cloud of mana surrounding him faded away as well. Hajime slumped to his knees and grimaced. He'd overexerted himself using Limit Break, leaving him with a pounding headache. Still, his eyes glowed with triumph. They'd done it.

"Hajime, are you all right?"

"Hajime-kun, I'll heal you right away, don't worry!"

Yue walked over and helped him stand, Kaori cast healing magic, and Shea and Tio ran up and hugged him.

"We did it, Hajime-san!"

"Wonderful, Master. Your murder methods are as creative and cruel as always. That sent shivers down my spine."

Kaori's healing magic soothed Hajime's headache, and he smiled at his comrades. A grumpy old man's voice interrupted their celebration.

"Hey, Young Haj. Next time you're about to blow the ocean up, tell me first. I thought I was going to die back there."

"Ah, Fish-san. Sorry. I was so focused on killing that thing that I forgot."

The explosion had blown the fishman away too. Hajime was so focused on the Devourer that he forgot the fishman was also in the water. He also hadn't expected an explosion. The interaction between the flamrock and the ocean had surprised him.

"Well, I won't deny killing Devourers is pretty taxing. You guys did a good job."

"If you hadn't saved us back there, we might really have died. Thanks."

"You're welcome. I was just repaying my debts, though, so don't worry too much about it."

"You're so cool, Fish-san. I'm glad of whatever coincidence brought you here."

"Young Haj, a series of coincidences is what we call fate. It was fate that you saved me, back in that city, just as it was fate that brought me here to save you."

Hajime and the fishman smiled at each other. It almost looked like they were communicating silently. The girls whispered.

"Is it just me, or does it feel like they really understand each other?"

"Is this what friendships between guys are like?"

"Hajime-kun, is a fishman really the first friend you made in this world? I know you didn't get along with people in Japan, but that doesn't mean you have to turn to other species!"

"They were like this last time, too. I guess it's the boys' version of girls' talk or something? Although he's talking to an old man, not a boy... Actually, he's not even an old man. He's just a fish."

The women were a little confused and creeped out that Hajime seemed closer to the fishman than to them. After a while, Hajime and the fishman's conversation seemed to come to an end.

"I'll be leaving, then, Young Haj. We'll meet again, if fate wills it."

"Yeah. Stay safe, Fish-san."

The fishman turned around and swam off. Just as he was about to vanish from sight, he stopped and turned to face Shea.

"Good luck. I know you've got a lot of rivals, but you can do it. Whenever you two have kids, let me know. I'll let them play with mine. I'll introduce you to my wife, too. Bye, then."

He turned back around and vanished into the deep blue sea.

Hajime and the others were stunned.

"He's married?!"

No one had expected that, and it took a while for their shock to wear off. Hajime once thought the fishman just liked wandering around, but it turned out he was actually a deadbeat dad.

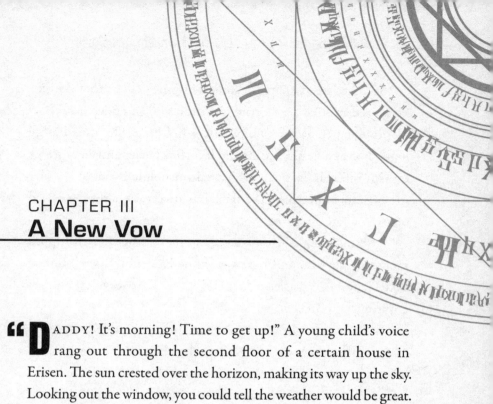

CHAPTER III
A New Vow

"**D**ADDY! It's morning! Time to get up!" A young child's voice rang out through the second floor of a certain house in Erisen. The sun crested over the horizon, making its way up the sky. Looking out the window, you could tell the weather would be great.

"Haaah..."

Hajime rolled over in bed. Myu ran to wake him up.

She jumped onto his bed and landed squarely on his stomach. Her body's full weight pressed down against him.

She might have been a little girl, only four years old, but people were heavy. She still weighed around 16 kilograms. If something that heavy slammed into a normal person's stomach, they'd groan in pain. Hajime barely felt it. Still, he wasn't too happy about being forced awake.

"Daddy, get up. It's morning. The sun's out."

"Hey, Myu. Good morning. I'm up, so you can stop slapping me now."

Myu had been happily slapping Hajime's cheek to wake him. He raised himself to a sitting position and lifted Myu off him. Her long emerald hair spilled out behind her. He smiled as he looked up at her. They really did look like father and daughter.

"Mmm... Hajime? Myu?" a tired voice called out.

Hajime pulled back the sheets to unveil Yue, sleeping curled up in a ball next to him.

Although she'd just awoken, her hair wasn't messy. It glimmered in the sun, and her eyes shone like rubies. She blinked. Like Hajime, she was naked. Her long hair fell over her shoulders, covering her porcelain-white skin.

"Why are you and Yue-oneechan always naked, Daddy?"

Specifically, Myu was asking why they were always naked when she woke them up in the morning. Hajime and Yue hadn't become nudists since returning from Melusine's labyrinth.

"You don't have any pajamas?" Myu asked innocently. She looked at Hajime with pity, and he exchanged glances with Yue. There was no way they could give an answer that would corrupt this pure girl's mind. After agonizing for a few seconds, Yue came to Hajime's rescue. She gave a very respectable, mature answer.

"Myu, you'll understand when you're older."

"I will?"

"Yeah, you will."

With that, they dodged a bullet. Yue would let Remia teach her own daughter about sex. However, Myu wasn't completely convinced. She tilted her head and, after a few seconds of thought, asked:

"Do you know because you're big over here, Daddy? But I don't have one of those... Does that mean I'll never understand?"

Myu pointed at Hajime's hard-on. Hajime hurriedly pushed her hand away.

"Myu, don't touch that. Listen up. You're a girl, so it's normal not to have one. Don't worry about it. In ten years, no in twenty years you'll... Actually, just never worry about it."

Hajime started spouting dumb things with a very serious face. Myu had no idea what Hajime was trying to say, but she nodded all the same. Satisfied, Hajime began combing Myu's hair with his fingers. Myu forgot all about the topic, and leaned into Hajime.

Yue watched the proceedings with an amused look. Hajime's surprisingly insatiable libido, combined with his overprotectiveness of Myu, made for an interesting mixture.

Hajime averted his gaze. The three of them sat in the morning sun until Kaori and Remia showed up, wondering why Hajime still hadn't come downstairs.

◦⫶◦ ◦⫶◦ ◦⫶◦ ◦⫶◦ ◦⫶◦ ◦⫶◦ ◦⫶◦ ◦⫶◦ ◦⫶◦ ◦⫶◦ ◦⫶◦ ◦⫶◦ ◦⫶◦

Six days had passed since they cleared the Sunken Ruins of Melusine and rode Tio back to Erisen. They were staying at Remia's house, and since their return, they were the talk of the town.

They'd spent the past six days mastering the new magic, and repairing and improving their equipment. With the great food and warm weather, though, they spent more time vacationing than preparing.

Still, six days was a long time, even for both training and vacationing. The reason for their extended stay was of, course, Myu.

Hajime wouldn't take Myu with him on his travels any longer. There was no way he could bring a four-year-old girl into a labyrinth on the other edge of the world.

Worse, the two remaining labyrinths were in even more dangerous locations. One was in demon territory, in the Frost Caverns of the Schnee Snow Fields. The other was on the Divine Mountain, of all places. Both would require the party to dive right into the heart of the enemy. It was impossible to leave Myu somewhere safe while he challenged those labyrinths.

Myu seemed to realize that, too. Every time someone tried to bring up the topic, she acted extremely spoiled and made it difficult to discuss. They dragged out their training longer than necessary just so they'd have an excuse to stay.

"Still, we really need to get moving soon. Haaah... I'm going to have to tell Myu. You think she'll cry? Actually, she'll definitely cry... Man, this sucks."

Hajime sat on the pier and sighed. He was transmuting equipment for their upcoming trials. When he first left the abyss, he couldn't have cared less about anyone in this world, but now he was depressed over parting with a single girl. He wasn't sure how to feel about that.

"This is all your fault, Sensei."

Although his words sounded harsh, there was a gentle smile on his face. Aiko's guidance had led to the shift in Hajime's thinking. He was no longer willing to sacrifice anything and everything for the sake of his goal.

As he watched Yue, Shea, Kaori, Tio, and Myu frolic in the water, he realized he was glad Aiko had lectured him. Had he simply abandoned Myu in Fuhren, decided to ignore Ankaji's crisis, or left Myu with Remia the moment they found her, chances were his comrades wouldn't be smiling so brightly.

Leaving the people he saved to their plight wouldn't necessarily have depressed Yue and the others. Still, he was certain they wouldn't be nearly as happy.

He didn't have any proof, but he was sure of it.

By taking Aiko's words to heart, he'd avoided going down what she called a lonely path.

"Guess she was right." Hajime smiled ruefully. He watched Myu skillfully evade the others in a strange game of tag. Although they were all overpowered beyond measure, and were working together to try and catch Myu, her swimming abilities kept her ahead.

I never thought saying goodbye would be so hard. Hajime couldn't lie to himself. He sighed for the umpteenth time. The moment he brought up the fact that he'd be leaving, he knew he would mar Myu's smile with tears.

As if sensing his worries, Remia swam up to Hajime. She stopped in front of his legs, which dangled in the water. Seawater dripped from her emerald-green hair. She'd tied it back in a single braid, and wore a light-green bikini. When they first met, she'd looked haggard, but thanks to the restoration magic from

Melusine's labyrinth, she was as lively as ever. It was hard to imagine she was old enough to be someone's mother.

Hajime could see why every bachelor in town wanted to be Remia's new husband, and why they'd even started a fan club for her and Myu. Her beauty rivaled Tio's, and she looked absolutely stunning in her bikini. Furthermore, because she was in the water, she was eye-level with his crotch. Hajime, who'd been worrying himself sick over Myu, was taken completely by surprise.

Remia placed a hand on Hajime's knee and looked up at him with an expression of gentle concern.

"Thank you, Hajime-san."

"Where'd that come from? I didn't really do anything deserving of thanks, I don't think." He looked quizzically down at Remia.

"Hee hee! Don't be silly. You're worrying so much for my daughter's sake. As her mother, it'd be wrong of me not to thank you."

"That's... I guess I can't hide anything from you. And here I was, trying not to be obvious."

"My! You do realize everyone's noticed? Yue-san and the others look as though they don't want to leave either. I'm so glad Myu was able to meet such wonderful people."

Remia turned to watch a topless Shea chasing after Myu, who'd stolen the upper half of her swimsuit. Remia turned back to Hajime and spoke in a more serious tone.

"Hajime-san. You've done more than enough. Everyone has, really. So, please, don't look so worried. Finish what you have to do."

"Remia..."

"She's grown up so much since she met you all. Even though all I did was spoil her while she was here, she's learned to care about other people. Myu knows, too. She knows you'll have to go. Of course, she's still young, and doesn't really want you to leave, but... Despite that, she's never once asked you directly not to go. She knows she can't keep you here forever, so..."

"I see. Man, I'm pretty pathetic to let a little girl worry about me. All right. I'll tell her tonight. We'll leave tomorrow."

Remia's right. Myu doesn't want us to go, but she also doesn't want to say that, because she doesn't want to make it harder for us. Realizing the depth of Myu's determination, Hajime steeled his own.

Remia smiled. "In that case, I'll make a feast for you all tonight. It'll be your farewell party."

"Sounds good. I look forward to it."

"Hee hee! Glad to hear it, *dear.*"

"Seriously, could you stop calling..."

Before Hajime finished, a frigid wind passed over them, and a voice colder than death interrupted him.

"Remia, you better not." Yue glared at Remia. She absolutely wouldn't allow her to marry Hajime. This scene had played out numerous times over the past week.

"Remia-san, when did you..." Kaori gasped. "I can't let my guard down around you!"

"Hmm, from this angle, it almost looks as if she's servicing master," murmured Tio. "Exhibitionism... Wonderful."

Everyone ignored Tio. Likewise, they ignored the nearly

naked bunny girl as she whined, "Hey, Myu-chan? Could you please give me my swimsuit back? People are starting to stare."

❖ ❖ ❖ ❖ ❖ ❖ ❖ ❖ ❖ ❖ ❖ ❖ ❖

Remia's smile didn't waver, despite Yue's bloodcurdling glare. It was impossible to tell what she was thinking when she smiled like that, and Hajime was still unsure if she was serious about marrying him, or just playing around.

Maybe that's just how widows tease people. Hajime's attention was diverted when he glimpsed Yue in her swimsuit. He'd seen that quite a few times already over the past few days, but it never failed to captivate him.

Yue was wearing a black bikini. It was the kind that tied in front, so it was pretty provocative. The black contrasted nicely with Yue's pale skin. She'd bound her hair into pigtails for once, making her look younger than usual. Hajime found the disparity between her innocent appearance and her mature swimsuit extremely alluring.

Yue only noticed Hajime's gaze in the midst of a fierce staring contest with Remia. She smiled seductively and turned to face him.

Unwilling to let herself be outdone, Kaori approached Hajime from the opposite side and took his arm. She blushed at her own boldness and pressed his arm into her white bikini. She looked up, imploring him to pay attention to her too.

At the same time, Shea came up to Hajime from behind and pressed her massive chest against him. Myu hadn't given back the top half of her swimsuit, so that was also a good way to hide her exposed breasts. Of course, pressing them directly against his back only made things harder for Hajime.

Tio, too, was dressed in a rather eye-catching swimsuit. But in her case, the effect was ruined by her disgusting panting. Hajime threw a piece of metal at her to knock her out of it. He might have thrown it a little too hard, as it literally knocked Tio out and left her floating like a drowned corpse in the sea.

Myu jumped out of the water, eager to join in the fun. She landed between Remia and Hajime, then threw herself into his arms. She raised Shea's bikini top up high, as if showing off the spoils of war, and placed it atop Hajime's head, apparently as a gift.

"M-Myu-chan?! Why are you... Wait! Don't tell me Hajime-san asked you to take it...? J-jeez! If you wanted my swimsuit, Hajime-san, you should have just asked... I wouldn't have minded."

"Hajime, take mine too."

"M-mine too! If that's what you're into, Hajime-kun... Ah, but it'd be too embarrassing to strip here. Come to my room later, okay?"

"Oh, my. I suppose that means you want mine as well... Would you prefer the top, the bottom, or perhaps...both?"

Hajime Nagumo sat there, a bikini top on his head, surrounded by girls pressing their swimsuits against him.

Water from Shea's swimsuit dripped down his cheek. Despite the excitement, his expression was as wooden as a board. This situation was beyond surreal.

The male onlookers were crying tears of blood. From that day onward, rumors spread across Erisen. "Watch out for that white-haired eyepatch kid. He's got a swimsuit fetish. That pervert ran around town with a girl's bikini top on his head."

That evening, Hajime finally told Myu that he was leaving. She gripped the hem of her dress tight, and tried her best not to cry. After a protracted silence, she finally spoke.

"I won't ever see you again?"

"......"

Hajime didn't know what to say. His goal was to return home to Japan. He still wasn't sure exactly how he was going to do that, or when he'd be able to.

Miledi Reisen had told him he needed to clear all the labyrinths if he wanted his wish granted. It was possible he'd be forcibly transported back the moment he beat the seventh. He doubted he'd return to Erisen before his journey was complete, so it was certainly possible this would be the last time Myu would ever see him. He didn't want to lie to her.

Before Hajime could come up with a reply, however, she followed up with another question. "You'll always be my daddy, right?"

Hajime gripped her shoulders and looked her squarely in the eye. "If that's what you want."

Myu held back her tears and squeezed out a smile. Yue and the others were taken aback. Myu's smile looked strikingly similar to Hajime's when he was up against a powerful foe. The two really were beginning to resemble each other.

"Then when I get older, I'll come find you, Daddy."

"Find me? Myu, I'll be going somewhere really far away, so..."

"But if you can go there, I can too. Because...I'm your daughter."

If Hajime could do something, she could too. Myu was certain of it. If her daddy wouldn't be able to come back to her, then she'd just have to find him.

Of course, there was no way Myu could understand that Hajime planned to travel across dimensions. Plus, it was unlikely that she'd conquer the labyrinths on her own and chase him to his world.

That would be nearly impossible, despite her determination.

Still, no one dared ridicule Myu's resolve. No one dared tell her it was impossible. They knew they shouldn't. No... They *couldn't*. Hajime finally understood what Remia meant when she said Myu had grown. Although they'd only spent a short time together, Myu learned a lot from Hajime and the others.

And now, they were going to leave her. Can I really just leave her like this? No, I can't. I definitely can't.

Hajime made his decision. He bound himself to yet another oath.

"Myu, wait for me."

"Daddy?"

Myu tilted her head quizzically. She sensed the slight shift in Hajime's demeanor, but didn't know what it meant. There was no longer any hesitation in Hajime's gaze, only his usual steadfast resolve. The same resolve Myu had learned to emulate.

"Once everything's settled, I promise to come back to you. We'll all come back to see you again."

"Really?"

"Yeah, really. Have I ever broken a promise?"

Myu shook her head. Hajime ruffled her hair.

"When I come back, I'll show you my home. You'll get to see where I was born. I bet you'll be surprised. My hometown's a pretty different place."

"I want to see where you were born, Daddy!"

"Looking forward to it?"

"Yep!"

Myu jumped up happily. Hajime's gaze softened as he looked at her. Now that she knew she'd be able to see him again, there was no reason to be sad. Still beaming, Myu leaped into Hajime's arms. Hajime lifted her up and hugged her.

"Don't do anything dangerous. Be a good girl, and wait with Mommy, okay? You're going to be good and help Mommy around the house, right?"

"Uh-huh!"

Hajime smiled at that, but his eyes silently apologized to Remia. *Sorry for deciding all that on my own.*

Remia met Hajime's gaze, shook her head, then nodded. *It's fine. Don't worry about it.* If anything, Remia was thankful.

Myu noticed Hajime and Remia exchanging silent glances, and thought of something. She tugged Hajime's sleeve to grab his attention.

"Daddy, is Mommy going to come too?"

"Uh, well, that depends... Remia?"

"What is it, dear? You weren't thinking of leaving me behind, now, were you?"

"Err, not exactly, but...my homeland's literally in a different world. You sure you wanna come?"

"Really, now. How could I stay behind if my husband and daughter are going? Hee hee."

Remia sidled up to Hajime. For a moment, she really looked like his wife.

Kaori and the others hurriedly stepped in, unwilling to let Remia get ahead of them. The solemn atmosphere from earlier evaporated. Kaori and Remia glared daggers at each other, while Yue quietly walked up to Hajime.

"Are you really going to take them?"

"Are you against it?"

Yue shook her head and gazed gently into Hajime's eyes.

"If that's what you've decided, then I don't mind."

"I see."

"But what if we get transported right away?"

She'd been considering it too. There was no guarantee that they could choose when to activate the magic that would return them to their world. It was certainly possible that Hajime wouldn't be able to fulfill his promise. If that really did happen, it would scar Myu forever.

However, Hajime just shrugged and smiled. Once he made his decision, there was no turning back. Yue knew his answer before she even asked. She smiled at Hajime, noting the determination in his gaze.

"I'll figure something out. One way or another, we'll return to see Myu, then show her Japan. If the spell takes us back without time to prepare, we'll just have to find a way to come here again. I'll hop between worlds as many times as it takes. That's all there is to it."

"Yeah... That's all there is to it."

The two shared a knowing smile. Yue was glad Hajime had found something else he treasured enough to protect. Hajime, too, was glad he was changing into someone kinder. And like that, the two were once again lost in their own world, flirting without a care for their surroundings.

Kaori and the others stopped fighting to glare pointedly at Hajime and Yue. They hesitated to interfere, but Myu had no such inhibitions.

She brazenly stepped between Yue and Hajime and begged Hajime for another hug. Even if he'd promised to come back, she still wouldn't see him for some time. She was going to make the most of her last hours with him.

•/• •/• •/• •/• •/• •/• •/• •/• •/• •/• •/• •/• •/• •/•

Myu and Remia saw Hajime and the others off the next morning.

A day and a half passed, and Hajime's group spent the entire time traveling the rust-red desert.

Brise roared across the dunes, heading toward Ankaji. Their eventual goal was still Haltina, but Kaori wanted to see if her newly-acquired restoration magic could repair Ankaji's damaged oasis.

As its name suggested, restoration magic restored things to

their original state. Although healing magic hadn't been able to remove the toxins from the water, restoration magic could bring it back to its pure state. Or, at least, Kaori hoped so.

Since Ankaji was more or less on the way, Hajime saw no problem with stopping there for a bit. Besides, the party hadn't had a chance to try Ankaji's famous cuisine last time.

Before long, the city's main gate came into view. Unlike last time, it was quite lively. A long line of caravans waited to be admitted. It looked like a proper center of trade.

"That sure is a lot of wagons."

"Yeah... This might take a while."

"Isn't that food and water they're carrying in?"

Kaori was correct. The wagons contained the emergency supplies Ankaji requested from Heiligh. They'd only just arrived. It seemed Lanzwi had also bought the food stores of every passing merchant. At least, every passing merchant who hadn't asked an exorbitant price.

Since their immediate water supply had been compromised, Lanzwi knew he needed to stockpile nonperishable goods. Not only did they lack drinking water, they also didn't have enough water to grow crops. He bought whatever food the royal treasury could afford.

Hajime drove Brise past the line of merchants shuffling uncomfortably in the sand and headed for the main gate. He had no intention of waiting for hours.

The merchants gazed in awe as a giant black box sped past. A few screamed in surprise, worried that a strange new monster had come to attack them. The guards brandished their weapons, wary of this unknown object.

A senior watchman walked out of the guardhouse to see what the commotion was, and instantly recognized Brise. He remonstrated his guards and ordered them to lower their weapons. Then, he sent a messenger to the palace.

Hajime and the others stopped in front of the gate and stepped out of the truck, heedless of the stares around them. As always, the men were first stunned by the girls' beauty, then amazed when Hajime seemingly made Brise vanish into thin air.

"I thought I recognized your strange vehicle! I see you've returned to us, Warriors of Ehit." The senior guardsman breathed a sigh of relief when he saw Kaori. Hajime guessed he'd seen Brise when Hajime brought Bize in, or perhaps when he left for the volcano.

The guard assumed it was Kaori, the "Warrior of Ehit," that used Brise to travel around. That was basically true, so Hajime saw no need to correct him. It made sense that Kaori was the best-known figure in their party.

"We have. The truth is, I've discovered magic that might help me purify the oasis, so I came back to try again. I'd like to speak with your duke about it, if possible."

"Can you really purify the oasis?!"

"I-I think so. I need to test it to be sure, but..."

"I should have expected as much from one of Ehit's warriors. Sorry for holding you up. I've already sent a runner to the duke. It's best if you wait here, so you don't miss each other. Once he hears you've returned, I'm sure he'll head straight over."

The soldier looked at them with great respect. *I guess that makes sense, since we saved his city,* Hajime thought. They were being treated like VIPs. He ignored the merchants' curious stares and let the guard lead them into the guardhouse's waiting room.

❖ ❖ ❖ ❖ ❖ ❖ ❖ ❖ ❖ ❖ ❖ ❖ ❖

Fifteen minutes later, Lanzwi burst into the guardhouse, panting heavily. He really had come running. Hajime again realized just how much this city respected them.

"It... Well, I can't rightly say it's been a long time. Regardless, I'm glad to see you're doing well, Hajime-dono. We began to grow worried when you didn't return. You and your companions are the saviors of my realm. It would have been quite a shame if you died without letting me thank you properly."

"I'm just a passing adventurer who happened to be here at the right time. And, as you can see, I'm doing perfectly fine. Thanks for your concern, though. At any rate, it's good to see that your emergency supplies made it here in time."

"Indeed. Thanks to the food being brought in now, and the reservoirs Yue-dono made for us, we should be able to last a while. With this, we'll manage to avoid starving to death, at least." Lanzwi smiled, looking tired. He'd worked nonstop these past few days to ensure his people had enough food. His exhaustion was clear, but so were the results of his efforts.

"Duke, how does the oasis look?"

"Warrior of Ehit... I mean, Kaori-dono... The oasis remains unchanged. We've managed to pump in more fresh water from underground and clear away some of the polluted water, but have otherwise made no progress. It will take at least half a year to remove all the polluted water and replace it with clean water. And it will likely take an entire year, or perhaps even two, to get the toxins out of the soil."

Gloom settled over Lanzwi. Then Kaori explained that she might be able to purify it herself, and his face lit up like the sun.

He clutched at Kaori's clothes. "Really?!" he yelled, with unbelievable zeal. She backed away and nodded hesitantly. Lanzwi cleared his throat and collected himself, realizing he'd acted improperly. He implored Kaori to attempt to purify the oasis right away.

That was what she'd been planning to do, so Kaori agreed, and the party headed to the oasis.

Like before, it was completely deserted. Normally, it was one of Ankaji's most popular destinations, but now there was no one. Lanzwi frowned as he looked at the empty oasis.

Kaori stepped up to the shore and began casting. Although they'd all obtained the ability to use restoration magic, Hajime and Shea possessed no aptitude for it, as usual. Shea, at least, could sort of use it. She was able to internalize the magic to increase her natural regeneration abilities. If she concentrated, she could increase her mana and stamina regeneration for some time. At this point, she was completely superhuman. Her body-strengthening abilities had grown, and she'd become much more skilled at manipulating gravity. Now, with the addition of automatic highspeed regeneration, she was basically a one-bunny army.

Kaori possessed the highest affinity for restoration magic, followed by Tio, then Yue. Yue was so accustomed to her own self-regeneration skill that she rarely used healing magic. For that reason, her affinity was much lower. She could heal herself without thinking, so having to actively cast recovery spells was hard for her.

On the other hand, Kaori was a Priest. Restoration and recovery magic were strongly linked, so affinity was highest. She could use restoration magic more efficiently, and at greater range, than either Yue or Tio. Unfortunately, she needed magic circles and an incantation to cast, so Yue's version was still more useful in combat.

Kaori began a long incantation. When she first started practicing, it took her seven minutes to complete one spell. Now, she could finish in three. The fact that she'd cut the casting time down by more than half proved she was plenty overpowered herself. Sadly for Kaori, Yue's strength was beyond even that. It stung her a little, but she'd already resolved not to wallow.

An air of tranquil majesty descended upon the oasis as Kaori's magic set in. Lanzwi and his attendants gulped. They felt as if they were witnessing some holy rite. They watched with nervous excitement as Kaori finished her chant.

"Tetragrammaton."

Eyes still closed, Kaori thrust her pure white staff over the water.

A second later, the tip glowed with lavender light. The orb of light traveled down her staff, across the water's surface, and fell into the center of the oasis. The entire oasis began to glow with faint purple light. Motes of it floated up from the water and vanished in the air. It looked as if all the world's evil had been purified and sent to heaven.

Everyone watched with rapt attention, so captivated that they forgot to breathe. Finally, the spell ended, and the light faded away. Silence stretched on for some time.

Hajime, supporting a spent Kaori, eventually nodded to Lanzwi. Lanzwi snapped back to reality and ordered his attendants to test the water. They hurriedly cast appraisal spells. Once they finished, they turned to Lanzwi with looks of disbelief. After a brief pause, they announced the results.

"The poison is gone."

"Are you sure?"

The man spoke again, this time with more certainty. "The oasis is clean! It's back to normal! It's been purified!"

They all cried out in joy. Lanzwi's attendants dropped whatever they held and hugged each other. Lanzwi took a deep breath, looked at the heavens, and closed his eyes.

"All that's left now is to purify the soil. Duke, have you already gotten rid of the poisoned crops?"

"No, we've just gathered them all in one place. There wasn't enough time or manpower to dispose of them. Don't tell me you plan on purifying those too?"

"If Yue and Tio are willing to help, I think we can. What do you two think?"

"Hmm... Not a problem."

"Very well. It would indeed be a pity to see the food go to waste after you worked so hard to grow it. Allow us to help."

Lanzwi bowed deeply. Not only had they purified his oasis, but they were going to save his soil and crops. Although it wasn't a duke's place to bow his head to others, it was the only way he could think of to show the depth of his gratitude. That was how much he loved his city and its people.

Hajime and the others graciously accepted his thanks and walked toward the agricultural district.

Just then, Hajime stopped and turned around. He cast about with Farsight, and spotted a group of people swaggering toward them. It looked like they wanted a fight. They were dressed differently from Ankaji's soldiers. From what Hajime could tell, they were the templar knights who protected this city's church.

They surrounded Hajime and his companions, forming a half-circle. A middle-aged man dressed in ostentatious white robes stepped out from their ranks.

Sensing the hostility in the knights' gaze, Lanzwi quickly interposed himself.

"Lord Zengen... Please step aside. Those people are dangerous."

"What is the meaning of this, Bishop Forbin? And what do you mean, they're dangerous? These good people have saved my dukedom twice now. They're heroes. I will not allow anyone to speak ill of them."

Bishop Forbin scoffed.

"Hmph. Heroes? Watch your tongue, Duke. The Holy Church declared them heretics. Defend them at your own peril."

Lanzwi sucked in a sharp breath. "Heretics? Preposterous! I've heard no such thing!"

Like most people, Lanzwi was a devout follower of Ehit. He knew what it meant to be branded a heretic, which was precisely why he couldn't believe his city's saviors were among their ranks.

"Of course you haven't. The decision was made just this morning. To think the heretics would choose to return now... Heh heh heh, perfect timing, wouldn't you say? It's as if Ehit himself delivered them into my arms. Clearly, this is a sign. He wants me to be the one to purge these nonbelievers. If I bring the pope their heads, I'm sure to be promoted..."

Forbin spoke his last few words so softly that Lanzwi didn't catch them. Still, it seemed that Hajime was a heretic. Lanzwi turned to his saviors. Hajime didn't seem the least bit surprised. He shrugged as if he'd expected this. He met Lanzwi's gaze, and his eyes silently asked, "What will you do?"

Lanzwi furrowed his brow, but before he could speak, Forbin continued with a sneer.

"Now, if you'll excuse me, I have some heretics to purge. I've heard you're quite powerful, but I wonder how you'll fare against a hundred templar knights? Now then, Duke Zengen, kindly get out of my way. Surely you won't do anything as foolish as stand against the Holy Church?"

Lanzwi closed his eyes. From Hajime's personality, and his strange powers, Lanzwi could easily guess why the Holy Church had branded him a heretic. They couldn't afford to let someone so mighty live, except under their control.

However, when he thought of how powerful Hajime and his comrades were, Lanzwi considered it suicide to stand against them. Hajime would wipe out the humans long before the demons could even get to them. Had the pope gone mad? This declaration reeked of political maneuvering.

Regardless of the reason, Hajime was Ankaji's savior. He and his comrades had healed Lanzwi's people, given them water, destroyed the monster lurking in the oasis, and now come back to purify their land.

Only a few seconds ago, he'd racked his brains to think of how he'd thank them. Lanzwi opened his eyes and smiled at Forbin. This was a good opportunity to make his allegiances clear. He looked sharply into the bishop's eyes, and solemnly shook his head.

"I refuse."

"What did you just say?" Forbin was so surprised his eyes nearly bulged out of their sockets.

It amused Lanzwi how certain the bishop had been that no one would dare disdain the Holy Church's authority. He repeated himself, his words backed by an unshakable will.

"I said, I refuse. These adventurers saved my people. I won't let anyone raise a hand against them, not even the Holy Church."

"Y-y-y-y-you godless bastard! Have you lost your mind?! Do you understand what it means to oppose the Holy Church?! You'll be branded a heretic, you know!"

Forbin's surprise transformed into rage. The templar knights looked at each other in confusion.

"Bishop Forbin. Do the archbishops and pope really not know what these adventurers did for us? Without them, poison would have destroyed this city. From what I've heard, they saved Ur, and even rescued the hero's party. How could such great people be branded heretics? I cannot imagine the Holy Church's decision is a sane one. I, Lanzwi Feuward Zengen, implore the Holy Church to reconsider its decision. Perhaps the news that they saved this city will convince the clergy."

"S-silence! Our decision is final! This is Ehit's will! Disobey him at your own peril! Duke, if you insist on protecting these heretics, I will brand you...no, all of Ankaji...heretics as well! Are you sure you want to do this?!"

Madness glinted in Forbin's eyes. It was hard to believe he was really a man of god. As Lanzwi watched coldly, Hajime walked up to him.

"Hey, are you sure about this?" he asked, with a worried expression. "You'll make an enemy out of Heiligh and the Holy Church. Shouldn't you do what's best for your people?"

Lanzwi looked down at his attendants. Hajime followed his gaze. The attendants gazed at them, closed their eyes, and, after a brief moment of consideration, made their decision. Their eyes glimmered with resolve.

"We won't go down that easy!"

At their reaction, Forbin reddened with anger and screeched a final warning.

"Are you certain?! You'll die here, you stubborn fools! Not just you, but your people, too! I'll turn this city into a sea of blood. I shall rain Ehit's divine wrath down on you wretched heretics!"

"None of my subjects are craven enough to turn their back on the heroes who saved them. You claim you'll bring down divine wrath? The god I believe in would reward such loyalty. Perhaps *your* faith is heretical, Bishop."

Forbin was so furious that he stopped yelling. A cold finality settled over his face. He raised a hand, ordering his knights to attack.

Before they could charge, something whistled through the air and clanged against a templar knight's helmet. The knight looked down and saw a pebble. It hadn't so much as dented his armor, so he tilted his head in confusion. Before he could ponder its meaning, more stones rained down on the knights. They clanged loudly against gleaming breastplates.

The knights looked up and saw Ankaji's residents surrounding them. It seemed they had hurried over when light flowed from the oasis. They arrived in time to see the entire exchange. Not only had Kaori healed and tended to their sick, but Hajime and the others braved the volcano to bring back enough stillstone. Moreover, their beloved lord had sided with Hajime and the others. Besides, the bishop looked clearly deranged, so they made their allegiances clear, hurling stones at the knights.

"Desist, citizens of Ankaji! These people have been branded heretics and enemies of god! Ehit himself desires their deaths!"

Forbin desperately tried to convince the people. He thought they hadn't heard the declaration, and hoped that informing them would be enough to calm their wrath.

The people did indeed stop, exchanging confused glances with one another.

Lanzwi turned and addressed them.

"My beloved citizens. Listen to me! These adventurers purified our oasis! Thanks to them, the symbol of our great city is clean once more! They even promised to purify our soil and crops! Because of them, Ankaji is here today, and will be restored to its former splendor! However, it is not for me to tell you what to do. Let your hearts decide whether our city's saviors deserve our scorn, or protection. I, at least, choose to stand with them!"

Forbin sneered. He was certain the people wouldn't trust Lanzwi's word over the Holy Church's. A second later, his face froze.

Clang! Clang! Clang! Clang! Clang! Clang! Clang! Clang!
The citizens had resumed throwing stones.

"Wh-what..." Forbin was at a loss for words. The citizens pressed forward, hurling insults with their stones.

"Fuck you! They saved our lives. We won't let you kill them!"

"The Holy Church didn't do a damn thing to save us, but now you want to kill the people who did?! You're no holy man!"

"They're no heretics! You're the real heretic!"

"This has to be some kind of mistake!"

"Protect Kaori-sama!"

"Defend our lord!"

"Kaori-sama, I'll lay down my life for you!"

"Dear adventurers, run now, while you still have the chance!"

"Hey, someone get Bize! Tell him to summon Kaori-sama's honor guard!"

It seemed that the citizens took Hajime's side. They hadn't forgotten who saved their lives. Their gratitude outweighed even their piety. No, that wasn't quite true. Rather, the nature of their faith had changed. They simply couldn't believe that their god, their ultimate object of worship, would want to harm his own warrior, or the people traveling with her.

In other words, their faith in god remained unshaken, but their faith in Forbin had dissolved. *I wonder, though, if anyone really trusted a bishop like that to begin with.* The crowd grew as word spread. As individuals, their strength was weak, but they already far outnumbered the knights. Forbin and his templars winced at their ferocity and stepped backwards.

"Bishop, this is Ankaji's will. Will you please ask the Holy Church to reconsider?"

"Tch... Don't think you can get away with this!"

Forbin ground his teeth in frustration. He shot one last hateful look at Hajime before turning on his heel and stalking away. The templar knights hurriedly followed. Forbin disappeared inside the church, looking for something to vent his frustrations on.

"Are you sure? I know it's a bit late to ask this now, but you could have stayed neutral."

Hajime looked at Lanzwi, a troubled expression on his face. Kaori and the others were worried as well. None of them wanted to cause Ankaji's destruction.

Contrary to Hajime's expectations, though, Lanzwi was unconcerned.

"I said it before, didn't I? This is Ankaji's will. Every man, woman, and child within these walls owes you their life. That's a debt they won't soon forget. If I'd let the bishop kill you, I guarantee the people would have killed me next. The last thing I want is a coup d'etat."

"We could have taken those guys easily."

Hajime scratched his cheek. Lanzwi smiled knowingly.

"I suppose so, which makes you five even scarier than the Holy Church. It's true that you're our heroes, but I also really didn't want to make you my enemy. You use magic I've never heard of, slaughter monsters that would trample my entire army... You even conquered a labyrinth in a few days' time. I can tell you care nothing for the Holy Church's authority, and I'm sure a hundred knights wouldn't faze you. I've already heard how you demolished a monster army, tens of thousands strong, and saved the hero party from enemies who nearly killed them. You truly are a frightening bunch. I imagine this is the most important decision I have made since I inherited the dukedom from my father."

Hajime wouldn't have blamed Lanzwi if he gave them up to the bishop. Still, after weighing the two options, Lanzwi chose to side with them. Even if it had been for the sake of his country, he rebelled against the Holy Church. That was an important decision.

Hajime smiled awkwardly. He'd expected this confrontation, but hadn't expected other people to resolve it without him.

I guess this is another result of avoiding a lonely path. Aiko-sensei really did have a point, Hajime thought as he watched Kaori and the others converse happily with the citizens.

•|• •|• •|• •|• •|• •|• •|• •|• •|• •|• •|• •|• •|•

Three days after the showdown with the bishop, Kaori, Yue, and Tio finished purifying the soil and crops. The whole party gathered atop a small hill overlooking the newly-sparkling oasis.

Now that it had returned to its original grandeur, smiling people filled the oasis. They sprawled along its edge, and children played in the water. Men fished along the pier, and lovers sailed in tiny rowboats. All sorts of people were present, but they had one thing in common... Smiles.

Hajime and the others were leaving Ankaji. Originally, the plan was to purify the city, try some of their delicacies, buy some local fruit, and leave. In the end, though, Lanzwi and the people of Ankaji insisted they stay two extra days.

The people were so grateful that, if Hajime had not told Lanzwi to keep his departure secret, they would have held a fare-well parade. He told only the duke and his family of his departure, and the party stopped for one last look at the famed oasis.

"Hey, you guys are gonna stand out if you stay dressed like that. Hurry up and put something on," Hajime said, turning to face the gate.

"Oh? Already tired of seeing so much skin?"

"Huh? Is that really true, Hajime-kun?"

"Look at Master's eyes, Yue, Kaori. He has not had his fill just yet, but he doesn't want us to stand out."

"Yeah, I guess I can't wear something like this to the front gate!"

Shea twirled around, showing off her belly dancer's outfit. She was wearing a choli top and harem pants. The provocative outfit would definitely attract attention.

It was apparently traditional in Ankaji, though. Lanzwi had given the garments to the girls, and the first time they wore them, Hajime could hardly look away. Outfits like those hit all of his buttons. For the first time, he'd been captivated not just by Yue, but by Shea, Tio, and Kaori too.

It really was the first time that had happened. Having finally tasted success, the other girls wore the outfits for an entire day. Naturally, Yue kept hers on as well, and successfully seduced him multiple times.

In the end, they'd worn the dresses for their entire stay. One of Hajime's fetishes had finally been revealed. He was both happy and a little troubled by the fact that they continued wearing the clothes for so long. He really needed them to change by the time they reached the gate.

⁂

On the road, two days after they left Ankaji, they encountered a band of brigands attacking a merchant convoy near Horaud. There, they reunited with someone they hadn't expected to see.

ARIFURETA:
ARIFURETA SHOKUGYOU DE SEKAISAIKYOU

FROM COMMONPLACE
TO WORLD'S STRONGEST

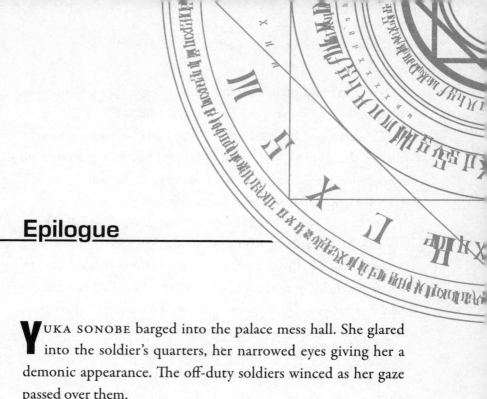

Epilogue

YUKA SONOBE barged into the palace mess hall. She glared into the soldier's quarters, her narrowed eyes giving her a demonic appearance. The off-duty soldiers winced as her gaze passed over them.

"Not here either, huh? Jeez... Why do they always vanish at the most important times?"

She tousled her chestnut-colored hair, her frustration plain for all to see. The soldiers jumped a little as she stomped away.

"They're not in the training grounds, not in the barracks, not in the mess hall... Did they go to town?"

Yuka marched off to the castle's main gate as she muttered. Her footsteps echoed across the hallway.

"Yukacchi!" Nana Miyazaki dashed after her.

"I couldn't find them. You?"

"No one in the mess hall. I just checked... Tamai-kun and

Taeko didn't find them either, so they're looking in other rooms right now. But I don't think they're in the palace."

"Makes sense. I just talked to Aikawa-kun, and he hasn't seen them either. Sheesh, where are they loitering? This is important. And they call themselves Ai-chan-sensei's bodyguards!"

Nana cradled her head in her hands and screamed.

Yuka and Nana—or, rather, the entire Ai-chan-sensei escort squad—were searching for David and his knights.

Aiko hadn't shown up for three days straight. According to the pope, she went to the main cathedral to have Hajime's heretic status rescinded. The pope claimed she'd have to stay there for a while, and that they wouldn't see her for a few days.

However, according to Shizuku, Aiko had something important she wanted to tell them. So naturally, they were suspicious. They asked to be let into the main cathedral, but Ishtar said friends of heretics weren't permitted inside, so they'd been cooling their heels.

After three days of no contact, however, the students were fed up. The elevator to the cathedral remained dormant, and none of the priests gave them straightforward answers. Tired of waiting, Yuka tried to seek out David and the others to demand an explanation.

David and his knights had been here yesterday, but today they were nowhere to be found. Yuka couldn't discover any trace of them. The only plausible explanation was that they went into town, but she found it hard to believe they'd fool around in the city with Aiko missing.

"I've got a bad feeling about this." Yuka ground her teeth and looked around warily. It was as if some formless evil was creeping up on her and taking her friends.

Just as the fear was starting to take over, someone called out to her. "Yuka? Nana?"

It was Shizuku. She glanced about the hall as though searching for someone.

"I wanted to ask if you'd seen David and the others... Although, judging by your expressions, that's a no."

"Nope. Looks like you didn't find the captain either."

Shizuku looked down sadly. Not only Aiko had vanished that night. Captain Meld and Princess Liliana were gone as well. Even Shizuku's maid, Nia, was nowhere to be found. A number of the other servants and knights were also missing, all friends of the students.

"Hey, Yukacchi, Shizukucchi... Are we going to be all right?"

"......"

Nana looked scared. Unfortunately, neither Yuka or Shizuku could reassure her.

They didn't know what was happening, and that vague unease had them on edge.

If only he was here...

If only that guy was around...

Yuka and Shizuku's thoughts turned in the same direction. They looked at the western sky, one man on their minds. He was ruthless, not always pleasant, and unbelievably blunt, but he was also the one person they knew they could trust.

⁌⁌ ⁌⁌ ⁌⁌ ⁌⁌ ⁌⁌ ⁌⁌ ⁌⁌ ⁌⁌ ⁌⁌ ⁌⁌ ⁌⁌ ⁌⁌ ⁌⁌ ⁌⁌

A number of figures stood in a wide, dimly-lit room. They looked like wraiths in the darkness. They were completely still, no one so much as twitching.

Farther inside, a short distance away, stood two others. Unlike the rest, they seemed human. Not sane, perhaps, but at least human.

There was a crazed look in their eyes.

"The preparations are finally complete. I'm getting excited. The moment I've been waiting for is almost here. I'm truly glad I was called to this world! I know now what happiness is!"

Laughter rang through the room. Although the voice spoke of happiness, its tone dripped malice. The speaker was clearly mad.

The figure next to them stared with cold eyes. They obviously didn't see the speaker as a comrade, but they too grinned cruelly.

⁌⁌ ⁌⁌ ⁌⁌ ⁌⁌ ⁌⁌ ⁌⁌ ⁌⁌ ⁌⁌ ⁌⁌ ⁌⁌ ⁌⁌ ⁌⁌ ⁌⁌ ⁌⁌

Around the same time, something happened in the kingdom on the continent's southern tip.

A massive army of monsters stood in formation. They were easily ten thousand strong. Waves of power rolled off them. Each monster was as powerful as the ones at the bottom of the Great Orcus Labyrinth. They could trample anything in their way.

Surprisingly, their numbers contained a few horseback riders. It was clear this gathering was no unorganized mob.

A single, massive monster descended from the heavens and landed before them. Its gleaming white scales looked majestic in the sunlight. A humanoid figure rode on its back. His red hair fluttered in the wind, and the men below cheered.

"The demon king has received a divine revelation! He has given our armies a single command... Destroy the heretics."

Although the man's voice was dignified, it was tinged with insanity.

The army burst into cheers.

"It is time we show them the strength of our faith. Let's teach the fools strutting about the Northern Continent who the true rulers of this land are!"

The monsters stamped the ground so hard the earth shook.

Interestingly, the figures hidden in the dim room spoke at the same time.

"Now then, let us begin. To achieve happiness, we must carve our story into the annals of history! Let me hear your war cries! It's time we fight, for the sake of our lord!"

•ı• •ı• •ı• •ı• •ı• •ı• •ı• •ı• •ı• •ı• •ı• •ı•

Eight thousand meters above sea level, a giant steel spire rose from the peak of the Divine Mountain. A weak groan echoed in one of its prison cells. Blood dripped from Aiko Hatayama's fingers. She stared at the ground, her brow furrowed in concentration.

She had drawn a magic circle with her own blood, and chanted dozens of different spells, but no matter how hard she tried, no matter which spell she chose, the shackles on her wrists cut off her flow of mana.

She slumped and looked down at her hands. They bore dozens of small cuts, one for each attempt.

"How many times do I have to tell you, it's futile?"

"Ah..."

Aiko shivered at the mechanical voice next to her. She looked up and saw a nun wearing a hood low over her eyes. The woman carried a tray of food.

Noticing that the nun had left the door open when she entered, Aiko made a mad dash for freedom.

"I believe I already told you it was futile."

"Agh!"

The nun punched Aiko in the stomach. The attack came so fast Aiko didn't even seen it. She gasped in pain and crashed into the wall.

"L-Let me out of here. What do you plan to do to my students?"

The nun didn't react. She robotically placed the food in the room and walked out.

"Wait! Please wait! At least tell me if my students are safe!"

The nun slowly closed the door, her expression unchanged. Just before she shut it completely, she stopped.

"This is the will of my lord. There is nothing you, who have been removed from the game, need to know."

With an air of finality, the nun shut the door.

Aiko struggled to her knees and cursed her own powerlessness. Something terrible could happen to her students, and she wouldn't know. Even though she was their teacher, she couldn't do anything to help.

Her thoughts turned to the boy who'd overturned one hopeless situation after another back in Ur. She looked at the moon through the small skylight, and murmured his name.

"Nagumo-kun..."

•/• •/• •/• •/• •/• •/• •/• •/• •/• •/• •/• •/• •/•

The nun heard Aiko's whisper as she left. She walked onto a nearby terrace and looked down at the ground below.

"Come if you dare, you anomaly. It will mean your end if you do."

The monster of the abyss continued onward to a place of betrayals, madness, and divinity.

It was as if he was guided by fate itself.

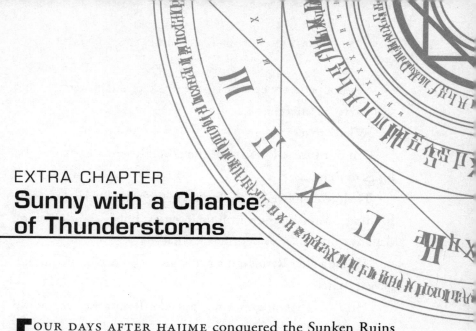

Sunny with a Chance of Thunderstorms

FOUR DAYS AFTER HAJIME conquered the Sunken Ruins of Melusine, the party was still resting at Remia and Myu's house.

It was pretty big by Erisen's standards, but still just a house. True, there were enough rooms for everyone, but the bathroom, laundry room, and other chambers weren't huge. The bathroom had a single shower, which was enchanted to take seawater from the ocean and convert it to freshwater. There was only enough space for two people.

Today, Tio and Shea were taking a shower together. Yue and Kaori had already finished theirs. Although they were always at each other's throats, they tended to group up for things like that. Tio found their relationship rather interesting.

"Hm? What's this?" Shea stopped undressing and turned to see what Tio was looking at, her rabbit ears tilting forward inquisitively.

Tio stooped between the clothes baskets and picked up what seemed to be a notebook.

"What's that?"

"I'm not sure. I found it in the corner there... Perhaps it belongs to Remia?"

Tio looked it over. It was bound in high-quality leather. Such bindings were common in human cities, but Tio didn't think dagons would have something like that.

"Was it a gift? Remia-san's really pretty, so maybe an admirer gave it to her."

"Hmm... That does seem plausible. I suppose we should return—huh?!"

Tio idly opened the notebook. When she saw what was written there, she froze.

"Tio-san? What's the matt—whaaaaaaaaaaaaah?!"

Shea came over and took a peek at the contents. In the notebook they'd thought belonged to Remia was written: *Yue's Diary.*

Tio and Shea stared at those two words in silence. Yue had never mentioned that she kept a diary, and no one had ever seen her writing.

After all, Yue didn't speak much. That wasn't to say that she didn't join in conversations, or play pranks, but she was certainly quieter than the others. If they read her diary, they would finally have a window into her enigmatic mind.

Tio and Shea gulped nervously, then exchanged glances.

"I know other people shouldn't rifle through someone's diary simply to satisfy their own curiosity..."

"Yeah, you're right. It's the most tactless thing you could do."

The pair nodded. They both agreed it was rude.

"But let's read it anyway!"

"This time, my curiosity is too great!"

Still, they also had no tact.

Shea was buck naked, and Tio was half-undressed. They squatted over the diary and flipped through the pages.

"Hmm... It seems Yue found this notebook at the end of the Great Orcus Labyrinth."

"Yeah. It looks like she wanted to start her own diary after reading Oscar-san's. That way, she'd have a written record of her travels with Hajime-san."

"However, it looks like she's too embarrassed to tell Master. If even he is unaware of this, it stands to reason that we wouldn't know."

Tio and Shea discussed Yue's reason for starting a diary. The next few pages were filled with accounts of special training Yue had done with Hajime, her night life with Hajime, her conversations with Hajime, the food she ate with Hajime, watching Hajime transmute things, surprising Hajime with sex, making Hajime's clothes, Hajime's sleeping habits, spending time with Hajime in the bath, Hajime's fetishes, Hajime's weak points, Hajime's...

"She's way too clingy!"

Over 90 percent of it was about Hajime. It basically detailed their month-long honeymoon. In just a few pages, Shea and Tio were throwing up. Naturally, they threw up sugar and rainbows, not vomit.

"Ugh. I feel like this is just rubbing their relationship in my face. Is all of it like this? Just accounts of her flirting with Hajime-san?"

"W-well, it might be... Wait, Shea, look, they're finally about to leave Orcus' house. Start from the part that says 'Our adventure starts here.'"

"Oooh, that means Reisen Gorge is next! That's where they met me! Hee hee hee... I wonder what Yue-san wrote about me?"

Shea urged Tio to turn the page, trepidation and excitement mixing on her face.

"No need to be so impatient," Tio said with a smile, and turned the page.

—O Month. X Day.
We found a worthless rabbit in the wild. I can't imagine
her having any value.

"Stop treating me like some kind of animal! And quit calling me worthless!" Shea slapped the diary. Tio calmed her down and continued.

—O Month. X Day.
I'm in charge of training the worthless rabbit. She's totally
in love with Hajime. I can understand why... He looked
really cool when he talked down the elders at Verbergen.
Still, I don't like the tricks she uses to get close to him. I'm
gonna trap her in ice again today...

—*O Month. X Day.*

I haven't been able to spend much time with Hajime these past few days. It's all this worthless rabbit's fault. I think I'll trap her in ice. I am Yue, a woman who never goes easy on crafty rabbits, even in training. Actually, this fog is pretty thick. Maybe I can kidnap Hajime without anyone noticing?

"Ugh, I definitely remember being frozen in ice every day. And could she stop calling me worthless and crafty all the time?"

"Shea, shouldn't you be more worried about the last thing she wrote? She was planning to kidnap our master."

Tio shuddered as she read about Shea's ten days of hellish training. She turned the page.

—*O Month. X Day.*

This worthless rabbit's surprisingly tough. She starts crying at the littlest thing, but she hasn't given up. The fire in her pale blue eyes burns bright. I can't help but admire her a little. That kind of pisses me off. Well, I guess I'll just trap her in ice again. Also, I'm running out of Hajimenium. I'm starting to suffer from withdrawal symptoms. I'm going to ride him all night once this rabbit's training is done. I am Yue, a woman who never lets her prey escape.

"Yue-san... I never knew you admired me... Hee hee hee!"

"You're looking at the wrong thing again, Shea. Our

poor master is about to be hunted down. What even *is* this 'Hajimenium'?!"

Shea blushed, but Tio grew even more worried as she read on. She flipped another page.

—*O Month. X Day.*
Hajime was delicious.

"She hunted him down! She really did it! When did she have time for that?! Poor Master... He was assaulted in the thick fog..."

Tio was beginning to pity Hajime, and fear Yue. She turned the page again.

—*O Month. X Day.*
I lost to Shea. I actually lost. I lost to a worthless rabbit.
How? What on earth is she? This doesn't make any sense.
She's crazy. She threw entire trees at me. She knocked
down my magic with her hammer, and every time she
jumped, the earth shook. This can't be happening...

"She's totally lost it! I've never seen her write like this...or talk like this! Is this really the same Yue?!"

"W-was it really that shocking to lose to me, Yue-san?"

Tio looked shaken. Shea, too, froze in shock. She couldn't believe the one glancing blow she landed by sheer luck had depressed Yue that badly. She wondered how much more shocking it must have been when Shea confessed.

Frankly, she was scared to keep reading. Still, Tio flipped the page.

—*O Month. X Day.*
We left the sea of trees and headed for the Reisen Gorge. In just half a month, we've already obtained a new comrade... The bunny girl sleeping next to me right now. She's sleeping so peacefully. Honestly, it's like she doesn't have a care in the world. She must have suffered a lot to make it this far. How can she still look so cheerful? Come to think of it, even when she begged us for help, she still looked just fine. She's always like that. Even in the most desperate situations, she's full of energy, serious, and earnest. This girl is strong. Her spirit is unbreakable... More so than mine, really. I think that's why I let her come with us, and confess to Hajime. She's still inexperienced, but depending on how this labyrinth goes...

"......"
Tio silently turned the page. There were tears in Shea's eyes.

—*O Month X Day.*
I hate Miledi.

"What happened to the serious tone from earlier?!"
"I mean, she was *really* annoying!"

—O Month. X Day.

Shea worked really hard. She's definitely one of us now.
I'm too embarrassed to say this to her face, so I'll write it
down here: she's like the little sister I wish I always had.
She's like my best friend, too. I'll protect Shea's future from
here on out. I won't let anyone take anything important
from her.

"Yue...san..."

"What a discovery. Yue is as fond of you as she is of Master."

A waterfall of tears ran down Shea's face. They dripped to the
floor in a steady rivulet. She'd never realized Yue cared so much.
Obviously, she'd known Yue treasured her, but not to that extent.
She wanted to run out and give Yue a giant hug, but she was still
naked, so she couldn't.

Tio gently patted Shea's head. After Shea calmed down, Tio
turned the page once more.

—O Month. X Day.

We found a deadbeat wild dragon. I never knew dragons
were this pathetic. She's a hopeless pervert. I can't believe I
looked up to their species once.

"Bwah?!"

"Tio-san?! Get a hold of yourself! It's not as bad as it sounds!"

Normally, Tio enjoyed being insulted, but insulting her
entire race just hurt, especially right after Yue wrote all those

nice things about Shea. Tio wanted to run out and prostrate herself before Yue to apologize for ruining her image of dragonmen.

—*O Month. X Day.*
The world knows about Hajime's strength now. The people from the Holy Church didn't look happy at all. Our journey's going to get a lot rougher from here. It's possible the Holy Church will declare him a heretic. Oh, and we can't forget Hajime kissed his teacher. Teacher-student relationships sound...fascinating. I will become Yue-sensei, the teacher who hunts students after school.

"No, don't!"
"You can't!"
The entries got funny again.

—*O Month. X Day.*
This dragon's even more perverted than I thought. I'm sure she's beyond saving. Still, I can tell she's trying to get to know us. I like that part of her. And the more I talk to her, the more I realize that she's actually really smart. Though it's kind of creepy how she sometimes looks at us like she's our mom. I don't think that's part of her weird fetish. It seems like she's remembering something really important to her when she looks at us. Like me, she lost her country and comrades... I'll need to ask her for that story sometime.

*What did she feel when she watched her country burn?
How does she plan on living from here on out? I'm sure
she'll tell me if I ask, but I'll wait a little bit. I haven't
opened up to her enough for that kind of question. She's
been open with us this whole time, so I have to do the same
before I go any further. Also, is it just me, or does she actually like being punished by Hajime? I-I am Yue! I may not
be able to change pain into pleasure, but nothing anyone
does to me can kill me! I can take it, Hajime!*

"Please don't!" Shea cried, as though to Yui herself. "If he actually beat you until you nearly died, he'd be a psycho!"

"......"

Tio just stared at the pages. She scratched her cheek awkwardly, not sure what to say. She was happy Yue thought so highly
of her, but she didn't know how to express her thoughts in words.

"Tio-san, let's keep reading."

Tio looked up to see Shea staring right at her. She'd read the
pages too. But Shea didn't say anything else, instead gazing gently
at Tio.

Now that I think about it, Shea is no different. She'd lost her
homeland and most of her family as well, but Tio understood
now that Yue had her own reasons not to ask either of them for
more information. Yue was waiting until she could share with
them before delving deeper.

"You're right. Let's keep going." Tio had also begun to cry.

—O Month. X Day.
I want a kid.

"Seriously?!"
"She even underlined it!"
She probably didn't like that Myu never called her Mommy, Shea thought.
Yue's frustration was evident in her handwriting. She'd pushed down on her pen really hard; they could see the marks it left on the page.

—O Month. X Day.
Myu's so cute. I want a kid. I want a kid. Specifically,
Hajime's kid. I really want one. Like, really want one. I
love Hajime, and I want his kid. I want a kid, I want a
kid, I want...

"Sh-she spent a whole five pages writing that..."
"Sh-she's actually insane. Only a madman would write something like this! Yue-san, I never knew you were a *yandere*!"
Tio's hands trembled. Cold sweat poured down Shea's back, and her rabbit ears pressed firmly against her head.

—O Month. X Day.
A wild Kaori appeared. I thought she was spineless, but
she's surprisingly determined. I like her spirit, so I guess
I'll crush her head-on. Also, I still want Hajime's kid.

*I am Yue. I won't hold back against any love rival, no
matter how weak.*

"Are we all just wild animals to Yue-san?"

"I'm more worried about her obsession with having Master's
child. How badly does she want a baby? We're in the middle of
conquering the labyrinths... Now's not the time to get pregnant!
I hope Yue understands that too... But the more I read, the more
scared I am that an entry will say 'I got pregnant.'"

"I-I get what you mean. Yue-san does do it an awful lot with
Hajime-san."

"Resisting her is futile."

Even the monster of the abyss stood no chance of beating
her. Yue, the vampire princess, was at her most dangerous when
seducing someone. Nothing could stand against her when she
was on the prowl.

Trembling in fear, Shea and Tio continued reading.

"Shea. Tio."

"Huh?!"

They stiffened in terror when they suddenly heard a voice
behind them. Their heads turned, creaking like badly-oiled
doors.

"Y-Y-Y-Y-Yue-san?! How long have you been there?!"

"Th-this isn't what it looks like, Yue! We didn't mean for this
to happen!"

Yue's merciless gaze bored into them.

"Did you read it?"

They couldn't answer. All they could do was sit there, trembling in fear.

Yue silently held out her hand. She seemed to want her diary back. Tio held it out reverently, as though it were some holy artifact. Yue took it and put it in her pocket. Then, both Shea and Tio prostrated themselves at her feet.

"We're so sorry!" they exclaimed simultaneously.

She made them raise their heads and shrugged.

"It's partly my fault for leaving it here. Don't worry about it."

They hadn't expected her to forgive them, so they felt even guiltier. They tried to apologize again, but Yue interrupted.

"Anyway, did you two finish showering?"

"Huh? O-oh... Not yet."

"W-we...were about to go in when we spotted this..."

For some reason, Yue's question scared them. They had an ominous premonition of what was to come.

"I see..." Yue replied, her golden hair beginning to flutter. "I am Yue. I won't hold back, even against my best friend or the woman I look up to."

The pair bolted. Shea tackled the bathroom wall, grabbing a bath towel to wrap around herself on the way. Tio hurriedly deployed a barrier behind her, then restored Remia's wall with her newly acquired magic. The two were in perfect sync.

They knew they needed to run until Yue's wrath finally subsided. Unfortunately, before they even made it a few paces, dark clouds rolled in, and thunder dragons filled the sky.

Shea and Tio's screams were loud enough for all Erisen to hear.

Yue opened her notebook and pulled a miniature pen from her pocket.

—*O Month. X Day.*
Today's weather, sunny with a chance of thunderstorms.
All in all, a good day.

She snapped her notebook shut, nodded in satisfaction, and went out to retrieve the companions she'd burnt to a crisp.

Tales From Arifureta: The Match Sellers

THE MATCH-SELLING BUNNY GIRL...

"Does anyone need matches? Matches for saaale!"

One harsh winter evening, a bunny girl wandered the streets, selling matches. Her weak voice rang out through the snow, and her ears drooped in the cold.

"Please, someone, buy my matches! Doesn't anyone need matches?"

She'd already spent half the day walking the streets, peddling her wares. She was so numb from the cold that she could barely walk. Her cries were practically a plea for help.

"Why won't anyone lend a poor bunny girl their ear...? I'm so cold!"

The bunny girl ducked into a nearby alley, hoping to get out of the wind and snow. But the dark, dingy alley provided no shelter for her frozen heart.

"*Sniff!* At this rate, I'll freeze to death. I guess I should use a match to warm myself up."

The bunny girl took out one of her matches. Just as she was about to light it, she noticed someone staring at her. A white-haired boy with an eyepatch was watching from the main street. Thinking she might finally have found a customer, the bunny girl called out to him.

"Would you like to buy a match?!"

The boy looked at her as if she were some strange creature. "Aren't you cold? You're shivering."

Of course I'm cold! I'm freezing to death here! So buy my freaking matches! The bunny girl once again tried to sell her wares to the boy.

"How about you put on some clothes?"

Indeed, despite the fact that it was the dead of winter, the bunny girl was dressed very skimpily. Her outfit was the main reason the villagers avoided her.

The scantily-clad bunny girl's eyes opened wide in surprise.

"How did I never realize?!"

I can just wear more layers! Her ears perked up.

The match-selling dragon pervert...

It was evening, in the dead of winter. A beautiful older woman shuffled down the street, carrying a basket full of matches.

"Ugh... I couldn't sell any matches today, either."

She hung her head, and a few people spared her pitying glances.

"It's far too cold out tonight. I suppose I have no choice but to light these matches to warm myself."

The woman stepped into an alleyway and lit one of her matches. The fire's gentle light warmed her frozen hands. However, the fire lasted only a brief moment before going out. The woman groaned. It seemed she would have to do something she'd hoped to avoid.

"Ascend in a swirling vortex of crimson fire—Blaze Tempest!"

A burning pillar of fire erupted in front of her. She hadn't wanted to use magic, but it was too cold not to. Don't ask why someone who could use fire magic was selling matches.

Finally warm, the woman let out a contended sigh.

"I found her! She's over there! You do this every night, you crazy pyromaniac! I'm taking you in! Men, tie her up!"

"Wh-what?!"

A horde of angry policemen surrounded the match-selling pyromaniac. She tried to run, but one officer, a young white-haired boy with an eyepatch, grabbed her and started spanking her. Despite being punished, she looked oddly happy.

Remember, kids, if you start fires in the middle of a city, you're likely to get arrested. So, don't be an arsonist.

The match-selling vampire princess...

"Do you want to buy some matches? You do, right? You absolutely want these matches."

It was a cold, windy night, and the girl pushed matches onto anyone who passed by. She had golden-blonde hair, red eyes, and a stunning figure. Most of the men nearby were more interested in her than the matches. However, if you didn't buy them, this beautiful girl would crush your balls. As most people weren't interested in exploring the world of extreme masochism, they gladly bought her matches. Thanks to that, the vampire girl did booming business. Even women weren't spared her wrath.

"Want some matches?"

"Huh? No, not really..."

"......"

The girl stared pointedly at a mother until she finally gave in.

"I-I'll take a box."

"......"

"I-I mean two boxes... No, three boxes, please..."

"Good. Thank you for your purchase."

The poor woman bought a box for each of her kids as well. At least the children seemed excited to have matches to play with. As she walked away, the vampire girl spotted her next mark. A white-haired boy wearing an eyepatch. She thought he struck a rather handsome figure.

"Would you like to buy some match—actually, would you like to buy me?"

She suddenly changed what she was selling. Most people would be suspicious of a girl abruptly volunteering to sell herself. The boy sensed that she was up to something and quickly walked away.

"Would you like to buy me?"

Unfortunately, he was unable to escape.

The match-selling demon...

"W-would you like to buy some matches?"

A girl stood on the street corner, selling matches. She seemed somewhat flustered.

At a glance, she just seemed desperate for customers. However, her gaze wasn't focused on the people milling about, but at a spot farther down the street. In fact, she made no motion to offer her matches to the people walking past.

Suddenly, the match-seller hid behind a nearby lamppost. Blushing, she peeked out to stare at that same spot down the street. She was acting extremely suspicious.

A passing child pointed to her. "Look, mommy, it's that girl again! She's always standing there..."

"Shh! Don't look at her. Don't talk to her either! She's a stalker!"

The match-seller didn't even notice the insult.

Finally, the boy she was waiting for appeared. He had white hair and wore an eyepatch.

"I-I can do this! Today's finally the day I'll sell him a match and confess to him!"

There was no particular reason that she needed to sell him a match to confess, but she was too panicked to realize that.

"Huh? Wait... What's this? He's not alone?"

As she pumped herself up, the match-selling stalker noticed something. Upon closer inspection, there was another matchgirl hanging off his arm. The stalker's face went blank, and the light went out of her eyes. Her nervousness forgotten, she marched boldly up to the white-haired boy.

"Hm? Who're you?" his companion asked.

"That's what I want to know! I'm the only match-seller he needs."

"Oh? So, you say you're the only match-seller worthy of him? Let me show you just how fleeting your life could be. You'll vanish faster than the flame on a match!"

Why they were so hung up on being match-sellers, no one knew.

The pair struck grandiose poses. A giant thunder dragon appeared behind one match-seller, while a demonic swordsman with a frightening mask appeared behind the other.

"Hee hee hee hee hee!"

"Aha ha ha ha!"

Their ominous laughter rang through the streets. There would be a fierce blizzard tonight. Oh... And the white-haired boy had long since gone home.

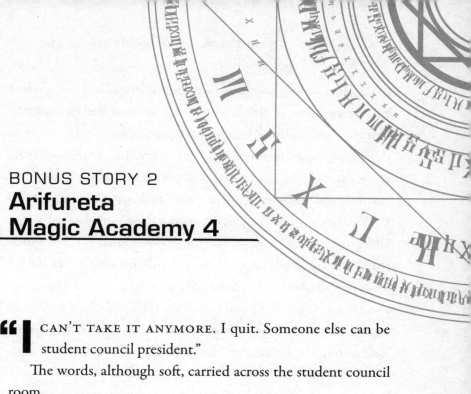

BONUS STORY 2
Arifureta
Magic Academy 4

"I CAN'T TAKE IT ANYMORE. I quit. Someone else can be student council president."

The words, although soft, carried across the student council room.

The other council members and the council advisor all stiffened. An unnatural silence followed.

Urged by his fellow members' piercing stares, Vice President Kouki Amanogawa hesitantly called to the president. "Sh-Shizuku? What's wrong? Did something happen?"

Shizuku's expression was unreadable, hidden by her bangs. "You want to know if something happened?"

Kouki quailed at her thunderous tone. The secretary, Eri Nakamura; accountant, Suzu Taniguchi; and advisor, Aiko Hatayama, flinched as well. Shizuku pointed to the stack of documents on her desk.

"Why don't you tell me what *didn't* happen? This is a stack of complaints people lodged against the academy. No other student council president in this academy's history ever had to deal with so many. And *this* stack is orders to repair, replace, and strengthen destroyed school facilities. That stack over there is order forms to replace goods taken without permission during academy events. Finally, that stack over there is receipts for events we've held. Worse, a certain teacher's...*and* a certain student's...fan clubs have grown so large that their club budget is greater than the sports club budgets are! Oh, and I almost forgot. See *this*? A student sent this letter. He's asking how he can steal Yue-sensei away from Nagumo. Apparently, if we don't reply, he'll bomb the school. There are hundreds more like that... Dozens for all the girls surrounding Nagumo. Hee hee... Our students are certainly wonderful young adults, don't you agree? Hee hee hee..."

Suzu and Eri shrunk back and hugged each other as Shizuku rattled off her problems. Aiko collapsed when she heard Shizuku's deranged laughter.

"C-calm down, Shizuku. I'm sure...I'm sure it'll be all right! We're here for you. We'll pull through this somehow—"

"Somehow?! You mean you'll make me do even more work, right?! Ha ha ha... Kouki, you really need to get better at telling jokes. Say that again and I'll kill you."

"Ahhh!"

Kouki crumbled. No one could blame him. Shizuku looked ready to go off on anyone who so much as looked in her direction. The accumulated stress of managing the student council had finally caught up to her. However, Shizuku was, above all, rational. When she saw her friends flinching away from her gaze, she realized she'd been unreasonable. She cleared her throat and tried to calmly—

Before she could say anything, the door slid open. The head of the public morals committee, Ryutarou Sakagami, walked inside, a stack of papers in his hands.

"Hey, Shizuku. Yue-sensei and the others blew up the school again. Here are all the complaints and—"

"I'll kill them."

With that ominous proclamation, Shizuku picked up her katana and stomped to the door. Everyone present knew she would really do it.

"St-stop, Shizuku!"

"Calm down, Shizushizu."

"Someone call a healer! We need someone who can heal broken hearts!"

"Sakagami-kun! Defend that doorway like your life depends on it! We can't let Yaegashi-san get out while she's like this."

Kouki tried to pin Shizuku's arms behind her, while Suzu and Eri held her back. Aiko hung onto Shizuku's sword arm for dear life. Sweating profusely, Ryutarou prepared to give his life to stop the student council president.

"Hmph! Let me go. Let me go, I said. I won't be satisfied until I've killed them at least once! They need to taste my pain!"

"You can't kill someone more than once! Besides, they'll be dead, so they won't be able to taste your pain!"

Kouki was absolutely correct. However, Shizuku really was at her limit. Taking care of Yue and the others' fights, then cleaning up after the riots each girl's respective fan club caused, had left her utterly exhausted. Sounds of fighting filled the student council room for a while. Finally, the dust settled, and Shizuku stood amidst a sea of corpses. Her enemies defeated, Shizuku declared, "Student council president elections are now open."

Translation: "I'm sick and tired of dealing with this! Someone else can handle these problems now!"

Kouki tried to talk her out of quitting, but Shizuku refused to listen. In a few days, she'd already set up special elections to decide the next president. At times like this, her unparalleled organizational skills shone. The candidates for the next student council president were as follows:

Candidate 1 — Yue

"If I am elected president, I promise to designate a room all students can have sex in."

The students' expressions stiffened when they learned that a teacher, of all people, was running for *student* council president.

Candidate 2 — Shea Haulia

"I want to make a government of the rabbit ears, for the rabbit ears, by the rabbit ears! In other words, turn the government into me and Hajime-san's love nest!"

The students retorted that no one would vote for somebody who clearly planned to use the student council for her own gain.

Candidate 3 — Kaori Shirasaki

"I-I'll do my best in Shizuku-chan's place! I promise to open a suggestion box where everyone can put opinions and requests. I know that, with Hajime-kun's help, the two of us will be able to make the academy a better place!"

Kaori was apparently planning on having only Hajime in her student council. The students sighed. They could easily tell what she was really after.

Candidate 4 — Perverted Dragon Headmistress

"If I am elected, I will make Mas—ahem, I mean, Hajime Nagumo—student council president! After that, I will utilize my powers as headmistress to turn the student council room into the headmistress' office! No one is allowed to—ah! Hey! Stop throwing things at me! Wh-who did that?! And who's firing advanced magic at me?!"

The students hurled insults at her. "Go back to your cave, you perverted dragon!"

Needless to say, Tio found said insults highly arousing.

In the end, the election resulted in Shizuku Yaegashi being chosen to serve another term. Because of the special election rules she herself had set up, she had no right to refuse the appointment. When Shizuku saw the results, she threw a tantrum.

"Noooooooooooooooooooooooooooooo! That does it—I'm dropping ouuuuuuuuuuuuuut!"

After her infantile outburst, she tried to flee.

"Th-the president's trying to run away! Everyone, chase her!"

"Without her, this school's doomed! Capture the president, for the sake of our future!"

"Guys, surround her! We've gotta make sure she can't escape!"

"This is an announcement for all little sisters of this school!

Launch the oneesama disciplinary squad! There will be a prize waiting for whoever can console her! Furthermore, you are permitted to take advantage of the chaos and touch her!"

The entire student body pursued Shizuku. Their fervor was surely a sign of how much they loved her.

However, despite her childlike tantrum, Shizuku was a crafty woman. She evaded her pursuers for a good three days and nights. Finally, after a concentrated effort combining the talents of the entire student body, they captured her. Her great escape was so impressive that international leaders applauded her skills. Unfortunately, that also meant her status as student council president was set in stone.

"I swear, I'll kill you all someday," Shizuku Yaegashi muttered to herself as she nursed a headache and started on today's pile of paperwork. She truly was the academy's hardest worker.

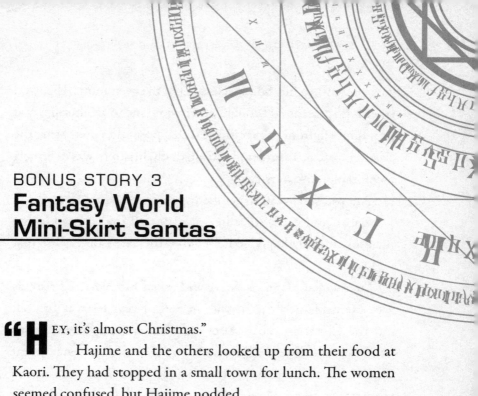

Fantasy World Mini-Skirt Santas

"**H**EY, it's almost Christmas."

Hajime and the others looked up from their food at Kaori. They had stopped in a small town for lunch. The women seemed confused, but Hajime nodded.

"Oh, yeah, you're right... At least, on Earth, it would be."

"Hee hee! Last year's school Christmas party was pretty fun. You only stayed for a bit, but at least we took pictures, and exchanged presents..."

Kaori smiled as she reminisced. Hajime, too, smiled faintly as he thought back to his days in Japan. Yue's eyebrows twitched. Shea grumbled to herself, while Tio smiled knowingly. Myu simply watched them with a blank expression on her face.

"Yeah, I definitely remember you and Yaegashi blocking the door and begging me to take a picture with you. Thanks to that, the whole class hated me on Christmas. Afterwards, even though it was supposed to be a Secret Santa exchange, you gave your presents to me. So, the class hated me even more. Then you jacked the present I'd brought and invited me to an after-party at your house in front of everyone. At that point, I'm pretty sure the class was ready to murder me. Yeah, that Christmas was definitely memorable. Also, terrifying."

"Are you sure we're remembering the same party?!"

Kaori couldn't believe her ears. But all the events Hajime mentioned really happened. He honestly feared for his life that night.

Yue tugged Hajime's sleeve and asked him what Christmas was. He explained that it was an end-of-year festival and left out the Christian roots. After all, what was important about Christmas was that a jolly man in a strange costume went around that night, giving presents to the good kids. That, and all the Christmas cake people ate. Kaori puffed out her cheeks and complained about Hajime's half-assed explanation.

"That's not all, Hajime-kun! If you're going to explain, explain properly. L-Like, mention how it's a holiday for lovers to deepen their bonds."

Kaori blushed at her own words. Yue and the others suddenly looked very interested.

"Hajime, did you do anything with Kaori that night? You know, the kinds of things lovers might do?"

"I already mentioned everything I did at that party. Back then, I just thought of Kaori as a troublemaker. There was no way I would have ended up spending Christmas alone with her. If I had... I probably wouldn't be standing here now."

"Th-that's mean, Hajime-kun!"

It hurt to have Hajime denounce her so casually. Worse, Hajime didn't seem moved at all by her pleading gaze.

"That's my line, you airheaded troublemaker. It would have been even worse if you'd only invited *me* to that after-party of yours, but as it was, that still caused me a huge headache. Especially considering the way you were dressed. I thought for sure you were out to kill me."

"O-out to kill you? Why would I do that?"

Wondering what Hajime meant, Kaori tearfully searched through her memories. *The way I was dressed? What was I even wearing that day? Oh, yeah...*

"U-umm... If I recall correctly, I was dressed in a Santa costume."

Kaori had indeed been dressed in a Santa outfit the day of the party. That in itself wouldn't have been a problem. Santa costumes were pretty common during Christmas. Kaori tilted her head, wondering what was wrong with her outfit. Hajime sighed. The worst part of all this was that he knew now that Kaori hadn't actually meant anything malicious by it.

"Back when you asked me how you looked, I just said it suited you. That was because I didn't want the other students to kill me. However, I'll be honest with you now. That costume of yours was really erotic."

"E-erotic?! You really thought that?!"

"Uh, yeah? Your skirt was so short I thought I might see your panties. There were heart-shaped cut-outs on the shirt, so

I could easily see your cleavage, *and* it was sleeveless. Plus, it fit so tightly I could see all your curves. Do you even know how many guys Yaegashi had to put down because they couldn't control themselves?"

Kaori buried her face in her hands. She was red all the way to the tips of her ears. She'd worn that outfit because her friends (mostly Suzu) had told her that she'd be able to make any man fall for her. Her delusions of snaring Hajime had given her the courage to wear such an embarrassing costume. When she thought back, she realized just how bold she'd been. But she didn't have too long to sit there squirming, because Shea and the others chose that moment to butt in.

"You really are crafty, Kaori-san. Really crafty. To think you tried to use revealing clothes to make Hajime-san fall for you. You're a natural-born terrorist!" Shea sniffed.

I don't want to hear that from you. You wear even less than that normally, thought Kaori.

"Hmm. I understand now. You wore a revealing outfit on purpose, so you could get off to everyone calling you a pervert. You are even more of a deviant than I am."

I am NOT! Also, there is no way I could ever be more perverted than you!

"You're so red, Kaori-oneechan. You look cute!"

You're cuter than I am, Myu. In fact, you're my only source of healing in this cruel world.

Yue stood up silently, eyes burning with fighting spirit.

"......"

She grabbed Kaori by the collar and dragged her out of the restaurant.

"Y-Yue? Where are you taking me? Actually, wait, let me go! I can walk myself!"

"We're going to buy clothes. Then to fight, seduction against seduction. Santa costume against Santa costume. I'll prove that you're not the only one who can be an erotic Santa."

"I never claimed I was! And I'm not that big a pervert! Stop lumping me in with you!"

"Heh."

"Hey, what was that laugh for?! Tell me, Yue!"

But Yue ignored her. Realizing what was about to happen, Shea and Tio followed them out. They took Myu, and left Hajime to pay the bill.

That evening, five figures in Santa outfits stood in front of Hajime. Aside from Myu, all of their outfits were revealing. Mini-skirts and sleeveless shirts abounded.

"Hmm. What do you think, Hajime?"

Yue twirled around, her skirt rising dangerously high. Shea and Tio struck alluring poses, emphasizing their massive breasts.

"Well, they do look good on you guys, but... If I saw you on the street, I'd think you were perverts."

"Huh?!"

Yue, Shea, and Tio stiffened. They turned to Kaori, who tried her best to cover herself with her hands. Kaori averted her gaze.

"You planned this, didn't you?"

"I didn't! In fact, I'm the one who told you guys not to do

this! But you kept insisting! And now I'm stuck wearing this too... It's so embarrassing!"

"Doesn't matter! This is your fault. Now pay for making Hajime sigh at us!"

Yue called forth a fierce tempest. Kaori had no real defense to speak of. She could only watch as her skirt flipped all the way up.

"Stop! He'll see my pantieeees! Ugh, fine, if this is how you want to play... Divine Shackles!"

Kaori pushed her skirt back down and sent chains of light at Yue's skirt.

"Hmph. Not good enough. Tio Barrier!"

"What are you doing? Aaah! They're twisting around me! I've never experienced bondage like this!"

Yue pulled Tio in front of her and used the dragonwoman as a shield. Kaori's chains mercilessly tied Tio up, emphasizing her breasts even more. She started panting heavily. Yue countered with another burst of wind. This too, was aimed at Kaori's skirt.

"Like I'll let you! Shea Barrier!"

"Whaaa?! Hey, Kaori-san!"

Kaori's chains wrapped around Shea and dragged her into the line of fire. Shea's skirt flipped past her stomach, revealing her plump thighs.

"Kaori-san! This is far too embarrassing! Please let me go!"

"Don't worry, the outfit you're usually wearing is just as embarrassing!"

"Hey, what the fuck did you just say, you little bitch?! Are you insulting the traditional dress of the Haulia?!"

Shea ripped off her chains and charged Kaori. Kaori fended her off with Binding Blades of Light.

Freed from her shackles, Tio squared off against Yue.

"If you're going to strip people, then it's only fair for you to be stripped in return!"

Tio grabbed Kaori's depowered chains and looked for an opportunity to flip Yue's skirt. In an inn at a small town in Tortus, four Santas tried their best to disrobe each other.

"Daddy, this coat is all fluffy!"

Meanwhile, Myu enjoyed prancing around in her Santa outfit.

"Myu, please grow up into a better woman than those four."

Hajime patted Myu's head while he watched the four girls try to strip each other by increasingly violent means.

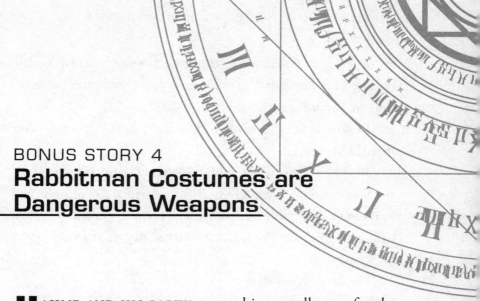

Rabbitman Costumes are Dangerous Weapons

HAJIME AND HIS PARTY stopped in a small town for the night. Despite the town's relatively modest size, there was a surprisingly large amount of people there. The girls looked around happily.

"So, this is the town famous for its textiles. Everyone's clothes look really well-made."

"Mhmm. The weavers here are very skilled."

Yue's crimson eyes darted from person to person. The quality of the cloth she saw impressed her. Back in the abyss, she sewed clothes for herself and Hajime. At first, it took effort to make even the simplest garments, but she'd improved a lot. Sewing had become something of a hobby. Hence her excitement about the rolls of colorful yarn, and the skilled weavers who knitted with them.

Shea and Kaori were quite excited as well. Shea was a master of household chores, so of course, clothes and sewing excited her, while Kaori was a high school girl, interested in fashion. While the others were fascinated by the town, the town was fascinated by Tio. Her exquisitely crafted dress was a traditional dragon-woman garment, rare outside Tio's village.

"Daddy, look at all their different clothes! I've never seen those kinds before!"

"Really...? Come to think of it, what do Dagons usually wear?"

Young though she might be, Myu was still a girl. She was just as interested in clothes as the others. Hajime looked up at the little girl riding his shoulders. She tilted her head and thought for a moment.

"Nothing, usually!"

"You guys are nudists?!"

Hajime noticed the girls' cold stares and quickly cleared his throat. In truth, Dagons usually wore some type of swimsuit, as they spent most of their lives in the water. On land, they put a robe or something over that, but that was about it.

Hajime could see the other girls were about to volunteer to strip for him if he wished. He really didn't want to have that conversation, so he turned to Myu for salvation.

"Do you want anything, Myu? Since we're already here, I can buy you some new clothes."

"I can buy anything?! Ummmm, ummm..."

Eyes sparkling, Myu looked for something. Hajime really did spoil her. Yue and the others stared pointedly. Hajime smiled, and agreed to buy them whatever they wanted too. After a few seconds of searching, Myu stared long and hard at her chosen article of clothing. Specifically, what Yue was wearing.

"Hm? What's wrong, Myu?"

Myu pointed at Yue. "I want what Yue-oneechan is wearing! I want to wear something like that too!"

"You want my clothes? But, Myu, there's so many cuter outfits here."

Yue's dress had frills everywhere and was plenty cute. But she'd designed it for travel and combat, so it wasn't the most elegant piece. However, Myu had seemingly taken a liking to it.

"But you're the coolest, Yue-oneechan! You look awesome when you're fighting with Daddy and using magic and stuff! Even though I'm daddy's daughter, I'm really weak. But maybe if I wear your dress, I'll get stronger!"

"Myu, you're so pure it hurts."

Myu's statement was so cute, it gave Yue a nosebleed. She plucked Myu off Hajime's shoulders and squished her soft cheeks. Myu squealed in protest, but Yue ignored her.

"M-Myu-chan, don't you think I look cool too? I can take out anyone with a single swing of my hammer! Enemies cower before me!"

"Myu-chan, I'm really good at holding enemies back! Here, let me show you my Binding Blades of Light!"

"In that case, allow me to show you the power of my breath. You've yet to see just how amazing I am, correct? My glorious breath will leave you astounded."

Everyone tried to impress the party's little princess. Myu squirmed her way out of Yue's grip and turned around.

"You're not...cool, Shea-oneechan. You're, umm...wild?"

Shea clutched her chest and collapsed with a moan. There was nothing more heartbreaking than being told you weren't cool by a little girl.

"And Kaori-oneechan's...weak."

Kaori clutched her chest and collapsed with a moan. There was nothing more heartbreaking than being told you were a pathetic weakling by a little girl.

"And Tio-oneechan... Y-you're okay!"

"What on earth is that supposed to mean?!" Tio retorted, and collapsed. There was nothing more heartbreaking than being pitied by a little girl.

Three girls lay on the ground in the middle of the town's main street. They looked up simultaneously when they heard footsteps approaching. Yue stood over them, grinning from ear to ear. She was hardly ever so expressive.

Shea and the others slowly got to their feet, their eyes glinting murderously. They had always known she would be the final boss.

Thinking it was her fault that her role models were fighting, Myu hurriedly stepped between them.

"U-umm, you all have really cool clothes too, Shea-oneechan, Kaori-oneechan, Tio-oneechan! So, umm... I know! Let's all trade clothes! That way, we'll all be able to wear each other's! It'll be fun!"

The four women exchanged glances and smiled awkwardly. Their petty rivalry had worried Myu. Hajime smiled, proud of his daughter's attempts to mediate. Then he grinned wickedly and turned to Yue.

"How about it? Why not try out Myu's proposal? You can all draw lots at random and wear whoever's outfit you pull. We're in a town of tailors, so they'll be able to adjust the sizes easily."

Myu looked up at the girls expectantly. There was no refusing her. Yue and the others quickly agreed. With a great deal of money and coercion, Hajime convinced a nearby tailor to make the girls' outfits right away. Once he finished, the girls went into the fitting rooms to change. The store was large, with plenty of other customers around. Hajime stood in front of the changing rooms, waiting to see who came out first.

"Daddy, look, look! I'm Yue-oneechan!"

It turned out to be Myu. She was wearing Yue's clothes. A frilly shirt, black skirt, white coat, and ankle boots. Hajime had to admit she looked cute. She flapped her arms, which were too short for the coat, and struck the same pose Yue did when she cast magic.

"Oh, it looks pretty good on you, Myu. You look more grown-up now."

Myu grinned and blushed.

"Myu, don't open the door while other people are still changing!"

Yue stepped out of the same fitting room. She'd gone in with Myu to help her change. Hajime muttered a soft "Wow..." as he saw Yue's outfit. He wasn't the only one, either. The other customers, and even the tailor who ran the store, were impressed. Yue was wearing Tio's kimono, an eclectic mixture of western and Japanese styles. She looked like a refined, elegant lady in it.

"Th-this is my first time wearing such an outfit... I must say, it's rather embarrassing."

"Your clothes are so frilly, Kaori-san! There's so much cloth, it's hard to move around."

Next came Tio and Shea. Tio wore Myu's one-piece. It was white, and adorned with ribbons and frills. Tio blushed as she looked down at herself. *It's rare to see that perverted dragon embarrassed about anything. Still, she looks cute in that.* Hajime said as much to Tio, which caused her to blush even more furiously and hide behind a clothing rack. The male customers got nosebleeds watching her.

Meanwhile, Shea was in Kaori's priestess clothes. She found the overabundance of cloth uncomfortable, but the outfit accented her figure nicely. Hajime had to admit she looked beautiful. The only one left was Kaori. However, even after a few minutes, she didn't come out.

"Hm? She's still not coming."

"Hmm. Wait here, I'll drag her out."

Yue smiled mischievously and barged into Kaori's changing room. There were a few loud thumps, and Kaori screamed.

"I can't do it! I can't wear Shea's clothes! They're practically underwear!"

"Don't worry about it," Yue replied.

After a moment of silence, the door to Kaori's changing room flew open, and Kaori was thrown out into the wild.

"Ugh, this is soooo embarrassing. Hajime-kun, please don't stare at me..."

Kaori tried to cover herself with her hands as she blushed to the tips of her ears. Rabbitman clothing was quite revealing, and Kaori's slender legs and ample cleavage were on full display. Hajime normally didn't notice the outfit, since Shea didn't seem to care how much skin she exposed. However, Kaori's embarrassment emphasized just how revealing it was. Quite a few customers fainted from blood loss after seeing how sexy she looked. The store became a sea of blood as Yue and the others swapped outfits again and again.

Shea's outfit looked smoking hot on anyone who wore it, and before long, the customers were drowning in their own nosebleeds. Hajime made a mental note to slaughter the men who'd gotten nosebleeds looking at Myu in Shea's outfit later. Once the outfit swap was over, Hajime gave his closing remarks.

"Yeah, I guess Shea's clothes really are sexy."

Traditional or not, they were rather revealing. And so, Hajime reconfirmed what he'd always known, but had forgotten.

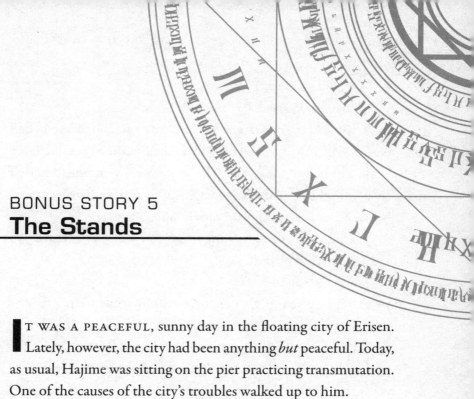

BONUS STORY 5
The Stands

IT WAS A PEACEFUL, sunny day in the floating city of Erisen. Lately, however, the city had been anything *but* peaceful. Today, as usual, Hajime was sitting on the pier practicing transmutation. One of the causes of the city's troubles walked up to him.

"Hajime-kun, can I sit next to you?"

"That you, Kaori? You know you don't have to ask permission for each little thing, right?"

Kaori blushed, and sat down close to him. Extremely close to him. Close enough that Hajime had a hard time concentrating on his transmuting. She was also in her swimsuit.

Hajime turned to Kaori, planning to tell her to respect his personal space, when she was blown off the pier. She flew through the sky, somersaulting multiple times, and fell into the water with a loud splash. Yue walked up and took the spot Kaori had vacated. Although she was expressionless as usual, Hajime could tell she was satisfied. She sat next to Hajime and stretched her bare legs.

"Yue, did you just...?"

"What are you making, Hajime?"

Looks like she's at it again today. Yue pretended she hadn't blown Kaori into the water and looked curiously at Hajime's work. But before she could do much more, Kaori pulled herself back onto the pier. She was dripping wet, and her bangs covered her face like a certain horror movie antagonist.

"Yue, do you have anything to say for yourself? I'll give you one chance to explain."

"Who are you?"

A vein pulsed in Kaori's forehead. Invisible sparks flew as their gazes met.

"Hee hee, you're a funny one, Yue. I can't believe you've forgotten about the girl you just threw into the sea. Is your memory really that bad?"

"Oh. I remember now, you're Kaori. You're so gloomy, I always forget who you are. You should try and do something about that."

"You're the one that needs to fix that leaky brain of yours!"

Kaori and Yue laughed. Yue got to her feet and they glared at each other. As always, strange creatures appeared behind both girls. A massive golden thunder dragon appeared behind Yue, while a demon in a terrifying mask appeared behind Kaori. The dragon let out a ferocious roar; a blizzard whipped around the demon as he tapped his sword against his shoulder. This was the reason Erisen hadn't been peaceful recently. The strange apparitions Yue and Kaori summoned caused it all. Hajime knew what came next. Kaori would yell at Yue for being a bully and attack her. Yue would reply that it was Kaori's fault for being sneaky and fight back. Their little catfights had become quite the spectacle, and many of Erisen's citizens came to watch.

"Look, they're at it again today too. Just what are those things behind them? They look like a dragon and a demon, but how do they appear and disappear like that?"

As Hajime watched them duel with a troubled smile, Shea walked up to him.

"Why do you look so unhappy?" he asked her. "You shouldn't try to understand those apparitions. Just accept them as part of life."

"What are you saying, Hajime-san? Those things only pop up whenever they fight over you. In other words, they're proof of their love!"

"They better not be. What kind of symbol of love is a dragon or demon?"

Shea folded her ears over her head and ignored Hajime's words.

"I love you just as much as they do, so how come I can't summon a love spirit? I want one of those weird apparition thingies too!"

That's what she's unhappy about? Hajime sighed as Shea scrunched up her face and tried to summon something.

"I think I already know, but what are you doing?"

"Trying to summon an apparition, obviously!"

I'm not sure that's something you can bring out by brute force... However, force was the only thing Shea could think to use. What happened to those things being a symbol of love?

Sky-blue mana swirled around Shea, and her hair began to flutter in the breeze. She let out an earth-shattering yell that sent nearby residents scurrying to safety. The sea around the pier grew choppy, and for a moment, Hajime honestly thought she might summon something. But in the end, nothing happened.

"Figures that wouldn't work," Hajime grunted.

"Awww. What a shame." Shea sank to her knees, and her rabbit ears drooped in disappointment. "Is my love not strong enough? No way," she muttered.

Hajime smiled and patted her fluffy ears. He continued playing with them until he was satisfied. "Well, I didn't think you'd be able to summon one of those anyway."

"I don't believe it. Do you doubt my love too, Hajime-san?"

When Hajime started patting Shea, her mood started to improve, but it took a nosedive when he said that. Hajime shook his head.

"I don't really...mean that in a bad way. I think those things are created from negative emotions. They're illusions born from the negative auras those two have."

"Haaah... Really?"

It wasn't a very scientific explanation, but it seemed that Hajime had at least given it some thought. Shea stared blankly at Hajime, wondering where he was going with this. Hajime pulled Shea close and ruffled her ears again.

"Basically, you're not the kind of person who would have one. Besides, even if you don't have a weird illusion behind you, you have two perfectly good bunny ears on top of you. You should be proud of those. At the very least, they're good enough for me."

"Ugh... I wish I had more experience. I never know what to say at times like these. If only I was more feminine..."

Shea blushed and fidgeted absently for a few seconds before deciding to lean into Hajime. Her ears perked up, and she pulled Hajime's hand closer.

"Ha ha. You don't let any opportunity slip by, do you, Shea?"

"Yeah. She got us there. Though it was a splendid surprise attack... I can't believe you would try and surpass your master."

"Huh?!"

Shea's ears shot straight up. She turned around to see Yue and Kaori smiling at her.

"Shaaaaaaaaaaaaaaaaaaaaaaah!"

"Rooooaaaaaaaaaaaaaaaaaaaaaaar!"

Kaori's demon and Yue's dragon growled ominously at her.

Shea bolted. Naturally, Yue and Kaori gave chase. For some reason, Erisen's residents cheered whenever they heard another explosion.

"I'm so glad this city is peaceful."

Rumbling thunder drowned out Hajime's words.

BONUS STORY 6
A Falcon's Daughter
is Still a Falcon

THERE WAS A LOUD BANG, and several flashes of crimson light raced through the sky. Hajime's railgun-accelerated bullets shot straight through the wolf-shaped monsters. Each bullet blew up a monster's head.

"Aww. Thanks to your Artifacts, we only ever get to fight in labyrinths, Hajime-san."

"That's just how it is. Master's Artifacts are so powerful that at long range, they make magic look like a joke."

Shea and Tio chatted while they watched Hajime mow down an entire pack of wolves. Kaori smiled awkwardly.

"I'm not sure you could even call those Artifacts... They're more like weapons out of a sci-fi story."

Yue tilted her head in confusion. "Sci-fi?"

"It's short for 'science fiction.' Basically, stories that are based off of science but aren't very realistic. There are guns in our world, but not the rail guns Hajime-kun's made. You'd only see some-thing like that in books or movies."

"Well, I had to use the cheat known as magic to make them work, so I'd say they're more fantasy than sci-fi."

Hajime walked up to the girls, reloading Donner. He'd al-ready wiped out the monsters. Myu sat on his shoulders. She seemed to be enjoying herself. She had front row seats to a mon-ster massacre, and it appeared she quite liked it.

"Daddy, I want to try using that thing that goes bang!"

Yes, Myu was really enjoying herself.

Kaori, who tended to be sensible about all things not involv-ing Hajime, furrowed her brow.

"Hajime-kun, you're a bad influence on Myu-chan. She's say-ing some really ominous things with a smile on her face now. I'm worried about what kind of woman she'll grow into."

"Well, you've got a point, but...this world's pretty dangerous."

"Yeah. You're being naïve, Kaori. It's kill or be killed. Even if your enemy doesn't look like they'll hurt you, kill them anyway. In fact, if your eyes meet, kill them. It's best to kill at least once a day. You can only get what you want by wading through a sea of blood and climbing over a mountain of corpses. That's the kind of place this world is."

"You're way too bloodthirsty, Yue! We're not in Fist of the North Star! It's true that this world is more dangerous than ours, but it's not *that* violent!"

Yue ignored Kaori and turned to Myu.

"Do you desire strength?" she asked in an imposing voice.

"Wait, Yue, that line's supposed—"

Before Hajime could finish, Myu interrupted.

"I do! I want to make bad people explode like Daddy!"

Yue nodded solemnly. "Very well. Then Hajime shall grant you strength."

She implored Hajime with her gaze to let Myu shoot Donner. Hajime's expression hardened. Not only would letting Myu shoot Donner be dangerous, it really wasn't a good idea to teach a little girl how to kill. He hesitated, a rare display of common sense.

Myu hopped off Hajime's shoulders, ran to Yue, and turned back to Hajime. She looked up at him with pleading eyes, and his common sense vanished.

"All right, you can shoot."

"Don't you think you gave in a little fast?!"

Hajime pulled some ore out of his Treasure Trove and began transmuting. Red sparks flew from his hands. All his guns had too much recoil for Myu, so he made a toy gun she could fire safely. He crafted this gun with even more care than Donner. He named the newly-forged toy gun Donna. It wasn't strong enough to kill anything, but was still powerful enough to have some fun. The toy revolver's exquisite craftsmanship showed just how skilled a Synergist Hajime really was. Myu's eyes sparkled as she looked at it. It was as if she'd received the birthday present she'd always wanted, although not many four-year-old girls wanted a revolver.

"All right, Myu, I'm gonna teach you how to shoot. But first, you have to promise you won't pull the trigger without my permission."

"I promise!"

Her cheerful reply was at odds with the murderous weapon she held.

"Haah... I'm not sure this is a good idea."

The wind swept Kaori's muttered worries away.

And so, Hajime began teaching Myu how to shoot. He set up a target ten meters away, and showed her the Weaver Stance.

"All right, Myu, this may be a weaker gun, but it still has a lot of recoil. If it hurts too much to hold, just let go."

Myu nodded. Then, without hesitation, she fired. There was a soft pop, and Donna bucked in Myu's hands. She didn't even scratch the target. Myu pouted, and Hajime consoled her with a smile.

"Don't worry. It's not that easy to hit a target. You'll get better with practice."

He pulled out another set of practice bullets.

"Hajime-san, Hajime-san, I want to try shooting too, if possible...!"

Watching Myu shoot had piqued Shea's interest.

"You have Drucken's bombardment mode, don't you?"

"I know, but that's different. I want to try the precision shooting you do."

"I told Myu this earlier, too, but it's not easy to hit a target."

Hajime was sure Shea didn't really want to practice precision shooting. If anything, he suspected she just wanted to experience the feeling of shooting a gun. Yue, Tio, and Kaori were all interested as well, judging by their expectant looks. Hajime sighed, shrugged, and lent the girls Donner and Schlag.

"Here I go! Take that!"

Shea wasn't prepared for the recoil, and her shot went wide.

"Hmm, despite the simple principles, this weapon is quite difficult to handle."

Thanks to Tio's draconic strength, the recoil didn't affect her, but her aim was still off.

"Kaori, the target's over there."

"I could say the same to you, Yue. You're supposed to shoot in front of you."

Neither Yue nor Kaori could hit their targets either. After a few shots, Yue at least got the hang of it enough to graze the target's edge.

"Well, I expected that," Hajime said with a wry smile.

What he didn't expect, though, was the speed at which Myu learned.

"Daddy, I need a new target."

Hajime had been watching Myu out of the corner of his eye to make sure she didn't do anything dangerous. So, he hadn't properly seen her shots. He pulled out some bullets, not realizing at first that she'd asked for a target, not more ammunition. He looked over at Myu's target, and saw that she'd pulverized it already.

"Myu, let's try putting the target a little farther away this time."

"Bring it on!"

Hajime made a mental note to speak with Tio about the kinds of language she taught Myu, and put the target twice as far out, twenty meters away. Myu took the stance Hajime taught her and fired.

Her first shot missed by a mile. Just as Hajime thought he'd overestimated her, he watched her second shot graze the edge of the target. Yue and the others were watching her now too. Myu's third shot was only ten centimeters from the center.

"Hey, are you kidding me?"

Myu's fourth shot hit the target dead center. Her fifth and sixth shots were a few centimeters off, but still bullseyes.

"M-Myu, you think you'd be interested in shooting a moving target now?"

"Yeah! I wanna try it!"

Within ten shots, Myu could shoot down the practice planes Hajime flew around for her. Even when he tried moving the planes in unpredictable patterns, Myu could read their movements after a few missed shots.

"Want to try sniping now?"

"Yeah!"

Myu held out her hand, and Hajime crafted a miniature sniper rifle for her. He gave it to her and showed her the proper posture. Myu did as instructed. She tucked in her elbows, stood up straight, and pressed the gun's stock against her cheek. She looked through the scope at her target—a dummy plane hovering a hundred meters away. No matter how good she was, no one expected Myu to hit this. But she exceeded all expectations. With a shot even a pro sniper would have been proud of, she shot down Hajime's dummy plane.

"Daddy, what's next?"

"Oh, uh, here, try this."

Hajime looked at Myu with newfound respect. She proceeded to cheerfully shoot down the next ten planes Hajime prepared. The moment she pulled the trigger, Myu's eyes narrowed into a falcon's sharp glare. Once he started moving the targets again, even Myu couldn't get them every time. Still, her accuracy was uncanny enough to leave Hajime and the others dumbfounded.

"Hajime-kun. Are you sure Myu-chan isn't your real daughter?"

At Kaori's words, everyone turned to Hajime. It was clear to everyone that her marksmanship was unparalleled.

"Mrgh, I'm not as good as Daddy yet. I was off by five millimeters."

"......"

Most people wouldn't even have noticed. After seeing his daughter's unbelievable talent, Hajime couldn't bring himself to deny Kaori's accusation. He simply stared into the distance, wondering what the future held.

AFTERWORD

THANK YOU SO MUCH for purchasing Arifureta, Volume 5.

It's everyone's favorite chuuni lover, Ryo Shirakome, here.

A lot happened in this volume. Hajime cleared two labyrinths, Tio made some big decisions, Kaori found her strength again, and the group parted with Myu.

It's nice that the cast keeps growing, but I'm beginning to worry that I'm not giving each character enough time and development. I hope I was able to give voice properly to everyone's feelings this volume. Oh, by the way, there's actually a certain someone I modeled Remia after. Can you tell who? I imagine most of you might have figured it out from the way she speaks.

As you may have guessed, she's based off my favorite character from Aria.

If you're wondering who that is, I recommend googling "Ara

ara ufufu" to find out. She'll surely bring warmth and comfort to your life too.

Kind of funny that I ended up using Arifureta's afterword to plug a different series entirely, huh? Personally, though, I'd just be glad if more people experienced the things I love... Well, I'll get back to plugging Arifureta now.

The first volume of the Arifureta manga, illustrated by RoGa-sensei, came out at the same time as this volume. It's being published by an imprint of Overlap too, and I've gotta say, it looks amazing. Like, seriously, it's so good!

You should all check it out! Now then, I'm running out of space, but I'd like to give everyone my thanks.

First and foremost, I'd like to thank Takayaki-sensei for his wonderful illustrations. I'd also like to thank my editor for listening to me ramble every day. Also, my proofreader, for catching my numerous egregious typos, and the rest of the publishing staff who made this volume possible. I'd also like to thank the illustrator of the manga, RoGa-sensei. You're amazing.

Lastly, I'd like to thank all of my readers. The ones from Narou, too. It's only because of you that all this is possible.

Let's meet again in the next afterword.

—Ryo Shirakome